Savannah is delighted to be back in her hometown of Sweetwater, surrounded by family and friends, even if it's only temporarily. The house in Nashville is in the process of being repaired after the fire. Baby Caroline is alive and well and getting bigger every day. And Rafe is all recovered, and is working for Tamara Grimaldi and the Columbia PD, at least for the time being. That probably won't last, but for now, Savannah's content.

There are flies in the ointment, however. Savannah's best friend from high school is back in town, and seems to be setting her cap for Savannah's brother Dix. Savannah has been rooting for Dix and Tamara Grimaldi to get together, and this new development doesn't make her happy. Sure, she loves Charlotte… but Charlotte already has a husband, and shouldn't need another one. She especially shouldn't need Dix, not when Savannah wants Grimaldi to have him.

And then there's the case Rafe is working on. Katie Graves was a teenager when she disappeared fifteen years ago. Now she's back—or at least her remains are. And the evidence in what looks like a case of homicide points squarely to one of Savannah's nearest and dearest. With another Martin on the hot-seat, and Rafe and Grimaldi duty-bound to serve the law, it's up to Savannah to keep her family safe and out of prison.

OTHER BOOKS IN THIS SERIES

A Cutthroat Business

Hot Property

Contract Pending

Close to Home

A Done Deal

Change of Heart

Kickout Clause

Past Due

Dirty Deeds

Unfinished Business

Adverse Possession

Uncertain Terms

Scared Money

Bad Debt

Home Stretch

Wrongful Termination

CONFLICT OF INTEREST

INTEREST

Savannah Martin Mystery #17

Jenna Bennett

CONFLICT OF INTEREST

Savannah Martin Mystery #17

Interior design and formatting: B. Gallagher
Cover Design: Dar Albert, Wicked Smart Designs

Magpie Ink

One

"Do you remember Katie Graves?" my husband asked.

It took a second, maybe more than one, before I placed the name in my memory. Then I nodded. "Of course."

We were sitting side by side at the island in Mother's kitchen in the Martin Mansion in Sweetwater, having dinner.

And I'm calling it my mother's kitchen, even though technically, it was my kitchen now. At least for the time being. Mother had vacated the premises over the weekend, to live in sin with Sheriff Satterfield, and had left Rafe and me, and baby Carrie, in sole possession.

We were eating at the island because the dining room table can seat sixteen and I hadn't felt like dealing with the antique splendor of it for just the two of us, and besides, the kitchen island was much closer to the stove and the food, and that made everything easier.

Rafe quirked a brow in my direction. "A bit of thinking for an 'of course,' wasn't it?"

I couldn't very well deny that. "I haven't thought about her in years. And I didn't really know her. I don't think I ever met her. But I remember what happened."

Rafe nodded and took another bite of chicken.

He's three years older than me, and must have been in high school at the time Katie Graves disappeared. I'd still been in middle school. But he had probably known Katie. Or at least known her better than I did.

"She was a year ahead of me," he said when I asked, "and didn't pay me no mind, but I knew who she was. Saw her in the hallways and the cafeteria."

"Pretty girl?"

"Pretty enough," Rafe said, "though that don't always matter."

No, it doesn't. Sixteen-year-old girls disappear sometimes even when they aren't pretty.

That's what had happened to Katie. She'd set out for school one morning, and never made it there. Her parents sounded the alarm when she didn't come home in the evening, but by then she'd been gone close to twelve hours, and she either had enough of a head start to be halfway to Canada, or whoever took her did.

Nobody knew what had happened, or if they did, they didn't talk about it. There was speculation that she'd run away from home, and speculation that she'd been abducted. For a few weeks, every parent in Maury County kept a tight rein on their children. As time passed, and no body appeared, people started leaning more toward Katie taking off on her own, and everyone relaxed again. Life went back to normal.

For everyone but Katie's friends and family, I guess.

"What about her?" I asked.

Rafe took another deliberate bite, and chewed and swallowed, before he answered. "The sheriff called. They found bones up in the hills near the Devil's Backbone."

The Devil's Backbone is a ridge of hills in the western part of Maury County. As for the rest of the statement… "They?"

He glanced at me. "You know they've been going over the Skinners' property since the murders."

The Skinner family—Art and Linda, their son AJ and their daughter Cilla, Cilla's boyfriend, along with Darrell and Robbie, Art's brothers—had all been murdered in their beds one night last fall. Rafe had been sent from Nashville to Maury County on Sheriff Satterfield's request, on loan from the TBI, the Tennessee Bureau of Investigations, to help out. Like Katie Graves, the Skinner boys had also gone to Columbia High, and Rafe had known them, or at least known of them. Like Katie, they'd all been older than me, so I hadn't.

At any rate, the Skinners had been involved in a fair few unsavory endeavors at the time of their deaths. Pearl, the gray pitbull terrier mix who had lifted her head from her pillow over in the corner of Mother's kitchen, and who was thumping her tail now at the mention of bones, was a casualty of the dog fighting operation they'd been running. We'd rescued her from being chained underneath Robbie Skinner's trailer back in October.

In wandering around the Skinners' adjoining properties, which took up a lot of space in the foothills leading up to the Devil's Backbone, we'd also run across a large scale marijuana operation, with several greenhouses. As a result, there had been agents from all sorts of alphabet agencies crawling all over the hills of Middle Tennessee over the past few months.

"Someone found bones on the Skinners' property?"

"One of the ATF guys ran across'em back in November," Rafe said. "Not a complete skeleton. Just the skull and most of the bigger bones."

I put down my fork. "What happened to the rest?"

He shrugged. "Animals, maybe. It's wild up there."

It was. Most of the land that belonged to the Skinners was just woods and a few dirt tracks. And yes, there are animals. No bears or anything like that, but raccoons and coyotes and various birds of prey, who might pick at a corpse and carry some of one away.

I steered my mind firmly away from the Skinners' dogs, and from Pearl. Much better not to go there. Not that she can help being what she is. But I'd be happier if I didn't think about it. "If this happened in November, why are we only hearing about it now?"

"The sheriff heard about it then," Rafe said. "He went up and gathered what they could find of the remains and sent them to the lab. It's the lab that's been dragging their feet getting back with the results."

Labs are notorious for that. It isn't the tests themselves that take a long time; it's waiting for the lab to find the time to do the testing.

And we were more than halfway through January now. If the bones had been discovered in November, there'd been Thanksgiving and then the whole Christmas season to get through, with holiday closings, annual Christmas parties, and the like. Not to mention the increased crime that usually happens around the holidays, that would have taken precedence over a few old bones. No, it was no wonder the sheriff hadn't heard anything before now.

I picked up my fork again. "Which of the Skinners' land was she found on? Has she been up there all this time? Ever since she disappeared?"

"I dunno yet," Rafe said. "The sheriff just called Tammy this afternoon."

Tammy is Tamara Grimaldi, formerly of the Metropolitan Nashville police department, homicide division, and since the first of the year, chief of the Columbia PD. Since two days ago, she was also Rafe's boss, at least for the time being.

It's a long story. And one that probably doesn't matter right now.

He continued, "The remains were found outside the city limits, but Katie disappeared from Columbia, so the sheriff wants somebody from the PD involved."

"And that's you?"

"I was part of the Skinner investigation," Rafe said, "and I went to school with Katie."

And the sheriff respected him. For a long time, a very long time, that hadn't been the case. For years upon years, my mother's boyfriend suspected Rafe of involvement in anything that happened in and around Maury County. And admittedly, he'd had some cause, since Rafe hadn't been the best behaved teenager. But it was nice that the sheriff finally saw him as a colleague, and not a suspect.

"Just out of curiosity," I said, "did they talk to you back when Katie disappeared?"

He arched a brow. Just one. And didn't say a word.

"Sorry," I added, since an apology seemed to be expected. "But the sheriff used to think you had a hand in everything that went wrong around here. I was just curious whether he'd talked to you about Katie back then."

"No," Rafe said. "It was Columbia's case. Not the sheriff's. I can't remember who was in charge of the Columbia PD sixteen years ago. But nobody talked to me about nothing."

After a second's pause he added, "The school did an assembly. The principal talked about it, and said if anybody knew something, to go tell the cops."

"But of course you didn't."

He shook his head. "Wouldn't have, even if I did know something. Not like I was gonna go volunteer information. Then they'd think I had something to do with it for sure."

Sadly, they probably would have.

"But like I said," Rafe added, and turned back to his dinner, "I didn't know Katie."

"No problem. I was just curious." I rearranged some of the broccoli on my plate with the tines of my fork. "Is it certain it's her?"

"The sheriff seems to think so. He called Tammy and told her he was gonna reopen a cold case from her jurisdiction because the body had turned up on the Devil's Backbone. And could she spare someone to help out, since there'd be overlap between her jurisdiction and his."

"And he asked for you."

"I figure there's a reason for that," Rafe said calmly, "and it ain't because I went to school with Katie."

No, it wasn't likely to be. Part of the reason Rafe was here—part of the reason Grimaldi was here—was that Sheriff Satterfield had wanted someone in charge of the Columbia Police Department who could figure out whatever the hell—pardon my French—had been going on there.

The reason there was a vacancy at all, was that the previous chief had been corrupt. He'd been removed back in October, in conjunction with the Skinner investigation. But when the head is rotten, there's quite likely to be some rot elsewhere too, and the sheriff wanted to root it out. He'd offered the chief's job to Rafe first. My husband had turned it down flat, without realizing what the sheriff was really after. Then the sheriff had approached Grimaldi, and she'd accepted. He'd probably been more open with her. And she had prevailed on Rafe to help. So now they were both here—and I was, too—and in addition to keeping the peace, and solving any crimes that came their way, they had to figure out whether anyone else in Chief Carter's old command, and Grimaldi's new one, was corrupt and had to go.

And that was most likely the reason the sheriff had asked to work with Rafe. Under cover of the Katie Graves investigation, they could discuss and confer and sniff out other things, as well.

"I start tomorrow morning," Rafe added. "Jarvis is pissed."

Detective Paul Jarvis was one of Rafe's new colleagues in the Columbia PD. And while we had no particular reason to think he was corrupt, or at least no more reason to suspect him than anyone else, I don't care for him. "Why?"

"High profile case," Rafe said, "lots of interest. He likes the attention."

"Is that your opinion of him after working together for two

days?"

"It's my opinion after seeing him throw a tantrum 'cause Tammy didn't loan him to the sheriff's department instead of me today. He slammed outta there at the end of the day like a five-year-old taking his toys and going home. Damn near ran me down in the parking lot."

"You're kidding."

He shook his head. "If he coulda gotten away with it, I think he'd'a done it. I'm guessing he was Chief Carter's pet investigator, and he figured it'd be the same with Tammy."

"And instead, you're the pet investigator." I smiled.

He gave me a look. "There ain't no pet investigator. The sheriff asked for me. You know why."

I did know why. "Why do you think Jarvis was Carter's pet investigator? Is Jarvis corrupt, too? Or is he stupid, so Carter assigned him cases he didn't want solved, because he knew Jarvis couldn't solve them?"

"He solved cases," Rafe said. "Tammy's going over'em, to make sure they got solved the right way, but he don't seem stupid."

Corrupt, then.

Or maybe he was neither corrupt nor stupid. "Maybe Carter kept him busy with as many investigations as he could, because he knew Jarvis was both smart and driven, and if he kept him busy with other things, maybe Jarvis wouldn't notice what Carter was up to."

Rafe nodded. "Could be. Either way, I'm on this one, and Jarvis ain't."

"Too bad for Jarvis," I said. Without a smidgeon of sympathy, I might add. "So the bones have been identified, and they definitely belong to Katie Graves?"

"You know as much as I do, darlin'," Rafe said and put his fork down. "The sheriff called and explained what he needed. Tammy said he could borrow me. The sheriff said to have me report for duty tomorrow morning. I guess I'll find out more then."

I guessed he would. However—

"It's not that late." Just going on seven, by the clock on the stove. "We could load the baby in the car and drive over to the sheriff's house. Just to say hello and see how they're doing."

"They're doing fine," Rafe said. "Prob'ly taking advantage of the peace and quiet to do what people do when they move in together."

I winced. "I wish you wouldn't put pictures like that in my head."

He chuckled. "If they're in mine, they might as well be in yours, darlin'."

I supposed. "I don't think they're having sex. Not at this time of night. They're not young anymore. And I bet Mother would like to see Carrie."

Rafe arched a brow. "Your mama saw the baby at lunch, didn't she?"

She had, but she probably wouldn't mind seeing her again. "Besides, I'm sure Pearl would like to see Mother."

Over on the pillow, Pearl's jaws split in a doggy grin and her tail thumped.

"See?"

"Shameless," Rafe told me, with a shake of his head. "You just wanna know what the sheriff knows, and you don't wanna wait until tomorrow to hear it. So you're using your baby and your dog as an excuse."

And I wasn't ashamed of it. "Aren't you curious?"

"'Course I'm curious. I'll find out tomorrow morning, though. I can live with being curious till then."

"I can't," I said. "You might find out in the morning. But I'll have to wait until tomorrow evening, when you come home, to learn anything. And besides, it'll be secondhand. I love you, but I'd rather hear it from the sheriff."

"'Course you would." He got off the stool and carried his plate over to the sink. "Fine. We'll take the baby and dog and go see your mama. But if the sheriff won't tell you nothing, don't blame me."

"He'll tell me something," I said, dumping my plate next to his. "Just leave the dishes. I'll deal with them when we get back. We don't want to get there too late."

"'Course not." But he didn't say anything more to try to dissuade me. Maybe he was curious, too. "You get the dog. I'll get the baby."

"Works for me." Pearl likes me better anyway. And while I think Carrie's too young to have developed a preference for one of us, she definitely likes her daddy very much.

So we loaded up both the baby and the dog—Carrie in the back seat with me, Pearl in the front with Rafe; better not to take any chances while the dog was getting used to the baby—and set out for town and Bob Satterfield's house.

The Martin Mansion sits north of town, on the Columbia Highway. The sheriff lives in a big turn-of-the-twentieth-century foursquare in the historic district. When I'd been growing up, it had been Bob, Pauline, and their son Todd, my brother Dix's best friend, in the house. Then Todd went away to college, and Pauline died. And Todd got divorced and came back. Most recently, he'd gotten himself engaged and had moved in with his fiancée, Marley, and her little boy, in the same subdivision where Dix lives. All through this, Bob had been living in the house. And now my mother had joined him there.

"Things change," Rafe said.

I nodded. They sure do. "How do you feel, being back?"

He'd also grown up in Sweetwater, in the trailer park on the other side of town. Unlike me, he didn't have fond memories of growing up here.

He shrugged. "Could be worse."

Of course it could. "I'm happy," I said. "It's nice to have help with the baby. And it's nice to see my family more. And we wouldn't be able to stay in the house in Nashville anyway."

The house we'd been living in in Nashville—it belongs to Rafe's grandmother, Mrs. Jenkins, who was here in Sweetwater—had experienced a fire a couple of weeks ago. Another long story, but the bottom line was that the foyer and most of the stairs were gone, along with a lot of windows and the front door. We couldn't secure the house, and we couldn't make it up to the—miraculously whole—second floor, where our bedroom and the nursery were. The house needed repair. So we'd decamped for Sweetwater, and left a construction company in temporary charge. It made for a dandy excuse for why we were here, too, if anyone asked.

Not that anyone had, so far. Or at least no one had asked me.

"Has anyone questioned you about what we're doing here?" I asked Rafe.

He shrugged. "Not to say 'questioned.' The subject came up. I told 'em you wanted to be closer to your family, what with the baby and all."

And that was as good a reason as any other. Especially since it was true.

It's a short trip from the Martin Mansion to the center of town where the sheriff lived. By this point of the conversation, we were already pulling up to the curb.

An American foursquare, in case you're unfamiliar with the term, is a big, two-and-a-half-story house with four rooms square on each floor, hence the name. Living and dining on one side of the house, with a butler's pantry between, and a parlor and kitchen on the other, with a staircase to the second floor. Four bedrooms upstairs, one in each corner, with the stairway on one side and a bathroom directly opposite. Up top, a big loft area, often with dormers. There's usually a big porch that runs across the full front of the house, and the front door can either be in the middle, with a central hallway running the length of the house, like in the mansion, or it can be on one side, and lead directly into the front parlor. In that case, you still have the four rooms, but no central hallway.

The sheriff's house was of the first variety. It's built of brick—yellow brick, not the red brick of the mansion—with a deep front porch perfect for sipping mint juleps, and a porte cochere, a sort of carport over the side entrance, where the sheriff's patrol car was parked. Mother's Cadillac was in the garage in the back, I assumed.

There were lights on in the parlor, so I didn't feel bad about dragging Carrie's seat out of the back of the car, grabbing Pearl's leash, and heading up on the porch with both of them.

I had to put the baby carrier down to push the door bell, and Rafe immediately picked her up, although Pearl showed her no interest whatsoever. Instead, she was busy sniffing the crack where the front door met the jamb.

A figure passed from the parlor into the hallway, and I waited while it made its way toward us. The light was on on the porch, and the hallway was mostly dark, so I couldn't see well, but the figure was too tall and too masculine to be my mother.

As the locks tumbled, I smiled sweetly. "Hi, Sheriff— Oh."

It wasn't the sheriff. Instead, it was his son Todd, also known as my brother's best friend, my high school boyfriend, and the man who had wanted to marry me before I married Rafe.

He gave me a fishy stare as my smile dropped. "Savannah." After a second he moved his attention to Rafe. "Collier."

Rafe nodded back. "Satterfield." From the set of his lips, I deduced that he thought the situation was funny.

"Pearl missed Mother," I said, and lifted Pearl's leash. The dog was currently sniffing Todd's trousers. He looked like he might have preferred to take a step back, but since that might look like an invitation to come in, he chose not to.

Not that there was a whole lot of bad blood between us at the moment. I'd been married to Rafe for more than six months. Todd had fallen in love with Marley Cartwright since then, and was supposed to be living with her. I thought we'd put all that behind us. Yet here he was, looking at us both like we'd crawled out from underneath a big rock.

There wasn't anything unusual about him directing that look at Rafe. I wasn't used to it, and he'd mostly stopped using it on Rafe, too, lately.

"Something wrong?" my husband asked.

Todd sighed. "No. Just having a talk with my dad."

"We can take Mother into another room if you want," I said.

He gave me a look. "She's already in another room. In another house."

"She isn't here?" Well, that would explain why I hadn't seen the Cadillac.

"She went to your sister's place," Todd said.

He still wasn't offering us the opportunity to come inside, which between you and me was quite rude. People in the South are generally very happy to extend hospitality, even to people they don't know well. Yet Todd was holding the door open but blocking the way inside.

"Are you sure you're all right?" I peered past him into the house.

"Do you want to come inside and check for yourself?"

I wouldn't mind, and said so. Rafe's lips twitched. "C'mon, darlin'. Let Satterfield talk to his daddy in peace. You can get your fix when I get home tomorrow night."

I stuck my bottom lip out, while Todd looked from one to the other of us, curiously.

"Savannah heard about the bones on the Devil's Backbone," Rafe said. "She wants the details."

"You're going to be working on that?"

Rafe nodded. "Your daddy wants someone from the Columbia PD to be involved. I worked on the Skinner case and I went to school with Katie."

"And my dad wants a liaison while he and Chief Grimaldi work on the other matter." Todd nodded. "Makes sense."

"Is that what you're talking about?"

He turned to me, and this time it was his lips that twitched. "No, Savannah. My dad and I are having a private conversation about personal things."

I grimaced. "Fine. Just… fine. I'll wait until tomorrow."

"Don't look like you have much of a choice, darlin'." Rafe put his arm around my shoulder. "Let's go. Say goodnight."

"Goodnight, Todd," I said. Not happily, but I said it. I mean, what was the big deal? It wouldn't have hurt him to spare five minutes for the sheriff to give me the scoop, would it?

But— "Goodnight." He gave Rafe a nod and closed the door. Rafe waited until we were off the porch and out of the yard before he chuckled.

"Guess he don't have a soft spot for you anymore, darlin'."

"I think that went away when I jilted him and married you," I said, as he opened the door and fitted the baby and carrier back into the car. The seat snapped in with a click, and he shut the door and then opened the front door for Pearl. I nodded to her. "Go on, sweetheart."

She didn't have to be asked twice, but jumped onto the front passenger seat and sat there, tongue lolling and canine grin on display, while Rafe shut the door behind her before we walked around the car.

I sent a disgruntled glance in the direction of the lighted windows of the foursquare, and Rafe grinned. "Sorry, darlin'."

"You'd think he could have spared five minutes for the sheriff to give us the information, don't you?"

"Maybe they're talking about something important," Rafe said, and opened the door for me. His voice was a little uneven from the laughter he was manfully holding back.

"What could be more important than me wanting to know about Katie Graves?"

Rafe chuckled. "Maybe he's knocked up his girlfriend." He shut the door behind me and reached for his own.

Maybe he had. But since they were already engaged and living together, surely that wasn't such a big deal. "Do you suppose Mother knows anything about it?" I asked when he'd fitted himself behind the wheel.

He gave me a look in the rearview mirror. "Satterfield knocking up Marley?"

I rolled my eyes. "I mean Katie Graves. If Todd knocked up Marley, that's their business. I don't care, beyond the fact that I hope they'll be happy together. Do you think the sheriff told Mother anything about the bones?"

"I don't imagine your mama'd be much interested in what happened to Katie Graves," Rafe said, and turned the key in the ignition.

I raised my voice over the sound of the engine. "I'm sure she would. She was pretty worried back when it happened. Everyone was, but Mother had two daughters, one of whom went to school with Katie."

My sister Catherine, roughly four years older than me and a year older than Rafe, would have been in Katie's class. Dix, meanwhile, falls halfway between the two of us, give or take a few months.

"Let me guess," Rafe said, "you wanna go to your sister's house."

"It isn't that late." Going on seven-thirty by now. "And we're already out. We might as well."

"Why not?" Rafe said, and put the car in gear.

Two

Catherine and Jonathan, with their three children, live in one of the newer family-focused subdivisions on the outskirts of Sweetwater. It's full of big brick McMansion-type family homes, with front-facing garages, small front yards, and privacy-fences in the back, surrounding the requisite trampoline and jungle-gym equipment. All of it along 15 mph winding roads where the kiddies can learn to skateboard or ride bikes without fear of being run down by speeding drivers.

It had taken us about ten minutes to get here, and now we were creeping along at a snail's pace while Pearl was peering out the window, grinning.

I don't know what she was grinning at, because there was very little to see. It was dark, and too late for any kids to be out playing. They were probably inside their respective homes, behind their lighted windows, either doing homework, playing video games, or getting ready for bed. We'd met two cars and seen one jogger since we entered the subdivision, but that was all. Nonetheless, Pearl was watching the world go by with a big canine grin. Maybe she knew we were going to see Mother, or maybe she just liked being in the car.

Rafe pulled up to the curb outside Catherine and Jonathan's place, where Mother's Cadillac was parked in the driveway. He cut the engine and opened the door. "You get the dog. I'll get the baby."

It made more sense for me to get the baby and him to get the dog, since he could walk around the front of the car to the front door where the dog was, and I could walk around the back of the car to the back door where the baby was. But the baby with carrier weighed more, and I didn't have to carry the dog, so I guess that was his thinking. And either way, it made no difference to me. "Sure."

We got our respective burdens and hoofed it up the driveway and across the grass to the front door, where I put my finger on the doorbell.

The summons was answered with excited shrieks and the pounding of what sounded like an army of small feet. It wasn't an army, but when the door was yanked open and I looked down into the delighted face of one of my small nephews, he turned out to be accompanied not just by his own sister and brother, but Dix's two little girls, too.

"Aunt Savannah!" They beamed at me. And looked past me. "Uncle Rafe! You brought Pearl!"

Pearl was clearly more exciting than either of us, including Carrie. Although I must admit that my heart melted a little when my nephew called my husband 'Uncle.' I know that that's what he was, technically—my husband would be my sister's children's uncle—but my instinct was still to be delighted any time anyone in my vicinity said or did anything that made it clear that Rafe was accepted and valued as part of the family.

I glanced at him as the children all fell on Pearl with exclamations of joy. He glanced back, a corner of his mouth curved up. And then he glanced down at the kids, swarming around his legs and the dog. "This OK?"

"It seems to be." Pearl didn't seem to be in any danger of devouring any of them. She had a gentle heart, but had had a tough life that had given her some scary habits, so I was never entirely sure how she'd handle the situations that came her way.

At this point, Jonathan wandered into the hallway and surveyed the churning mass of children and dog outside his front door. He arched his brows and put his hands on his hips.

"Move on inside," I told the kids before Jonathan could say anything. "We're letting all the warm air out."

I moved forward, and they moved back, swarming into the hallway. Rafe brought Carrie inside, and we were finally able to close the door behind us. Jonathan nodded to Rafe and turned to me. "Something wrong?"

I shook my head. "We drove over to the sheriff's house so Pearl could visit with Mother. He said she was here. We decided to stop by."

Jonathan didn't seem to think this was strange at all. "Your mother's in the family room with Catherine. The kids and I are upstairs."

In the media room above the garage, I assumed. Where the big TV and toys were.

"And Dix?"

"On a date," Jonathan said. "We're kid-sitting."

He turned to Rafe. "Up or down?"

My husband smiled. "I'm just gonna go say hello to Margaret Anne. Gotta rack up those points when I can. I'll be up after."

"Beer's in the fridge," Jonathan said and turned so he could shoo the kids ahead of him toward the stairs. Little Cole, the youngest of their three, dug his heels in.

"I want Pearl to come!"

"I'll bring her with me later," Rafe told him. "She came to see your grandma, so we gotta do that first."

Little Cole looked mutinous. "Then I wanna go see Grandma, too. And stay with Pearl."

Jonathan shrugged. "Have at it." He left Cole there and ushered the other kids—Cole's siblings Robert and Annie, and

Dix's daughters Abigail and Hannah—toward the stairs.

They headed up while I handed Pearl's leash to Cole. "Here. You can take her in to your grandmther while we take our jackets off."

Cole beamed, and then shrieked as Pearl saw her opportunity to take off down the hallway once I relinquished her leash. Cole held on, and slid after her in his stocking feet, like a slightly wobbly water skier. Pearl's nails scrabbled on the wood floors.

"Slow down!" Jonathan bellowed after them, but of course Pearl didn't listen, and Cole had no way to stop her. She weighed more than he did, and was solid muscle. All Cole could do was hang on.

They disappeared through the door into the kitchen with Jonathan in pursuit. Cole's shrieks of laughter faded behind the wall.

"Oops," I said.

Rafe shrugged. "They'll be fine. I'm sure the house is child-proof."

It probably was. Although maybe not dog proof.

If anything needed doing, Jonathan would take care of it, though. I shrugged out of my winter coat and handed it to Rafe, who put it next to his own in the closet before he picked up the car seat with Carrie. "Go on."

I went, down the hallway where Cole had slid, through the door to the kitchen and into the family room, where Pearl was trying to express her love for Mother with a series of exuberant tongue-swipes.

Mother sputtered. "Down, Pearl! Down!"

Pearl dropped to her haunches and sat there, quivering with mad joy while she grinned at Mother.

"Good girl," Mother managed, and swiped one hand over her shiny face while she extended the other to pat Pearl's huge head. "Good girl."

Cole giggled. Catherine's lips twitched, but she managed to hold back her own, no doubt hysterical, laughter.

I let Rafe approach with Carrie while I detoured into the kitchen, snagged a paper towel from the roll, ran it through a small trickle of water, and brought it into the family room. "Here."

Mother took it and dabbed gently on her complexion. "Thank you, Savannah."

"No problem." I dropped down next to Catherine on the sofa and exchanged a glance with her while Mother was hidden behind the paper towel. Both of us were on the verge of losing our cool.

"Sorry, Margaret." Jonathan gathered up Cole and the dog, and took them both through the kitchen and out. "Join us when you're ready," he told Rafe over his shoulder.

My husband nodded and put the baby carrier down where Mother could see it. "Coming."

He winked at me, grinned at Catherine, and patted Mother on the shoulder before sauntering out. He didn't stop at the refrigerator for that beer Jonathan had told him was there, so he must have decided he didn't want one.

When his footsteps had faded up the stairs, Mother folded the moist paper towel delicately into a square and deposited it just on the edge of a tray sitting on the coffee table. The tray was glazed ceramic, so the towel wasn't likely to bother it.

"Sorry about that," I said.

"It wasn't your fault, darling," Mother told me.

Catherine cleared her throat. "Sorry." I could hear a little of the suppressed laughter in her voice, but she kept a straight face. "My son, my fault."

"My dog," I said. "I was the one who handed him the leash."

"My dog," Mother corrected. "Although I appreciate your taking care of her. It's easier to settle into Bob's house without her."

No doubt. While Pearl loves Mother with single-minded passion, she's less enamored with the sheriff. Not that she growls at him or anything. She just likes him less than she does Mother. And the change of scenery might be tough for her, just a couple of months after being moved from the underside of Robbie Skinner's trailer and to the Martin Mansion. Better for everyone concerned to just keep her where she is for the time being.

I wiggled a little further into the sofa. "We stopped by and he told us you were here."

"You should have told me you were coming," Mother said, "and I would have stayed there. But Todd stopped by, and wanted to talk to Bob in private, so I decided to make myself scarce for a while."

"Is something wrong? With Todd, I mean?"

"Not that I know about," Mother said, and leaned back in the chair. "Is something wrong with you?"

"Of course not. Why would you…? Oh, because we came to see you? No, nothing's wrong. Rafe told me that he's going to be working with the sheriff for a while, on loan from the Columbia PD—" Where he was, technically, on loan from the TBI, although no one but the family, Grimaldi, and Sheriff Satterfield knew that, "and I didn't want to wait until he comes home tomorrow night to hear the scoop about the case."

"What scoop?" Catherine wanted to know. "What case?"

I turned to her. "They've found Katie Graves. Or what's left of her."

Catherine stared at me, her mouth open, as all the color drained out of her face.

My brother Dix and I take after Mother's family, the Georgia Calverts. We're both on the tall side, with fair hair and blue eyes. Catherine looks more like our father and the Martins: shorter, rounder, and with dark hair and gray eyes. Her skin is usually more on the sallow side, a legacy of our great-great-however-many-greats-grandmother Caroline—baby Carrie's namesake—who had an affair with one of the grooms while her husband was off fighting the Damn Yankees.

But I digress. Catherine was pale. Paler than she usually is. "Katie?" she said. "They've found Katie?"

I nodded. And between you and me, if I'd realized she was going to take it the way she did, I would have tempered my language a little when I told her the news. Maybe not used the expression 'what's left of her.'

"I hadn't heard anything about that," Mother said, with a faint frown. Faint because frowning can cause wrinkles, and my mother doesn't want them. As an aside, she looks damn good for fifty-nine-and-a-half.

"I don't think it's a secret," I said. At least Rafe hadn't acted like it was. Once they started investigating tomorrow, word would get around quickly, anyway. "Although I don't think it's common knowledge yet, either."

"What happened?" Mother asked, while Catherine still just sat there and stared at me like she'd seen a ghost. Or heard about one.

"To Katie? I don't think anyone knows. But she obviously didn't run away. Or if she did, she didn't get far."

Neither of them spoke, and I added, "She was found up in the hills near the Devil's Backbone back in November."

"The Devil's Backbone?" Mother repeated, with another faint frown line between her brows.

"The ridge of hills to the west of Columbia. Where the Skinners lived." And died.

Mother knew about the murders, of course—everyone did—since Rafe had been down here investigating them. And since that kind of thing doesn't happen in our quiet county with much regularity. Or at all.

Catherine made a little sound, and I turned to her. She

stared back at me, a hand covering her mouth.

"Are you going to be sick?" I asked, worried.

She shook her head. "She was found on the Skinners' property?"

"That's what Rafe said. That one of the ATF agents who was up there looking at the pot houses found—" *What was left of her.*

I amended it on the fly to, "—her bones."

"Dear me," Mother said faintly. Catherine went from sallow to faintly green.

"Sorry." *Sheesh.* I'd had no idea they were so sensitive. And what did they expect, after fifteen or sixteen years? Of course there was nothing left but bones.

I gave them a few seconds for their stomachs to settle, and then I added, "The sheriff sent the bones to the lab back in November. With the holidays, I guess they didn't get around to testing them until now."

"But it's definitely Katie?"

I'd asked Rafe the same thing. "I think so. But I didn't get a chance to ask the sheriff, because Todd was there. I guess Rafe will get all the details tomorrow." And then I'd get them from him.

"Did he know Katie Graves?" Mother asked as, down in the baby seat, Carrie kicked her legs.

I shook my head. "They went to school together, but she was a year older than him, and he said she didn't pay him no… um… any attention."

Mother gave me a look, and I smiled apologetically. My husband's language is a bit more colorful than mine, in several different ways, and sometimes I quote him. "No," I said now, "he didn't know her personally."

Mother nodded, and it might have been my imagination, but I thought she looked relieved. Maybe, like me, she's always worried that someone will come along and accuse him of something.

"You went to school with Katie," I turned to Catherine, "didn't you?"

She looked at me for a second before she nodded. "Rafe was a year below me and Dix a year below him. You were still in middle school."

Yes, thank you. I knew that. "Did you know her? Beyond just going to school with her?"

There was another slight pause, like it took a few extra seconds for her to process anything I said. Or as if she had to think about it. "Not well. She was from Columbia, I was from Sweetwater. I already had my circle of friends by the time we got to high school. She did, too. But we had some classes together. I guess we spoke once in a while."

So nothing to really explain the green tinge to her skin, or the shock. But maybe she just had a squeamish stomach and didn't like the idea of Katie rotting up in the hills all these years. Hard to blame her for that. I didn't much like the idea, either.

Or maybe something else was going on, that I didn't know about. Like, there was another reason why her stomach was extra sensitive.

"You aren't pregnant, are you?"

Her eyes widened, and she dropped the hand from her mouth. "Have you lost your mind? Of course not!"

"It's not a crazy idea," I said. "You're only thirty-two. It's been almost four years since Cole was born. If you were going to have any more children, now would be time to have them." Before either she or Cole got much older.

"You don't think three is enough?"

Three was enough. If she wanted it to be enough.

Catherine shook her head. "I'm not pregnant. From here on out, I think any new grandchildren will be on you and Rafe. I'm pretty sure Dix and I are done."

"Dix might want another child. When…" I caught myself and changed it to, "if he finds someone else and they get serious about each other."

Mother gave me a fishy stare, like she suspected I knew something she didn't. Which I was pretty sure I did. Dix and Tamara Grimaldi were working on some kind of relationship. I wasn't entirely sure what kind of relationship it was, but I thought it was romantic. Although I wasn't sure Mother had caught on, and I certainly didn't want to be the person to let the cat out of the bag.

"Well," I said, "he's on a date, isn't he? Jonathan said that's why you're babysitting."

Catherine nodded. "I wouldn't expect any babies from that union, though."

Oh, really? "Who's he out with?" It wasn't Todd, since Todd had been at his daddy's house. Maybe Darcy, our half-sister, who also happened to be the receptionist at Dix's law firm?

"Charlotte," Catherine said.

My jaw dropped, and it took me a few seconds to find my voice. "My Charlotte? Charlotte Albertson? Whitaker? That Charlotte? Dix is on a date with her?"

Catherine nodded.

"But she's married!" I said.

Yes, she'd been in Sweetwater on her own since just after Christmas, with her two kids but not her husband. Although there could be all sorts of reasons for that, not necessarily that they were having marital problems. Maybe one of her parents was sick. Or maybe she'd just wanted to give the kids some extra time with their grandparents. I had no idea what was going on, honestly, since Charlotte hadn't seemed inclined to talk to me about it. I'd reached out a couple times, but she'd always had an excuse for why she couldn't get together.

And now she was on a date with my brother?

"Why would Dix agree to go out with her?"

"You'd have to ask him," Mother said, and from the set of her lips I deduced she wasn't any happier about this than I was.

Here's the thing. I loved Charlotte—who had been my best friend through elementary school, middle school, and high school, when she had dated Dix while I'd dated Todd. I wanted her to be happy. I certainly wouldn't have had a problem with her dating Dix under other circumstances. I hadn't minded when they dated in high school. But at this point I'd invested a lot in the Dix/Grimaldi relationship, and the last thing I wanted was for Charlotte to get in the way of that.

Plus, she already had a husband. The least she could do was get rid of him first, before she started looking for another.

"Maybe she's just trying to talk him into hiring her for the office," Catherine said, but in a tone that made it doubtful.

"Is she still doing that?" She'd done it a couple of weeks ago, when she'd first arrived back in Sweetwater, but I'd assumed, after Dix explained to her that Darcy isn't just the receptionist but our sister, that she'd have stopped angling for Darcy's job.

"She's angling for something," Catherine said. "But I'm not sure what it is."

Me either. Especially since there weren't any other jobs to be had at Martin and McCall. The staff consists of Darcy, Dix, Jonathan, and Catherine, when she isn't taking care of kids. All family members. Three lawyers plus a paralegal-slash-receptionist. I had no idea what Charlotte thought she could do around the office, without any kind of legal background. They could make their own coffee, and Darcy already did the filing.

Mother muttered something, which isn't like her. I glanced at her, but she was bent over the baby seat, lifting Carrie out, and I couldn't see her face. "Hello, there," she cooed at my daughter, "aren't you pretty?"

Carrie has her father's dark, curly hair and dusky skin, but long-lashed eyes of a startling clear blue that she either got from me and the Georgia Calverts, or from Rafe's mother LaDonna. Either way, Carrie looks just like a doll. And is, in fact, very pretty.

I let Mother focus on her and turned my attention back to my sister. "Rafe and the sheriff are starting to work the case tomorrow. By now, it's obvious that Katie didn't run away, so I guess they'll have to try to figure out what happened to her."

"They tried that sixteen years ago," Catherine said. "If they couldn't do it then, what makes them think they can now?"

I had no idea, but cold cases do get solved sometimes. It was possible that this would be one of them.

If nothing else, at least they could stop trying to figure out whether she'd left on her own or not, since it was pretty clear that she hadn't.

Unless she had left on her own, for whatever reason, and had ended up near the Devil's Backbone. And had broken her leg or something like that, out there in the woods, and had starved to death in the Skinners' back forty.

Part of me thought I'd almost rather have it be quick and brutal. Someone took her, and killed her. She didn't suffer for interminable days or weeks by herself, out in the wilderness, hoping against hope that someone would come by and find her before it was too late.

"Now you're turning green," Catherine observed. "You OK?"

I nodded. "Just had an uncomfortable thought. I should know better than to let my mind wander like that."

Catherine arched her brows, but didn't ask me to elaborate. I was grateful, since I didn't want to think about it anymore. "How are you doing?" she asked instead, and I was happy to accept the change of subject.

"We're fine. Rafe's all healed after the fire." He'd gotten some minor burns while trying to get the rest of us out of Mrs.

Jenkins's house in the middle of the night, but they had healed nicely over the past week, with lots of cream and lots of kisses. "He's been working with Grimaldi for the past two days, and this afternoon the sheriff asked to borrow him for this Katie Graves thing."

Catherine nodded. "And you? Are you settling in OK?"

I was happy to be back in my childhood home, and told her so. "I should probably start looking for work, but since I'm not sure how long we'll be here, I guess I'll just keep my license in Nashville for now, just in case we end up going back there."

When I'm not taking care of Carrie or sticking my nose in where it isn't wanted, I have a real estate license. I had planned to transfer it down here permanently, but now that it looked like the move might not be permanent, I'd decided to just wait and see what happened. Carrie was still young enough that I could make a good case for staying home with her, and besides, we lived for free at the mansion. Rafe's salary, which the Columbia PD was paying at the moment, was more than adequate to keep us in the manner to which we had become accustomed.

It wasn't the manner to which Mother was accustomed, needless to say, or for that matter the manner to which Catherine and Jonathan were accustomed, but we were doing just fine.

"You could go back to school, you know," Catherine said. "You dropped out before you got your degree, but you didn't have a whole lot left. You could finish up, and then pass the bar and come to work with the rest of us."

At the law firm my grandfather started, on the square in Sweetwater.

I shuddered. "No. Thank you. I'm not a lawyer at heart."

She leaned back. "What are you, at heart? Because if you'll forgive me for saying so, the real estate doesn't look like it's working out all that well."

It wasn't. I'd only sold a handful of houses in the time I'd had my license. Competition between realtors is stiff, at least in Nashville, and I'd been brought up to be a lady. Which meant I wasn't equipped to take up the fight for the clients, listings, and dollars.

"Maybe things will be different here," I said, optimistically. "Where people know me, and the Martin name still means something."

"You're not a Martin, dear," Mother told me. "You're a Collier now."

And the Collier name meant the opposite. I made a face. "Whose side are you on?"

"Yours, darling. Always." She smiled.

I smiled back, even though I wanted to snort. "Maybe I'll just take the opportunity to write that historical bodice ripper I've been thinking about since Elspeth Caulfield died."

Yet another long story. Elspeth Caulfield was a local woman, someone we had all gone to school with. She also happened to be the mother of Rafe's son David, who was born when Rafe was eighteen, and who was living with his adopted family in Nashville. Rafe hadn't even known about him until recently.

But back to Elspeth. Under the *nom de plume* Barbara Botticelli, she had also been a fantastically successful writer of bodice ripper romances, and one of my favorite authors. I figured, now that she was no longer writing, there was a vacancy in the market I could fill. I could call myself Romilda Romaine, or maybe Vanessa Vermicelli.

"Savannah Semolina," Catherine said. "Or Jane Jamocha." Jane being my middle name.

I gave her a quelling look. "I have come up with a title for it. *Bedded by the Bedouin.* I'm planning to put Rafe in a robe and turban and use him for inspiration."

My mother and my sister gave me identical looks of horror.

"It worked for Elspeth," I said.

Catherine's lips twitched. "Elspeth hadn't seen your husband naked since she was sixteen. It's a little different."

Maybe it was. "It's something to think about, anyway." I think I would like to become a fantastically successful author of bodice rippers.

"If you ask me," Catherine said, "thinking about it is about all you should do."

Three

We ended up going home before Dix arrived to pick up his girls, so I didn't get a chance to ask him what the hell—excuse me, heck—he thought he was doing, going on a date with Charlotte Albertson.

"Can you imagine?" I fumed to Rafe on the way home. "I mean, what's wrong with him? She's still married. She has no business going on dates. He has no business taking her on them. And isn't he supposed to be involved with Grimaldi?"

"I dunno," Rafe said, expertly driving the car along the dark road toward the mansion. "Is he?"

I stared at him. "Isn't he?" They'd certainly spent a lot of time together since Sheila—my sister-in-law—died. And there was that one time when Dix wanted to go work out with Rafe, because—I had assumed—he'd wanted to beef up for Grimaldi. Like Rafe, and like a lot of law enforcement, at least the people who take it seriously, she's in good physical shape. And Dix, being a desk jockey and a small-town lawyer, maybe isn't quite so buff.

Rafe gave me a quick look over his shoulder. I was still in the rear of the car, with Carrie, and Pearl was up front, sitting tall and watching the world go by outside the windows. "Haven't you asked?"

"Not straight out." Or maybe I had, and they just hadn't given me a straight answer. Grimaldi had a way of ignoring the questions she didn't like. And I don't really feel comfortable asking my brother about his sex life. "She moved down here, didn't she?"

"To help the sheriff root out corruption in the Columbia PD," Rafe said.

Well, yes. But— "Don't you think it was a little bit because Dix is here, too? I mean, they didn't have any chance at a normal relationship with him here and her in Nashville. I assumed that was part of the reason she took the job."

Even after I'd learned the real reason Sheriff Satterfield had offered it to her, I had assumed that.

Rafe shrugged. "You're gonna have to ask her."

"She won't answer. She never does."

"Then I guess you'll just have to wait and see," my husband said, without any sympathy at all.

I changed the subject. "Did I tell you that I've come up with a title for that Barbara Botticelli ripoff I've been wanting to write? *Bedded by the Bedouin.* Would you mind dressing up in a robe and turban and be my inspiration?"

Unlike Catherine and Mother, and their joint looks of horror, he grinned at me in the mirror. "Sure thing, darlin'. I'm always happy to be inspirational."

"My hero," I said.

The grin widened. "What would my name be in this one?"

After the first few moments of shock and distaste when we first made the connection, he'd taken the fact that Elspeth had used him for inspiration in stride, and by now, he thought it was funny. Or at least he thought it was funny that I wanted to.

"Not sure," I said. "When Elspeth—or Barbara Botticelli— wrote her Sheikh romance, the hero was named Hasan something." I'd been reading it around the time I first met Rafe, or met him again, a year and a half ago. "Lady Selena—or maybe Serena; I can't remember—and Sheikh Hasan."

"I wanna be Raoul," Rafe said, and I squinted at him.

"Really? Why?"

He glanced back at me. "Like I said, it's easier to answer to something that's similar to your own name."

He had told me that once. When he was in character as Ry'mone, small-time gang banger and gun procurer.

I shook my head. "You won't have to answer to it."

"You weren't gonna call me Raoul when we're in bed tonight?"

Absolutely not. "Why would I want to make love to Raoul when I have you?"

Elspeth had to make do with Hasan, or Mac the Black MacGregor, or whoever—I couldn't remember the names of all her romance novel heroes anymore—but I didn't have to, because I had Rafe. And I was not about to call him Raoul. Or anything else.

"Good answer," he told me. "But you want the robe and turban?"

"I'd rather have you naked. I'll imagine the robe and turban."

He grinned. "That works for me."

It worked for me, too. Or would, once we got around to it.

But since that was a ways off—I'd have to take care of the baby first—I changed the subject again. "I don't suppose Jonathan said anything interesting?"

"About what?" We approached the driveway to the mansion, and Rafe started to decelerate.

"Nothing in particular. Just interesting in general."

"No," Rafe said, and took the turn into the driveway gently. "We talked about basketball."

And that wasn't interesting at all, at least not to me. "Catherine and Mother were both pretty shocked that Katie Graves's remains had been found. Catherine even more so than Mother. She turned green."

"What did you tell her?" He glanced back at me as we

rolled slowly up the driveway toward the mansion.

"Just the little bit that I know. That someone with the ATF found the bones before Christmas, and now she's been identified."

"To turn her green," Rafe clarified, and pulled the car to a stop at the bottom of the steps. "If you grab the baby, I'll take the car to the garage and bring the dog back."

That made sense, so I reached for my door handle. "I don't think I said anything to turn her green. Except that I said 'what's left of her.'"

"That'd do it," Rafe said, as I swung my legs out. When I'd shut my own door and gone around the rear of the car and opened the back door to reach for Carrie, he added, "I'll stay out for a couple minutes. I imagine the dog probably has some business to take care of."

She probably did. It was getting close to bedtime, so she might as well get her evening bathroom break taken care of. "I'll be upstairs."

"I'll come find you," Rafe said, and rolled off as soon as I'd closed the door. I hoisted the baby carrier over my arm and climbed the couple of steps to the front door.

He did indeed come find me, after getting the dog settled and, I'm sure, after walking through the house and making sure all the windows and doors were securely locked. By then, Carrie was in her little footed pajamas, yellow with ducks all over them, and was having her final meal of the day in the rocking chair in her room.

Final, because the next time she woke me up, it would be after midnight. She still got me out of bed a couple of times every night. Somehow, my body seemed to have adjusted to this, since I didn't feel so much like a zombie anymore. For a first few weeks, when she'd been nursing every couple hours around the clock, I'd been a walking disaster.

Rafe stopped in the doorway to watch for a moment. The look on his face was, as always, a mixture of amusement and tenderness, with a little awe thrown in for good measure. And just a touch of heat, since I was, after all, flashing my breasts at him.

After a minute he told me he was going to get ready for bed, and I nodded. He disappeared into the bathroom, and I glanced down at Carrie. Her eyelids were getting heavy, those long, inky lashes fluttering against her cheeks.

By the time Rafe came back, all washed and brushed and ready for bed, she had fallen asleep. I shifted her up to my shoulder and patted her back until she gave a sleepy belch, and then I got to my feet. "I'm going to put her down."

"I'll be over here."

Of course he would. I wandered over to the port-a-crib we'd brought with us from Nashville, and lowered Carrie into it. There was a hundred-year-old baby bed somewhere in the attic, that I and Dix and Catherine and several generations of Martins before us had slept in, and I kept thinking that I should go dig it out so Carrie could take her rightful place in it. But so far I'd ended up just putting her down in the port-a-crib whenever it was time for a nap.

I left the door open and wandered into the bathroom next door to brush my own teeth. By the time I got back to my own room, or our room now, Rafe was underneath the covers, his skin a warm golden brown against the white sheets, and one arm curled under his head with muscles—very nice muscles— bunching.

"Hello, Raoul," I told him, as I posed in the doorway in a suitably romantic fashion. One that would have looked better in one of the confectionary nightgowns I used to wear, dripping with ribbons and lace, and that probably didn't look quite so alluring in the simple cotton camisole and pajama pants I wore to bed these days, to make nursing easier.

He grinned. "I thought you said you weren't gonna do that."

"I'm not." I dropped my arm from the door jamb and headed across the floor. "I don't want Raoul. I want you."

"I want you, too. C'mere." He turned to me as I slipped between the sheets, and tumbled me onto my back. His knee moved between my legs. One hand came up to cup my cheek. "I don't wanna share you. Even with Raoul."

Nice to know. I felt the same way. Meaning that even if Catherine was right and Elspeth hadn't actually seen Rafe naked in fourteen years, I wasn't at all happy about her fantasizing about him all this time.

"I don't want to share you, either," I told him. Perhaps, when it came to it, not even with the reading public.

But I could make that decision later. For now, I had more important things to focus on. I wound my arms around his neck and pulled his head down so I could kiss him. And that was all either of us said for a while. Or at least all either of us said that I want to share in print.

He got up and went to work as usual the next morning. Except I guess instead of heading for Columbia and the police department there, he headed for the Maury County sheriff's department and Bob Satterfield instead.

I wasn't awake when he left. As usual, Carrie had been up a few times overnight, and as usual I was dead to the world when the alarm went off. The irritated beeping was loud enough to drag my gluey eyelids apart, but when Rafe turned it off and then bent over me and whispered, "Go back to sleep," I did. He walked out while I was snoozing.

By the time I—or rather Carrie—got hungry and woke up the second time, it was after eight, and the house was empty except for the two of us (and Pearl). There was a faint aroma of coffee in the air, but as I discovered when I got down to the kitchen, there was no coffee in the machine. And since I'm not actually supposed to have much coffee, I heated some milk for a cup of hot chocolate instead—milk is good for the baby, chocolate is good in general—and consoled myself with that. It didn't make it any easier to wake up, but it made up, to at least some degree, for not getting any coffee.

All that done, and once I was dressed and ready to face the day, I gave Pearl a dog biscuit and left her on her pillow in the kitchen, and then I walked myself and Carrie over to the converted carriage house that serves as the Martin Mansion garage, and strapped the baby and the car seat into the back of the Volvo and headed for Sweetwater proper.

Eight hours of interrupted sleep had done very little to ease my irritation when it came to Dix and Charlotte. How dare he take her on a date? How dare she go? How dared either of them do it without running it by me first?

Granted, it was really none of my business, and no reason either of them should have to run their respective love lives past me… but when one of them was my best friend from high school, and the other was my brother, and I had an investment in both of their happiness—with other people—it seemed like informing me was the least they could do.

I started with Dix. Charlotte had been avoiding me since she came back to Sweetwater, and besides, while there was a time in my life I would have gone to her first, that had changed. Dix was my brother. I started there.

Or rather, I tried. I drove to the square and parked the car in an empty space outside Martin and McCall Law Offices, hauled the baby seat from the back of the car, and went inside. Only to be informed that Dix wasn't on the premises.

I put the carrier on the floor. Carrie wasn't very big, but in combination with the seat she got heavy pretty quickly, and I didn't see why I should have to stand there and hold her aloft when the seat would be perfectly fine on the floor. "Where is he?"

"He had an appointment," Darcy said, smiling at the sight of the baby. She came around the desk and squatted in front of her. "Hello, Caroline!"

Carrie gurgled and Darcy laughed. "Yes, you are a pretty girl."

"What kind of appointment?"

Darcy tilted her head and looked up at me. Standing, she's a couple of inches taller than me, but since she was squatting, I could actually look down at her. Her brows, as elegantly drawn as her mother's, pulled together. "What's wrong?"

"He went on a date last night," I said.

Darcy nodded. "I know. He arranged to have Catherine take the girls. I would have done it, but I was having dinner with Patrick."

Patrick Nolan, Darcy's beau, is a police officer with the Columbia PD. One of Tamara Grimaldi's underlings now, and one of Rafe's coworkers.

I waved it aside. "He went out with Charlotte Albertson!"

Or Charlotte Whitaker, but here in Sweetwater, she'd probably always be Charlotte Albertson, just as I'd always be Savannah Martin, even though we were both married now. And besides, if Charlotte's separation from Richard stuck, she might become Charlotte Albertson again.

"Your friend from high school?" Darcy got up and legged it back behind the desk. "I thought you liked her."

"I used to," I grumbled, "before she went out with my brother."

"Didn't she go out with your brother in high school?"

"Yes, she went out with *our* brother in high school. That doesn't mean I want her going out with him now. At least not until she's properly divorced." And preferably not then, either.

"For what it's worth," Darcy offered, "I didn't get the impression that he was all that excited about taking her out."

"Then he shouldn't have asked her!"

"I got the feeling she asked him. And that it was more of a friendly dinner than anything romantic."

Friendly? "Catherine said she's still angling for a job here. Although there's nothing for her to do and she isn't family."

"Maybe she thinks, if she marries Dix, she will be family," Darcy said.

I folded my arms across my chest. "That's a lot of trouble to go to for a job." And besides, if she married Dix, she wouldn't have to work. Sheila hadn't worked.

"Maybe that's what she's looking for," Darcy said when I'd aired this thought. "Someone to support her the way her husband does. Or did."

"If so, I think she'll be disappointed. Not that Dix is poor. But he's a family practice lawyer in a small town. Richard is a cosmetic surgeon in a big city. I'm sure he makes a lot more money than Dix."

Darcy shrugged. "Why don't you go ask her?"

"That was going to be my next stop. I wanted to talk to Dix first."

She nodded. "Well, I'm sorry you can't. He'll be back after lunch, but that's a few hours from now."

"I'll just go look for Charlotte." I bent and snagged the handle of the baby seat.

"Thanks for stopping by," Darcy said. "And for bringing the baby."

I headed for the door, and told her over my shoulder, "Now that we're settled, at least for a while, and Rafe's recovered and back to work, you and I should grab lunch or dinner sometime so we can catch up."

"I'm always happy to see you," Darcy said. "And the baby."

"I'll text you. We'll figure out a time and place."

She nodded. "Looking forward to it."

I was, too. It was nice to have another sister. We weren't as close as I was with Catherine, since I'd only known that Darcy was family for six months or so, and Catherine and I had been sisters for twenty-eight years, but I enjoyed her company. And since she was also Rafe's cousin a few times removed on his father's side, we had that in common, as well. Really and truly, for having discovered one another late, I thought we were doing just fine.

Outside, I put Carrie and the carrier back into the Volvo, and got behind the wheel. And was just about to pull away from the curb when the door to Audrey's On The Square, the only designer boutique in Maury County, opened. "Savannah!"

I put the car back in park and turned off the engine before I got out. "Audrey."

"I thought that was you." My mother's best friend, as well as Darcy's mother and Rafe's aunt or cousin of some sort, beamed at me.

"I was just looking for Dix," I explained after I'd given her the expected hug. "But Darcy said he wasn't in the office. So now I'm going to look for Charlotte."

"Your friend from high school?"

I nodded. "She and Dix went on a date last night. I want to know why."

Audrey got a sort of funny look on her face. "I'm sure for the usual reasons."

Well… yes. Probably. But— "She's still married to Richard. She only left him after Christmas. She can't possibly have had time to get a divorce yet. The usual reasons don't apply when she's still married."

"Be that as it may," Audrey started, and then shook her head. "How's Rafe?"

I told her he was fine. "On loan to Sheriff Satterfield. They found what's left of Katie Graves up in the hills by the Devil's Backbone."

Her eyes widened. "The girl who disappeared all those years ago? Back when y'all were kids?"

I nodded. "She went to school with Catherine. With Rafe and Dix, too, but she was Catherine's age."

"And now she's back?"

"I imagine she was always there," I said, although I had no way of knowing whether that was true or not. But it made sense to think that she'd been there ever since she disappeared. The thought of anything else was upsetting.

Audrey shook her head and clicked her tongue. Her wedge of thick, black hair swung. "Dear me. I remember all the hoopla when she went missing. Margaret was frantic."

No doubt. I remembered some of that myself, but Audrey had probably seen, or noticed, more of it. Mother would have tried to keep some of her hysteria hidden from her children, probably, but she was likely to have cut loose with her best friend. "The sheriff wants Rafe to help him figure out what happened."

"Good for Bob," Audrey said, with a glance over her shoulder at the store. "I should get back inside. But I saw you out here and wanted to say hello."

"And I'm glad you did." I've always liked Audrey. And now that I knew she was related to Rafe, I liked her even better. "Mrs. Jenkins OK?"

"Aunt Tondalia is fine," Audrey said. "She's coloring in the back room. I'd tell you to come inside and say hello, but I know you have to go. Maybe the two of you can stop by some night, with the baby."

I was sure we could. "I'll let you know."

Audrey nodded and turned back to the door. She was just wearing a thin silk shirt with polkadots, along with a skirt and shoes, so I didn't blame her for wanting to get back inside where it was warmer. "Drive carefully."

I wasn't going far, but I told her thanks, and went back to

the car. And drove the two or three blocks to the big, white Victorian where Charlotte had grown up.

Last time I'd been by, a couple of weeks ago, Charlotte's mother had been out in the yard watching her grandchildren play. Today the front lawn was empty, just an expanse of dead yellow grass and a few spiky sticks of vegetation where the flower beds would be in warmer weather.

I parked at the curb and hauled the baby out of the car. We made our way through the gate, up the walkway, onto the covered Victorian porch, where I rang the doorbell.

After a minute, the door opened, and Mrs. Albertson peered out. "Oh," she said after a beat. "It's you."

Like the last time I'd shown up unannounced, she seemed less than happy to see me. It had struck me as strange then, and still did now, since when we were younger, the Albertsons had always seemed happy that Charlotte and I were friends. "Hi, Mrs. Albertson." I gave her my best smile. "Is Charlotte home?"

I inched forward. She stood her ground instead of stepping back. "No. She's out."

Not much sense in trying to force my way into the house, then. I stopped. "Where'd she go?"

"She didn't say," Mrs. Albertson said. That also seemed strange to me, but it wasn't like I could call her on it.

"Any idea when she'll be back?"

She shook her head. "You can try to text her."

I could, and probably would. Although it hadn't worked the last time I tried. Or the time before that. Or the time before that.

But there was no point in saying that, either, so I just nodded. "Thank you."

I turned and started to make my way down the couple of steps again. The door shut and the deadbolt locked with a sound of finality before I'd even gotten down on level ground.

"That was weird," I told Carrie as I put her back into the Volvo. She pursed her lips and blew a bubble.

After getting back behind the wheel, I sat for a moment and thought about what to do next. I'd tried to find Dix, and he hadn't been there. I'd tried to find Charlotte, and she hadn't been there, either.

The only thing left to do, as far as I was concerned, was talk to Tamara Grimaldi. I hadn't seen her for a couple of days anyway. Not since Rafe started work. I should probably check in with her and make sure everything was copasetic.

Decision made, I put the Volvo in gear and rolled off toward Columbia.

It isn't a far drive. When I was a teenager, we'd gone by bus to high school in Columbia every morning. It took twenty minutes or so. When I was driving myself, and I didn't have to stop every few minutes, it took less. In no time at all, I was pulling up outside the police station in downtown Columbia, pulling the car seat with the baby out of the car, and walking into the lobby.

The same woman as last time I'd been here was on duty behind the desk over in the corner. She gave me a polite look, and then a second look. And then a smirk. "He isn't here."

"I know he isn't here," I said. And because I didn't like her—she had ogled Rafe when we were here two weeks ago—I added, "When he left me in bed this morning, he was going to see Sheriff Satterfield."

After this reminder that I shared a bed with him and she didn't, I finished up with, "I'd like to see Detec... um... Chief Grimaldi, if she's available."

She gave me another smirk, so maybe she thought the fact that I'd felt it necessary to stake, or remind her of, my claim on Rafe was amusing. "I'll see if she's in."

She punched a couple of buttons on her phone. I waited. "Chief Grimaldi. Mrs.... um... Collier is here to see you."

Grimaldi said something, and the young woman nodded. "Yes, ma'am." She put the phone down and told me, "She'll be right out."

I thanked her and took the baby over to the sitting area. I hadn't even managed to get my butt planted in a chair before the door to the inner sanctum opened and Grimaldi came through.

Four

As usual when she was working, the detective, or police chief now, was wearing a suit. One with pants instead of a skirt. Other than when she was the maid of honor at my wedding, I'm not sure I've ever seen Grimaldi in a skirt.

She's tall, a little taller than me, with an olive complexion, black curls cut short, and a somewhat prominent nose. And although we've been friends for the best part of a year and a half now—and she was maid of honor at my wedding—she still intimidates me just a little.

I pushed it aside. "Hello, Detec… um… Tamara."

She gave me a nod. "Something wrong?"

Yes. And no. "Nothing important. If this is a bad time, it can wait."

She shook her head. "It's not a bad time. Come on back."

She held the door while I grabbed the car seat with the baby and walked through. And then I followed her down the hallway to the chief's office at the rear of the building. Once there, I put the baby on the floor, removed the blanket I kept over Carrie in the car, and started unwinding my own scarf. It was January, and while it rarely gets very cold in Middle Tennessee in the winter, it was cold enough for a scarf.

Grimaldi walked around the desk and sat down while I shrugged out of my coat and put it over the back of the chair I planned to sit in. "What's going on?"

"I'm irritated," I said, sitting and folding one leg over the other.

She arched her brows. "With me?"

"No. You didn't do anything to me." After a second I added, "Should I be?"

"No reason I can think of." She leaned back in the desk chair. It gave a squeak and she grimaced. "Your husband isn't here."

I nodded. "I know. He told me Sheriff Satterfield borrowed him for a few days."

"It'll probably be longer than that," Grimaldi said. "Cold cases can take a long time to solve."

"Except it's sort of warm now." Or so I assumed. With the discovery of Katie's bones, the case had heated up.

"The evidence is still fifteen years old," Grimaldi said, and she had a point. "Do you remember the girl who disappeared?"

I shook my head. "She was Catherine's age. Four years older than me. And she wasn't local. To Sweetwater, I mean. Catherine knew her, and Rafe knew who she was, and maybe Dix did, too. They all went to high school in Columbia by then. But I was still in middle school. I don't think I'd even heard her name before that day."

Grimaldi nodded.

"Rafe told me one of the ATF agents who was up on the Skinners' property looking at the pot houses found her."

"It was before my time," Grimaldi said, since she had only been in the police chief's job for a couple of weeks by now. "But that's what the sheriff said."

"Did he say anything else?"

She gave me a sort of jaundiced look. "Are you here to fish?"

I wasn't. "Fishing is secondary." But fun nonetheless. "I didn't actually come to talk about Katie. I'm interested, though. I remember when it happened. How freaked out everyone was.

Especially Mother, and all the other mothers. I don't think we went to school for several days after it happened."

"That's probably normal," Grimaldi said. "At that time, nobody knew what had happened. At first, I'm sure your mother, and all the other mothers, were afraid it was going to turn into an epidemic. That someone was targeting teenage girls. When that didn't turn out to be the case, everything went back to normal."

It had. Until now. "Is it certain that it's Katie?"

"Again, it's not my case and I wasn't here when the bones were found. All I know is what Sheriff Satterfield told me on the phone yesterday. But he didn't sound like there was any doubt. I think there might have been dental records involved."

"So the sheriff suspected it was Katie all along?" He must have, if he'd gone to Katie's dentist to ask for dental records. And yet he hadn't said a word about his suspicions. Not at Thanksgiving, not during Christmas.

"There aren't that many open missing persons cases in this area," Grimaldi said. "And although I don't know—it's outside my jurisdiction—there might have been things found with her—with the bones—that gave him the idea. Clothes, maybe a backpack. She was on her way to school when she disappeared, right?"

I nodded. "I guess I'll have to wait until Rafe comes home tonight to get the details."

"I'm afraid so," Grimaldi said. "I'll have to do the same, if it comes to that. Wait for the report. Other than loaning the sheriff's department one of my investigators, I have nothing to do with the case."

And about that… "Rafe told me Jarvis was upset because he wasn't picked."

"Jarvis got the consolation prize," Grimaldi answered. When I looked as brightly inquisitive as I could, without actually sitting up and begging, she sighed. "We had another unnatural death in town a few days ago. It looks like a suicide—older man with terminal cancer, overdose of pain meds—but I had to give Jarvis something to do, or he'd be banging around here all day giving me attitude. Besides, we might as well take a good look, as there are a few interesting details."

I looked even more brightly inquisitive, if that was possible, and she gave me a jaundiced look. "The details are none of your business, Ms.... Savannah."

"I'm just curious," I said. "Is it anyone I know?"

"I wouldn't think so," Grimaldi answered, "although I suppose it's possible. The obituary ran this morning, so I'm not telling you anything that isn't public knowledge. His name was Scott Mason, and he was around sixty. Ring any bells?"

It didn't, and I said so. "Is Jarvis happy about his consolation prize?"

"Not as happy as he'd be with the Graves investigation," Grimaldi answered. "But he's enough of a cop to give it a good look, so I can't really complain."

Probably better not to.

"If you didn't come here to talk about the Katie Graves case, why are you here?"

Oh. Right. I shifted on the chair. "Did you know that Dix went out on a date last night? With Charlotte Albertson?"

There was a pause. I wasn't sure whether the detective—chief—was flabbergasted or hurt or just confused as to why I would tell her this. Her face gave nothing away, so it was impossible to guess what she was thinking.

"No," she said eventually, after what felt like an eternity, but which was probably just five seconds or so, "I didn't know that."

We sat in silence another few seconds.

"Charlotte Albertson. That's your friend from high school, isn't it?"

I nodded. "It's Charlotte Whitaker now. She's been living with her parents since Christmas. I saw her, very briefly, the last time I was down here. Other than that, she's been avoiding me."

Or that was how it felt.

"She came to Audrey's shop looking for a job a couple of weeks ago. Darcy said she'd been trying to get Dix to hire her since then, too. I guess maybe this—having dinner with him—was more of the same."

"Could be," Grimaldi said.

I squinted at her. "Aren't you upset?" Or was she upset and just didn't show it?

She looked back at me. "Why would I be upset?"

"Didn't you hear me? He went on a date with her!"

"I heard you. Your brother's a grown man. He can date anyone he wants to."

After a second's pause, not long enough for me to gather my wits and say anything, she added, "It's been more than a year since his wife died. If he feels ready to start dating again, I'm happy for him."

"Well, I'm—!" I stopped, since I couldn't very well say that I wasn't happy for him. I was. I didn't want him to be alone forever, and losing a spouse is hard. Dealing with Sheila's death, and the circumstances of it, hadn't been easy. I was glad he was moving on.

I just wasn't happy he was moving on with Charlotte. I wanted him to move on with Grimaldi.

"I thought the two of you..." I said, and trailed off. Suggestively. Waiting for her to pick up the ball and run with it.

She arched her brows. I huffed. "You know what I'm trying to say. You and Dix have been spending a lot of time together since Sheila died."

"I wouldn't call it a lot of time," Grimaldi said judiciously.

Compared to what, exactly? "You've come down here to visit him. He's gone to Nashville to visit you. And it isn't a quick drive. You have to really want to see someone, to spend more than an hour driving to where they are just to have dinner. And for all I know, you've been sleeping together—and don't tell me if you have, because I don't want to know."

Her lips twitched, but she didn't say anything.

"I thought you took this job, at least partly, because Dix was here. Or because the job was closer to Dix."

She opened her mouth. And closed it again. And opened it again. "I did take the job partly because it was here. And partly because the sheriff asked for my help. And partly because I thought it would make for a nice opportunity to work with your husband."

And while that was gratifying and all— "Then how can you be OK with the fact that Dix went on a date with someone else?"

"We don't have an exclusive relationship," Grimaldi said.

My eyes widened. "This wasn't the first time Dix went on a date with someone other than you?"

Because while I'd known he was seeing her occasionally, I hadn't known he was seeing anyone else.

Grimaldi looked uncomfortable. "As far as I know, you brother hasn't been on a date with anyone else since his wife died."

Well, if not Dix, then— "Have you been on a date with someone else?"

"I'm not sure that's any of your business," Grimaldi said.

I sniffed. "If you've been stringing my brother along while you've been dating other people, it's absolutely my business."

She smirked. I scowled. "Look. I like you. I made you my freaking maid of honor when I married Rafe. But Dix is my brother. And I don't want him to get hurt."

"I'm not hurting your brother," Grimaldi said. And didn't

say anything else.

I folded my arms across my chest and stuck my bottom lip out. "Well, I don't like it. I don't like that he was on a date with Charlotte yesterday, and if you've been dating someone else, I don't like that, either."

"Maybe you should talk to him about it," Grimaldi said.

I lost my breath at the sheer unfairness of it. "Do you think I haven't tried that? I went to the law office first thing this morning. He wasn't there. Then I went to Charlotte's house. She wasn't there, either. And that's when I ended up here."

"Have you tried calling?" Grimaldi asked.

I hadn't tried calling. And I wasn't about to, not while I sat in her office. But once I was back in my car, just wait. My fingers would be smoking, that's how fast they'd be dialing Dix's number.

But meanwhile— "I can't believe you're so calm about this!"

Grimaldi looked at me, and for a second her eyes weren't calm at all. Or maybe I imagined it, because it was what I wanted to see. At any rate, her voice was even when she said, "Your brother is a free operator. He can date anyone he wants. He isn't married anymore, and he and I don't have the kind of relationship that would stop him from dating someone else. And if you have questions beyond that, you're going to have to talk to him about it."

"Don't worry," I said, my teeth gritted, "I will."

Grimaldi nodded. "Anything else?"

I shook my head.

"Then you should probably go," Grimaldi said. "I have work to do."

She didn't sound upset with me, so that was something, anyway. I got up and started to put on my coat. "Let me know if you want to go grab some dinner or something one night. With or without Rafe. And as long as you don't mind if the baby comes."

"I'm always happy to see the baby," Grimaldi said, with a glance at her. "Is she doing OK?"

I moved on to winding the scarf around my neck. "She still wakes me up twice a night. But other than that, she's fine. Getting bigger. I think she was thinking about turning over during tummy time yesterday."

Grimaldi's lips twitched. "Tummy time?"

"It's when you put the baby on the floor and let her stay there for a while. It's important for development. It's how they learn to hold their heads up, and eventually to crawl and such."

Grimaldi nodded. "I'm glad everything's OK."

Everything was not OK, but I didn't bother saying so again. "I'll see you later." I hoisted the baby carrier from the floor.

"I'll see you out," Grimaldi said and got up from the desk.

I knew the way, but it probably wasn't good for me to be wandering around inside the police station on my own. Especially since Grimaldi knew me, and might suspect that I might fall into temptation to snoop. Not sure I'd risk doing that inside a police station, but there was probably interesting information here.

I put it out of my head as she opened the door to the hallway and held it for me. "I forgot to tell you," I said as I moved past, "I've decided on the title for the trashy historical romance novel I might be writing."

Grimaldi's brows arched. "I didn't know you were thinking about writing a trashy romance novel."

"I've been thinking about it ever since Elspeth Caulfield died. She made millions writing sex scenes about my husband. Now that she's no longer writing, I figure her readers are probably going through withdrawal." I would be, if I didn't have Rafe to keep me busy at night. "Besides, her publisher could probably use another Barbara Botticelli."

"I think there's probably a little more to it than just the sex scenes," Grimaldi said, as we walked side by side down the hallway toward the lobby, "but I'll bite. What's the title?"

I told her the title I'd come up with, and watched her mouth curve. "That's trashy, all right."

"Barbara had some real doozies. *Apache Amour. Tartan Tryst. Pirate's Booty.*"

Grimaldi laugh-snorted. "That last one's hard to beat."

It was. "I'll lend it to you, if you want to read it." And as long as she could keep from imagining Rafe naked.

"I might take you up on that," Grimaldi said and opened the door to the lobby. "Thanks for stopping by."

Oh, sure. "If you're going to kick my brother's butt, can I be there to watch?"

"I'll let you know," Grimaldi said. "Have a good day, Savannah."

She closed the door and headed back toward her office while Carrie and I made our way across the lobby and out.

Back inside the car I let the engine run for a minute while I pulled out my phone and dialed Dix's number. It rang twice, and then went to voicemail. I don't know why I was surprised, since nothing else had worked out the way I'd wanted it to this morning. "It's me," I told the recording. "Your favorite sister. Call me when you have a chance."

No sense in yelling at him by voicemail. That would only ensure that he probably wouldn't call me back.

So here I was, in the middle of Columbia. I couldn't get hold of Dix or Charlotte, to chew either of them out. Grimaldi had given me no satisfaction whatsoever. She'd even refused to trash-talk Dix with me, so there'd been no relief there. I supposed I could go unburden myself to Mother, but that would entail telling her about my hopes for Dix and Grimaldi, and I wasn't sure I wanted to do that. Mother would probably prefer Charlotte over Grimaldi as a potential daughter-in-law, and if she did, I didn't want to hear it.

I was officially at a loss for what to do next. I could go home, and feed Carrie, and give her tummy time before putting her down for a nap. And then I could sit there and twiddle my thumbs—or start work on *Bedded by the Bedouin*—while she slept.

Or I could occupy myself out here in the world for a bit longer.

I glanced at the clock on the dashboard. It was getting close to lunch. I lifted the phone again and punched in Rafe's number.

"I'm in Columbia," I told him when he picked up. "Want to meet for lunch?"

His voice sounded amused, and a little regretful. "Can't. I'm working."

"I'm sure Sheriff Satterfield won't mind if you eat."

"I'm up at the Skinners' place."

So not really nearby. "I could pick up a sandwich and come up there," I offered.

He chuckled. "You just wanna look at the crime scene."

I did want to look at the crime scene. If it was a crime scene. But that wasn't the only reason, or even the most pressing, why I wanted to see him. "I'm upset," I confessed. "I can't get hold of Dix or Charlotte. He's not in the office. She's not home. And neither of them are answering the phone or responding to texts. And when I went to see Grimaldi, she told me that Dix is a big boy and he can date who he wants."

There was a second's pause. "Well, what did you want her to say?" Rafe asked reasonably. "Not like she's gonna tell you he can't. They ain't married."

No. And at this juncture, not likely to be.

"I just want to yell at someone."

"Sorry, darlin'." His voice was amused. "If you're just gonna yell at me, I ain't telling you where to find me."

"Not you. There's no reason to yell at you."

He didn't answer, and I added, "I just want to see you. And I wouldn't mind seeing the crime scene. Or wherever Katie's bones were found, if that's what you mean by the crime scene. Can I pick up a couple of sandwiches and come meet you? I need a hug."

He chuckled. "Sure, darlin'. I'll meet you at Robbie's place. You remember how to get there?"

I did remember how to get there. "It'll be thirty minutes or so." Between picking up the sandwiches and then making the drive across the county.

"It'll give me time to walk back," Rafe said easily.

"What kind of sandwich would you like?"

He requested roast beef and cheddar, and then we hung up so I could go buy sandwiches and he could start making his way back to Robbie's trailer from wherever he was at the moment.

I'd made this trek with sandwiches once before. That had been during the Skinner investigation, and I had shown up outside Robbie Skinner's trailer to find Pearl the pitbull running loose. Animal Control had taken her away after the murders, along with the other Skinner dogs, but Pearl had gotten away from them and made her way back, and I had run across her when I showed up to feed my husband. I'd tossed her the sandwiches I'd been carrying so she wouldn't attack me, and she'd ended up protecting me against the big, scary guy who showed up next.

The big, scary guy had been Rafe, so I hadn't been in any danger, but of course Pearl hadn't known that.

This time, as I came bumping up the rough track and out into the clearing where Robbie's old trailer was situated, there was no dog there to greet me. Rafe, on the other hand, was leaning against the side of a boring, tan Chevy with extra antennae and government plates. If you looked closely, you could see the line of blue lights in the tinted rear window.

This must be one of the plain police cars Grimaldi had told him would be at his disposal if he decided to come to work for the Columbia PD. I guess it wouldn't look that professional for one of the investigators to be driving around on the muscular Harley-Davidson that's Rafe's usual mode of transportation, although I'm sure he'd prefer it.

"Nice car," I told him, after I'd pulled up next to it and opened my door. "C'mon in. We might as well be comfortable." And it was a little too cold for a picnic on the (dead) grass.

He grinned at me, but opened the back door to say hello to Carrie before doing anything else. He tickled her tummy, she gurgled, and then he popped the pacifier back into her mouth.

"Bring her," I told him, and although he arched a brow, he lifted her from the car seat and snuggled her against his chest as he shut the back door and folded himself into the front seat. I exchanged his roast beef and cheddar for the baby, and indicated the cup of sweet tea sitting in the console. "Knock yourself out."

"What about you? Ain't you gonna eat?"

"I had my sandwich on the way. I figured I'd feed Carrie while we sit here." I unbuttoned my coat and blouse while I juggled the baby.

"That could make it hard to concentrate," Rafe said, but he took a bite of the sandwich and washed it down with a swig of tea.

I got Carrie situated before I told him, "I'm sure you'll manage."

We sat in companionable silence for a few minutes, while Rafe and Carrie swallowed, and Rafe chewed. While he focused on his sandwich, I updated him on my conversation with Grimaldi. Since there wasn't much else to say about that particular matter, I moved on to what he was doing. In a roundabout sort of way.

"I can't believe Robbie's trailer is still here. Shouldn't someone have moved it away, for evidence or something?"

"You can't really confiscate a crime scene," Rafe said, around bites of sandwich. "Most of'em are stationary."

Sure. But— "This one isn't." It was an old Airstream that had seen better days, and it had wheels.

"Where were they gonna take it?" Rafe wanted to know. "Besides, it belongs to somebody."

"Who?"

He shrugged. "Robbie's daughter, I guess. She'd be his next of kin, so she'd inherit everything."

She would. And she was damned lucky her mother had taken her and moved out before the murders, or twelve-year-old Kayla and her mama would have been dead, too.

"Were the bones found on Robbie's property?" I asked, winding my way in the direction I wanted to go.

Rafe gave me a look that told me clearly that he saw straight through me and knew exactly where I was headed. But he answered anyway. "Not sure exactly."

I squinted at him. "But you were back there, right? Where they were found?"

He nodded. "The site's back in the woods apiece. And it's on Skinner land, but nobody knows for sure where the boundaries are between Robbie's land, and Darrell's and Art's."

There'd been three Skinner brothers. Art was the eldest, in his late thirties when he died. Darrell was the youngest, and I think Rafe had told me Darrell was two years older than him, so Darrell had been thirty-three or thereabouts. Robbie, whose trailer we were parked outside, had been in his mid-thirties.

"You're here," I pointed out. "Not at Art's trailer, or Darrell's. So does that mean she was found closest to Robbie's place?"

He nodded. "But that don't mean it's Robbie's land back there. I don't think Robbie's trailer sits in the middle of Robbie's patch of ground. It's much nearer the road, for one thing. Everything back in there," he indicated the trailer and what lay beyond it, "for miles and miles belongs to the Skinners."

Probably not for miles and miles. But I got the gist of what he was saying. The property extended back a long way, up into the hills, while the public road through this area was just down the long driveway, a football field's distance or so away. Robbie had set his trailer much closer to the road than the back end of his property.

And since that was so— "So Robbie's trailer could be sitting almost on the edge of Darrell's property. Or Art's. Is that what you're saying?"

Rafe nodded. "Nothing out here's marked. They've got fences and no trespassing signs on the edges of their property, but Robbie didn't protect his land from Darrell, or vice versa."

I nodded.

"Besides, I don't think it makes no difference where she was found. The Skinners always were thick as thieves. And back when Katie disappeared, Darrell was eighteen or so. Robbie mighta been twenty-one, maybe, and Art maybe twenty-three or -four. It woulda been their daddy's property back then."

That made sense. Darrell, Robbie, and Art would only have come into their chunks of land when their father, the original owner, passed away and they divided it up among themselves. So just because Katie had been found on Robbie's land, if it was Robbie's land now, didn't mean that Robbie was any more likely to have killed her than Darrell or Art.

And that was if anyone had killed her at all. She might have gotten lost, broken her foot, and died of exposure.

"What time of year did she disappear?" My memory wasn't quite good enough to recall the details. It hadn't been summer.

Katie had been on her way to the school bus, so it had been during the school year. But I couldn't recall whether it had been cold or warm, rainy or dry.

"October," Rafe said, "if memory serves."

So the exposure theory wasn't much of a possibility. Sometimes it's cold in October, but it's usually not cold enough to kill you. "I don't suppose it was possible to tell from the bones how she died?"

"Not that I've heard," Rafe said. "I ain't seen'em personally."

"I guess you don't even know whether you're investigating a murder or an accident."

He shook his head, but qualified it with, "Hard to imagine she coulda died out here and nobody found her for sixteen years, if it wasn't deliberate."

Perhaps. Then again, if one of the Skinners had killed her, leaving her in the middle of the woods would have been a risk, too. Yes, it was private property, but someone might have come along and found her, even so. It would have been smarter to bury her, if they'd known she was there.

"Not everybody bothers," Rafe said, when I pointed this out. "Remember Eugenio Hernandez?"

Not someone I was ever likely to forget, and not just because he'd almost killed Rafe. "He dumped the bodies of the girls he killed in the woods, and didn't bother to cover them up." And last summer, I had spent half a day walking those woods—back in Nashville, not anywhere around here— looking for those remains. One of the more disturbing half days I've ever spent.

"He didn't dump them on his own property, though," I added.

"Nobody ever said the Skinners were smart," Rafe told me, and crumpled the empty paper that had been wrapped around his sandwich. "Thanks for lunch."

"My pleasure." I put a drowsy Carrie up on my shoulder and began to pat her back. "How about we take a walk?"

He shook his head, even as his lips twitched. "You ain't dressed for that, darlin'. And you can't take the baby into the woods."

"I have a sling I can put her in. She'll probably fall asleep. And I'm good at walking in heels." They weren't even very high heels, really. Maybe two inches, if that. And the booties covered my ankles, so I wouldn't have to worry about twisting anything.

He looked at me. I smiled brightly, and did my best to look like I'd be just fine walking through the woods in my cashmere coat and suede booties. Like there was nothing I'd like better.

He sighed. "Fine. But when you wish you were back home, don't blame me. I ain't carrying you back."

"You won't have to. Although you might have to carry the baby."

"I'll carry the baby," Rafe said and reached for his door handle. "I just won't carry you. C'mon. Let's get this show on the road."

Five

Five minutes later, we were on our way into the woods. My elegant coat was flapping around my calves, getting snagged on twigs and brush, and Rafe had the baby slung across the chest of his new leather jacket, the one he'd bought to replace the one that had burned to a crisp in the fire two weeks ago. The baby sling sported images of cute zoo animals—yellow giraffes, blue elephants, brown monkeys, and green crocodiles on a hot pink background—and it clashed with the black leather, but somehow he pulled it off anyway, and didn't just manage to look like a good father, but really hot, too.

At first, we kept to paths we'd already traveled back in October when the Skinner investigation was ongoing. This was where Rafe and I had walked on the day when we'd stumbled over the Skinners' pot growing operation. A few minutes into the walk, we ended up outside the same pot house we'd discovered then.

When we'd been here in October, there'd been traps on the path to the greenhouse, and generators keeping the plants at optimal light and temperature inside the building. Now, everything was silent. There was a notice on the door that sported the logo of the ATF—I didn't stop to read it, but I could guess what it said—and when I squinted through one of the big windows on my way past, the plants were all gone. The ATF, or somebody, must have brought a tractor trailer or two up here, and loaded up all the marijuana plants for transportation elsewhere.

"Empty," I told Rafe's back.

He nodded. "It's all shut down. Everything they could find."

We kept walking. The next thing we came to was the track the Skinners had used to get their generators and building materials up to the grow site—probably the same track the ATF had used to remove the plants. Last fall, we'd followed this track to another greenhouse. This time Rafe cut across it, and ducked into the trees on the other side.

We weren't following a path anymore, although he seemed to know where he was going. If he needed to take his bearings, he didn't stop to do it, just kept moving into the trees, in a mostly straight line. The ground rose, and then fell. The trees were close together, and there was a slight wind under an overcast sky. Not quite cold enough to snow, but not too far off, either. I stuck my hands in my pockets, wishing I'd thought to bring gloves when I left the house this morning.

When I did, I hadn't expected to be making a cross-country trek, though.

We might have been walking for fifteen minutes or so when I saw a piece of yellow crime scene tape hanging from a tree to my left. It moved a little in the breeze, or I probably wouldn't have noticed it. I slowed down and looked around. "Here?"

There were a couple of pieces of yellow tape in the other direction, too. One strand hung between two trees, and another draped over a bush a little farther to the right.

"Up ahead," Rafe said, and kept going.

"But the crime scene tape…"

"Outer perimeter." He stepped carefully over brush and broken twigs. I scurried to catch back up so I could hear what he was saying. "There's a big area, like a football field, that got searched, and then a smaller area, right around where the skull and big bones were found, that was picked over pretty good. We're inside the big area. The small area is up ahead."

I nodded, and followed. He didn't sound winded at all, but I'll admit that I was a little short of breath. I hadn't moved much in the two months since the baby was born, and I was out of practice.

Of course, wearing the booties with the two-inch heels over this uneven ground didn't do me any favors, either.

After another couple of minutes, we came to another piece of crime scene tape. Rafe stopped and waited for me to catch up. "Here's the crime scene."

It was a much smaller area—maybe twelve feet by twelve: your standard room size in a house—and it was surrounded by crime scene tape on all four sides. Or at least it had been surrounded at one point. Now, a couple of months later, the yellow tape stretched from tree to tree only in a few places, and was left flapping from branches and twigs around most of the perimeter.

"This was where the skull and bigger bones were found," Rafe said, pointing. "Some of the smaller bones were probably in the bigger area we just walked through."

I felt weird about that, about the fact that I'd walked across ground where some of Katie's bones might have been discovered. It made me want to pick up both my feet at the same time, but of course that was impossible, so I did my best to ignore the feeling.

Instead, I looked around. The location felt remote, but honestly, we hadn't walked that far. "It isn't that long a distance from Robbie's trailer."

Rafe shook his head. "Far enough that nobody'd be likely to wander out here, but not so far that she couldn't'a made her way back if she was hurt."

Just what I'd been thinking. It wouldn't have been a comfortable walk, or crawl, with a broken leg or other injury, but it ought to have been manageable. If Katie had been out here by herself, and had gotten hurt, she should have been able to make it back to civilization without dying.

"'Course," Rafe added pensively, "Robbie's trailer might not'a been there sixteen years ago."

That was a good point. If Robbie and Darrell Skinner had been in their late teens or early twenties at the time when Katie disappeared, they might have been living at home with their parents. Robbie's trailer could have been moved to that spot much later.

I glanced up at Rafe. "You knew the Skinners, didn't you?"

"Not to say knew," Rafe said, peering into the area beyond the crime scene tape. "Darrell was a couple years older'n me, and the other two were older'n that. And none of'em liked me much."

No, I remembered him saying that. That the Skinner boys had been the kind of good old boys Southern hillbillies who didn't like black people. Or mixed race people. Or, I'm sure, rich people, or educated people, or anybody else who was different than them.

"I guess you didn't spend any time up here when you were younger."

He shook his head. "They woulda chased me off their property with a shotgun if they'd seen me."

No doubt. The signs warning that trespassers would be shot were still lining Robbie's driveway. There was no reason to think he hadn't felt the same way sixteen years ago. "Maybe Katie trespassed and somebody shot her."

"Katie wasn't black," Rafe said. "And they'd'a found something else to do with Katie if they'd found her."

I winced. "I don't suppose there's any way to know...?"

He shook his head. "Not from bones."

"I don't suppose there were any bullets found?" If someone had shot Katie, and she'd fallen and bled to death, the bullet would have stayed with the body while it decomposed, and then the bullet would still have been here with the bones when the ATF guy found them.

"Not inside the perimeter," Rafe said, squinting at it, measuring with his eyes. "It's a big area, though. Easy to miss something."

"I don't think a crime scene crew is supposed to miss anything."

He shook his head. "But they're human."

Yes, they were, and humans sometimes make mistakes. And miss things.

"Besides," Rafe added, "the perimeter's arbitrary. Not like when you have a confined crime scene with walls and borders of some sort. Here, some guy prob'ly just said, 'Let's string the tape between those big trees there and there,' and that became the area that was searched."

"So you're saying there could be something outside the area that wasn't found?"

He shrugged. "Might be worth taking a couple hours to look."

Now?

Honestly, I had wanted to see the place, so it was nothing more than I deserved, I guess, if he made me spend all afternoon staring at the ground looking for clues, but it wasn't how I wanted to spend the next few hours.

He looked at me, and his lips curved. "Don't worry, darlin'. I wouldn't ask you to do it."

"If you're going to do it by yourself, it'll take all day." Or worse, all week.

He shook his head. "I'd pull in a couple other people if I had to. We could knock it out in a couple hours, if I had two or three other people."

"I'd be willing to help," I said, "but preferably not until I'd put on better clothes." And shoes. "And it would be good if I could find a sitter for Carrie."

Rafe nodded. "Not sure the sheriff'd be happy about you stumbling around out here looking for clues, darlin'. But I'll keep it in mind."

He turned his back on the crime scene. "Ready to go?"

I guess I was. There wasn't anything more to see her. "How's the baby?"

He peered down at her. "Sleeping."

"Warm enough?"

He nodded. "Seems to be." He tested her cheek with the tip of a finger. "Yeah. No problems."

"Then let's head back." I turned my back on Katie Graves's final resting place, and started to make my way through the trees.

We'd only walked a few yards beyond the bigger perimeter of the search when Rafe said, "Hold on a second."

I stopped. "Did you forget something?"

He shook his head. "Saw something shiny."

He wandered off toward the right, or right-forward. Northwest, if I were any judge of direction. Robbie's place was more southwest, based on where I thought the sun was. It was still overcast, but I could see a sort of glow behind the clouds. That might have been what had reflected off whatever shiny thing Rafe thought he'd seen.

He didn't walk far. About the length of a tractor trailer away, he stopped and looked down. By that point, I'd started to follow, and I was about ten feet away when he held up a hand. "Don't."

I stayed where I was. "What is it?"

"Looks like a ring." He stuck his hand in his pocket and came up with his phone. After taking a couple of photos, he bent, with one hand holding Carrie to his chest. "And maybe a couple of bones."

Ugh. My stomach did a slow turn while he straightened and

turned to me. "C'mere, darlin'. Take the baby so I can get down there and take a look."

I didn't want to come any closer, but I didn't think I had a choice. And I certainly didn't want Carrie to drop from the sling while he was bending and fetching, and there was a real chance of that. Unless he kept his hand on her, but that would make it hard to pick up whatever he'd found.

So I made my reluctant way through the shrubs and dead grass and let him transfer the sling with the baby from around his neck to around mine. Carrie made a couple of squeaky noises, but once she was nestled close to me, she settled back down into sleep.

Rafe squatted, meanwhile, and took a couple more photographs with his phone. I squinted at the area he was photographing, and nodded. "That looks very much like a ring." And maybe a small bone. Like a finger bone.

Which made total sense if I thought about it. But since I didn't want to think too hard about what the finger was doing so far from the rest of the body, or how it had moved so far away, I banished the thought from my head. "Are you going to pick it up?"

He sat back on his heels. "Might as well. There's no point in leaving it and then getting somebody else out here to pick it up when I can do it."

No point at all. "Do you have something to carry it in?"

"My pocket?" Rafe said.

"I meant before you put it in your pocket." That's what they usually do with evidence, isn't it? Pack it up carefully before they take it to the lab to analyze it?

He shook his head. "After all these years of being out here, ain't like I'm gonna be messing up any clues if I don't wrap it up tight."

I guessed not. And besides, he was the professional and I wasn't. So I didn't say anything else, just watched as he used a pen he pulled from his pocket to wiggle the ring out of the ground. Part of me expected him to tell me that all it was, was the ring off a can of beer, but after putting it in his palm and peering at it for a second, he nodded. "Definitely looks like something somebody'd wear."

He held his hand out and I bent forward for a closer look. Yes, it looked like a ring someone would wear. And furthermore, it was familiar.

Rafe brow arched when I said so, and I amended my statement. "I mean, I know what it is. I've seen them before. Those were popular around the time when Katie disappeared. I had one, and I think Catherine did, too." Or at least I remembered seeing something very similar in my sister's room. "They were some sort of friendship ring, I think. You could get them with combinations of initials on them. Ready-made, not the way you'd engrave your names on a wedding band, you know? They were just cheap aluminum rings you'd buy at the mall, with the initials already there."

Rafe nodded. "Whose initials did you have on yours? S & T?"

I shook my head. "This was several years before Todd. I was probably twelve or so. Mine said S & C."

His lips curved. "For Savannah and Charlotte."

I nodded. "I don't suppose you had one?"

He shook his head. "No, darlin'. No ring with initials or a woman's name until this one."

He lifted his left hand, with the wedding band I'd put there in June. The wedding band with my name inside it.

I took a second to enjoy the warm and fuzzy sensation that being married to him always gave me, and then I asked, prosaically, "What does that one say?"

"Looks like a D & C," Rafe said, peering at it. "Maybe an O. It's gonna have to get cleaned before we can say for sure, I think."

He handed it to me. I looked at it and nodded. After a decade and a half out in the woods, through rain and snow and mud and everything else, the ring was encrusted with dirt. But even so, the D was pretty clear. The C—or maybe O—was the thing in question.

I shifted it back and forth. "Looks more like a C to me. But it isn't a K, at any rate."

"C for Catherine?" Rafe suggested.

I suppose it might be. No one had ever called my sister Katie, or Kate or Kathy, or anything other than her full name. But that didn't mean that Katie Graves's first name couldn't have been Catherine, with a C. "D for Darrell?"

Rafe shrugged, but not because he disagreed. "That'd make sense."

It would, since the ring was found here, on Skinner property.

"I don't suppose Katie was involved with Darrell?"

"If she was," Rafe said, "the information ain't in the file."

No, that would be too easy.

"And it isn't like you can ask him." Since Darrell was as dead as Katie now.

He shook his head. "We should get back."

I nodded. "What about the… um… bones?"

He glanced at the ground and then at me. "Those are twigs, not bones."

I squinted at him.

"See for yourself." He bent and picked something up. It was small and brown, and I didn't want to touch it. When I put both hands behind my back, Rafe rolled his eyes and held it up in front of my nose. Close enough that my eyes crossed when I tried to focus on it.

"A little more distance?" I leaned back. "Yes, that's a twig."

"Told you," Rafe said and dropped it before wiping his fingers on his jeans.

"So the ring might not have anything to do with Katie."

He shook his head. "If it was Darrell's, he mighta dropped it. Before Katie died."

"Why— Oh." If it had been after, he would have seen Katie. And if he hadn't had anything to do with her death, he would have notified the police. Or so I would hope.

"C'mon." Rafe put a hand on my back and began to nudge me forward.

We hit the dirt track after a few minutes of walking, and then adjusted our direction toward Robbie's greenhouse and the path back to Robbie's trailer.

Neither of us said much on the way back. I guess we were both pondering the ring, and what it was doing there, and whether it had belonged to Katie, and had gotten separated from the rest of her body at some point, or whether it had been Darrell's, and had gotten there some other way.

Back in the clearing, Rafe helped me get the sling with the baby over my head, and we transferred her into her car seat in the back of the Volvo. Her eyes blinked a couple of times, and her lips pursed and made sucking motions, and I thought for sure she was going to wake up. But Rafe popped a pacifier into her mouth, and she settled back down again. I closed the door carefully and turned to him. "Thanks for showing me around."

His lips quirked. "Anytime. Thanks for lunch."

"I guess I'll head home," I said. And clarified, "Back to the mansion."

He nodded. "I'm gonna get this ring to the sheriff. See what he wants me to do with it."

"Katie's parents might be able to identify it," I suggested, "if it was hers."

"Not sure he's gonna wanna do that. He went to see'em yesterday, and Katie's mama didn't take the news well."

It wasn't the kind of news anyone would take well. Although after a decade and a half, they must have had their suspicions that she wasn't coming home. At least not alive.

"The sheriff will know what to do," I said. "And it might not have anything to do with anything. It might be Darrell's ring."

Rafe nodded. "Might. I'll follow you outta here…"

He trailed off and turned toward the driveway. I hadn't noticed anything, but after a second or two, I picked up the sound his keener ears had heard. "Someone's coming."

My first instinct was to run and hide. I'm not sure why, except maybe because the last time I'd been standing in this spot, we'd been in the middle of a homicide investigation involving seven deaths, one of which had occurred just a few feet away, and we had no idea who the killer was.

Rafe nodded. "Guess I won't be leaving just yet."

The sound of a car engine came closer, and we watched as a blue sedan crested the driveway and bumped into the rough patch of ground Robbie had used for his parking lot. It came to a stop a few feet away. After a couple of seconds, the driver's side door opened, and a man got out.

He looked from Rafe to me and back before he said, "I'm Doug Miller. One of you with the sheriff's department?"

My husband nodded. "What can I do for you, Mr. Miller?"

The guy glanced at the car. "My wife… we called the sheriff, and he said somebody was up here. My wife wants to see where her daughter was found."

Some of the color drained out of my face, or at least it felt that way. This is one of those parts of police work I don't think I'd be good at. Telling people their loved ones are dead, or just dealing with those that are left behind, must be the hardest part of the job. I glanced at Rafe to see whether he looked as uncomfortable as I felt, but he just nodded. "I'll be happy to take you back. It's a bit of a walk."

By now Mrs. Miller had exited the car, too, without waiting for her husband to come around and fetch her. She was a faded brunette in her late fifties, and where she and my mother were probably around the same age, Mrs. Miller looked ten years older, and like she'd been through the wringer. Her face was devoid of makeup, and it didn't look like she'd taken the time to comb her hair today.

Even so, she gave Rafe a stare. "We don't mind walking."

"Now, now, Laura," Mr. Miller said, his tone like an audible pat on the hand. "He wasn't saying we couldn't go."

Mrs. Miller pretty much ignored him in favor of pinning Rafe with a glare. "She was my daughter. I want to see where she died."

My husband's voice was even. If her attitude bothered him, he didn't let it show. "I'll take you there. I'm just letting you know you'll have to hoof it for a while. Through the woods."

Mrs. Miller nodded. After a second, so did Mr. Miller. I cleared my throat. "I'll just get going. I'll see you at home later."

Rafe nodded.

"I'm Rafe's wife," I added. "I brought him a sandwich for lunch." Just in case they thought I'd had some ulterior motive for coming up here. Like, I wanted to gawk at the place where their daughter had died. "I'm so sorry for your loss."

Mrs. Miller stared at me for a moment. It was quite uncomfortable, but now that she was looking at me and not Rafe, I got the impression that the stare and pause wasn't so much confrontational as because it took her that long to process what I'd said and formulate an answer for it. The world was probably coming at her with a bit of a delay right now. I remembered that feeling from times in the past, when someone I knew had died. "I lost Katie a long time ago."

But finding out that she was never coming home was still not easy. How could it be?

I didn't say so, just nodded. "Excuse me." I exchanged a glance with Rafe and walked around to the driver's side of the

Volvo. As I reversed and circled and reversed again, the Millers locked their car and then all three of them walked toward the woods. By the time I had gotten my car all the way turned around and was on my way down the driveway, they had disappeared behind Robbie Skinner's trailer.

Six

By the time I made it back to the mansion, Carrie decided she had slept long enough. She wanted more food, and then we spent some time on the floor, having tummy time and back time. Pearl stayed in the parlor with us, keeping a close eye on the baby from the pillow Mother had put in the corner for her.

It was at this point that Dix finally deigned to call me back. I saw his name on the screen and felt my blood pressure rise. "It's about time you called."

"Hello to you too," my brother answered. "What's got your knickers in a twist?"

"Specifically? You did."

He sounded sincerely confused. "Me? What did I do?"

"You went on a date with Charlotte Albertson," I said. And as I said it, realized that maybe it was Charlotte who had gotten my knickers in a twist, not Dix.

There was a beat. "Yes," Dix said eventually. "If you want to call it that."

"What would you call it?"

Dix didn't answer, and I added, "That's what Catherine said it was. That you went on a date with Charlotte. Did you go somewhere there was food?"

"Yes," Dix said.

"Did you eat? Was there anyone else with you?"

"Yes," Dix said. "No."

"Then you were on a date."

He sighed. "Fine. What's the problem?"

What was the problem?

I was very close to explaining the problem, at a decibel only Pearl would be able to hear, but I forced myself to calm down. "She's still married."

"I know that," Dix said.

"And you don't have a problem with it?"

I could hear a sort of audible squirm. "It wasn't that kind of date."

"What kind of date was it?" I lifted my hand before he could say anything in response, never mind the fact that he couldn't see me. "Don't answer that. I don't want to know. I thought you and Grimaldi were dating."

"Tamara?" He sounded surprised. I don't know what that meant, but I didn't think it could be good.

"Haven't you two been seeing each other on and off since last year sometime?"

"On and off," Dix agreed.

"Is there a problem?" Were they off? Did they have periods of on, and periods of off?

"No," Dix said. "No problem."

"Well, when I couldn't find you this morning—I drove to the office, and you weren't there—I went to Columbia to see Grimaldi. And I told her you'd had dinner with Charlotte."

Dix sighed. "What did you do that for?"

"I thought she deserved to know," I said piously.

"What did she say?" He sounded more curious than angry.

"That you're a free agent and you can date anyone you want."

There was a pause.

"If you screw things up…" I said, my voice threatening.

"I'm not going to screw anything up." The assertion was accompanied by an audible eyeroll. "And have you thought that maybe this is none of your business, Savannah? That we're all adults and can handle our own affairs?"

"I don't doubt that you can handle your own affairs," I said, with heavy emphasis on 'affairs'; Dix sighed, "but Grimaldi is my friend, and so is Charlotte." Even though I felt less friendly toward her at the moment. Not only was she ducking my phone calls and texts, but she was dating my brother, again, when I didn't want her to. "And you're my brother. I want all of you to be happy. And since I don't see either Grimaldi or Charlotte being interested in being sister-wives, you're going to have to pick one of them. And that'll make the other one unhappy."

Dix had nothing to say to that.

"Are you going out with her again?"

"Which one of them?"

It was my turn to roll my eyes. "Either. Both."

"No. Not both."

Marvelous. "You're pissing me off," I told him, and heard him choke back a laugh.

"Your husband's rubbing off on you, Sis. Don't let Mother hear you say that."

"Mother loves Rafe," I said.

"And while she'll put up with that kind of language from him, she won't take it from you."

No, she wouldn't. "Good thing I was talking to you and not Mother." Unless he was threatening to rat me out because I had, in turn, pissed him off.

"Good thing," Dix agreed, so apparently he wasn't. "Don't fret, Savannah. I've got it under control."

Sure he did. But since there was nothing I could actually do, except continue to harangue him, and that wasn't working, I stopped what I was doing. For now. "Anything else going on in your life?"

"Nothing you need to worry about," he told me. "Anything

else you want to ask me before you get off the phone and let me work?"

Actually, yes. "Back in 10th grade, the first time you and Charlotte were dating, did you give her one of those rings that were popular back then, with your initials on it?"

There was silence from the other end of the line. "No…?" Dix said eventually, his voice wary. "Was I supposed to?"

"No." Although it would have been OK if he had, I guess. I'd been fine with them dating back then. It was them dating now I had the problem with. "It just crossed my mind."

I could practically hear his eyebrows rise. "It just crossed your mind to wonder whether I gave Charlotte a ring with our initials on it a dozen years ago? Out of the blue?"

"Not entirely out of the blue." I explained how I'd gone up to the Skinners' property and Rafe had shown me where Katie Graves's bones had been found. "Did you hear about that?"

"Catherine told me when I picked up the girls last night," Dix said.

"Well, Rafe and I discovered a ring in the woods this afternoon. It had the initials D & C on it."

There was a beat. "No," Dix said. "I didn't give Charlotte a ring with our initials on it. We didn't start dating until a couple of years after Katie Graves had gone missing. I'm not sure those rings were still popular then. And even if I had given Charlotte one, how would it have made its way up on the Devil's Backbone? Neither Charlotte nor I had any connection with the Skinners."

That was true. "I guess it must have been Darrell's ring." That made more sense anyway. I guess I was just a little hung up on the Dix and Charlotte thing at the moment. As soon as I'd seen the initials, their names had crossed my mind. I hadn't mentioned anything to Rafe, since it had been a harebrained idea at best, but not so harebrained that I'd been able to forget it entirely. Maybe now I could. "Thanks."

"Don't mention it," Dix said. "Anything else?"

I told him there wasn't. "Would you like to get together and have dinner some night? Unless you're going out with Charlotte again?"

"That would be nice," Dix said, without telling me whether he had plans to go out with Charlotte or not. "But not on a weeknight. The girls have homework."

That didn't seem to have bothered him last night, but I refrained from saying so. There was no point in it, other than to rile him up. "Just let me know. I'm sure Rafe would like to spend time with you."

Dix hesitated. "That sounded like a threat. Is there something you aren't telling me?"

I thought about assuring him that no, of course there wasn't. And then I realized that it wouldn't hurt for him to worry a little about it. So I didn't answer, just smiled. "Talk to you later."

I hung up before he had the chance to say anything else. And while I didn't think the remark would cause him much loss of sleep, I felt a little better about the whole thing.

Rafe made it home in time for dinner. I guess the Katie Graves investigation wasn't so high priority, or so hot, that he couldn't afford to take some downtime. With an active killer out there, and the chance that he—or she—might kill again, I guess things would have been different. I'd watched Grimaldi, and for that matter Rafe, burn the midnight oil many a time in the middle of an investigation.

But not this time. This time I heard the engine of the incognito Chevy come up the driveway around six-thirty, and a few minutes later he came through the back door. Pearl, the consummate guard dog, came awake out of dead sleep to throw herself at the door, teeth bared and fur raised.

"It's me," Rafe said, unnecessarily.

I nodded. "I heard the car go by."

"I was talking to the dog." He bent to pat her on the head. By now, she was wagging her entire back half, her jaws split in a doggy grin as she greeted him.

He shut the door, slid the bolt home, and then came over to where I was standing by the stove stirring a big pot of chili. I'd been cold when I got home from the Skinner excursion, and some nice, hot chili had sounded like just the thing.

Apparently Rafe thought so, too, because he breathed deeply. "Smells good."

"Chili."

"I was talking about you." He leaned in to nuzzle my neck. I grinned. This was a standard exchange, one that happened at least once a week.

He turned to where Carrie was sitting, in her bouncy seat on the island, safely away from Pearl and the floor, and tickled her. And then he asked, "How long until dinner's ready?"

I glanced at the clock. "About ten minutes."

He nodded. "I'm gonna grab a quick shower."

"Take your time," I told him. "It'll stay warm until you get back."

He wandered off, down the hallway to where he'd leave his leather jacket—probably draped over one of the newel posts—and up to the shower. I watched him walk away, as I thought how sad it was that I couldn't just drop everything and join him. That kind of spontaneity had pretty much gone out the window with Carrie. I was lucky to get a shower every other day myself; taking twenty minutes under the spray with my husband was out of the question.

But then I looked at her, at her beautiful face and dark curls and bright blue eyes, and knew that it was worth it. Rafe and I could have sex tonight, if I could keep my eyes open for it. I didn't need to join him in the shower.

So I spent the ten minutes he was upstairs stirring the chili and fixing the coleslaw I intended to accompany it, and by the time he wandered back in, with his little bit of hair still damp and his feet bare below a pair of faded jeans that hung low on his hips, we were ready to eat. I even had a bottle of Corona sitting on the island next to his bowl. It matched the logo on the T-shirt he was wearing. The soft blue shirt was a special favorite of mine, since he'd been wearing it the first time we made love. Or at least he'd been wearing it until we made love. After that, he'd been all soft skin and hard muscles.

But I digress. I cleared my throat and looked away, trying to convince myself that the flush of color in my cheeks was from slaving over a hot stove, and not from picturing my husband naked. He chuckled, since he knows me well enough to have interpreted the lingering look I'd given him when he came in. "Later."

I nodded. "How did it go with Katie's parents?"

He grimaced as he got comfortable at the island. "Only she was Katie's parent. That was her second husband. They got married after Katie disappeared."

Ah. "I didn't realize that." Although maybe I should have, since they didn't have the same last name as Katie. Then again, that kind of thing is pretty common these days.

"He didn't say a lot about it," Rafe said, starting to doctor the bowl of chili I put in front of him. He sprinkled some cheese on it, and then reached for the sour cream. "Just that he wasn't Katie's dad, and he married Mrs. Miller five years after Katie disappeared. Katie's mother didn't say anything at all."

"She was probably in shock." I grabbed the cheese and sprinkled it liberally over my own bowl of chili before I, too, reached for the sour cream.

Rafe nodded. "I was afraid we were gonna have to carry her out of there. That she'd have a total breakdown once we got into the woods. But she didn't. Just stood there and stared at the place for ten minutes with tears running down her face.

Didn't say a word."

I winced, mostly in sympathy this time. "It has to be the worst thing in the world, to lose your child. Children aren't supposed to die before their parents."

Rafe nodded. "I'm thinking I might never let her leave the house without one of us."

He was looking at Carrie. I looked at her, too, and thought about losing her, about being in Mrs. Miller's position and standing there, looking at the place where my daughter's bones had been found.

And nodded. "Yes. Let's just never let her leave the house alone."

One corner of Rafe's mouth turned up. I smiled back and nodded to the bowl of chili in front of him. "Eat. It's a long time since lunch." And he'd probably used up some energy since then. On thinking, if nothing else.

He nodded and brought the first spoonful to his mouth. We ate in companionable silence for a few minutes, until I told him, "I asked Dix about that ring we found."

Rafe arched a brow, but didn't stop eating to ask me why.

"I know it wasn't very likely that the D & C on the ring were Dix and Charlotte, but I figured it couldn't hurt to ask."

Rafe nodded.

"He said he never gave Charlotte a ring like that, and that it wasn't his."

Rafe swallowed. "I didn't think it was."

I hadn't, either. I'd just needed to cross off that possibility. "My sister had a ring like that. Or at least I think I remember seeing one in her room once. I suppose it could be hers. Although I don't think she'd be any more likely to have been wandering around the Skinners' property than Dix or Charlotte. And anyway, her best friend back then was Angela. I think she was dating a guy named Greg."

Greg, who had gone off to Chicago after high school, and

had become an engineer.

"It's prob'ly Darrell's ring," Rafe said.

Or maybe Katie's. "Did you show it to the Millers?"

Rafe nodded. "Mr. Miller didn't know Katie back then, but her mama said it didn't look familiar. Not sure she took her eyes off the ground long enough to be able to tell, but that's what she said."

After a second he added, "She had no idea what her daughter mighta been doing up on the Devil's Backbone. So far as she knew, Katie didn't associate with the Skinner boys."

"But she knew who the Skinner boys were."

He smirked. "I imagine every mama in Columbia knew who the Skinner boys were. Just like every mama in Sweetwater knew me."

And warned their daughters about him. "If Katie had been involved with one of the Skinners," I said, "maybe Darrell, would she have told her mother?"

Rafe shook his head. "I don't imagine so. If I was a girl, and I was gonna get involved with Darrell Skinner, I'd make damn sure my mama wouldn't find out about it."

I nodded. I didn't remember Darrell, but I'd take Rafe's word for it. "It's a shame he's dead." Or we'd be able to ask him about the ring, and whether he'd been involved with Katie.

Rafe made an agreeable sort of noise. "Guess I'm gonna have to figure out who inherited Darrell's stuff, and see if I can get permission to go through it. Just in case he's got something of Katie's tucked away in his trailer."

"Does Darrell's stuff still exist?"

"I imagine it does," Rafe said. "Everything looks the same at Robbie's place. I don't figure anyone's done any cleaning at Art's or Darrell's, either."

I thought for a second. "Kayla inherited Robbie's property and his belongings, most likely. She's his daughter, so she'd be next-of-kin."

Rafe nodded.

"Darrell didn't have a wife or kids—"

"That we know of."

I nodded, "and Art and Linda are both dead, along with their children. Cilla had a baby."

"That's prob'ly who'll inherit after Art and Linda," Rafe agreed.

Likely so. The baby was living with Cilla's boyfriend's parents, I thought. Another couple who had lost their child, albeit a lot more recently. Cilla and… what was his name? Matt?—hadn't been much older than Katie, either.

"But Darrell didn't have anyone. Who inherits his stuff?"

"Less'n he had a will," Rafe said, "and you'd know this better than I would, I imagine it'd be Robbie's daughter and Cilla's baby. They're the only two surviving members of the family."

It had been a few years since I dropped out of law school to marry Bradley Ferguson, but I thought he was probably right. It was easy to check, though. I peered at the clock on the stove, and then grabbed my phone.

"Who're you calling?" Rafe wanted to know, but he wasn't so interested that he stopped eating. Since my mouth was full and I was trying to swallow before my sister picked up the phone, I didn't answer, just let the response speak for itself.

"Savannah?" my sister's voice said. I'd switched the phone to speaker so Rafe could hear, too, and over by the wall, Pearl's head rose and she looked around. "Something wrong?"

I swallowed. "Not at all. Am I interrupting your dinner?" Because I was interrupting my own.

"Almost," Catherine said. "We're just about ready to sit down. What do you need?"

"I just had a quick question. We're sitting here talking about the Skinners, and…"

"I don't know anything about the Skinners," Catherine

interrupted me.

"I didn't think you did. This is more of a general question. For a lawyer."

I imagined her brows rose. "In that case, go ahead."

"We're trying to figure out who inherits after Darrell. Robbie's daughter gets his property, and Cilla's baby gets Art's and Linda's. But if Darrell didn't have a wife or children, who inherits his stuff?"

There was a pause. "Why?" Catherine wanted to know.

I gave the phone a look. "Does it matter?"

I didn't wait for her to answer, just added, "Rafe wants to go through the trailers. He's trying to get permission from next of kin, and we need to know who to talk to about Darrell's stuff."

"Why does he want to do that?"

I gave the phone another look. "Because Katie Graves was found on Skinner property. And there was a ring nearby that had the initials D & C on it. We're thinking the C is for Catherine and the D for Darrell."

My own Catherine made a noise. I guess she was agreeing, or maybe encouraging me to go on, but it sounded more like she'd swallowed wrong and was choking. I gave it a second, and when she sounded like she was going to be all right, I continued, "Rafe wants to get into Darrell's trailer and see if there's anything there connecting him and Katie."

"Yes," Catherine said. "Unless Darrell had a will, or a wife or child, it's likely Robbie's daughter inherits. She'd be closest. Cilla's daughter is one more generation away."

I didn't say anything, and she added, "Spouse first, then child. Then grandchild. If no spouse or children, parents. If no parents, siblings, and then nephews and nieces."

"So his niece," Robbie's daughter Kayla, "would become his heir before his niece's baby."

"Yes," Catherine said.

"I appreciate it. That's what I thought, but I wanted to be sure. It's been a while since I went to law school."

"Been a while since I went to law school, too," Catherine said.

"True. But you practice law every day. I practice real estate." And at the moment, baby tending.

She didn't respond to that. "Anything else I can do for you?"

"I don't think so."

"Great," Catherine said, and I got the feeling she was trying to get off the phone. Maybe their dinner was getting cold.

"Just one more quick thing."

She didn't hang up, but she didn't say anything, either.

"Didn't you have one of those rings, with initials on it, when you were a teenager?"

"Yes," Catherine said.

"Do you still have it?"

She hesitated. "I don't think so. But I can look. Why?"

"No reason. Whose initials?"

She didn't answer immediately, and I clarified, "I was just wondering whether Greg gave it to you—that was the name of the guy you dated in high school, right?—or maybe you and Angela had matching rings? You were best friends, weren't you?"

"Yes," Catherine said.

"Yes, you and Angela had matching rings?"

My sister was starting to sound impatient. "You expect me to remember this fifteen years later? High school was a long time ago."

It was. For both of us. "Sorry," I said. "I didn't mean to keep you. I can tell you don't want to talk about this right now. Go enjoy dinner with your family."

She must have realized she'd been impatient and unhelpful, because she apologized, too. "Sorry, Savannah."

"No problem," I said. "We appreciate the information. And if you come across the ring, I'd like to see it."

"I'll see what I can do," Catherine said. "But as long as it isn't an emergency, I have to have dinner with my family first. I'll see you later, OK?"

I told her that would be perfectly fine, and disconnected the call. And glanced at Rafe. "I guess she was hungry."

He nodded. "So it sounds like Kayla would be Darrell's heir as well as Robbie's."

That's what it sounded like. And while the Skinners hadn't been wealthy, they'd probably done OK, between their legal and illegal activities. Not to mention all the land they owned between them. It was a big inheritance for a twelve-year-old girl.

"Guess I have to call Sandy," Rafe said, reaching for his own phone.

"Robbie's ex?"

He nodded. "Hush for a minute, and let me do this."

No problem. I started clearing the table, or island, while he dialed and then waited. Unlike me, he didn't put the phone on speaker, so I could only hear his side of the conversation.

"Sandy? This is Rafe Collier. We met back when Robbie… Yeah, that's right. I'm back in Maury County working on something else, and I wondered whether you'd give me access to Darrell's trailer. It's still there, right?"

Sandy must have said something, because he nodded. "Yeah. Something else. Nothing to do with Robbie or the murders."

He hesitated a second, and then he added, "Word's gonna get out soon anyway, so I might as well tell you. Back in November, one of the ATF agents found human remains on the property. They've been identified as Katie Graves."

There was more silence from Rafe while Sandy spoke. I heard her voice very faintly, but not well enough to make out any of the words. Not that it was difficult to guess what she was saying. I would have been saying the same thing in her position, and besides, I could extrapolate from Rafe's answers.

"Yeah, the girl who disappeared fifteen or sixteen years ago. You'd'a been older…"

Sandy spoke again.

"No," Rafe said, "I'm not thinking that Robbie had anything to do with it. If somebody did, it's more likely it'd be Darrell than Robbie. That's why I wanna take a look at his trailer."

Sandy spoke.

"Yes," Rafe said, "I could probl'ly get a judge to sign off on a warrant for all three homesteads if I asked. Right now I'm more interested in Darrell's, so if you'll give me access there, maybe Robbie's place won't even come into it."

My lips curved. That was very nicely put. Very nicely indeed.

Rafe saw my expression and raised a brow at me before he said to Sandy, "No, I don't need the key. I doubt the place is locked." And if it was, he'd still be able to find his way inside.

"'Course I'll let you know what I find. Or you can be there yourself, if you wanna see what I'm doing."

Sandy must have said no to that, because Rafe nodded. "No problem. I'll just call you after, then. Tomorrow afternoon, most likely."

He disconnected.

"She's worried about Robbie," I interpreted.

Rafe shook his head and placed the phone on the granite countertop. "She's worried about Kayla."

"But she worried that Robbie had something to do with Katie's death." And if he did, what that would do to Kayla.

He nodded. "If Darrell did something to Katie, chances are Robbie and Art knew about it."

Chances were. "But if Darrell, or Robbie or Art, did something that resulted in Katie's death, it would be very stupid to leave her where she was found."

"The Skinners weren't the brightest tools in the shed," Rafe said.

"And while that may be true, it's hard to believe that they were stupid enough to leave a girl they killed out in the open on their own property. And for sixteen years, too. I mean, I realize they were reclusive, but they had dealings with people. For the dog fights and the marijuana operation, at least."

Rafe nodded. "Just as hard to believe she coulda been there for fifteen years and them not noticing, though."

That was also true. If an ATF agent had found her within a month of the murders, it would be almost impossible to live on the same property for sixteen years and not stumble over her.

"So you'll be going to Darrell's trailer tomorrow?"

"After lunch," Rafe said. "I've got Nolan and Vasquez coming out in the morning to walk a grid with me. Just in case we find something around the drop site."

The drop site being where Katie was found, I assumed. I wondered whether he had a reason to think it was a drop site rather than a murder scene, but decided he couldn't possibly know one way or the other. Calling it a murder scene implied she'd been killed, though, and we didn't know that for sure, so maybe drop site was the safer description, at least for now.

"How about I stop by with some sandwiches again? For Nolan and Vasquez, too."

"I never turn down food," Rafe said.

Good. "Then it's settled." And I'd have the opportunity to not only see Nolan and Vasquez, both of whom I liked, but to see whether they'd found anything in their grid walk, as well as—maybe—talk my way into Darrell's trailer.

I gave Rafe a big smile. "Why don't you take Carrie and go to the parlor? I'll clean up the kitchen and be out in a couple of minutes."

He nodded. And rose and grabbed the baby, bouncy seat and all. "Don't think I don't realize what you're doing," he told me on his way to the door.

Seven

I spent the next morning with Carrie. We did our morning ablutions and had our morning meal, and then we took a walk across the fields with Pearl, to give the dog some exercise. The Columbia Highway, which runs past the mansion, isn't really conducive to pushing a baby carriage—too much traffic—so loading the baby up in a carrier and walking across the fields made more sense. I got some exercise, too, which was probably good for me. The experience of hiking through the woods with Rafe yesterday had been more draining than it would have been before I got pregnant, so I should probably do something to try to get back into shape.

After we got back, Carrie got tummy time while I packed sandwiches for the lunch run. Since this was a planned event instead of an impromptu attempt to inveigle myself into Rafe's investigation, I made my own sandwiches today instead of buying them. There was plenty of food in the fridge, so I put roast beef and turkey and ruffled lettuce and cheese on whole wheat bread, enough for four, and loaded it all up into a picnic basket I fished out of the pantry. The mansion is roughly a hundred and eighty years old, so you can find practically anything you could possibly need here. The attic is chock full of treasures—if you consider former generations' castoffs treasures, and I do—and one day I intend to go up there and look through it all, with a more discerning eye than I had when

I was a kid.

But that wouldn't be today. Today I dug the picnic basket—I think it dated from the 1950s, judging from the gingham fabric on the inside—out of the pantry, and put sandwiches in it. And added some pasta salad, and some chips, and a few water bottles plus a thermos of coffee. And a little before noon, I loaded the basket and Carrie into the Volvo, gave Pearl a biscuit and told her to be good, and headed for the Devil's Backbone.

This was my first time getting a look at Darrell's place. Back in October, I'd gone with Rafe to Robbie's trailer a few times, and we'd ended up in the back forty once, and were lucky to have escaped. At that time, we'd driven past Darrell's driveway, so I knew where to find it, but it was my first time to turn in and follow it.

It turned out to be a carbon copy of Robbie's driveway. Long, narrow, winding, surrounded by trees, and decorated with *No Trespassing* signs sporting images of automatic weapons.

Like Robbie's driveway, it opened up into a clearing with a trailer.

Unlike Robbie's old Airstream, this one was a seventies model travel trailer, white with orange stripes along the side. And it was smaller, the kind of thing you take for a camping trip. It was clear that neither brother had worried much about how he lived.

Rafe's car, the tan Chevy, was parked next to the trailer. So was a patrol car with the Columbia PD logo on the side. I parked beside it, and got out. "Hello?"

There was no answer. Both the cars were empty, so that meant they were probably already inside the trailer.

I went over to it and knocked on the door. "Lunch delivery."

But nothing happened. "Rafe?" I reached for the door

handle, and then thought better of it. If he'd been in there, he would have heard me knock. If he didn't answer, he probably wasn't here yet. He and Nolan and Lupe Vasquez must have walked from here through the woods to the crime scene—or search area—and they weren't back yet.

It was cold, so I went back to the Volvo and got in before I fished my phone out of my purse and sent him a text. *I'm here. I have sandwiches. Where are you?*

The message came back a minute later. *On our way back. Stay there.*

No problem. I was not stupid enough to grab the baby and try to make my own way through the woods without any clue where I was going. They'd get here when they got here, and until then, I was happy to wait.

They must have been close by, because it was less than ten minutes before first Patrick Nolan, and then Lupe Vasquez, and finally Rafe, made their way out of the trees behind the trailer. I got out of the car and went to greet them.

Nolan, tall and lanky, gave me a polite nod. He's courting my sister Darcy, so I guess he figures he has to be nice to me. Or maybe he genuinely likes me. Who knows?

His partner Lupe Vasquez is his direct opposite. Short where he's tall, compact where he's lanky, and female where he's male, she's about ten years younger than he is, a few years younger than me, and quite nice. She gave me a friendly smile. "Hi, Mrs. Collier."

"Nice to see you again," I told her, and included Nolan with a glance, before I looked past them both to Rafe. "Find anything?"

He shrugged. "A few small bones. Might just as easily be raccoon or squirrel as Katie's, but we picked'em up. No guns, knives, bullets, anything like that."

"No clothes," Lupe Vasquez added.

I glanced at her, and she added, "It's only been sixteen

years. Some of her clothes should have survived, even out here."

That was true. I mentioned the attic earlier. There were pieces of clothing up there from a hundred years ago, still in good shape.

Of course, those pieces of clothing had been somewhat protected by being inside, dry and mostly temperate, for a century. Anything that had been out here in the hills for sixteen years wouldn't be in good shape anymore, but it should still be here. Hundred percent cotton might break down in a decade and a half, if exposed to the elements—or maybe not; I don't really know—but chances were good that Katie had been wearing something that wasn't a hundred percent cotton. Plastic buttons on her shirt, if nothing else. A zipper. Some form of shoes with rubber soles.

And she'd disappeared on her way to school. Where was her book bag?

"Were there no clothes found with the bones?" I asked Rafe.

"Nobody told me about any clothes."

"So she was naked when she was killed? Or was dumped?"

He shrugged.

"Do you know what she was wearing when she disappeared?"

"I looked it up. Jeans, sneakers, striped shirt, blue jacket with a hood."

Some of that would have survived for sure. If the bones had lain here undisturbed, the clothing and shoes would have, too.

If they'd been here in the first place.

"I brought sandwiches," I told Nolan and Vasquez, while Rafe headed for the Chevy to put whatever little bones he had in his pocket somewhere better. "And coffee."

"I'll take that." Lupe Vasquez was wearing a heavy lined parka over her uniform, but she still looked cold. The tip of her nose was pink.

I glanced at the trailer. "Rafe will probably say no if I suggest going inside to eat." And neither of the cars was big enough for all of us. Unless I kept Carrie on my lap, which I supposed would be OK. "How about we all pile into the Chevy and have some food? I'd offer up the Volvo, but the car seat takes up half the back seat." And their patrol car would have a window or screen between the back and front seats, I assumed—I've been in a patrol car a time or two—and that would just be weird.

They nodded. I grabbed the picnic basket from the Volvo and handed it over. Nolan stepped up to grab it. And then the two of them headed for the Chevy while I walked around to the other side of my car to get the baby out of her carrier.

Vasquez and Nolan took the back seat, with the basket between them. Rafe slid behind the wheel, and I took the passenger seat. Vasquez passed out sandwiches and Nolan poured coffee and handed out water bottles. And we munched in contented silence until everyone was warmed up and the food was mostly gone.

"So now what?" I asked.

"Now we search the trailer," Rafe answered.

"Looking for what?" Vasquez wanted to know, and he glanced at her in the mirror.

"Katie's clothes, for one thing. Anything that don't look like it belongs to Darrell Skinner."

We sat in silence a moment, all of us looking at the trailer.

"It's going to be tight in there," I said.

He nodded. "I don't suppose I could talk you into going home?"

I should have seen that coming. "I will if you ask nicely. Although I was hoping you'd let me stay and help with the search."

"There ain't gonna be enough room for a baby and four adults in there, darlin'."

No, there wasn't. It would be tight enough with just the three of them.

"I'll stay out here with Savannah for a bit," Lupe Vasquez offered, "if you two want to get started."

Nolan gave her a look. Rafe gave me one. Then they both nodded.

"Sure," Nolan said. Rafe didn't say anything, but his look was eloquent. The two of them exited the Chevy and walked side by side toward the trailer. Rafe grabbed the handle, and the door must have been unlocked, because he was able to just pull it open. He nodded Nolan inside, and followed a second later himself. The door closed behind them.

I turned to Lupe Vasquez, who had finished packing up the remains of lunch and was now in the process of moving from the back seat to behind the wheel so we wouldn't have to talk from front seat to back seat and back. And I was just about to say something when the door to the trailer opened again. Rafe hopped down the couple of steps to the ground, put his hands on his hips, and scowled at us.

Or, I suppose, at me.

I rolled down the window. "What?"

"Did you go inside while you were waiting?"

"No," I said. I'd thought about it. But I hadn't actually done it.

"What's wrong?" Lupe Vasquez wanted to know. She was still standing outside the car, in the process of moving from the back to the front.

Rafe scowled at her, too. It must be a general sort of scowl, and not directed at anyone in particular, since he couldn't possibly suspect her of having gone inside the trailer without letting him know. "See for yourself."

She closed the door and moved toward the trailer. I decided that the invitation included me, as well, and got out of the Chevy with Carrie in my arms. "What's going on?"

"Better if you just see for yourself," Rafe told me, in a voice that was deeply disgusted. Meanwhile, Lupe Vasquez jumped up and disappeared inside the trailer.

I arched my brows, but walked past him and stuck my head through the door. And looked around. "Oh."

Rafe nodded. "Yeah."

"I don't suppose this was how the sheriff's office, or the ATF people, left it?"

He shook his head. "I don't imagine so."

"And he wasn't just a messy housekeeper?"

"I imagine he was," Rafe said, "but this is more than messy housekeeping. This looks like somebody blew through and turned the whole place upside down looking for something."

It did. It looked exactly like that. All the cabinets and drawers stood open. The seats were off the banquette in the kitchen, exposing the storage areas below the seats. They were open, too. The floor was a mess of cups and plates, clothes and shoes, dirty magazines and shampoo bottles. Patrick Nolan and Lupe Vasquez were picking their way across the floor, carefully.

"For your information," I told Rafe, "I texted you as soon as I realized you weren't here. I wouldn't have had time to do this between the time I arrived, and the time you came back."

"I didn't think you did, darlin'." Although he was still scowling.

"This probably could have happened anytime between October," when Darrell died, "and now." The trailer had been sitting here empty, and everyone in the county knew that Darrell was dead and the place was unoccupied. There are always going to be people looking to see how they can benefit from a tragedy.

Rafe nodded. "And I don't know that it didn't. But the timing's suspicious."

"With it just getting out," in the past few days, "that Katie's remains have been found up here, you mean? Who would have thought to search Darrell's trailer, though? And for what? I mean, if Darrell killed her, and Darrell's dead, what would be the point?"

"Same point we're making," Rafe said. "Looking to see if Darrell did it."

"Yes, but you're the police. It's your job to figure out what happened to Katie. Who else would care, at this point, whether Darrell did it or not? I mean... I'm sure the Millers want to know what happened. Hell—heck—*I* want to know what happened! Most people in Columbia probably feel the same way. But I don't see why anybody would think to turn Darrell's trailer upside down to find out."

Certainly not the Millers. Katie's mother had given me the impression of someone who was on the ragged edge of a nervous breakdown. She would have spent last night clutching wet tissues and sipping brandy.

Rafe shrugged. "Somebody did it. Whether it has to do with Katie or not. And if whoever it was found what he was looking for..."

I stated the obvious. "It won't be here anymore."

"We're still gonna have to search." Rafe said, with a scowl at the trailer. "This just makes it harder. I'll try to make it home for dinner, but if I don't, don't wait for me."

"How about you just let me know?" I said, since I could see that he had a terrible job in front of him. "Audrey had suggested that maybe we could come over to their house tonight, so I guess I should tell her that it doesn't look likely."

He nodded. "Maybe in a couple days. Saturday might work."

Because even if he hadn't figured out what was going on by then, he probably wouldn't be working on Saturday night. Not on a cold case where there was no danger of anyone else getting hurt.

"I'll tell her," I said. "Good luck with it."

He nodded. "Thanks for lunch, darlin'." He leaned in and brushed a kiss across my mouth, and dropped another on Carrie's head. And then he went back inside the trailer, and I made my way to the Volvo, and went back the way I'd come, with my snooping instincts unsatisfied.

Back in Sweetwater, Audrey was sad not to see us for dinner, but happy that we'd committed to Saturday. "Would *Coq au Vin* be all right?" she asked, sounding a little worried. Maybe because it was the first time she'd have us over for dinner, and she wanted to make a good impression.

"Of course." I've known her my whole life. Even if the food was bad, it wouldn't change how I felt about her. And I'm sure Audrey's *Coq au Vin* would be far superior to anything Rafe would get at home. I mean, I can cook, but I don't often attempt anything ambitious. Or anything French. "Would you like me to bring something? Wine?"

"I'll handle the wine," Audrey said, "but if you'd like to bring something for dessert, feel free."

We settled on a time, and then a customer wandered in and I wandered out, and glanced at the door to the law office. Since I was here, I might as well stop in and say hi.

Darcy was at the front desk, as usual, and as usual, she got out of her chair to come over and coo at the baby. I'd informed her recently that she should think about having one of her own, so I refrained from doing it again, just told her, "I saw Nolan just now."

"Oh?" She flushed. I guess she must really like him, if just the mention of his name was enough to make her blush.

"Up on the Devil's Backbone, by Darrell Skinner's trailer. They were about to go through it when I left."

Darcy moved back around the desk. "He was one of the people who was shot this fall, right?"

I nodded. "The youngest of the Skinner brothers. I guess he'd have been around your age. Not that that matters, since you didn't grow up here."

Like Rafe's son David, Darcy had grown up with adoptive parents, and had only made it to Sweetwater a few years ago. Unless she'd run across Darrell since she got here, she wouldn't have known who he was. And I didn't think she'd be the type he'd try to pick up. Attractive, sure. But a bit too dark-skinned for a good old Southern boy with prejudices, no matter how pretty she was.

"Patrick grew up here," Darcy said. "And he's my age. He might have known Darrell."

He might, and I wondered why that hadn't occurred to me. "I'm sure Rafe will ask him. Or Nolan will mention it."

It might already have happened. They'd spent some time together this morning, walking the perimeter of the crime scene, and if it hadn't, they would be spending more time in each other's company this afternoon, sifting through the contents of the trailer. Rafe was sure to ask both of them what they knew about Darrell and the other Skinners, if he hadn't already.

"We're having dinner with your mother on Saturday," I said. "Unless there's a reason she wants only me and Rafe—and the baby—the two of you could join us. She's making Coq au Vin, so it shouldn't be a problem with the food."

Darcy's lips curved. "I don't think you can invite me to my mother's house without asking her first, Savannah."

"Of course I didn't mean for you just to show up," I said. "I figured you could ask her. Or hint. You're her daughter; I'm sure she'd be happy to have you to dinner anytime you want to come."

"I'll talk to Patrick about it," Darcy said, "and we'll see."

After a second she added, "We usually go out on Saturday nights, if he doesn't have to work. But I don't think he'd mind spending the evening with my mother. And you."

No reason why he should. I'm likeable. And they could still go back to her place, or his, and do whatever they'd been planning to do after dinner. Same as if they'd had dinner in a restaurant.

"Good," I said. "Hopefully we'll see you, then."

She nodded. "Did you need something?"

When I looked blank, she added, "Here? Did you stop by to see someone? Your brother? Your brother-in-law? Your sister isn't here."

Oh. "No, I was next door at Audrey's and decided I should say hello. I don't need to talk to anyone in particular." Although if Dix was here…

Darcy's lips curved, as if she'd guessed what I was thinking. "Go on back. He's alone."

"Can I leave the baby? I don't think this'll take long." Especially as I'd already vented most of my frustration over the phone.

"Sure," Darcy said. "Bring her over here."

I brought the car seat around the desk, and left them both to walk down the hallway to my brother's office in the back. The door was closed, and I knocked on it. When there was no answer, I turned the knob and pushed the door open. "Dix?"

"He left," Jonathan's voice said behind me, sounding amused. "He heard your voice out front, and slipped out through the back door."

Damn. I mean… darn. He must really not want to see me. What did he think I was going to say or do, that I hadn't already covered over the phone?

"Coward," I told Jonathan.

He grinned, and then the grin fell away, and he gave me a concerned look. "Everything all right with you?"

"Of course." Why wouldn't it be? "I just wanted to chew him out about Charlotte again."

Jonathan nodded, but said, "So you and Rafe are... um...?"

Um... what?

He tried again. "Yesterday, when you called Catherine... was she able to help you? When she came over last night?"

When she... what?

"Oh," I said, before I'd even thought it through, "that. Sure. She was a big help. Having a new baby is tough. I'm sure you know that. And then the move down here. I like Sweetwater. Rafe doesn't, so much. So it's a bit of a strain on him, being here. But we're doing all right."

"I'm glad to hear it," Jonathan said sincerely, and gathered me in for a hug. I hugged him back, and tried not to feel guilty that I was, for all intents and purposes, lying to him.

Not that what I'd said wasn't true. Having a new baby *is* tough, and Rafe wasn't altogether happy to be back in Sweetwater. But I hadn't called Catherine for help last night. She certainly hadn't come by, and by not telling Jonathan that, I felt like I was enabling my sister in whatever the hell—heck— she was doing.

But at the same time she was my sister, and until I knew what was going on, I owed her my loyalty. So when Jonathan let me go, I did my best to smile naturally. "Thanks."

He smiled back, and it looked like he couldn't tell the difference. "Anytime. Rafe seemed all right the other night, but after Catherine rushed out just after dinner yesterday, and didn't come home for hours..."

"I'm sorry," I said, even as I envisioned stringing my sister up by her eyelids. "Yes, we're all fine. Thank you for letting us borrow her."

"Of course." Jonathan smiled again, and then glanced at his door. "I should get back to work. I just heard your voice out here, and thought I'd make sure things were all right."

"I appreciate it." I leaned in for another hug, this time because I was afraid my expression would give me away if I didn't. How dare my sister use me—and the freaking well-being of my marriage!—as an excuse for ducking out on her husband?! "I guess she's home?" Since she wasn't here.

Jonathan nodded. "She was tired this morning. After being up so late…"

I growled, but was able to catch myself before I let it out. Instead, I pasted a bright fake smile on my face. "I'll drive over there and see if there anything I can do to help."

"That's kind of you," Jonathan told me.

"Oh," I pried my teeth apart so I wouldn't accidentally break something by grinding them too hard, "it seems the least I can do."

He went back inside his office, and I stood there for a moment, with my fingernails digging into my palms, before I'd calmed down enough to walk down the hallway to the lobby again, and give Darcy a mostly natural smile. "He ducked out the back, the big chicken."

Darcy smirked. "I'm sure he'll come back when he sees you leave."

"And when he does," I told her, as I gathered up the car seat with the baby and headed for the front door, "you tell him that the longer he avoids me, the worse it's going to be when I catch him."

"Yes'm." Darcy was grinning by now.

"She hasn't been back, has she? Or called?"

"Charlotte?" She shook her head. "Not that I've seen."

"Let me know if she shows up." I thought—briefly—about stopping by the Albertsons' house on my way to Catherine's, but discarded the idea. I was too angry with my sister right now to be able to deal with anything else, even if I was angry with Charlotte, too. And giving Charlotte the full blast of what I was feeling right now would be unfair. Not that I wouldn't blast her too, once I got around to it. But at the moment, I wanted to blast Catherine more.

Darcy said she would pass my message along to Dix, and then she watched me walk out the door. I scanned the square while I walked to the Volvo and buckled Carrie into the back seat, but saw no sign of Dix. Nor was it logical that I would. He wouldn't be standing around the square, freezing in his shirtsleeves while he waited for me to drive away. He was probably inside one of the stores. Audrey's, or the café, or one of the others. But unless I wanted to walk around and eliminate them one by one, he could stay where he was. I had bigger—or at least more important, or more imminent—fish to fry.

Even so, I raked the plaza with a fulminating glare. If he was watching, there was no reason not to let him see how angry I was. Even if that anger was, mostly, directed at someone else right now.

And then I got into the car and vented some of my feelings by backing out of the parking space too quickly—after I made sure no one was in my way—and peeling around the corner with a squeal of tires. Rafe would have been proud.

Eight

A part of me was worried that Jonathan might have called Catherine—all loving innocence—to tell her that I was on my way to see her, and just so she wouldn't decide to duck out to avoid me—much the way Dix had done earlier—I called her myself on my way over.

She didn't answer, of course. I hadn't expected her to. She'd probably screened my call—especially if Jonathan had gotten to her first—and decided not to talk to me. So I left a message. One that reverberated with threat and dire consequences, and got progressively less calm and more heated as it went on. "It's Savannah. I'm on my way over to your house. And you'd better be there when I show up. And if you're not—if you're legitimately somewhere else right now—you'd better call and tell me where you are. Because if I get there and you're not home, and I haven't heard from you, I'm turning right back around and driving back to town, and then I'm telling Jonathan that you weren't anywhere near the mansion last night, and *how dare you tell him that my marriage is in trouble as an excuse to get away from him for a couple of hours—!"*

By that point I realized I was screaming, and Carrie was whimpering in the back seat, so I disconnected, and spent the rest of the drive breathing deeply and forcing my blood pressure down from the danger zone and talking sweetly to my daughter.

Catherine didn't call back, and when I pulled up in front of her house, she was waiting to let me in. She held the door open while I stalked across the threshold and into the house, exuding righteous anger and indignation, but she wouldn't meet my eyes. I waited until she'd shut the door behind me, and then I turned to her, ready to blow her into next season. Only to realize that I'd managed to calm myself down enough that yelling wasn't necessary.

I was still a bit miffed, though. "What the hell were you thinking?"

She looked at me, but didn't answer.

"Doesn't our family have enough misgivings about me and Rafe? Did you have to tell your husband that my marriage is on the rocks? Couldn't you have come up with a different excuse?"

"I had to think fast," Catherine said.

"And that was the first thing that came to mind?"

In considering it, I guess maybe it would have been. That didn't make me feel any better. "I can't believe you did that. You know that if Mother hears about this, she'll think the worst!"

And while she adored Rafe now, there was no denying that she hadn't had such a great opinion of him for a long time. If she thought we were having trouble, she might go back to not liking him again.

Or considering how things were at the moment, maybe she'd stop liking *me*. I wasn't sure which possibility made me more upset.

I opened my mouth, but before I could ask, again, what Catherine had been thinking, my daughter did the same thing. Opened her mouth and let out a whimper, and then a cry.

My breasts tingled, a sure sign that it had been a while since I'd fed the baby.

"She's hungry," I said, distractedly.

Catherine nodded. "Come in and sit down in the family room."

I hesitated. I was still angry enough not to want to be comfortable in my sister's home. But since it was either nursing the baby here, or leaving and driving back to the mansion with a screaming infant in the backseat, and without talking to Catherine first, I chose the lesser of the two evils. Get my daughter fed, even if acting like everything was all right made me feel like I was giving up an advantage.

We ended up in the same cozy area in front of the fireplace where we'd sat the other night. While I made myself and Carrie comfortable, Catherine walked away.

I figured she'd be right back, but after a few minutes, when she didn't reappear, I raised my voice. "Catherine?"

There was no answer. My eyes narrowed. But since I couldn't really get up and walk around while nursing the baby, I was forced to stay where I was and wait. And try to determine whether she was somewhere else in the house—upstairs, maybe—or whether she'd done a Dix, and slipped out the door while I wasn't looking.

Everything was so quiet that I had just about come to the conclusion that I was alone in the house when she came back into the room. I raised my brows. She sighed. "I should totally take advantage of the fact that you can't run after me to leave."

"I know where you live," I pointed out. "If you won't talk to me now, I'll find you later." Or just camp out here until she came back. I was warm and dry, I had a diaper bag full of paraphernalia for Carrie and Catherine's refrigerator and pantry I could raid, and she'd have to return eventually.

She nodded. "That's what I decided. That I'd rather get it over with now."

"Good." I waited. Catherine didn't say anything. "So where did you go last night? And why couldn't you tell your husband about it? Is this the first time you've used me as an excuse to get away from him, or is it a habit?"

"I'm not trying to get away from him," Catherine said irritably, and dropped into the sofa opposite where I was sitting. "Or only last night. For a couple of hours."

"Don't tell me the two of you are having problems?" I unlatched the baby and moved her from one side to the other.

"Of course not," Catherine said haughtily, as if such a thing was inconceivable.

"Then why did you need to get away from him?"

She sighed again, annoyed this time. "I wasn't trying to get away from him. I just had something to do that I didn't want him to know about."

"So you were trying to get away from him. Why? And don't tell me you're working on a Valentine's Day surprise, because I won't believe you."

If it had been two months ago, I might have accepted Christmas as a reason, but not Valentine's Day.

"I hadn't thought about that," Catherine said, sounding calculating, and then, when I scowled at her, she added, "Fine. I needed to go somewhere and do something, and I didn't want him to know where and what. So I said the first thing that came to mind. That you needed me to come over and hold your hand."

"I get all that," I said. "That makes sense. I called, and you used me as an excuse. And while it pisses me off that you lied about my marriage, I can see why it came to mind. But what was it you wanted to do? And why was it so sudden?"

And that's when, for the first time, it occurred to me to wonder what had set her off in the first place. So far, I'd been too incensed by the fact that she'd lied about me and Rafe having problems to really think things through. Now I did.

We'd been on the phone, talking about inheritances and how children and grandchildren inherited before parents or siblings. We'd determined—or I had—that Robbie's daughter

Kayla would be her uncle Darrell's heir, which was the reason I'd called: to figure out who Rafe needed to talk to about access to Darrell's trailer. And then…

"Oh, my God!" My eyes opened wide, and Catherine winced. "You lied to me! You do know something about the Skinners! You went to Darrell's trailer and tossed it!"

She shushed me, frantically. I have no idea why. There was nobody in the house but her and me, and of course Carrie, who was much too young to realize what was going on.

I did stop shrieking, though, mostly because it hurt my throat to make noises that were so high pitched. "Why? What do you know about Darrell and Katie?"

"Nothing," Catherine said. "Or nothing about Katie or what happened to her."

"But Darrell?"

She squirmed. There was no other word for it. "I knew Darrell."

I stared at her. For long enough that the squirming intensified. "You never told me that," I said eventually.

"When would we have talked about Darrell Skinner?" She followed it up with, "Certainly not back then. You were twelve!"

Meaning that I would have been too young to understand whatever had been going on. Which must mean it was either sexual, or something else too adult for a twelve-year-old. Drugs, alcohol…

"How about three months ago," I asked, "when he was killed? You might have mentioned it then. Didn't I ask you whether you knew the Skinners?"

I'd asked everyone else, so surely I must have asked Catherine, too.

"I didn't," she said. And added, "Not anymore."

That was probably true, actually. It was impossible to imagine my sister the way she was now—lawyer, wife, mother of three, upstanding citizen of Sweetwater—having anything to do with people like the Skinners.

Hell—heck—it was hard to imagine my sister the way she'd been in high school having anything to do with the Skinners, too. She'd been our mother's daughter, and although she hadn't been as concerned with toeing the line as I had been, she certainly hadn't come across as pushing the boundaries quite as far as getting involved with Darrell Skinner.

"How did you even know Darrell? Wasn't he older than you?"

"Two years," Catherine said. "When Katie disappeared, I'd just started junior year. Katie, too. Dix was a freshman and Rafe a sophomore. Darrell had graduated. And you were still in middle school."

Then. "I'm not twelve anymore," I told her. "Whatever you did, I'm not too young to understand it anymore."

Or at least I would try my best. From what I knew about Darrell and his brothers, they didn't sound like people I'd ever want to associate with, then or now, but I'd keep an open mind.

Catherine sighed. "It was the usual, you know."

The usual? "He was hot and you were horny?"

The words just fell out of my mind, I swear, straight onto my tongue, and out of my mouth with no stopover in-between. I didn't realize what I'd said until Catherine looked shocked. "Sorry," I added. "I just meant—"

She gave me a look. "Do I give you a hard time about your husband?"

My husband? "Keep Rafe out of this. We're not talking about why I married Rafe." And it hadn't been because I was horny. Although I'll admit he was hot. But that was a side benefit. "We're talking about why you, apparently, got involved with Darrell Skinner in high school. And for the record, when I was in high school, I dated Todd Satterfield." Not Rafe.

"And I dated Greg," Catherine said. "But you knew who he was. If he'd crooked his finger at you…"

I shook my head. "I wouldn't have dated him." Not at sixteen. In fact, I'd thought long and hard about it at twenty-seven. It had come down to necessity in the end—not because I was pregnant, but because being with him, with all the problems that came along with it, was still a thousand percent better than trying to be without him.

"Well, I didn't really date Darrell, either."

No kidding.

The words came through my head in a sarcastic tone, so I decided to keep them to myself. "What did you do?" Not that I couldn't venture a good guess.

She squirmed. "It was just once."

I nodded encouragingly.

"He was charming, and I was a little drunk, and I wanted to know what all the hoopla was about…"

"Oh, my God," I said, as my jaw dropped unbecomingly. "You lost your virginity to Darrell Skinner!"

"No, no. God, no. It wasn't that bad."

I breathed out and hiked my jaw up. Just to have it drop again when she added, "I'd already lost my virginity to Greg. But I wanted to see what I was missing."

"Gah!" I clapped my hands over my ears. Or tried, until I realized that I was still holding Carrie. "Don't tell me that! What's wrong with you? I don't want to know that!"

Catherine shrugged. We sat in silence for a minute, maybe even two, as I processed this info. Then I opened my mouth, just to make sure I had all the information correctly. "So you were going steady with Greg. And you slept with Greg. And then you slept with Darrell Skinner, but without going steady with him."

"That's about the strength of it," Catherine nodded.

And meanwhile, I hadn't slept with Todd Satterfield in high

school. I hadn't slept with anyone until I was engaged to Bradley Ferguson in college. Because a lady doesn't sleep around, and besides, what man is going to pay for the cow if he can get the milk for free?

But this wasn't about me. It was about my sister, and her teenage exploits. Exploits I'd had no idea had occurred until this very moment.

"So last night," I said, "when I told you that Rafe was going to go through Darrell's trailer, you decided to lie to your husband and run up to the Devil's Backbone after dinner—in the dark, alone, to a murder scene!—to go through Darrell's belongings looking for… what exactly?"

"He had a collection," Catherine said.

"A collection of what?"

She winced. "Panties."

"Panties." I knew the word. I even got the appropriate, or corresponding, image in my head. But my voice was still flat.

She nodded. "Girls' panties. Girls he'd taken to bed. He collected their underwear."

I blinked. "That's a little creepy, frankly." Like something a serial killer would do. Kill women and keep their underpants as trophies.

Only Darrell didn't kill anyone; he just slept with them.

Except maybe Katie. He might have killed Katie. And perhaps even kept her underpants.

"Excuse me," I told Catherine and reached for my phone. Rafe should know this. He was surely still in the process of sifting through the years of accumulated debris littering the floor and every flat surface of Darrell's trailer. If Darrell had had a collection of girls' panties, Rafe should know about it. And if Katie's panties were among them, well…

Catherine watched me with mounting unease. "What are you doing?"

"Calling Rafe," I said, punching in the number. "He needs

to know about this."

"Have you lost your mind? You can't tell Rafe!"

How could I not tell Rafe? "If he has Katie's underwear..."

"He doesn't have anybody's underwear," Catherine said.

I lowered the phone to my lap before I could put the call through. "It wasn't there?"

Not surprising, perhaps, that Darrell would have gotten rid of his collection in the fifteen or sixteen years since he graduated from high school. It isn't something any self-respecting grown man would keep.

"It was there," Catherine said. "It isn't there now."

"Oh, my God." I gaped at her. "You stole evidence?"

"I removed something that might implicate me in a crime," Catherine said.

"You stole evidence. Oh, my God."

I just stared at her, speechlessly, for a moment. Then, as my brain caught up, I added, "Even if your underwear was there—your underwear from sixteen years ago!—how would that implicate you in anything? First they'd have to test it, and match it to you. Unless you have your DNA on file somewhere, I don't see how they could do that. But even if they did, all it would prove is that Darrell got his hands on your panties somehow. It doesn't even prove that you slept with him."

Catherine rolled her eyes. "Of course it does."

I shook my head. "It's strongly suggestive. But it isn't proof. You're a lawyer. You should know that."

When she didn't answer, I added, "Not that it's a crime if you slept with him. Greg might have had something to say about it back then, or Mother, but you were free to sleep with anyone you wanted."

If she'd been underage, and he'd been a legal adult, a case could be made for statutory rape, but I couldn't imagine any judge with sense ruling that way when a sixteen-year-old girl said she was sleeping with the eighteen-year-old guy willingly.

And besides, Darrell was dead now, and Catherine was thirty-two, so the whole thing was moot.

"For the sake of argument," I asked, "why didn't you just take your own pair of panties? Why take all of them?"

"Can you remember what kind of panties you wore when you slept with someone more than sixteen years ago?"

Again, I hadn't slept with anyone back then. My first sexual experience had come at twenty-one or so. And no, I couldn't remember what I'd taken off before getting into bed with Bradley the first time.

I could vividly remember what Rafe had peeled off me the first time we'd made love, but that was only a year and a half ago, and besides, a totally different story. I could remember pretty much every detail of that night.

But I put it out of my mind, since I didn't need the distraction. "So you didn't remember which pair was yours. And you took all of them."

She nodded.

"I don't believe this," I said. "You realize that if Katie's underwear was there, you took that too?"

"Of course," Catherine said.

"And if it was there, it might have something to do with why she was killed?"

"Why would…? Oh."

I nodded. "There were no clothes found with the bones. And no clothes anywhere else within the search perimeter. So she was either naked when she died, or someone undressed her afterwards. If her panties were in Darrell's collection, that could mean that she was naked because they had sex."

There was a pause. "You're saying Darrell killed her," Catherine said.

Of course I was. "He's the obvious suspect, isn't he? She was found on his family's property. He was the closest to her in age. His brothers were both older. He and Katie went to school together, at least for a couple of years. They probably knew each other. Apparently he had a reputation for sleeping with girls. Enough girls that he had a whole collection of their panties."

I had heard the same thing before, as well. Not about the panty collection, but that Darrell had a hard time keeping Little Darrell in his pants. He hadn't grown out of it after high school either, from what I knew about it.

I'd seen a picture of him once, if it came to that. Never the man himself, not that I could recall, but the picture had been enough to show me that he'd been both good-looking—if you liked the type—and charming, judging by the cocky grin he'd aimed at the camera. The picture had been taken at least ten years after he left high school, but it wasn't hard to imagine that he might have gotten plenty of attention back then. Teenage girls—or at least some teenage girls—are suckers for good-looking bad boys.

"None of that is proof that he killed her," I added. "So far, it isn't even certain that she was killed. But the circumstances are suggestive."

Catherine nodded reluctantly.

"Rafe needs that collection. If there was some sort of sexual relationship between Darrell and Katie, it might explain what she was doing up there, thirty minutes away from Columbia, on a school day."

Catherine looked mutinous, and I added, "You went to school together. Did Katie have a habit of skipping? Was she absent a lot?"

"Not that I can recall," Catherine said. "But we weren't friends, Savannah. Just acquaintances. I didn't really know her. We just had some classes together."

"Can you remember if she had a boyfriend? Not Darrell, but someone else?"

Catherine shook her head. "We really weren't close,

Savannah."

"I guess I'll have to ask Yvonne," I said.

Catherine looked confused. "Yvonne McCoy? She's Dix's age, isn't she? She wouldn't have been old enough to… Yes?"

I nodded. "She had a thing with Darrell back then. Or at least she did while she was in high school. He was older. It was at the end of Rafe's senior year, which was Yvonne's junior year, so Darrell might have been twenty or twenty-one, maybe?"

Catherine nodded.

"She finally dumped him when she got tired of the cheating. Do you remember Marcy Coble?"

"Yes…?" Catherine said, but she sounded far from sure.

"Same age as Dix and Yvonne. Cheerleader. Also slept with Darrell when she was in high school and while he was—supposedly—dating Yvonne."

Catherine winced.

I twisted the knife a little more, "Did you happen to count the number of panties you found last night?"

She shook her head.

"I bet there were a lot."

Catherine didn't answer.

"A lot?"

She sighed. "Yes. A drawer full."

"Where are they now?"

"In my car," Catherine said. "In a box."

"What are you going to do with them?"

It seemed as if she hadn't thought about that, because she didn't answer.

"You can't keep them here," I pointed out. "You have three small children and a husband. You don't want any of them to find your box full of old panties."

Catherine hesitated. "Maybe I can just burn them."

"Destroy evidence? Won't you be disbarred for that?"

She didn't answer.

"Just give me the box, please. I'll give it to Rafe."

"He'll arrest me," Catherine said. I opened my mouth, and she added before I could say anything, "You're right. I committed a crime. Two. I broke into someone else's home and stole something."

"He won't arrest you," I said. "At least not as long as he gets the panties back."

Words I'd never thought would come out of my mouth.

Catherine sighed. "Fine. Take them and give them to your husband. And tell him I'm sorry and to please not arrest me. I have children."

I promised I would do everything I could to talk my husband out of arresting my sister—not that I thought he'd try—and Catherine took me out to the garage. And while I strapped Carrie into the car seat, Catherine transferred the box of panties—it had to have been a small drawer, because the box wasn't that large; bigger than a shoe box, but not much—from her minivan to the Volvo.

"It'll be all right," I told her, as she stood there and wrung her hands.

She nodded, but I'm not sure she believed me. "I don't know what I was thinking, Savannah. I mean, you're right. I broke the law. I could, and maybe should, be disbarred."

"Nobody's going to disbar you over something like this," I said, although between you and me, I had no idea whether that was true or not.

Catherine didn't contradict me, at any rate. Although she might just have been too wrapped up in her own thoughts to really register what I was saying. "I just panicked, and it was all I could think of to do. If word got out that I'd been involved with Darrell Skinner in high school..."

"It was high school," I said. "Nobody would hold that against you now. You've been an upstanding citizen for fourteen years. Besides, I married Rafe. You having a fling with Darrell Skinner in high school can't compare to me getting knocked up and marrying LaDonna Collier's good-for-nothing colored boy."

Catherine winced. "People don't still call him that, do they?"

Not if they know what was good for them. Or at least not around me.

"It's been a while since I heard it," I admitted. "Although I have no idea what people say when I'm not around. But it helped when word got out that he worked undercover for the TBI and wasn't just a criminal for his own sake."

"Yes," Catherine said dryly, "I can imagine."

"At any rate, I don't think he'll arrest you for this. I'll do my best to talk him out of it if he wants to."

"I appreciate it," Catherine said, and on that note she went into the house, and I got into the Volvo and headed home.

Nine

Rafe had warned me he'd be late, so I wasn't surprised when he didn't make it home by dinnertime. Instead, I pushed dinner off another hour before I got busy cooking, and because I did, there was hot food ready to go on the table by the time he pushed open the back door, looking dirty and grumpy and like he'd had a very long day full of annoyances.

"Dinner in fifteen minutes," I told him cheerfully as I walked over to give him a welcome-home hug and kiss. The black leather jacket was cold under my hands, but his lips were warm against mine and lingered a little longer than strictly necessary. "You have time for a quick shower," I added, breathlessly, when he let me go.

He grinned. "Wanna join me upstairs?"

I would love to join him, but Carrie was awake and food was simmering on the stove, and I couldn't easily leave either to go have shower sex with my husband, no matter how appealing the idea was. "I'd better not. Rain check."

"I'll hold you to that." He dropped another quick kiss on my lips, greeted Pearl and Carrie, and headed through the kitchen and out the other side. I heard his steps walk down the hallway and into the foyer, and then I heard them stop. "What's this?"

The box. I'd left it sitting beside the door.

"Oh," I put the wooden spoon down on the spoon rest next

to the stove—my mother would never condone placing a used cooking implement directly on the granite—and hurried down the hallway. "I was going to tell you about that. It's a long story. But…"

I screeched to a halt when he turned to me, a pair of panties hanging from the index fingers on both hands—one pair was red and lacy, the other white cotton with little red hearts all over them.

"Yard sale?" One of his eyebrows was arched.

"Darrell Skinner's collection," I said, and watched all the amusement go out of his eyes.

He dropped the panties carefully back into the box, and if he would have wiped his hands on the outside of his jeans, I wouldn't have blamed him. Instead, he put them on his hips and faced me. "Explain."

"I will. But they're not going anywhere, so you can get a shower first, and then I'll tell you over dinner."

"This better be good," Rafe said. But that was all he said before he stalked across the foyer and started up the stairs.

"I thought about driving back up to Darrell's place earlier, to give them to you then," I told his back, since part of his annoyance was probably that I hadn't called him earlier. "But I figured the three of you had enough to deal with without any more surprises. And anyway, I wanted to do this in private."

He gave me a scowl over his shoulder as he reached the top of the stairs. "Save it. I wanna wash."

"Then go wash. Dinner will be ready when you come back down."

I headed back toward the kitchen, while over my head, his footsteps went into the bedroom and then, a few seconds later, across the hall and into the bathroom. As I stood at the stove stirring ground beef, I heard the water kick on in the shower upstairs.

When he came back down the hallway ten minutes later, he

was clean, dressed in a pair of faded jeans and another soft T-shirt that stretched tight across his chest and shoulders, and his feet were bare against the old plank floors. He was still scowling, though. And he was carrying the cardboard box, which he put in the middle of the island before quirking a brow at me. The request—order—to explain was implicit.

"Long story," I said. "Don't leave it there. We need room to eat."

He moved it off the island to the counter beside Pearl, and leaned against the cabinets next to it, his arms folded across his chest. In case I haven't mentioned it recently, he has great arms. Great chest, too. Everything else is pretty nice, as well.

"How did you guys do this afternoon?" I asked. "Did you find anything exciting?"

"No," Rafe said. "Don't try to change the subject."

"I'm not changing the subject. We're still talking about Darrell Skinner and what may or may not have been in his trailer."

"There was nothing in Darrell's trailer."

Not true. There'd been a whole lot of things in Darrell's trailer. I'd seen them, all over the floor when I'd peeked in earlier. "Anything that belonged to Katie? Her clothes? Her shoes? Her backpack?"

"No," Rafe said. "We spent the whole afternoon going through every inch of that trailer, and there was nothing there that didn't belong to Darrell. Best as I could tell."

Yes, at this point it would be hard to tell whether a particular something belonged to Darrell or one of his brothers, with nobody around to claim it one way or the other. But at least none of Katie's things had been found inside.

"Food's ready." I smiled brightly as I dished up Spaghetti Bolognese on two plates, and grabbed the basket with the garlic breadsticks.

Rafe's eyes narrowed, but he took his plate and walked the

couple of steps over to the island. "Don't think I can't tell that you're stalling."

"I'm not really stalling." I pulled out the stool next to his. "I just want us to be able to talk it through without stopping. So I thought it was better if we made small talk until we were ready to sit down."

"I'm sitting down," Rafe said, taking his fork in one hand and a breadstick in the other. "Talk."

I sighed. "Fine. After I left you, I went to Audrey's. We're going to her house on Saturday night, to have dinner with her and your grandmother. I suggested that maybe Darcy and Patrick Nolan could join us, too. Although that was later, after I'd gone next door, to the law office."

Rafe arched his brow.

"I'm not stalling." Although I was, a little. "I spoke to Darcy for a minute, and then I went back to talk to Dix. And guess what?"

"What?" Rafe said.

"He ran out the back door to avoid me!"

His lips twitched. "Sorry."

"He's the one who's going to be sorry when I catch him!"

I scowled as I bit into my own breadstick and chewed, and for a few seconds, the sound of eating was the only thing competing with the ticking of the clock on the wall and the hum of the refrigerator. Then I swallowed and continued. "Jonathan told me that's what he'd done. Dix, I mean. And then he asked—Jonathan—if everything was OK. And I said of course it was; why wouldn't it be? And he said that with the way Catherine had run out of their house and over to ours after I called her last night, he'd feared the worst."

And OK, he hadn't said exactly that. Not in those words. But that had been the gist of it.

"Our house?" Rafe said.

I nodded. Of course he knew as well as I did that we hadn't

seen hide or hair of Catherine last night.

"So you went to see her."

"Of course I did. After I called to let her know she'd better be there, or I was going to tell Jonathan she'd lied to him."

"And she gave you the box?" He glanced at it. "How'd your sister end up with Darrell Skinner's collection of girls' underwear?"

"She went to his trailer last night and took them," I said.

Rafe stopped chewing to look at me. And swallowed before he said, "Come again?"

"She went there last night and took them. Looked for them, and found them, and took them. That's why the trailer looked the way it did when you got there this afternoon. I guess she was in a hurry." To get home before her husband called me and asked to speak to her.

"I hope she had the sense to wear gloves," Rafe said, "'cause I asked for a forensic tech to go up there and dust for prints."

Of course he had.

"Maybe I should have called you earlier."

"That mighta been good," Rafe said.

We ate in silence for a minute. Until Rafe added, "So tell me exactly what it is that I've got there, and how your sister knew about it, and why it was important enough that she'd drive all the way up to the Devil's Backbone in the dark to commit burglary?"

Right. I took a breath. "So it turns out that Darrell Skinner had a bit of a reputation with the ladies."

Rafe nodded.

"My sister heard this, and although she'd already lost her virginity to this guy named Greg she was dating in high school, she slept with Darrell anyway, because she—and I quote— 'wanted to see what all the hoopla was about.'"

His lips twitched.

"Over in the box are Darrell's trophies. The underwear of the girls he slept with. I guess he sent them home commando after he was done with them. Anyway, one of the pairs belongs to my sister, and she didn't want anyone to find them."

By now Rafe was chuckling, and who could blame him?

"But she couldn't remember which pair was hers, so she took them all."

At this point he was laughing outright, and it was nice to see. Catherine wouldn't have enjoyed it, but it doesn't happen that often, so I did.

"I can't imagine what went through her mind," I said, half irritated and half amused myself. "She ought to know better. She's a lawyer, for God's sake. She can't go around breaking into other people's houses and stealing evidence."

"As it happens," Rafe said, mostly wiping the grin off his face, but not quite, "Darrell's trailer had security cameras."

I stared at him. "Oh, my God! You have film of my sister breaking and entering?"

He shook his head. "Lucky for Catherine, the generator's been turned off, with nobody living there. The camera's weren't running last night."

I breathed out.

"I'm gonna have to interview her, though. Officially and on record. And I don't imagine she'll like it much."

No, I couldn't imagine she would, either. "Will that cause problems for her?"

"Not less'n I have to charge her with something," Rafe said. "I ain't going after her over a box of girls' underwear."

Good to know. "You have my permission to put the fear of God in her if you want to. I can't believe she'd tell her husband you and I are having problems just so she could go up there and rescue a pair of panties she wore sixteen years ago."

The corner of Rafe's mouth turned up. "We'll survive."

Of course we would, but that didn't mean I had to like it.

I took a bite of breadstick and chewed. And said, "Did you know that Darrell kept trophies?"

"Not till now," Rafe said, winding pasta around his fork, "but then I never slept with him."

No. The girls would know, but maybe no one else did. Although I would have expected Darrell to brag about it. Why else keep the panties? "It's kind of creepy, if you ask me."

He shrugged. "At least he didn't kill'em first."

No, But even so...

I looked at him. "You got around some in high school." And since, but we wouldn't discuss that. "Did you ever keep trophies?"

"Women's underwear?" He smirked. "No, darlin'. My mama brought me up better'n that."

I nodded.

"Besides, there never was nothing I wanted to keep. Not until I slept with you."

"You kept my underwear?" I sure hadn't noticed that.

He grinned. "No, darlin'. I didn't wanna keep your underwear. I wanted to keep you."

Awww. "That's so sweet. I never wanted to keep anybody until you, either."

"You wanted to keep Bradley."

"Not for long." I added, "I was young and stupid. Maybe Darrell was, too."

"I don't think Darrell ever grew out of being stupid," Rafe said, implying that I had, which was nice of him.

And maybe he was right. About Darrell, I mean. At thirty-three or so, Darrell had still had his collection of panties somewhere where my sister had been able to find them. He might even have added to the collection in the years since high school.

"So what happens now?" I asked Rafe.

"I gotta talk to your sister and make it official. I guess I gotta go through the evidence—" He shot the box a disgruntled look, "although I don't know what good it's gonna do me…"

No. Not like he could send all the pairs of panties to the lab and ask for DNA tests. Not only would it be a horrible waste of resources, but the results were likely to be inconclusive. Most of these girls weren't likely to have their DNA on file. And in addition to that, it probably didn't matter who Darrell had slept with in high school. Even if Katie's underwear was in the box, it wouldn't tell us anything—or much of anything—we didn't already know. Darrell was implicated in Katie's disappearance already, given that she was found on his family's land. If he'd slept with her, that might be one more indicator that he might have killed her, but it certainly wasn't conclusive one way or the other.

"I don't suppose Katie's mother…?" I trailed off.

He arched a brow. "You really want me to carry a box of Darrell Skinner's trophies to the Miller house and ask Katie's mama if she can identify her dead daughter's panties from sixteen years ago?"

When he put it like that, probably not. If Catherine couldn't remember what she'd worn to sleep with Darrell, Katie's mother was even less likely to remember. And besides, the woman was grieving. Showing up with a box of girls' panties would add insult to injury.

"So it's a dead end."

Rafe shrugged. Might have been a yes, a no, or a maybe. Maybe he didn't know.

"But you didn't find Katie's other clothes," I said, "or her shoes or her book bag, at Darrell's."

He shook his head. "Nothing there that belonged to anybody but Darrell, that I could see."

"If he killed her, even accidentally, and got rid of all her other clothes, he probably wouldn't have kept her panties, anyway."

"Probl'ly not," Rafe agreed.

"You knew him a little bit. What would he have done if he'd accidentally killed a girl?"

"Not called the cops," Rafe said promptly. After a couple of seconds he added, "Prob'ly called Robbie and Art, and between'em, they woulda dealt with it."

"What would that mean? Dealt with it?"

"Gotten rid of the body and anything that could tie either of'em to the murder," Rafe said.

Like Katie's clothes and backpack. Which were still missing. "You'd think they could have done a better job with the body, in that case."

Rafe nodded, looking dissatisfied. "I dunno that we'll ever figure out what happened to Katie Graves. If nobody saw nothing back then, and there's no evidence now, we might never know."

Maybe not. But— "Maybe someone knows something they don't know that they know. Or someone knows something, but they haven't been willing to share it yet. But maybe as they get older…"

"Deathbed confession?" He didn't look enamored with the idea. "I suppose. It's too late for Darrell, though. If he killed Katie, he'll never confess to it."

No, he wouldn't. And if the other Skinners helped him hide it, they'd never confess, either. If the Skinners had been responsible for her death, we'd never know for sure.

"How do you want to spend the rest of the evening?" I wanted to know. We'd spent enough time rehashing what had happened to Katie Graves. "How about we watch a movie? Something mindless, with lots of explosions."

"Works for me," Rafe said and got to his feet.

The next morning, he set off to talk to my sister and get her statement. I offered to come along, but he told me it was official business and my services wouldn't be needed. Which made me a little miffed, but since he was right, there wasn't much I could do about it.

"What else are you doing today?" I wanted to know.

"I figured I'd have a talk with Yvonne," Rafe said, "see if maybe she can put some names to some of those panties."

I arched my brows, and he added. "Not the panties themselves. Just the girls who mighta worn them."

That made more sense. "Can I come along?" I asked. "I haven't seen Yvonne in a while." And besides, I was curious. And, in addition to that, I had nothing else to do.

"Official business, darlin'."

I pouted, and he added, "Though there's nothing keeping you from going to Beulah's on your own. And if you happen to be there when I get there, I imagine I'll sit down and talk to you for a minute."

Good enough. "About an hour?"

"Something like that." He dropped a kiss on my lips before he headed for the door. "See you later."

"Good luck," I told his back. "Make sure my sister understands that you're not happy about this."

He didn't turn around, but he did lift his hand in acknowledgement of what I'd said.

So he left—I heard the Chevy drive away a minute or two later—and then I got Carrie and myself ready to go, and, with fifteen minutes or so to spare, fired up the Volvo and headed out.

Beulah's Meat'n Three is a small cinderblock building that sits on the road between Sweetwater and Columbia. It's been there for as long as I can remember, and judging from the architecture—or lack thereof—was probably put up sometime in the fifties. Beulah Odom ran it for as long as I've been alive, until sometime last year, when she died of a heart attack that might or might not have been induced. The jury is still out on that one, or rather, there's not enough evidence one way or the other for an arrest and trial, from what I can gather.

Beulah left the place to her employee and protégée, Yvonne McCoy, one of the waitresses. She had no children of her own, and apparently she disliked her sister-in-law and niece enough to want to make sure they didn't inherit. They didn't take that lying down, of course, so for a while last year, it was touch and go whether Yvonne would get to keep the place, or whether she'd end up in prison for murder.

That's where the heart attack comes in. The Otis Odoms contested the will. When that didn't work, they claimed that Yvonne had poisoned Beulah to get her hands on the restaurant. They even had poor Beulah dug up and reexamined. When that proved inconclusive, they backed off, and Yvonne went ahead and reopened Beulah's, but I've been waiting for the other shoe to drop, and I dare say Yvonne has, as well.

She went to high school with Dix—and Catherine and Rafe, but in Dix's class—and she's always had a sort of crush on him. That didn't stop her from sleeping with Rafe once, at sixteen or so. And it certainly didn't keep her from being involved with Darrell Skinner, before and after Rafe, as well as more recently. And that, of course, was what Rafe wanted to talk to her about.

He was already there when I arrived, sitting at a table in the back facing the door. You might think that was so he could look for me, but in reality, he's learned to always keep his back to the wall so no one can sneak up on him.

When he saw me, he smiled, and that was nice, too. I wended my way past the other booths and small tables, with a friendly nod here and there to people I recognized who were looking at me, and slid onto the seat across from him. "Fancy meeting you here."

Ten

He grinned. "Likewise, darlin'."

He'd been here long enough to snag a cup of coffee. I wriggled out of my coat and then went about uncovering Carrie, who gurgled at her daddy and shook her little fist to make the toy strapped around her wrist rattle.

"Hi there, pretty girl." He grinned at her, too.

Let me tell you, having a baby is a great equalizer. There were still people in town who were shocked and appalled that Margaret Anne Martin's perfect youngest daughter—that would be me—had married LaDonna Collier's screwup of a son. There were people who objected because of class—I'd grown up in the mansion on the hill, while Rafe had spent his childhood in the trailer park on the other side of town. There were people who objected because of race—if I've neglected to mention it, Rafe's daddy was black—and there were people who objected because I truly am a very nice girl, at least on the outside, and while Rafe is also very nice on the outside, in a totally different way, he has something of a past.

Mostly people just objected because they're ugly people who can't be happy about anyone else's happiness unless it fits into their very narrow confines of what's proper.

But Carrie changed all that, at least for a few of the old biddies who were probably giving my mother haughty looks at the grocery store.

Not all of them, by any means, but a few stopped by the table to smile at the baby—it was impossible not to; she's adorable—and to give me polite congratulations and Rafe sidelong, sort of avid, looks. He was invariably polite, even to people who had probably called him horrible names growing up. I was, too—not like I could let him outdo me in the properly-brought-up department—although I'll admit it wasn't always easy. By the time the last little biddy had returned to her table, and had put her head together with her friends' to whisper about us, I had about chewed my tongue off.

Rafe grinned at me. "Glad that's over."

I nodded. "Another few months, and they'll probably stop caring."

"I imagine it'll prob'ly take a little longer than that, darlin'. Ten years from now, if I step a foot outta line, somebody's gonna say something about that nice Martin girl and how sad it is her no-good husband wasn't better brought up."

Maybe. "I love you," I said. "And you were brought up perfectly well. You have better manners than I do."

He shook his head. "Just more bad behavior to make up for."

"I really don't care what a lot of ignorant people think," I told him, but I kept my voice low, since he seemed to. Care, I mean. "If they don't like us, and don't like us being together, and don't like you for marrying me and me for marrying you or both of us for being happy, that's their problem."

"Until they make it ours." He looked around instead of at me. "We're gonna be living here now. At least for a while. It didn't matter what people thought as long as we were in Nashville. But now we're gonna be here. I gotta deal with these people. There ain't nothing I can do about before—"

"What happened before was not your fault." Or at least not very much of it. He couldn't help being born in poverty, to a fifteen-year-old girl whose father had shot her boyfriend for being black, and then proceeded to take that fact out on his grandson until he stumbled into the Duck River and drowned when Rafe was twelve. That kind of thing leaves marks, and affects things. There's no way around that. "Or, let's put it this way: you had plenty of help."

"I put Billy Scruggs in the hospital all on my own," Rafe said, "and myself in prison for it."

"If you'd only come clean about the reason you fought him back then, that might not have happened."

He shrugged. "Water under the bridge."

"You're the one who brought it up," I pointed out. "We'll be all right. And if you really don't want to stay here after…" I couldn't really articulate exactly what we were waiting for, not out loud, so I changed it to, "after, then we'll go back to Nashville. The house will be fixed by then, and you can go back to work with Wendell and Jamal."

He nodded. "Here's Yvonne."

It was a warning to stop talking as well as a head's up to brace myself. I twisted on my seat. Yep, here was Yvonne.

She's two years older than me, one younger than Rafe, and she's pretty much the picture you'd get in your head when I say 'small town waitress.' Buxom, reasonably pretty in a slightly hard way, with big hoop earrings and a bright red ponytail. Now that she owned Beulah's, she had exchanged the waitress uniform of snug black skirt and white shirt for a blouse and a nice pair of jeans. They were tight, too. When you've got it, you might as well flaunt it.

"Hello, princess." She gave me a grin in passing—she likes me OK, just not as much as she likes my husband—before leaning toward him. "Hello, handsome."

"Yvonne." He puckered up, since there wasn't anything else he could do. I rolled my eyes as she took her time kissing him before turning on the baby.

"Hello, precious! Oh—" She turned to me, "she's beautiful!"

"Thank you," I said, while Rafe added, "She looks like her mama."

She didn't. She looked more like him, at least to me. Although she had my eyes, bright blue against dusky skin. Either way, she was undeniably pretty. Although I appreciated the compliment nonetheless.

Yvonne scooted her butt into the booth next to Rafe, the better to be close to him. "What can I get you two for breakfast?"

"Are you taking our order yourself?" I asked, since that certainly was above and beyond the duty of a restaurant owner. She had wait staff for that.

"For my favorite customers?" She dimpled at Rafe. "Of course."

I'm pretty sure that plural was an afterthought, but I was glad to be included. And honestly, Yvonne likes me. If Rafe wasn't my husband, I don't think she'd mind another night with him—in fact, she's told me as much—but she likes me just fine.

We ordered breakfast, and Yvonne took herself off to the kitchen to put in the order. "C'mon back when you're done," Rafe told her. "I wanna ask you something."

Her brows arched. "Official business?"

He nodded.

"Just a minute." She walked off. A minute later she walked back, with the cup of tea I'd asked for, and scooted in next to me this time. I guess maybe she realized he'd want to see her face when they talked, or maybe she'd copped enough of a feel and was satisfied for now. "What's going on?"

"It's about Darrell," Rafe said.

"Still?" The single word question implied a lot of things. Like, 'Darrell's dead.' And 'his killer was caught.' And 'the case is closed.' And 'why are you still wanting to talk about Darrell?'

"Something new's come up."

Yvonne arched her brows.

"I guess word hasn't gotten out yet," I said, and Rafe shook his head.

"We're trying to keep a lid on it. The more people know, the harder it's gonna be to get somewhere. Although the news is gonna explode pretty soon, I figure."

He kept his voice low, but I didn't think he had any illusions about being able to keep this a secret much longer. Someone was likely to overhear, and then the gossip mill would start grinding. But that was no reason to broadcast anything as loudly as possible, either.

He turned back to Yvonne. "Back in November, one of the ATF agents found bones on the Skinners' land."

Yvonne opened her mouth, and closed it again when he added, "Human bones."

She stared at him.

"The sheriff sent'em off to the lab, and it turns out to be Katie Graves."

"Oh, God." Yvonne lost a shade or two of color in her cheeks.

"Did you know Katie?" I asked.

She shook her head. "Not beyond going to school with her. She was couple years older than me, and we didn't travel in the same circles."

"Nice girl?" I asked, since Yvonne had associated with Rafe and Darrell Skinner back then, and hadn't been the textbook—or Sweetwater's—definition of 'nice.'

She nodded. "She seemed to be. I never heard about any trouble."

I hadn't, either, and at the time she disappeared, if there had been anything like that associated with Katie, I'm sure it would have come out.

"Did Darrell know her?" Rafe asked.

Yvonne shook her head, but qualified it with, "Not that he ever told me. Although he might have. Darrell knew all sorts of people."

Including my sister Catherine. Yvonne hadn't been looking at me when she said it, though, so she probably hadn't been insinuating anything. I took a sip of tea and kept my mouth shut.

"I was up there going through his trailer yesterday," Rafe said, "looking to see if I could find anything that tied him to Katie. What can you tell me about a box full of girls' panties?"

"Oh, Lord." Yvonne flushed. "He was such an asshole, you know? Women liked him, and he liked being liked, and he liked getting laid, and he thought it was funny to send them home without any underwear. Some kind of power trip, I guess."

"So there'd be a pair or two of yours in there?"

"More than one or two, I imagine," Yvonne said, her lips curving, "but I slept with Darrell enough that I'd be naked if I gave up a pair of panties every time he got some. That was more for the girls who only came around once to see what the big deal was about."

Like my sister.

"Any names for any of those girls?" Rafe wanted to know. "Was Katie one of'em?"

Yvonne shook her head again. "I have no idea. If she was, he never mentioned her. And it woulda been before he and I started having anything to do with each other. I was just fourteen when Katie disappeared."

And seventeen when she'd slept with Rafe, and Darrell and his brothers had gone after him for it.

"Who do you remember?" Rafe asked.

Yvonne thought back. "There was me. And Marcy Coble. He cheated on me with her. Andrea Larkin, I think. Cindy Meyer."

Another C, someone who might match the initial on the ring we'd found.

Although if these had been one-night-stands, girls who wanted to—in Yvonne's words—know what the big deal was about, it wasn't likely that Darrell would have put any of their initials on a ring. Even one he could buy for a couple of dollars at the drugstore.

Rafe must have gotten what he wanted, or all he could expect to get, from this line of questioning, because he changed the subject. "Did you ever spend any time walking around the Skinners' back forty?"

"All that area back behind the trailers, you mean?" Yvonne shook her head. "They had camp-outs back there when they were kids. And they ran off-road vehicles through there. They probably went hunting or trapping. We'd go back in there to party sometimes, when we were younger. Light a fire and bring some beer and…"

She must have remembered that he was law enforcement now, because she shut her mouth with a snap and a flush of color in her cheeks.

Rafe chuckled. "It's all right. I've prob'ly done it, whatever it is."

He might have. But even so, she didn't finish the statement. "We never went far, though. Just beyond where we couldn't see the house anymore. Why d'you ask?"

Rafe shrugged. "I was just wondering how likely it was that Katie woulda been lying out there for sixteen years with nobody noticing."

"I can't imagine how," Yvonne said. "I guess it would depend on how far out the bones were."

"Not that far. Close enough to the pot houses that an ATF agent found'em."

Granted, he or she must have been wandering pretty far afield, because the bones hadn't been in spitting distance of the nearest pot house—Robbie's—at all. But still, the agent had found them, and without walking more than a quarter mile or so.

Yvonne's voice had turned flat. "You're thinking that Darrell and the others knew she was out there, and they didn't say nothing."

"If she'd been in that spot for sixteen years," Rafe answered, "it's hard to imagine how they couldn't'a known."

There was silence for a moment. As it lengthened, I thought about things I could say to break it, since it's rude to let a silence linger. But better judgment triumphed over good manners, and I kept quiet.

"Is that something Darrell woulda done?" Rafe asked eventually. "Could he have killed her in the first place? And if he did, would he have left her there to rot?"

Yvonne shrugged, sort of helplessly. "How the hell do I know? I don't think so. First of all, Darrell wouldn't have killed her. He wasn't like that. Robbie liked to take his fists to women, so I could see Robbie, maybe, killing her accidentally. But not Darrell. He didn't mind using his fists, but not on women. And I don't think any of them would have left her there, if they killed her. They wouldn't have called the cops, but they'd have carried her farther away from the house, or they would have buried her, or put her in the chipper, or something."

My stomach did a slow turn. I don't know if Rafe's did, but if so, his voice showed no sign of it. "I appreciate it."

Yvonne nodded, and swallowed. And sat for a moment without saying anything. "You think Darrell did this?"

Rafe took his own moment before he answered. "I'm not sure what I think. Something about it don't sit right. A whole lot of somethings don't sit right."

With me either. But I don't think that's what he meant.

While I took a tiny sip of tea to try to calm my stomach, he went on. "But she was out there on Skinner property. Hard to imagine that don't mean something."

Yvonne nodded, reluctantly. And looked up, and looked relieved. "Here's your breakfast. I'll leave you alone to enjoy."

She scooted out of the booth as one of the waitresses deposited the food on the table.

"Thanks for taking the time to sit with us," I said politely.

Yvonne managed a smile, but it wasn't a happy one. At least not until Rafe gave her his best panty-melting grin and added his thanks. "I appreciate the time, sugar."

Then she rallied enough to smolder back at him. "You know I always have time for you."

I rolled my eyes, but I did it behind her back. And I waited until she'd walked away and we were alone, before I said, "You know, I figured out why you don't have a panty collection of your own."

"Didn't we already talk about this?" He was busy coaxing ketchup out of the old-fashioned glass bottle for the little mound of fried potatoes on his plate, and didn't even look up at me.

I nodded. "We did. But I figured it out. You melted them right off, didn't you? Until there was nothing left to keep."

He looked up, bottle in hand. And stared at me for a second before he chuckled. "Sure, darlin'. Whatever you say."

"For the record, feel free to incinerate mine any time."

"When I get home tonight, I'll be sure to take you up on that." He put the ketchup down and picked up his fork. "For now, I'd better keep my strength up. It takes effort, incinerating panties."

No, it didn't. It came naturally to him, with no effort at all. But he was probably hungry from all the calories he'd burned last night, so I didn't say anything about it, just let him dig in.

We separated outside Beulah's thirty minutes later. Rafe to drive north to the Columbia PD with the cardboard box of panties, and me to head south toward Sweetwater. I asked him what he planned to do for the rest of the day, and he said he'd take the evidence—the box of panties—to the lab, and then he'd check in with the sheriff. If Bob Satterfield didn't have any particular tasks for him to do, maybe he'd go over some of the old evidence in the case and re-interview some people.

I nodded. "I guess I'll just go home for a bit. Or maybe I'll see if Charlotte is home. She still isn't answering my texts."

He tilted his head to look down at me. "You bored, darlin'?"

I was, a little. I was a stay-at-home mom with an infant. My life revolved around the baby. And while that was lovely, it wasn't full of excitement.

Which was probably a good thing, actually.

"What happened to," his lips twitched, *"Bedded by the Bedouin?"*

I made a face. "Nothing."

"No progress?"

"I haven't even started. Every time I think about sitting down and trying to write something, Carrie wakes up. Or Pearl has to go out." Or he came home. "And besides, who am I to think I can write a romance novel? I don't have any skills. I dropped out of college to marry Bradley."

"You got me," Rafe said. "Didn't I do a good job of inspiring you last night?"

He'd done a fine job. Fine enough that I wasn't sure I wanted to share the events of last night with anyone else. "That's part of the problem. It's bad enough that Yvonne lusts after you. Not sure I want her—and every other woman in Sweetwater—to read about what you can do in bed. If that gets out, I'll have to beat them off with a stick."

Not to mention that my mother would have a heart attack. And while my mother can be annoying, I don't want her dead.

Rafe grinned, but didn't take the bait. "Do what you want,

darlin'. I'm gonna go."

"Have fun," I said, a bit enviously. Not only did he have something to do, something clear cut, but he'd probably enjoy it.

"You too." He leaned in and gave me a kiss. And then I watched him walk across the parking lot to the Chevy, and waved as he drove past me, before I got behind the wheel of the Volvo and headed out, too.

Eleven

Charlotte was not home. Or if she was, her mother lied about it. "Sorry, Savannah. She left early."

"What's going on?" I wanted to know, my voice a little demanding due to my frustration. "Has she found a job or something? Or does she just not want to see me?"

Mrs. Albertson flushed uncomfortably. "I'm sure it's not you, Savannah."

I waited, but she didn't elaborate, which made it sound like, yes, it absolutely was me. "When do you expect her back?" I asked, when it became clear that she wasn't going to say anything else.

She looked past me, out to the street, sort of longingly. Probably wishing I was out there instead of right in front of her. "I'm not sure."

"She didn't say?" Or her mother just didn't want to tell me?

"I'll let her know you stopped by," Mrs. Albertson said, without answering the question.

Fat lot that would do, when she hadn't responded to a text or phone call in days. But since there was nothing I could do about it, short of pushing Mrs. Albertson aside and searching the house myself, I accepted defeat. Not entirely gracefully, but I did it. "Thank you. I'll wait to hear from her."

Mrs. Albertson looked relieved. "Thank you, Savannah."

"No problem," I said. "But for the record, I think it's lousy of her to make you do her dirty-work."

Her jaw dropped, and I added, "Feel free to tell her I said that. She's acting cowardly, and after twenty years of friendship, I would have expected better."

I seemed to have struck her speechless, so I turned on my heel. "I'll see myself out."

Not a problem, since I was on the front steps, and 'out' in this case meant down the walkway and through the gate. By the time I got to the car, and turned to look back at the house, Mrs. Albertson had gone inside and shut the door. And upstairs, in what used to be Charlotte's room, the curtain fluttered, as if someone had stepped back hastily when I turned.

It didn't have to be Charlotte, of course. Her children might be sleeping in her old room. That might actually make sense. Or it could just be hot air from the vent below the window fluttering the curtain. But I scowled up at the window anyway, before I yanked my door open and got into the car. I hadn't even bothered to take the car seat with Carrie out of the back this time, since I'd expected exactly what happened to happen, and I'd figured I'd be back in the car within a minute of getting out.

I was tempted to peel away from the curb with a squeal of tires worthy of Rafe, but there was no sense in giving vent to my feelings beyond what I already had. So I put the car in gear and rolled sedately down the street. On the next street over, I passed Sheriff Satterfield's house, and decided, on a whim, to see if Mother was home.

There was a good chance she wasn't, I realized that. Mother has standing appointments at the spa in Columbia, for massages and haircuts and facials. She also has friends she gets together with for lunch, including Audrey. And of course she has children and grandchildren. There was no reason to think she was sitting around with nothing to do, the way I was. But I pulled up to the curb nonetheless, got the baby out of the back seat, since I didn't know how long I might be staying this time, and wandered up the path to the front porch.

It took a minute or two from the time I knocked until I heard footsteps inside, but then she peered through the window and blinked at me. And opened the door. "Savannah, darling! Something wrong?"

"Nothing at all," I said. "I just don't have anything to do, so I figured I'd stop by and say hello. I was just around the corner at Charlotte's house, so it was on my way home."

"Ah." She glanced over her shoulder. It took only a second, although it was a second too long, before she stepped back. "Of course, darling. Come on in. Rafael isn't with you?"

I shook my head, moving across the threshold with the baby. "We had breakfast together at Beulah's, and then he went to work."

"Let me take your coat, darling." She whipped it down my arms and off before I had a chance to say anything one way or the other. After it was hung—properly, on a hanger—in the closet, she gestured me forward. "Come into the parlor. Can I get you something to drink?"

"I'm fine," I said, putting the baby seat down and unwinding my scarf. "Like I said, I just came back from Beulah's."

"*As* I said, dear." She lowered her derriere onto the sheriff's pale green loveseat without taking her eyes off me.

I'd been taught how to do that in finishing school, too, but I glanced at the sofa to make sure it was there before I parked my posterior on it. "So what's going on with you?"

She looked startled. "What would be going on?"

I probably looked startled, too. But before I could tell her that I hadn't meant anything by it, I heard steps on the staircase from the second floor. When I twisted to look at the hallway, the sheriff was on his way down, tying his official law-enforcement tie as he went. "Oh."

It seemed I had caught them *in flagrante delicto*, as it were. Taking it easy on a Friday morning instead of going in to work early. Mother blushed delicately. I cleaned most of the amusement off my face before I gave Bob a polite smile. "Good morning, sheriff."

"Morning, Savannah." He sat down next to my mother on the loveseat. She glanced at him, and blushed harder. I suppressed—or did my best to suppress—a grin. They looked like two kids who had been caught making out.

"Sorry to interrupt," I told Bob. "I was in the neighborhood and thought I'd stop by. I didn't realize you'd still be here."

"Swing shift," he answered, putting his hand on my mother's thigh. She looked from it to me to him and back to it, but made no move to get rid of it. After a moment she put her own hand over it.

I pretended I didn't notice, just smiled politely at the sheriff while I watched the byplay out of my peripheral vision.

"Where's your husband?" Bob asked.

"He went to work." I explained how we'd had breakfast together and then he'd headed for the Columbia PD. "He took all of Darrell Skinner's trophies into evidence."

"Darrell Skinner's trophies?" the sheriff repeated.

"Girls' underwear he collected. From the girls he slept with when he was younger."

The sheriff arched his brows, but didn't ask me any more questions. He probably thought I didn't know anything else. And it was just as well, since I knew things I didn't particularly want to share with him. Especially in front of my mother. "Is he coming back this way?"

"He said he'd check in with you afterwards. And if you didn't have anything for him to do, maybe he'd start re-interviewing people."

The sheriff nodded, looking pensive.

"Something wrong?" I asked. "I can text him and ask him to drive back to Sweetwater, if you want."

He hesitated for a second, and then he shook his head. "I'll call him myself. It's nothing he needs to come back for. Just an update from the lab. I can tell him over the phone."

I looked politely expectant, but he didn't say anything more. After the silence had gone on for a little too long, I realized he wasn't going to share the update with me, whatever it was, and that I'd have to ask Rafe later whether it was anything interesting.

I pushed up from the sofa. "I guess I'll just move along, and let the two of you enjoy the rest of your morning in peace." And as a side note, it was the last time I'd stop by without warning at this time of day. I had assumed Mother and the sheriff were sharing a bed—why else would they need to shack up?—but I didn't need the reminder right in my face like this.

They both nodded. "Let me see you out, darling," Mother told me. The sheriff lifted his hand, and she got up from the loveseat with a little twinkling look at him. There was little doubt in my mind that as soon as I'd cleared out, they'd go back to their necking. Or worse.

"Sorry," I told her, *sotto voce*, when we were standing in front of the door to the outside and I was shrugging into my coat while she was admiring the baby. "I didn't realize he was home this morning. If I'd known, I wouldn't have interrupted."

"Don't be silly, darling," Mother told me, but without assuring me that I hadn't interrupted, "you're always welcome."

"Next time you want to fool around, why don't you hang a piece of rope on the doorknob or something, so I'll know not to disturb you."

And if anyone had told me I'd have to give my mother this piece of advice, I would have called him or her a big, fat liar.

She looked very, very prim. "That's ridiculous, darling. If I hadn't wanted to open the door, I wouldn't have."

I guess that was true.

"Well, from now on, just ignore me if I knock on the door while you're in the middle of something."

Mother smiled. "I'm always happy to see you, Savannah. And little Caroline." She shifted her attention to the baby for a moment, and then back to me. "So where are you off to now?"

"I'm in town," I said, "I might as well go see if I can get hold of Dix. Did I tell you that he skipped out of the office when he heard me coming yesterday?"

"That's terrible," Mother told me, but I could tell she thought it was funny.

I scowled at her. "Yes, it is. And when I do get my hands on him, I plan to tell him so."

"Good luck, darling." She glanced over her shoulder. "I should go and make sure Bob has everything he needs."

Bob could probably fend for himself. He'd done it for the decade or so since Pauline died. But I liked to fuss over my man, too, so I just nodded. "I'll talk to you later."

"Of course, darling," Mother said, and shut the door. I took the baby seat and trudged down the walkway to the street and the Volvo again.

This time, before I opened the door to Martin and McCall on the square, I sat in the car for a minute and dialed Darcy on my phone. "Don't say my name," I warned her, as soon as she'd done her chirpy, professional greeting.

"Sa... Sure." A moment passed, and then she added, "Why?"

"Because I don't want Dix to know I'm here. I don't want to give him another chance to run out the back door rather than face me."

"OK," Darcy said, but she sounded amused.

"Is he there?"

He was. In his office.

"Good," I said. "When I walk in, pretend you don't see me. I'm going to leave the baby up front with you, and then walk back to Dix's office." All without saying a word. "With any luck, he won't realize I'm coming until I'm standing in his doorway."

"Sure," Darcy said.

My eyes narrowed. "Do you have a problem with that?"

"No." Her voice was uneven. "No problem."

"Good. I'm on my way."

I dropped the phone back in my purse and exited the car, slinging the purse over my shoulder before I took the baby seat out of the back and made my way over to the door to Martin and McCall. A quick look through the glass showed me that Darcy was alone in the front office. I pushed the door open and maneuvered myself and the baby carrier through, as quietly as it's possible to maneuver a women and a thirty pound baby carrier through a hundred-year-old door with a glass panel in the front.

Darcy looked up at me, amusement dancing in her eyes.

I put the index finger of my free hand to my mouth to make sure she hadn't forgotten what I'd told her less than a minute ago.

She nodded, and watched, eyes alight, as I tiptoed across the lobby and put Carrie down next to her. "I'll be right back."

I mouthed the words more than said them, and she nodded. I left them both behind and moved off down the hallway, making sure to stay on my toes, so my heels wouldn't click against the floor, and to keep on top of the runner in the middle of the floor, so it would muffle my footsteps.

The conference room was empty. So was Catherine's office across the hall, although the light was on, so she might be around. In fact, as I approached the door of Jonathan's office, I saw that she was there, bent over his shoulder, looking at something on the computer screen.

The both lifted their heads when they saw me coming, and I put my finger to my mouth again. Catherine looked surprised—she hadn't been here yesterday—but Jonathan grinned.

I turned my back on them both and moved to Dix's closed door, and the question of whether to knock or not presented itself.

Surely, if he'd been with a client, Darcy would have mentioned it? I probably didn't have to act professionally, and throwing the door open to scare the crap out of him had a certain appeal.

On the other hand, just because he'd acted childishly yesterday, didn't mean I should stoop that low today.

So I did the mature thing, and applied my knuckles to the wood. "Yes?" Dix's voice said from inside. I twisted the knob.

It turned, and I pushed the door open and stepped through.

Dix looked up from what he was doing. "Oh," he said. "It's you."

I smiled. Sweetly. "Have a minute?"

He sighed and put his pen down. "Sure."

I left the door open—as incentive not to lose my temper and yell—and crossed the floor to the two chairs parked in front of Dix's desk. One of them was piled high with paperwork, but the other was empty. I sat down. And contemplated him.

He contemplated me back.

"I don't like you going out with Charlotte," I said.

He nodded. "So noted."

"Are you going to do it again?"

"I don't see that being any of your business," Dix said.

"You're my brother. She's my best friend." Or was. Until Grimaldi, or maybe Rafe. And until this. Now I was angry with her. "I don't like it."

"You don't have to like it," Dix said. "It's my business, not yours."

I changed my tactic. "I can't believe you're doing this to Grimaldi. She uprooted her life in Nashville, and quit her job—a job I happen to know that she liked—and moved down here, and now you're going to dinner with somebody else!"

"Tamara's and my relationship is also none of your business," Dix said, and of course he was right. Although it didn't feel that way.

"She's my friend. And you're still my brother. I want you to be happy." Together.

"Let us worry about that," Dix said.

This wasn't working, either. I wasn't getting anywhere. "You're frustrating me, Dix."

He grinned. "I'm your brother. It's my job."

"Can't you be the nice brother who tells me things?"

"Not about this. Sorry, Sis."

Fine. I was just about to accept defeat when the door to outside opened, up front, and then I heard a familiar voice. "Morning, Darcy."

"Morning," Darcy answered, sounding surprised. "Savannah didn't say you were coming. She's back with Dix."

"I didn't know she was gonna be here. Or that I was." I imagined him bending over the baby seat to greet his daughter. And while he sounded perfectly nice, there was an edge to his voice that gave me the idea that he was angry.

Dix must have noticed the same thing, because he gave me a look across the desk. I got to my feet, just as Darcy said, "You can go ahead and go back. I don't need to announce you."

By the time I got to the door, he was already halfway down the hallway toward me. And the first look at him told me that I hadn't been wrong about his state of mind. His eyes, always dark, were flat and black, and his jaw was tight.

"What's wrong?" I wanted to know, stepping out in front of him. He had to stop, perforce, and took the time to drop a kiss on my cheek.

"Nothing you need to worry about."

It was practically like listening to Dix. Who had gotten up from his desk and made his way to the doorway, too. "Rafe." He held out a hand. After a second's hesitation, Rafe took it, and Dix added, "If you're here to yell at me about Tamara, you can forget it. Your wife already did."

Rafe glanced at me, and then back at Dix. "Tammy can take care of herself. She don't need me doing it for her."

No, she didn't. Or me either, for that matter. Not that that was likely to stop me.

"So what can I do for you?" Dix wanted to know.

Rafe shook his head. "I wasn't looking for you."

And he hadn't been looking for me either, according to what he'd told Darcy. "Jonathan?" I suggested. "Catherine?"

By now, they'd both abandoned whatever they were looking at, and had joined us in the hallway. Or Jonathan was in the hallway, while Catherine was hanging back, still inside his office. I was starting to get a bad feeling about this.

Rafe gave Jonathan a polite nod, and then looked beyond him to my sister. "Got a minute?"

Catherine hesitated.

"I got some questions," Rafe added.

Catherine glanced at Jonathan, and then back at Rafe. "We already spoke this morning."

Jonathan's eyebrows winged up, so he must have left for the day by the time Rafe showed up at their house earlier. Now that I thought about it, I think he had a habit of going to the gym before going to the office. He's tall and lean, so he's probably doing something to stay in shape.

At any rate, this was obviously the first he'd heard of his wife's conversation with my husband. And he didn't seem too pleased about it.

"More questions," Rafe clarified, although I would have

thought that was obvious.

"But I told you everything I know!"

He arched a brow, and Catherine flushed.

"What's this about?" Jonathan wanted to know. He looked from Rafe to Catherine and back, and then took a step closer to her, protectively. I saw Rafe's lips tighten, but he didn't say anything. Not about that.

"Your wife is helping me with the Katie Graves case," he told Jonathan instead.

Jonathan glanced at her. "The girl who went missing? I thought you didn't know her."

"I didn't," Catherine said.

"So why does he want to talk to you?"

She didn't answer.

Jonathan looked from one face to another again. From Catherine, looking flushed and uncomfortable, to Rafe, looking annoyed, to Dix, looking as confused as Jonathan, and finally to me. I probably looked guilty. I felt a little guilty, to be honest. Not that I could have done anything different. Catherine stole evidence from Darrell Skinner's trailer. I hadn't had a choice but to tell Rafe.

But that guilt made me question him now. "What's going on?"

He looked at me for a second. Then he sighed. "I decided to take a look at the box of..." He hesitated slightly, "—of evidence before I logged it in."

I nodded. It seemed like a reasonable thing to do.

He turned to Catherine. "You didn't take a good look before you scooped 'em all into the box, did you?"

"It was dark," Catherine said defensively, while Dix muttered, "What evidence?" in Jonathan's direction, and Jonathan shook his head. Catherine added, "And I was in a hurry."

"What did you find?"

I was the one who asked, but Rafe didn't respond to me, just kept his eyes on Catherine. "And after you left, and went home, I guess you didn't take a look then, either?"

"It was late. And I didn't want to bring the…" She faltered. After a second, she continued again, "—the evidence into the house." Where Jonathan could see it and ask her about it, I assumed. She didn't say that, but it was implied.

Rafe nodded. "Well, you missed the fact that Darrell marked'em all."

"All what?" Dix asked in the silence that followed. Nobody answered.

"Marked them?" Catherine repeated. The flush was gone now, and she looked paler than normal.

"Name and date. On every single pair."

"Pair of what?" Dix said, but by this point he probably didn't expect an answer. He looked thoroughly confused, and so did Jonathan. Rafe and Catherine only had eyes for each other, and although I knew what they were talking about, I was too busy looking from one to the other of them, following the conversation, to take the time to explain anything to my brother and brother-in-law.

"Do I need to spell it out?" Rafe wanted to know, and Catherine finally got a little shot of color in her cheeks again. She shook her head.

Rafe glanced around. "Where d'you wanna talk?"

Catherine hesitated for a second before gesturing to the conference room. Rafe headed that way. Catherine made to move, too, but was stopped by Jonathan's grabbing her arm. "What's going on, Catherine?"

For a second, it looked like my sister contemplated throwing his hand off. Then she sighed. "It's stupid. I'll tell you later."

"Do you need a legal representative?" Dix wanted to know, a tiny wrinkle between his brows. He was probably just looking for an excuse to sit in on the discussion to see what was going on, but it was clever of him to think of it. Rafe, as a representative for the sheriff's department and Columbia PD, was probably conducting an official interview about an official case, and although he's my husband, it probably wouldn't be a good idea to take that lightly.

On the other hand, I'm sure I don't have to tell you that the dynamic of this thing—my husband against my sister, brother, and brother-in-law—didn't exactly give me warm and fuzzy feelings inside.

Catherine hesitated, but ended up shaking her head. "I can represent myself."

Jonathan looked like he wanted to argue, but Dix nodded. "We're both out here, if you change your mind."

With their ears pressed to the crack in the door, no doubt.

I ducked into the conference room after Rafe, and looked around.

The last time I'd spent any time in this room, was back in the fall for the denouement of Darcy's parentage. It was going to be hard to top that, frankly, but I had a feeling he'd give it a good shot.

"What's going on?"

His eyes were a sort of opaque black I hadn't seen in a long time. It was the way he used to look at me back when he didn't want me to guess what he was thinking. Before we'd gotten involved, or as involved as we were now.

"You heard me. I have some more questions for your sister."

"About the… um… evidence?"

He nodded.

"Darrell marked everything?"

"Sure did."

"I guess… Would it be accurate to assume that there are more than one pair of panties with Catherine's name on them in the box?"

"You can assume that," Rafe said.

I had my mouth open to ask him just how many pairs there were—and how big the lies she'd told me, since it was obvious that she hadn't slept with Darrell just once—but then Catherine stepped in from the hallway and, after a beat, pulled the door shut behind her.

"Darlin'," Rafe told me, and nodded to it.

I didn't want to leave. I wanted to hear what Catherine had to say first. So I ignored my husband's directive to get out. "You lied to me," I told my sister. "And then you lied to Rafe."

She flushed. "I didn't have a choice."

"Of course you had a choice! The other option was to tell the truth."

"I couldn't do that," Catherine said.

I thought about asking why, although the answer was obvious. Whatever she'd kept back would make her look bad. "Well, you're going to have to do it now."

"Savannah…" Rafe tried again.

I glanced at him over my shoulder. And then I looked back at my sister. "I'd like to hear the whole story. If Catherine doesn't mind."

She sighed. Rafe sighed, too. And then we stood in silence for a while—it probably felt longer than it actually was—until she said, "Fine. Stay. That way I'll only have to say it once."

I was pretty sure she'd have to say it again, to Jonathan if not Dix, but now wasn't the time to point that out. "Do you mind?" I asked Rafe. It seemed polite. He was here in his official capacity, and he might not want his wife sitting in on his interview with her sister.

For the first few seconds I was sure he was going to tell me he minded, that he didn't want me in here. Then he sighed. "If Catherine don't mind, I guess it don't matter to me."

"Thank you," I said, to both of them. "I'll be quiet."

Rafe gave me a look, one of those 'I'll believe it when I see it' looks, but he didn't say anything. Instead he pulled out a chair and nodded to Catherine. "Have a seat."

I scurried over and grabbed a chair, too—on the short end of the table, where I could see them both but where I might not look like I was on anyone's side in particular—and waited for the fireworks to start.

Eleven

"I'm gonna record this," Rafe said, pulling a small device out of his jacket pocket and setting it on the table.

Catherine eyed it with a marked lack of enthusiasm, but she nodded.

"State your name for the record, please."

"Catherine Marie McCall," Catherine said.

Rafe launched right into it. "So when we spoke this morning, you told me you'd had a one night stand with Darrell Skinner back in high school—or when you were in high school and he had graduated."

Catherine nodded. Rafe glanced at the recorder, and she cleared her throat. "Yes."

"You wanna amend that?"

"First tell me what you found in the box," Catherine said. She had put her hands in her lap, and from the way she was sitting, I was pretty sure she was winding them together like Lady McBeth trying to rub off the bloodstains.

Rafe arched a brow. "I don't have to tell you nothing, you know."

"I know. But I'd like to know exactly what you found before I give you my statement."

"So as you can fit what you tell me to what I already know?"

"No," Catherine said, but her cheeks flushed.

"For God's sake," I interjected, "just tell him the truth, Catherine. Nobody cares if you banged Darrell Skinner one time or twenty when you were in high school. It was sixteen years ago and he's dead. What does it matter?"

They both looked at me. Catherine was clearly unhappy. Rafe might have looked a slight bit amused, or maybe not. "If you're gonna be in here," he told me, "you're gonna have to be quiet."

"Sorry." It just seemed like a stupid thing to lie about. Especially now, after she'd been caught. Red-handed, so to speak.

Rafe turned his attention back to my sister. "Like I told you, I went through the contents of the box. Darrell marked every pair of underwear with a name and a date. Your name shows up nine times. Unless you brought spares, that's a little more than once."

"Maybe they belonged to the other Catherine," I suggested, before I remembered that he'd told me to be quiet.

"The other Catherine spelled her name with a K," Rafe answered.

"Really? Katie Graves spelled her name with a K?"

He nodded. "Now let me talk to your sister. You ain't on the hot seat here. I didn't find your underwear in the box."

No. And wouldn't.

But I zipped my lips, mentally, and turned my attention back to Catherine. Who heaved a sigh. "Fine. I slept with Darrell more than once."

Nine times, per Rafe's count. Perhaps more than nine. Yvonne had said Darrell didn't collect her underwear. Maybe Catherine, too, had been so regular that he stopped bothering after a while.

"Any reason you didn't just tell me that?" Rafe wanted to know.

Or me, I wanted to ask, but this time I remembered to keep

my mouth shut.

"I didn't want anyone to know," Catherine said, which was stating the obvious. "I guess I was ashamed."

Rafe leaned back in his chair. "I ain't the morality police, you know. Nobody's gonna give you a hard time for sleeping around in high school. 'Specially me. I got no room to talk."

No, he didn't. Although, honestly, I didn't think he'd slept with the female equivalent of Darrell Skinner nine times in high school. The only two girls I knew for sure he'd spent time with were Yvonne McCoy and Elspeth Caulfield. So maybe he didn't quite have the past I tended to attribute to him.

But we weren't here to talk about Rafe's teenage escapades.

"So you and Darrell had a relationship?" I asked, to get the conversation going again.

Rafe shot me a look, but didn't warn me again to be quiet. Maybe because I'd asked what he, too, wanted to know.

"I suppose," Catherine said. "I mean… we weren't going steady or anything. I was going out with Greg. Darrell was just…"

Different. And I understood the appeal of different. I also understood the appeal of 'good in the sack,' even if that particular aspect had eluded me, by quite a lot, in high school.

"So the two of you slept together more than once," Rafe said, and Catherine nodded. A little reluctantly, but she did. When Rafe glanced at the recorder, she said it out loud. "Yes."

"And you didn't want nobody to know. Even fifteen years later. When Darrell's dead."

"No," Catherine said.

"What's any of this gotta do with Katie?"

"Nothing."

It might have been my imagination, but it sounded a little too prompt. Rafe must have thought so, too, because he arched a brow.

They're very expressive brows, if I haven't mentioned that.

Catherine flushed, but persisted. "Nothing. Really. My relationship with Darrell had nothing to do with Katie."

"Did he sleep with her, too?" Rafe pushed. "Is that it?"

"Don't you know if he did?" I asked. "I mean, you've got the box. If he slept with her, wouldn't a pair of her panties—?"

And then I stopped, with an audible gulp, when my husband shot me a look that could have flayed the top layer of skin right off my nose. "Oops."

Catherine looked from him to me and back. When Rafe turned that same look on her, she gulped, too.

"Cut the crap," he told her brusquely, and I'm sure, if she hadn't been a lady and my sister, he would have couched it in stronger terms. "Yeah, a pair of Katie's panties were in the box. Or at least a pair of panties with Katie's name and a date."

I opened my mouth to point out that that didn't mean anything. I would have probably stopped myself from speaking, even if he hadn't continued, "The same date that's on one of your pairs."

My jaw dropped, and this time I couldn't have kept quiet under threat of torture. "Oh, my God! You slept with Darrell *and* Katie? At the same time?!"

Rafe made a noise. I would have said it was laughter, except his face showed not a single hint of humor.

"No!" Catherine said, flushing beet red. "No, of course not. I'd never... no."

"So he went from you to her, or vice versa?" On the same day?

She squirmed on the chair and avoided looking at me. "I don't know what he did."

"Well, did you know he was sleeping with Katie?"

"No," Catherine said. "Not until now."

"Did you think he was being faithful to you? Or was he sleeping with other people, and you knew about that, but you just didn't know about Katie?"

"Savannah," my husband said, his voice edged with worn patience.

"Sorry. Sorry." I leaned back and mimed zipping my lips. "I'll be quiet, I promise. Don't kick me out."

He gave me a jaundiced sort of look, but he turned back to Catherine. "At the time Katie disappeared, were you still sleeping with Darrell?"

"No," Catherine said.

"Wouldn't the dates on the—?" I broke off and slapped a hand across my mouth before I could finish the sentence. But really, wouldn't the dates on the underwear tell him that?

He gave me a look, but didn't answer. Just turned back to Catherine. "So you broke up with him before Katie disappeared? Or did he break up with you?"

"I broke up with him," Catherine said.

"Because he got involved with Katie?

She shook her head. "People were starting to talk, and Greg was getting suspicious."

"So you didn't know about Darrell and Katie?"

"No," Catherine said.

"You sure about that?"

"Yes," Catherine said. "Of course I'm sure."

Rafe looked at her for a second, probably trying to determine whether he should push her farther, but he must have decided against it. "How'd Darrell take it? When you broke up with him?"

"He couldn't care less," Catherine said, her cheeks turning pink. "Told me he was getting plenty of action elsewhere, and he didn't need me."

I winced. Even if Catherine hadn't really cared—even if Darrell had just been different and good in bed—that couldn't have been fun to hear.

"But you don't know if any of that action came from Katie Graves?"

Catherine shook her head, her face still flushed.

"Anything else you wanna add?"

"No."

"Then I guess we're done. For now." He reached for the recorder on the table.

"What does that mean?" I asked, before Catherine could. "For now?"

My husband glanced at me, in the process of pulling the little device closer. "The investigation ain't over. I might be back."

"Why? You can't seriously think that Catherine had anything to do with what happened to Katie Graves. Why would she?"

"Yes," Catherine agreed, "why would I? Even if Darrell was sleeping with her—and I'm not saying he was, or that I knew about if he did—why would I kill her? Over Darrell Skinner?"

She laughed, but it sounded strained. Not much like a laugh at all, really. More like a failed attempt at sounding like it didn't matter.

Or a fake laugh.

"How about this?" Rafe looked at her with the recorder still in his hand. I had no idea whether it was running at this point or not, but I guessed it was. "How about if maybe it wasn't your idea to break up with Darrell?"

Catherine opened her mouth, and Rafe went on without giving her a chance to speak. "Maybe you liked him more than you try to make it sound like you did. We all know he wasn't your type, and with the way you were brought up, I'm having a hard time believing that you were only interested in the sex."

He paused, maybe to give her a chance for a rebuttal, but when she didn't take it, he went on. "There had to be some sort of reason why you'd risk getting involved with him. Your mama would have a screaming hissy-fit if she found out, and while he got around some, he was still just a teenager. It's hard to believe he was that good in bed."

I opened my mouth, and closed it again.

"So maybe you were in love with him," Rafe said, "and that's why you risked it. But maybe Darrell didn't feel the same way. Maybe he didn't mind fooling around with you, but you weren't important enough to him for anything else."

A flush of color rose in Catherine's cheeks, and it was hard to blame her.

"And then maybe he met Katie. And maybe Katie was important enough for something more. And maybe you didn't like that. Maybe you thought that if Katie was gone, he'd come back to you."

"That's crazy," I said, since it seemed like Catherine was unable to get her vocal chords to cooperate. "You can't be serious."

He half turned to me. "Why not? It wouldn't be the first time something like that happened."

Well, no. It wouldn't. But— "Catherine already had a boyfriend. She was dating Greg."

"And sleeping with Darrell," Rafe said. He turned back toward Catherine. "The last time you slept with Darrell, was the first time he slept with Katie."

Per the evidence of the purloined panties, I assumed. It sounded like the title of a risqué Nancy Drew mystery. Maybe I should write that instead of *Bedded by the Bedouin*.

"Are you sure there's nothing more you wanna add?"

Catherine shook her head, looking pale, and after a second Rafe turned the recorder off with an audible click. "Thanks for your time," he told her.

Catherine took a breath. It shuddered. "Can I go?"

He nodded. We both sat in silence while she got up and headed for the door. She had to catch her balance on the back of one of the chairs on the way: evidence of how badly shaken she was.

Rafe and I sat in silence until the door had had shut again behind her. Once it had, I turned to him. "You can't be serious about this."

He looked at me.

"She's your sister-in-law!" I said.

"And she had motive for wanting to get rid of Katie."

He waited for me to contradict him, but when I didn't—because I couldn't—he continued. "She mighta had means and opportunity, too. She was in Columbia at the same time as Katie disappeared. It was the beginning of the school day, and they went to school together. Catherine woulda been there. And she had probably started driving herself to school, so she had a vehicle."

She had, yes. My father was still alive back then, and our parents had given her a car for her sixteenth birthday.

"For all I know," Rafe said, "your sister cruised down Katie's street and offered to give her a ride to school. Katie woulda had no reason not to say yes. They were classmates. And then—"

"Stop it!" I put my hands over my ears. "This is crazy. Catherine would never kill anyone."

"Two days ago," Rafe reminded me, "you wouldna believed she'd have anything to do with Darrell Skinner."

No, I wouldn't. But to believe her capable of murder was stretching belief too far.

And because it made me upset to think about it, I changed the subject. "Did you talk to the sheriff?"

Rafe nodded. "He called."

"I think I accidentally interrupted him and Mother having a private moment earlier. I knocked on Charlotte's door, and she wasn't there, so I decided to stop by and see Mother." I made a face. "They were very nice about it, but it felt awkward."

"More awkward for your mama than for you," Rafe said, and he might be right about that.

"Anyway, the sheriff asked about you. He said he had something to share with you."

"News from the lab," Rafe said.

"What kind of news?"

He hesitated. And then decided it probably couldn't hurt to tell me. "More information about the bones."

"It's still Katie," I said, "isn't it?"

"Yeah," Rafe answered. "It's still Katie."

"Have they discovered how she died?"

He shook his head. "Still no sign of COD."

COD stands for cause of death, for those of you unfamiliar with the lingo. I'd heard that phrase more times than I care to remember in the last year and a half.

If there was no sign of COD, then Katie hadn't been bashed over the head hard enough to crack the skull, and if she'd been stabbed, the knife hadn't nicked any of her ribs. Or at least none of the ribs that had been found. "What, then?"

"Turns out they were never frozen," Rafe said, and I wrinkled my brows.

"Were they supposed to have been frozen?"

He looked at me the same way I'd looked at him, only more patiently. "If they'd been out there on Skinner land for sixteen winters, they'd'a been frozen at some point, darlin'. Prob'ly more than once. We usually get a good freeze or two every year, even if we don't get much snow."

That was true. Sometimes we did get snow. Every three to five years or so, we'd get several inches. But he was right, it was a rare winter when the temperature didn't dip below freezing at least once or twice.

"They can tell that from bones?"

He nodded. "Seems so."

"What does it mean? If the bones were never frozen?"

"I figure it means she was kept somewhere else until recently," Rafe said, "and put on Skinner land after the first frost this year."

Huh. "So you're saying the Skinners kept her body hidden somewhere—somewhere with enough cover and heat that the body didn't freeze—for sixteen years, and then, for no reason, decided to put her in the woods sometime this fall."

Rafe nodded. "And that don't make no sense."

No, it didn't. If the body was safely tucked away somewhere, why move it? It wasn't like they knew they were about to be murdered and their homesteads combed through. And if they had known, surely they would have left Katie somewhere more remote, where a wandering ATF agent wasn't likely to stumble over what was left of her.

"So what does that mean?"

"That somebody else likely put the bones there," Rafe said. "Maybe somebody who thought they could pin Katie's disappearance on Darrell or one of the other Skinners now that they're all dead and can't say differently."

"Chief Carter?" He'd been responsible for the Skinner murders. It wasn't a stretch to wonder whether he'd had something to do with Katie's, as well.

Rafe shook his head. "Carter wasn't here when Katie disappeared."

"Do you know that for sure?"

He nodded. "I asked the sheriff. Carter came to Columbia just a few years ago. Long after Katie died."

OK, then. So we were looking for someone who had been here in the area sixteen years ago, and who had killed Katie and held onto the body all these years. Someone who had seen the opportunity to pin the crime on the Skinners posthumously. Maybe someone with a beef with one of the Skinners in particular, unless it was just a matter of opportunity...

"You've lost your mind," I said.

Rafe arched a brow at me.

"Entirely aside from the fact that my sister wouldn't hurt a fly, where would she have kept a body all these years? She was sixteen when Katie disappeared. She lived at home. It wasn't like she could bring it to the mansion and hide it in the basement. Someone would have noticed. We were all living there."

"Like you're always saying," Rafe said, "there's all sorts of stuff in the house. Prob'ly stuff nobody's looked at for decades."

While that was certainly true, I think someone would have noticed a decomposing body in the past decade and a half. When I'd told him we have items on the property that have been there for a century or more, I didn't mean that nobody ever went up to the attic or down to the basement, or for that matter into the outbuildings.

And it's not just the family wandering around the property, either. Local school children come to look at the old slave cabin. Mother opens the house for the occasional wedding, or magazine shoot, or music video. Hell—heck—Rafe and I had had our own wedding on the grounds less than a year ago, with guests crawling all over the place. There was no way Catherine could have hidden a body from the rest of us for sixteen years.

And the realization that I was sitting here actually going over the possibility in my head, was sobering. And crazy.

I turned back to him. "You can't be serious about going after my sister for this!"

He sighed. "I ain't going after nobody, Savannah. The evidence is there. She was involved with Darrell. Her underwear's in that box nine times. Nine! That's a relationship, whether you wanna call it that or not. And after he slept with Katie, there's nothing. I gotta look into it, whether she's your sister or not."

"But the fact that she's my sister matters. You know Catherine. You know she couldn't have done this."

"That don't mean I can ignore evidence," Rafe said.

"But if you know that the person the evidence points to can't possibly have done it—!"

He shook his head. "You're gonna have to let me do my job, darlin'."

Well, yes. I would. But— "The sheriff probably won't like this, either." Or at least he wouldn't like it once my mother figured out what was going on.

"That can't be helped." He got to his feet and took one step closer to me, where he could lean down and kiss me. I thought about turning my face away, piqued, but even when I disagreed with what he was doing, every atom in my body stood up and begged as he came closer. Withholding affection was never going to be an option for me when it came to Rafe.

So he kissed me, and I kissed him back, and a little later he straightened. "I gotta go."

I nodded. Speech was beyond me right then.

"I'll see you tonight."

I nodded. And watched as he opened the door and walked out.

Part of me had been afraid that Jonathan and/or Dix were lying in wait in the hallway outside. Such turned out not to be the case, or if they were, they didn't say anything. The next thing I heard was Rafe's voice in the distance saying goodbye to Darcy, and Darcy responding in kind, and then the front door opened and closed.

Twelve

I stayed where I was. I was still a little weak in the knees, and anyway, I didn't particularly relish coming face to face with either of my sisters, my brother, or my brother-in-law.

It didn't last, of course. Half a minute later, Darcy walked through the door with my daughter's baby carrier over her arm like a shopping basket. "What on earth happened?"

"Long story," I said, and was about to launch into it when Dix sidled around the door jamb. He must have heard Darcy moving around, and decided to join us.

"What the hell, Sis…!"

"Don't look at me," I protested. "He's doing his job. Take it up with the sheriff. Or Tamara Grimaldi. If you're still on speaking terms."

Darcy put the baby seat on the conference table and pulled out the chair Rafe had been sitting in. Getting comfortable, she folded one long leg over the other. "Did he really accuse Catherine of murder?"

"Not in so many words." But yes, he pretty much had.

"That's crazy," Dix said. "What the hell…!"

"He knows that." At least I hoped he did. I hoped he wasn't so busy following the clues that he forgot that this was my sister he was looking for evidence against.

"I was probably in the car with her that morning, you know," Dix said. "She'd drive both of us to school."

She would, now that I thought about it. However—"Sixteen years later, there's no way that you can remember specifically whether you were there or not that morning. You could have overslept. You could have been sick. Or had a dentist appointment. You might have gotten a ride with someone else."

"Yes," Dix said, "sure, but..."

I arched my brows and he ground to a frustrated halt. "Fine. You're right. I can't recall that morning specifically. Whose side are you on?"

That was a good question. If my husband was serious about looking at my sister for murder, where did my loyalties lie? I loved my husband... but he'd only been my husband for seven or eight months. Catherine had been my sister for twenty-eight years.

If she'd been guilty, that would be a different matter, of course. If she'd actually committed murder, I would be able to justify siding with my husband against her. But of course she hadn't.

"It's not about sides," I said finally. "He has a job to do. He has to look at the evidence. He doesn't actually think that Catherine did anything to Katie. But what would it look like if he ignored her? Like he was doing favors for his wife's family, right?"

Dix had to admit that it would look exactly like that. "But that doesn't mean I like it!"

No. And I didn't like it, either. Even if I understood it. Or at least I understood it when I put aside my own feelings of loyalty to Catherine and the rest of the family and looked at the situation as unemotionally as I could. "I'm sure he'll find some kind of evidence soon that points to someone else. He'd have to, since Catherine didn't do it."

"It's not that easy to prove you didn't do something," Dix said. "It's a lot easier to prove that you did." After a second he added, "If you did."

"So he'll find the evidence to prove someone else did it, and not Catherine."

Dix looked unconvinced, but before he could say anything else, Jonathan and Catherine also appeared in the doorway.

"What the hell, Savannah—!" my brother-in-law said. He had his arm around his wife. Her eyes were red, as if she'd been crying. From that, and the arm around her shoulders, I assumed that not only was Jonathan now up to speed with what had been going on in the conference room while the door had been closed, but Catherine had confessed to him about Darrell and the panty raid and everything else.

"I know," I said. "I know. He doesn't really think Catherine did anything wrong. He just has to look at the evidence and follow the clues that are there."

"To my wife?!"

"The fact that she's your wife, or my sister, or his own sister-in-law, doesn't really matter."

"The hell it doesn't!" Jonathan said.

I shifted my attention to Catherine. "If you'd only left that stupid box of underwear alone, this wouldn't be a problem, you know. He'd have found them when he and Nolan and Vasquez looked through Darrell's trailer—"

Darcy shifted in her seat when she heard Nolan's name, so maybe she hadn't realized he'd been involved in that.

"—but you wouldn't have looked so damn guilty. If he'd connected the dots and asked you about it—" Which he probably would have done, given that her name was written on nine of those pairs of panties, "you could have made it out to be no big deal. 'Sure, I spent a week or two sleeping with Darrell Skinner in high school. It was no big deal and ended amicably.'"

"It did end amicably!" Catherine said. When I kept looking at her, she added, "OK, so maybe it wasn't exactly amicable.

But it wasn't like I'd commit murder over it. I didn't like him that much!"

"I'm surprised you liked him at all, to be honest. I wouldn't have thought he'd be your type."

"He wasn't," Catherine said. "That's what I liked about him."

Ah. Yes, I could relate to that. The same thing I liked about Rafe in the beginning, pretty much. That he wasn't the type I was supposed to get involved with.

"Didn't it bother you that he slept around?"

"Yes," Catherine said. "But when I was sneaking up there, afraid that somebody'd see me and report me to Mother and Dad, it wasn't like I could make a big deal out of it."

No, I guessed not. "What about Katie?"

"I have no idea what happened to Katie." She shook her head. "For God's sake, Savannah, don't you know me better than that?"

"I didn't mean that," I said. "Of course I know you wouldn't have hurt Katie. I told Rafe as much. I wondered whether you knew that Darrell started seeing her."

"No," Catherine said tartly, "and furthermore, I have no way of knowing whether he did or not. Nor does your husband. Just because her underwear was in that box once, doesn't mean Darrell had anything to do with her again."

I guess that was true. We might all be postulating a relationship that just hadn't existed. Katie must have survived the encounter, anyway, and gone on to live longer, because if the date on the pair of panties had been the same date she'd died, Rafe would have had all the evidence he'd needed right there.

"You've done this type of thing before, Savannah," Jonathan said.

When I turned to look at him—what type of thing?—he added, "Can't you look into this and figure out what happened?"

"Get in my husband's way while he investigates? I don't think he'd appreciate that, do you?"

"*We'd* appreciate it," Jonathan said.

Well, yes. I'm sure they would. But that wouldn't help my homelife if Rafe got it into his head to be annoyed with me.

On the other hand, there had to be something I could do to help him reach the right conclusion, but hopefully without getting in his way. Sometimes it actually is easier to be a civilian when you're trying to solve a crime. People will talk to you when maybe they won't talk to someone who's officially in charge. Some people have a problem talking to the police.

And besides, with his past and reputation in Maury County, Rafe might not have the easiest time getting people to open up to him anyway.

"There's going to be a memorial service tomorrow morning," Darcy said. "For Katie. At the funeral home on Broad Street in Columbia."

We all turned to her. "How do you know that?"

"Patrick told me. He and Lupe are working crowd control."

"I guess Grimaldi expects there to be a big turnout." If she wanted officers there to direct traffic.

Darcy nodded. So did Dix, so maybe he'd spoken to Grimaldi in the past twenty-four hours, and heard the same thing. He hadn't mentioned that earlier. I gave him a narrow stare, but then Jonathan spoke to me again, and I had to stop scowling at Dix.

"Maybe the real killer will be there."

"That only happens in mystery novels," I said, although between you and me, for at least a couple of the funerals I had attended, the killer had shown up, too.

Then again, most homicide victims are killed by people they know, so not a big surprise, maybe.

"I'm not sure I'd recognize the killer if he did show up. I

haven't lived here for a long time, and I didn't know Katie. I have no idea who she associated with."

They all deflated.

"But I'd be happy to go to the memorial if someone can keep the baby for me." Since I assumed Rafe would also want to go to the memorial.

Catherine raised her hand. "Under the circumstances I probably shouldn't be going anyway."

Maybe not. "I'll come with you," Darcy told me, "if you don't want to go alone."

I didn't mind going alone, but if she wanted a chance to see Nolan, I wasn't going to deprive her of it. Besides, the company would be nice.

"I think if Jonathan or I showed up," Dix said, "we'd be accused of being ambulance chasers, so we'll just stay away."

That would probably be best. "If you don't have any connection to Katie's family, there's no reason for you to be there. Although I'm sure there'll be a whole lot of curious people who just don't want to miss the event of the season," like Darcy and me, "so in that sense, you could feel free to go."

"I have kids at home, too," Dix said, "and no need to burden my sister with them. We'll stay home."

Burden? "Excuse me," I said coldly, "but I'm not burdening my sister with my daughter." She'd volunteered, and besides, they were the ones burdening me with this trip to Katie's memorial service.

Not that I wouldn't have been tempted to go on my own if no one had brought it up. In fact, if I'd known that it was happening, I probably would have gone on my own, even with the baby. I had started to feel a bit invested in Katie's fate even before Catherine had become a (not very serious) suspect.

"When does it start?" I asked Darcy.

"Patrick has to be there by nine, so maybe ten?"

More like eleven, probably, but I wouldn't mind getting

there by ten. It would give me time to talk to people, if anyone seemed inclined to talk to me.

"How about I pick you up at a quarter of?"

"Make it half," Darcy said, "just in case we have to hunt for parking."

Good point. If as many people turned up as I expected they would, we could be walking a while after parking the car. Maybe I should just park at Darcy's little rental house outside Columbia and walk from there.

"We'll figure it out tomorrow," she told me. "I'll call Patrick and see what the parking situation looks like after he gets there."

It sounded like a plan. "I should let the rest of you get back to work."

"Not so fast," Jonathan told me. I had never noticed this bossy, somewhat menacing streak before, but then his wife had never been on the hot seat in a homicide investigation, either.

I sank back down in my chair. "Why?"

"What can the rest of us do to help?"

How was I supposed to know? "You realize this isn't my job, right? I don't usually work homicide cases. I've stumbled over a few dead bodies in my time, but it's Rafe's job to work the case."

"If he hauls my wife off to prison," Jonathan growled, "it won't be because I didn't try hard enough to stop it."

"He won't." For God's sake. "Nobody really thinks Catherine had anything to do with this. He just has to look at the evidence."

"And the evidence apparently puts her right in the crosshairs." Jonathan gave her a look, one that spoke volumes. She had her head bent and didn't see it, but I did. "I won't have it. There has to be something we can do."

"Honestly," I took a breath, "the best thing you can do is stay out of this. If Catherine hadn't gone up to Darrell's to look for those pairs of panties, you—or she—probably wouldn't be in it at all. She made herself look twice as suspicious. So just stay out of it. Let Rafe and the sheriff do their jobs. Obviously, if you think of anything that might help, let them know. Or let me know, and I'll pass it on. But otherwise, just pretend like it doesn't concern you. Because it won't, in the end."

"Easy for you to say," Jonathan muttered, but he didn't say anything else. Instead, he glanced from Darcy to Dix and back. "I think we're just gonna go home. Neither of us can focus on work right now."

My brother and other sister both nodded.

"Do you want me to forward any calls," Darcy asked, "or take messages?"

Since they were busy talking, I decided to leave again, and made it all the way to my feet this time. "I'll see you in the morning," I told Darcy as I grabbed the handle of the baby seat.

She nodded, and went right on talking to Jonathan and Catherine about their schedules. Dix hesitated a second before he got up, too, and followed me toward the front of the building.

He waited until we were in sight of the front door before he opened his mouth, and he kept his voice low so it wouldn't carry back to the conference room. "How much of that was true?"

I stopped to look at him. "How much of what? What I told Jonathan and Catherine?"

He nodded.

"Most of it. Getting involved will only make things worse."

"That your husband doesn't consider our sister a viable suspect," Dix said.

I hesitated, since I honestly wasn't sure how to answer that question. "Let me put it this way. He knows Catherine. He's probably less inclined to believe her guilty than someone he doesn't know. And the evidence is all circumstantial and mostly theoretical."

Dix nodded.

"But Catherine made it worse for herself by breaking into Darrell's trailer and removing his property. That didn't improve the way she looked at all."

Dix nodded.

"He has to investigate. I don't think he ultimately thinks Catherine is guilty, but he can't not look into it."

Dix lowered his voice another notch or two, to just above a whisper. "What if he doesn't come up with any evidence against anyone else?"

"Then I don't know what he'll do," I admitted. "But the absence of evidence against someone else isn't evidence against Catherine. And I don't think any of them—Rafe or Grimaldi or the sheriff—is going to take Catherine to trial on circumstantial evidence. Someone else, maybe. But not Catherine."

Dix nodded. "And if she went to trial, it would be the DA's office who'd prosecute. And I could probably talk Todd out of it."

"You probably could." Two years ago, I could have, too. But that was before I married Rafe, and jilted Todd in the process. Still, he might do it for Dix.

"This sucks," Dix said.

It did. "Maybe I'll discover something at the memorial tomorrow."

"When's the last time you saw a murderer confess at the memorial?" Dix wanted to know, and when I didn't say anything, he nodded. "Yeah, me either."

He walked back toward the conference room. I let myself and Caroline out the front door into what was now the chill of the early afternoon, and walked back to the Volvo.

I spent the rest of the afternoon at home, doing essentially nothing. I changed and fed Carrie, I fed myself, she spent time on the floor, she napped. While she did that, I pulled up a blank document on my computer screen, typed *BEDDED BY THE BEDOUIN* at the top, followed by *Chapter 1*, and then I sat there and waited for the next sentence to present itself.

It didn't, of course. I couldn't focus on the imaginary adventures of some woman I hadn't even named yet, and the sex appeal of some imaginary guy in a headdress—no matter how much he looked like Rafe—when I had Katie's murder and my sister's potential arrest swirling around in my brain.

So I turned the computer back off and climbed up to the attic. On my way past, I checked in on Carrie, who was sleeping sweetly in her crib, her cheeks rosy and her breath even. She wasn't likely to wake up for another hour, at least, so I'd have plenty of time to root around up there.

The mansion, as I've mentioned before, was built in the 1839 to 1841 timeframe, and is a two story, red brick building with big, white pillars across the front. Your typical antebellum plantation house, in other words. It has around 5,000 square feet, and an attic across the top floor that's bigger than my apartment used to be, before I moved in with Rafe.

And there's stuff up there from when the mansion was built. There's antique furniture throughout the downstairs, too, but a lot of pieces ended up in the attic. So did a lot of clothing, as it went out of style.

The old household ledgers and such, from back when the Martin Plantation was a working plantation, in the years before the War Between the States, have been donated to the local historical commission for display. At least one ledger lives in the old slave cabin, so the school children who come to see it can also see how the money was spent—or wasn't—back in the day.

But I wasn't up here for any of that. I had no idea what I was looking for, or where it would be, if it was even here to begin with, but it was much more recent stuff. It wasn't likely to be in the far recesses of the attic, where the really old things were. Unless Catherine had deliberately tried to hide something—and if she had something she desperately needed people not to see, it would have been easier to get rid of it— anything pertaining to her high school years would be close to the staircase.

So I started there, opening boxes and checking the pockets of clothes. Since Mother occasionally rented out the mansion for special occasions, anything personal had been removed from the bedrooms downstairs. Whatever Catherine hadn't wanted—like the pretty dresses Mother had bought for her to wear as a teenager, which Catherine had eschewed in favor of more socially acceptable jeans and shirts—ended up here.

There was nothing of interest in any of the pockets. A dried-out Chapstick, a piece of very old chewing gum, a quarter and a penny. An—I arched my brows—old condom, still in the wrapper. Size large, lubricated. If I wanted to take something away from that, I could surmise that someone—maybe Greg, maybe Darrell—had been reasonably well endowed, but maybe not too good at foreplay.

If Darrell had a reputation for making the earth move regularly, the condom might have been intended for Greg.

There was no way to know now, anyway, and no reason I needed to know. I left the small package where it was and kept digging.

Catherine's books, including high school yearbooks, were all packed into a couple of cartons, and I set them aside for later. The yearbooks, not the other books. There was nothing among Catherine's offerings that could rival *Apache Amour* or *Pirate's Booty*, so I wasn't interested in reading any of it.

One smaller box within a bigger box contained cards and notes and a few photographs. Letters from our mother's mother in Georgia—immediately identifiable by not just the spidery elegant handwriting, but the return address on the envelopes—

and cards from Catherine's best friend Angela, whenever they were separated over the summer. Angela's ancestry was Greek, if I remembered correctly, and some of the cards showed pictures of pretty, white buildings against a blue sky, and the ruins of what I assumed was the Acropolis. We have a life-size replica of the Parthenon in Centennial Park in Nashville, that I've looked at many times—it's the closest I've come to the real thing—but since the replica is of the Parthenon the way it would have looked before time and the Germans destroyed it, and the card showed the temple the way it looked now, it wasn't easy to make the match. But I was pretty sure I was looking at a picture of the Acropolis.

By this point, my fingertips were starting to get numb. The attic wasn't heated, and I'd probably spent twenty or thirty minutes up here. If I wanted time to look at what I'd found before Carrie woke up, I might just want to drag my finds downstairs and go through them in the heated comfort of the parlor.

So that's what I did. Balanced the box of correspondence on top of the stack of yearbooks, and staggered down the stairs with them, shutting the door behind me. For now, those two areas seemed like they'd have the best potential for finding anything interesting, and if there wasn't anything there, I could always come back upstairs later, or tomorrow, and look for something else.

Downstairs, I dumped my hoard on the table in the parlor, before curling up on the peach velvet loveseat that had been sitting there for a hundred years, at least. The central heat seeping into my bones from the register by the window felt lovely as I sorted envelopes and postcards from the box, and while Pearl snuffled a little on the pillow in the corner.

Let me just mention here that I did feel a little guilty. These were Catherine's personal possessions, and I had no business reading her correspondence with her friends and family. She'd probably feel violated if she knew.

On the other hand, she had left these things here at the mansion instead of taking them with her to her own house, so maybe they weren't that important to her.

In the end, it didn't turn out to matter. The box gave me no further info toward proving that Catherine had, or hadn't, had anything to do with Katie Graves's disappearance and death. And if I'd thought about it, I probably would have realized it. These were letters and postcards Catherine had received from friends and family. There wouldn't be anything in any of them pertaining to this. If Catherine had written anything down concerning either Darrell or Katie, it would have been in correspondence she had sent to someone else—probably Angela—and not on postcards Angela sent Catherine.

The handful of photographs showed Catherine and Angela, Catherine, Dix, and me, Catherine and Greg, and a couple of shots of a group of kids around a campfire somewhere in the woods. There was no way to know one way or the other—one hackberry tree looks very much like another—but I did wonder whether it had been taken on the Skinners' property. Yvonne had mentioned something about campfires, hadn't she?

I peeled my eyes, but didn't see Darrell Skinner anywhere among the faces. On the other hand, I didn't see Greg, either.

And as I peered from tiny face to tiny face, I realized that I didn't really know what Katie Graves had looked like. I had the photograph of Greg and Catherine in front of me, and it was just a few months since I'd seen a picture of Darrell with Yvonne. An older Darrell, but I was pretty sure I'd have recognized him, had he been in the photos. Maybe he'd been the one taking them.

Or maybe Greg had.

But I didn't have a clear idea of what Katie had looked like. I remembered the headlines in the local papers back when she died, and pictures of a girl with long, dark hair, but beyond that, I couldn't bring her features to mind. At least half the girls in the picture had long, dark hair, and sixteen years had blunted my recollection of Katie's face.

The yearbook took care of that. I grabbed the book for Catherine's sophomore year, and turned over the pages until I got to the Gs. Katie's name turned out to be Kathryn, not Katherine—same sound, different spelling—and she did indeed spell it with a K, so the ring we'd found near the dumpsite hadn't belonged to her. And if it had belonged to Darrell, he hadn't worn it to commemorate his relationship with Katie.

She looked up from the page with solemn, dark eyes. As Rafe had said once, when I asked, she'd been pretty enough, with long, straight hair parted in the middle, and steady eyes under straight brows. Not striking or even particularly noticeable, but with even features and a bland, somewhat unformed face.

Unlike some of the girls, she wasn't wearing a lot of makeup or fake eyelashes, and she also didn't have any of the nose- or eyebrow rings or colored hair some of them sported. She just looked like an average girl, the kind you can find millions of in high schools all across the country.

With her face in mind, I took another look at the pictures from the woods, and thought maybe she was there, in the background, half hidden behind another girl with blond curls and a big grin. It was hard to be sure, though. But I put the photos aside so I could ask Catherine about them later.

Other than Katie's face, the yearbooks didn't reveal much of interest. Catherine showed up a few times, with and without Greg and/or Angela. I knew both of their faces from seeing them around the house growing up, and from the photographs in Catherine's box. And Katie showed up once or twice, surrounded by people who weren't my sister, or anyone else I knew. So at least Catherine hadn't lied about that. Other than that one outing in the woods, where they were both depicted,

Catherine really didn't seem to have had much to do with Katie in high school.

In one of the photos—the school newspaper staff—Katie was sitting next to a curly-haired blonde with lots of teeth, whom I recognized from the picture in the woods. Her name turned out to be Lynn Jeffries, and I made a mental note to find out whether she was still around, and whether the cops had spoken to her, then or now. If she and Katie had been friends— and they might have been, since I'd seen pictures of them together both during school activities and off-time—Lynn might have some idea whether Katie was, or would have been, involved with Darrell Skinner.

At that point, Carrie started making noises, so I packed everything up neatly and stowed it all away on a bottom shelf in the bookcase, where Rafe might not notice it.

Not hidden, not precisely—because hiding it would make me feel like I was keeping things from my husband—but not anywhere where he was likely to notice it, either, unless I drew his attention to it. And then I went to get my daughter and to start cooking dinner.

Thirteen

Rafe kissed me goodbye on Saturday morning just as usual. I kissed him back, like nothing was wrong. We'd spent the evening the same way, carefully tiptoeing around the elephant in the room. Neither of us brought up Catherine and the conversation in the conference room earlier. I didn't even ask him how he'd spent the rest of his day, since I didn't want to hear that he'd been digging for evidence against my sister.

We spent the evening watching TV and not saying much. We went to bed as usual. Carrie woke up in the middle of the night, as usual. Rafe got up before me, as usual, and when he was ready to go, he came over and kissed me. I peered up at him out of sleepy eyes. "It's Saturday. How come you're up so early?"

"Places to go, people to see," he told me, as he shrugged a long-sleeved Henley over a short-sleeved T-shirt, both of which covered all those lovely muscles and that warm skin.

I squinted. "You're wearing a lot."

His mouth curved, but he didn't take the bait. "I'm taking a K9 and a handler up on the Devil's Backbone to walk the Skinners' property. See if we can find anywhere they mighta kept Katie's body for fifteen years."

I thought we'd agreed that it wasn't likely the Skinners had done that, but I guess I ought to be grateful that he was looking at possibilities other than Catherine. And since it sounded like he'd stay busy for most of the day—the Skinners had a lot of property—and he wasn't likely to notice that I went to Katie's memorial service, my semi-guilty conscience (and perhaps a little FOMO, fear of missing out on anything he might discover) prompted me to ask, "Would you like me to bring you lunch in the middle of the day?"

He shook his head. "Thanks, darlin', but I don't know where I'm gonna be when it's time to eat. I could be miles from any of the Skinners' homesteads by then. Better if I just fend for myself."

"Don't forget we're having dinner with your grandmother and Audrey tonight," I reminded him.

He nodded. "I don't figure I'll be neck deep in any new murders or ready to make any arrests by then, so that oughta be fine."

Good to know that my sister was safe for today, anyway. "You'll be home in time to get ready, then?"

He said he would, and that's when he kissed me before heading out. I kissed him back, since it's impossible not to, and then I stayed in bed while he let Pearl out so I wouldn't have to, until I heard the Chevy drive away. Carrie was still asleep, so I took a quick three-minute shower—the only kind of shower I got these days, unless Rafe was around to watch the baby—and got ready for the day. By eight-thirty, I was on my way to Catherine's house with Carrie, so I could drop her off and then go pick up Darcy by nine-thirty.

Catherine must have been waiting, because she opened the front door as soon as I got out of the car. "Everything OK?"

"Of course," I said. "Why wouldn't it be?"

I hauled the car seat out of the car along with Carrie's suitcase-sized bag full of diapers and clothing changes and bottles and pacifiers, and slung it over one shoulder while I took the baby seat over my other arm. It kept me nicely balanced as I staggered up the walk to the front door, but I will admit that I felt a bit like those poor little donkeys you see in videos from Peru or Nicaragua, laden down with sticks and sugar cane.

As I got closer to the door, I saw that my sister seemed to have spent a sleepless night. She had bags under her eyes almost as big as the one currently weighing down my shoulder, and her eyes were bloodshot.

"You look terrible," I told her.

She grimaced. "Thanks ever so."

"What's the matter? Don't you feel well?" Had she changed her mind about taking care of Carrie for a few hours?

"I'm fine," Catherine said, reaching for the diaper bag. "Just waiting for your husband to come haul me off to prison."

I relinquished the bag and put the car seat down on the floor in the foyer before closing the door behind us to keep the cold air out. "I wouldn't worry about it. Not today. He took a cadaver dog and a K9 handler up to the Skinners' property to see whether they could figure out where Katie may have been kept. It'll take them the best part of the day, I figure. It's a big property."

"Kept?" Catherine repeated, still stuck on what I'd said a couple of sentences ago.

"Before she was dumped in the woods. Oh, don't you know about that?"

Maybe Rafe had told me about it after she had left the conference room yesterday. I couldn't remember, to be honest. The whole encounter wasn't that clear in my mind. "Yes, apparently she was kept somewhere else until recently."

"Alive?" Catherine said, her eyes wide. That particular thought hadn't occurred to me yet, and now I wished it hadn't. How horrible, if she hadn't been killed right away, and instead had been kept somewhere, alive, while the search had been going on, and after, when we'd all decided she must have run away.

Then I shook it off, since that hadn't been what Rafe had meant. "No, no. Not as far as I know. She's been dead long enough that there was nothing left but bone, so I think she was killed pretty much right away. No, this had something to do with how the bones have never been frozen, so she can't have been lying outside, where she was found, for sixteen years."

Catherine looked relieved, and I couldn't blame her. The other option was unpalatable, to say the least.

"Anyway," I said, "he told me he expected it to take most of the day. And we're having dinner with Audrey and Mrs. Jenkins tonight, so I don't think you have to worry about being arrested later, either. Just relax."

"Easy for you to say," Catherine muttered, and I guess it was, so I changed the subject.

"You should have everything you need for Carrie in the bag. I'll probably be back by noon or twelve-thirty. I don't imagine the service will last longer than that, do you? People will mostly do their socializing before the service starts, surely. And if there's a graveside ceremony after, I don't think Darcy and I will follow along for that. It's probably more appropriate to leave that for the family."

Catherine nodded.

"Before I go, I wanted to show you something."

I dug in the pocket of my coat and came up with the two photographs I'd found yesterday, of the group of teenagers around the campfire in the woods. I handed them to her, and then, as she looked at them, leaned in to point. "That's you. And that's Angela, I think. And isn't that Katie Graves in the back there, behind the blonde with all the teeth?"

"Lynn somebody," Catherine said. "Where did you get these?"

I told her they'd been in a box in the attic, along with all the other stuff Mother had cleared out of Catherine's room after Catherine got married.

She eyed me balefully. "You went through my things?"

"They were just up in the attic," I said. "I didn't think you'd care. It's all stuff you left behind when you moved out."

"But it's *my* stuff!"

"I wasn't stealing it," I said. "If it's that big a deal, I'll put everything back where I found it. I just wanted to ask you about the pictures."

"Those are my personal belongings!" Catherine said. "I can't believe you would rifle through my things!"

I put my hands on my hips. "This carrying on makes it sound like you've got something to hide. And it's totally out of proportion to what happened. All I did was go up to the attic in the house where I live, and look through some boxes of old stuff."

"You think I killed Katie!" Catherine shrieked. "You're looking for evidence to give to your husband!"

"That's ridiculous," I said. "Of course I don't think you had anything to do with Katie's death. And I didn't show the pictures to Rafe. I just want to know when and where they were taken."

Now that she was holding them against her chest, in some sort of belated attempt to prevent me from looking at them, I could see that there was something written on the backs of the photographs, though. Something I hadn't noticed yesterday. "What's it say on the back?"

"Nothing!" Catherine said.

I reached out. For a second or two I was afraid she was going to take off running, but she must have realized that she was acting crazy, because when I took hold of a corner of one of the photographs, she let me tug it out of her hands instead of holding on until it ripped.

I turned it over and looked at the date scrawled there, in Catherine's rounded teenage girl cursive. "Late August? The month before Katie disappeared?"

She nodded.

"Where?"

"Up in the hills," Catherine said, as reluctantly as if I'd pulled the words out with pliers.

"The Skinners' property?"

She shrugged. "It was up there somewhere, but I'm not sure exactly."

"Were you sleeping with Darrell at this point?"

Catherine flushed. "Yes."

"Was Katie?"

"I have no idea whether Katie ever slept with Darrell," Catherine said waspishly.

"Rafe said…"

"He found one of her pairs of panties in Darrell's collection. Yes. So either Darrell slept with Katie, or your husband lied."

"He wouldn't do that," I said.

Catherine turned her nose up so she could look at me down the length of it. She's several inches shorter than me, so it didn't work too well. "Are you sure about that? You can't tell me he's never lied before."

No, I couldn't. But he didn't make a habit of lying to me. At least I didn't think so.

Although Catherine wasn't likely to be swayed one way or the other by that, so I let it go. "Do you want to keep the pictures, or should I put them back in the box?"

"Don't you want to show them to Rafe?" Catherine asked.

"Not if you don't want me to."

She looked surprised, and I added, "They don't prove anything one way or the other. The date is a couple of weeks, at least, before Katie disappeared, so she obviously walked away from this evening in one piece. I was just curious."

"You can put them back in the box," Catherine said. "And if Rafe wants to see them, feel free to show them to him. If nothing else, it proves that Katie and I could be in the same place at the same time without me killing her."

It did. Although if Catherine was sleeping with Darrell and Katie hadn't started yet, Catherine wouldn't have had any reason to harm Katie at this point.

Not that she'd harmed her later. Of course not.

I tucked the pictures back into the pocket of my coat. "I should go. I don't want to be late."

Catherine nodded. "Carrie and I will be fine here."

"Are you alone?" I looked around. It was pretty quiet, and neither of the kids had come running to greet me.

But she shook her head. "Jonathan went to the gym. The boys are upstairs watching cartoons. Annie slept over with Abigail and Hannah."

"I appreciate you doing this." Taking on the care of my daughter when she might have had a free hour or two on her own, was going above and beyond, in my opinion.

"It's no problem," Catherine said. "I'll probably never have another baby of my own, so it's nice to spend time with yours. And give her back when I'm done."

No doubt.

I turned toward the door. "I'll be back as soon as I can."

"Take your time," Catherine said. "Try to find another viable suspect so I can get your husband off my back."

I told her I'd try to do just that, and then I left my daughter with her and walked back out in the cold January morning to pick up my other sister.

Darcy lives in a small rental house on the south side of Columbia. It's a little ranch, and a far cry from Catherine's sprawling subdivision McMansion, but it's cute, and she seems happy there. When I pulled up in front, the bright blue door opened before I'd come to a full stop, and Darcy walked out.

Like me, she looked ready for a funeral, in tall, black boots and a sober wool coat.

I sometimes wonder whether anyone who sees us together think we're sisters. I suspect not. We're both tall, although Darcy has me beat by a couple of inches. She gets that from Audrey, just like I get my extra height from the Georgia Calverts, and not the Martins.

Darcy is also thinner and more athletic looking than me. Her hair is short and dark where mine's dishwater blond and longer, and her eyes are brown, courtesy of my father. I sometimes fancy I can see a little of him in her face, just enough to soften the sharper angles of Audrey's bone structure, but there, too, I look more like Mother, so I don't imagine Darcy and I look that similar. She's always looked more like Rafe, and once we discovered that her mother was his second cousin or some such, that made a lot more sense.

Anyway, she's my sister, and I love her. When she got into the car next to me, I gave her a big smile. "Morning."

She smiled back, looking amused. "You're awfully happy for someone who's going to a funeral."

"I've had some interesting experiences at funerals," I said. Like almost getting run down in the parking lot of a funeral home in Nashville back in November. "Did I ever tell you about the time the victim's current boyfriend and ex-boyfriend came to blows over the casket? Literally? They knocked it over and everything."

Darcy shook her head, her eyes huge.

"It was last year sometime." The story—not a bit of it made up, I swear—kept us busy until we'd made it to Broad Street. Darcy doesn't live that far from the center of town, since the center of Columbia isn't that far from anything to begin with.

"I don't think anything like that's going to happen today, though," I said. "Under the circumstances, I'm sure everyone will be very well behaved."

Darcy nodded. With the funeral home up ahead, as evidenced by the bright orange cones in the middle of the street, I started looking for a parking space.

"Besides," I added, "I'm not sure Katie had one boyfriend, let alone two. Darrell Skinner's dead, so he certainly won't be doing any fighting."

"Good to know," Darcy said.

There were no open spaces along the street, and I ended up pulling to a stop next to Patrick Nolan, who was directing traffic into and out of the funeral home. He smiled politely at me, and then bent down to give Darcy a beaming grin. "Hi there."

"Hi," Darcy answered, blushing.

"I didn't think I'd see you this morning."

"Me, either," Darcy said.

I would have been happy to sit there letting them make eyes at each other for a while, but by now an Escalade had pulled up behind me, so I told Nolan, "I'm sorry to interrupt, but where can we park?"

"You going to the funeral?"

I nodded.

"The parking lot here's full," Nolan said. "You can try to find something on the street, or there's a parking lot on the next block—Vasquez is up there—and I think there might be some spaces left there."

"We'll see you on the way back," I told him, before I lowered my foot on the gas and we rolled off, with the Escalade behind us.

A block farther on, Officer Lupe Vasquez, shorter than Nolan by about a foot, waved us into a parking lot, and I found an empty space and slotted the Volvo in. The Escalade moved past, so whoever it was wasn't here for the memorial. Or maybe he or she thought she'd have better luck finding parking somewhere else.

We greeted Lupe Vasquez before we walked back to the funeral home, and then I had to wait while Darcy greeted

Nolan again, up close and personal. While she crossed into the middle of the street, I stayed on the sidewalk and looked at the place where we were going.

At one point, the building that housed the Kovacz Funeral Home must have been a lovely old home. It was another foursquare, like the one Sheriff Satterfield and Mother lived in, in Sweetwater. This one looked like it might have been built a little earlier, as it had more Victorian touches, and was less Craftsman-like. The windows were arched at the top, even if they weren't as tall and skinny as the traditional Victorian windows.

Unfortunately, the two on the top floor looked like they were painted over, and in the same virulent mustard-olive color as the walls. I had seen that exact color come out of my daughter more than once in the two months she'd been with us. And as fond as I am of my daughter, that didn't make me appreciate the color any more.

There was a steady stream of people climbing up to the porch and going inside, though, and when we made it through the double doors ourselves, I realized that there wasn't just Katie's memorial going on, there was another visitation taking place, too. Two arrows in the foyer pointed in different directions: Graves to the right and Mason to the left.

The vast majority of people were headed right, and I felt kind of bad for Mr. or Ms. Mason, for being so thoroughly upstaged in death.

The name sounded familiar, but I couldn't place it. Maybe I had come across it in Catherine's yearbook yesterday afternoon. I'd looked at a lot of pictures and read a lot of names.

Although it isn't an uncommon name, so maybe that was all there was to it.

It wasn't any of my concern, anyway. I was here for the Katie Graves memorial, so the Mason visitation didn't matter.

We joined the throng going right, and entered what had probably been a formal parlor or maybe a dining room back when this had been a home a hundred years ago.

It was already full of people, more than an hour before the service was scheduled to start, and the buzzing of voices was like being inside a beehive. I tried to block it out as I scanned the room, but it wasn't easy.

There was no casket, not that I'd expected one. There were only bones left to begin with, and I knew they hadn't found all of Katie up there in the hills. The skull and most of the bigger bones, was how Rafe had put it. A full size casket would be ridiculous.

There was a small box sitting there, though. Pretty wood, with some metal filigree accents on the corners. They'd either fit the bones inside, or maybe cremated them. Or maybe the box was empty and Katie's remains were still at the lab. Maybe only her skull was inside. The box was about the right size for it.

The idea was a bit troubling, so I shunted it aside. "There's Mrs. Miller," I nudged Darcy, "in the navy blue dress. She was Katie's mother. The guy on the other side, with the mustache, is her husband."

Darcy glanced at me. "Not the girl's father?"

I shook my head. "They married after Katie disappeared. Not sure how much later. And I don't know what happened to Mr. Graves. I don't even know whether there ever was one. Mrs. Miller might have been a single mother. Or maybe they broke up after what happened to Katie. That kind of thing can be hard on a family."

Or so I've heard. And if the police had done their job at the time, they'd probably looked at Katie's father and his relationship with his daughter after she disappeared. They'd be fools not to, since fathers sometimes do kill their daughters.

Darcy nodded. "We should go pay our respects."

We should. I'd already done that when I met the Millers up on the Devil's Backbone a few days ago, but it would be appropriate to do it again now.

So we made our way toward the front, slowly. There were so many people packed into the room that it made moving extremely difficult. Especially since most of those people were standing in the aisles and around the perimeter of the room instead of sitting in the rows of chairs that were provided for the purpose.

We were about halfway there when I heard a familiar voice. "I'm afraid I can't comment on an ongoing investigation."

My head came up, like a pointer scenting game, and I scanned the crowd.

Yes, there she was, just a few feet ahead of me and to the right, speaking to a woman in her early sixties: a short, plump, older version of my sister Catherine, with dark curls shot through with gray.

I reached out and grabbed Darcy by the arm, and elbowed a couple of people out of my way to get there. "Morning, Detec… um… Chief Grimaldi. Have you been promoted to the crime beat, Aunt Regina?"

"Goodness me, no," my father's sister said with a shudder. "Just curious, you know."

I nodded. I was curious by nature, too, and would probably have cornered Grimaldi myself, to ask for news. And Aunt Regina had the additional incentive of being the society columnist for our local paper, the *Sweetwater Reporter*.

"Hello, Savannah." She leaned in.

I folded her in a hug, and then indicated Darcy, who was hovering a foot away. "Here's Darcy."

Aunt Regina embraced her, too. "Hello, dear."

"Um…" Darcy said, looking stiff and uncomfortable. "Hello."

"I'm your aunt, too, you know," Aunt Regina told her, but

she didn't press the point, just turned back to me and Grimaldi. "I didn't think I'd see the two of you here."

"Rafe's working the case," I said. "The sheriff asked Grimaldi if he could borrow him, and she said yes."

Aunt Regina nodded approvingly. "Is he here?" She looked around.

Grimaldi shook her head. "I'm the official representative for law enforcement today. Collier's up on the Devil's Backbone with a dog and a handler, and Sheriff Satterfield has other things to do. Meanwhile, I've got an open homicide case in this room, and another on the other side of the foyer."

That's right. That's where I'd heard the Mason name recently. It was earlier this week when Grimaldi told me she'd assigned Detective Jarvis to the Scott Mason case as a consolation prize for missing out on the Katie Graves investigation.

"How's that going?" I asked.

Grimaldi shrugged. "It's still just a suspicious-looking suicide. That might be all it'll ever be."

Maybe. But if it kept Paul Jarvis happy and out of Rafe's hair until the Katie Graves investigation was over, that was all that mattered.

"I was planning to stick my head in there at some point," Aunt Regina said. "I went to school with Scott. Haven't had anything to do with him in the time since, but I'm here. I might as well go pay my respects."

"I'll go with you if you want," I said. I had no connection whatsoever to Scott Mason, but I'd already spoken to Katie's mother and stepfather the other day, and besides, one funeral is better than two.

"In a little bit, dear," Aunt Regina said and patted my hand. "Where's that beautiful baby of yours?"

I explained that I'd left Carrie with Catherine. "I can't really expect her to behave herself somewhere like this, and I'd hate to have her start screaming in the middle of the eulogy."

"That wouldn't be good," Aunt Regina agreed, and glanced over her shoulder. "I should make my way to the front and give my respects to Katie's parents."

"Take Darcy with you," I told her. "I already spoke to them a couple of days ago." And it would give me a chance to have a word with Grimaldi.

Aunt Regina nodded, and twitched her arm through Darcy's. "Come along, dear."

She tugged Darcy behind her toward the front of the room, and left us standing there.

Fourteen

I watched for a second, to make sure Darcy didn't look too terribly uncomfortable—while she was getting more used to being related to the rest of us, she hadn't spent a whole lot of time with Aunt Regina and Uncle Sid so far.

When I'd reassured myself that she didn't need rescuing, I turned back to Grimaldi, who was watching me with a resigned sort of expression on her face. "What are you doing here?"

"I'm curious," I said. "It's my husband's case. And my sister knew Katie."

"So why isn't your sister here?"

Good question. But— "She's babysitting my daughter," I said, since, if Grimaldi hadn't been told that Catherine was a suspect yet, I didn't want to be the one to tell her. "She doesn't like funerals as much as I do, I guess."

"Uh-huh." She sounded like she didn't believe me. After a glance around, she added, "Let's go out in the hallway. Too many people here."

The people were the reason I was here, but I didn't bother saying so. She might have something to tell me, or something to ask me, something she wanted privacy for, and I wasn't going to quibble one way or the other. So I just followed in her wake toward the back of the room and through one of the double doors out into the foyer. Grimaldi moved several yards from the open door before she gave a little shake, sort of the same way Pearl does when the air outside is cold or it's raining. I deduced the detective—chief—was happy to be out of the crush of bodies.

Not that we were alone in the foyer. There were several other groups or pairings of people standing about, who must have had the same idea we'd had. But at least we weren't in the middle of a crowd so tightly packed that we were actually physically touching other people.

I gave her a bright, inquisitive sort of look.

She gave me a jaundiced one.

I made a wild guess. "Someone told you."

"That your sister broke into Darrell Skinner's trailer and walked away with his collection of girls' underwear? Yes. Someone did."

"Rafe?" I said.

She shook her head.

"The sheriff?" Because he probably knew by now.

"No," Grimaldi said.

"Catherine? Jonathan?"

"Your brother."

My eyes widened. "You're talking to Dix?"

"Of course," Grimaldi said.

She must be less upset about the Charlotte situation than I was, then. Not that I'd given Charlotte a single thought in the past twenty-four hours.

"What did he say?"

"That your sister couldn't possibly have killed anyone, and it was crazy to try to go after her for it."

She said it in the tone of voice of someone quoting.

"I agree with him," I said.

"Of course you do. As it happens, it's a waste of time to tell me what you think. Either of you. I'm not in charge of the investigation."

"It's a joint investigation," I pointed out. "Between the

sheriff's office and the Columbia PD. Rafe's the main investigator, and he works for you."

"If you want to be technical about it," Grimaldi answered, "he works for the TBI. Which takes the jurisdiction out of both of our hands."

I guess it did, although I hadn't thought about that. "It isn't a TBI investigation, though. Is it?"

"Not officially," Grimaldi said. "But your husband is a TBI agent, and the sheriff did call him in to assist. And there's a connection to the Skinner case. Your husband worked that, too. For the TBI."

He had. So maybe it was a TBI case. Technically.

"Whatever," I said. "Catherine's home with the kids. Including mine. Enjoying the fact that Rafe's up in the hills with a dog and won't be arresting her today."

Grimaldi nodded.

"Hopefully he'll find some kind of evidence that the Skinners kept the body somewhere for fifteen years before they removed what was left of it and dumped it in the woods, and then he won't be arresting her at all."

"Before or after they were killed?" Grimaldi asked, and then held up a hand. "Don't answer that."

I rolled my eyes. "Before, obviously. They couldn't do it after. And you don't have to tell me that it makes no sense. I know that. But it doesn't make any sense that Catherine would have kept it for fifteen years, either. She was living at home when Katie disappeared. One of us would have noticed if she'd brought home a body."

Grimaldi didn't respond to that, and I went on. "And besides, if she'd dumped the bones in the woods after the Skinners died, to pin Katie's death on them, wouldn't she have grabbed that box of underwear at the same time? Rather than waiting until now? And for that matter, if she did it because she was angry with Darrell and wanted to implicate him in Katie's murder, why wait until he was dead? If she had Katie's body, why not dump it on his doorstep back then? When he was alive to go to prison for it?"

I had to stop to draw breath, and noticed that a couple of people were looking at me sideways. Before I could tell Grimaldi that this probably wasn't the time and place to talk about it, the detective—chief—had taken me by the arm and was pulling me away, toward the quieter area around the Mason memorial. "Let's get out of the way a little bit."

I nodded. Good idea.

The Mason room was much calmer than the one where the Graves memorial took place. Another parlor, a bit smaller, and there were only a handful of people inside, sitting quietly and talking. Unlike Katie, Mr. Mason had a casket, with a blanket of white lilies draped across. Next door, pictures of Katie were scrolling slowly on a big screen, while here, a couple of photographs in frames showed the deceased at various times of his life: a young boy on a bike, a young man holding up a fish, a middle-aged man with his arm around a teenage boy.

That teenage boy, now a few years older than me, made his way across the floor to us. Grimaldi muttered something, and then pasted a pleasant smile on her face. "Mr. Mason."

"Chief Grimaldi." He nodded politely, although he might have looked worried for a second. "Something going on?"

Grimaldi shook her head. "Just paying my respects, Mr. Mason. Detective Jarvis is still working on your father's case."

Mr. Mason looked relieved. "Any news?"

"None I'm at liberty to share," Grimaldi said, glancing around the room.

Mr. Mason started to look worried again.

This is where that Southern Belle upbringing kicks in. I didn't know Mr. Mason, but he looked uncomfortable, and I've been trained to make uncomfortable people feel more at ease. It's part of my job description as a Southern female. So I smiled brightly and stuck my hand out. "Mr. Mason. I'm Savannah Martin."

He took my hand, of course. You can't do otherwise. Or you can, but it would be rude, and I'm sure he didn't want to be rude. "Scotty."

His palm was a little moist—nerves, maybe—and I stuck mine in my coat pocket when he let go, so I could surreptitiously wipe it dry. "I'm sorry for your loss."

"It wasn't unexpected," he told me, "but it's still hard."

I nodded sympathetically. "Of course it is. I lost my father a few years ago myself. It's never easy to lose a parent."

Beside me, Grimaldi looked inscrutable. She'd lost her mother at fourteen, to violence, and had probably had a harder time of it than either Scotty or me. We were adults, with—I assumed—lives of our own. She'd been a child.

"At least it's the natural order of things," Scotty said. He glanced at the door, and the foyer beyond, before he returned his attention to me. "Harder for parents to bury their children."

No doubt. Not at all the natural order of thing, for a parent to have to bury their child. And worse yet, with the circumstances of Katie's death. "Did you know Katie?" I asked.

Scotty looked like he might be in his early thirties, and he was obviously local, so it seemed logical to assume that he might have attended Columbia High around the same time as Katie.

He nodded. "She lived around the corner from me. We took the bus together."

"I was younger," I said. "But my sister knew her, and my brother and my husband were both at Columbia High at that time, too."

Another tactic that's been ingrained in my Southern Belle self. Find common ground with people. Establish connections.

He contemplated me in silence for a second. "Martin?" he said eventually. "From Sweetwater?"

I nodded. "My sister Catherine was in Katie's class. My brother Dix is two years younger. And my husband's in-between."

He looked blank, so maybe he didn't keep up with the *Sweetwater Reporter*'s society page. Aunt Regina had done a big spread on my wedding to Rafe last June, with pictures and everything. It was easily the story of the season.

I waited politely for it to click, and when it didn't, I said, "I married Rafe Collier last year."

His mouth opened. And shut again without anything coming out. Then he opened it again, and managed a sort of strangled, "Congratulations."

"Thank you." I smiled sweetly.

There was a long silence, aside from the buzzing of voices from the foyer, punctuated by Scotty Mason clearing his throat. "He's... um... the guy who went to prison after high school, right?"

I nodded brightly. "Right. We're very happy together."

There was another silence, before— "We just wanted to pay our respects," Grimaldi said. She gave him a pleasant nod and me a more peremptory one, toward the door.

"Nice to have met you," I told Scotty. "I'm sorry about your father."

We left him standing there blinking after us.

"That was weird," I told Grimaldi when we were back outside in the foyer.

She shrugged. "Some people are uncomfortable with law enforcement, even when they don't have anything to hide."

And some people are uncomfortable with my husband, or the mention of my husband, just because.

"I don't suppose there's any connection between Scott Mason's death and Katie's?"

Grimaldi shook her head. "Why would there be?"

"It's all going on at the same time," I said. "Doesn't it make sense that two things going on at the same time might be related?"

"But they're not going on at the same time," Grimaldi answered. "Katie Graves disappeared sixteen years ago, and was probably killed pretty much immediately. Her body was found in November, and she was identified a few days ago. Scott Mason died of an overdose of prescription painkillers last week. At that point, Katie hadn't been identified yet, and no one but law enforcement knew that the bones had been found, so she wasn't the reason he did it. And if you're thinking that he dumped her in the woods in October, there's absolutely no way he'd have been able to make that trek. He'd been bedridden since last fall. The man was dying. If he hadn't killed himself, he'd be dead soon, anyway."

"So why are you having Jarvis investigate his death? It sounds like he had every reason to do away with himself."

Grimaldi didn't answer that, and I added, "It sounded like Scotty knew Katie, anyway."

"Look around," Grimaldi said, indicating the foyer and, beyond, the visitation room. "Everyone here knew Katie."

I guess that was true. She and I hadn't, but most people probably wouldn't go to a memorial service for a person they didn't know.

So having known Katie wasn't proof of anything, not in this crowd. Guess I'd have to look beyond Scotty Mason and his father to clear my sister of suspicion.

"Are you staying for the service?" I asked.

Grimaldi shook her head. "I've shown up and done my duty to both families. I'm going to head out."

I glanced around at the foyer, keeping an eye out for Lynn Jeffries, the blonde from the photographs. "I want to talk to some more people, so we'll stick around. I'll let you know if anything exciting happens."

"I won't hold my breath," Grimaldi said.

"You'd be surprised at what can happen at funerals."

She shook her head. "Bet I wouldn't."

Perhaps not. "How about lunch one day next week? You get to take a lunch break, right?"

"I usually just grab something at my desk."

"Well, if you want to get out of the police station one day, let me know. I'd be happy to drive up and meet you."

We arranged that she'd call me and we'd make plans, and then she headed for the door to the outside, and I headed for the door to the Graves memorial.

By now, Aunt Regina and Darcy had made it all the way up to the front, and were talking to Mrs. Miller. I squeezed past the throngs and made it to Darcy's side before the conversation was over. "...still there," Mrs. Miller was saying. "Doug moved in after we got married—"

She stopped talking to peer at me.

I smiled politely. "Hi, Mrs. Miller."

She didn't smile back, just stared at me, fixedly. "You look familiar."

"We met a couple of days ago, outside Robbie Skinner's trailer. I'd just brought my husband lunch, and you..."

She nodded. "We came to see where Katie'd been found. Sorry."

"No problem," I told her. It isn't every day a mother has to trek through the woods to see the spot where her dead daughter's bones had lain. "You had a lot on your mind."

"Is your husband here?" She looked around.

I shook my head, and felt kind of bad that I had to. She was probably hoping that he'd discovered something. "He's up there on the Devil's Backbone with a K9 handler and a dog."

There was a sound on the other side of me, and when I turned that way, I saw Scotty Mason. He must have departed his own event across the foyer to pay his regards to the Millers. "Oh. It's you again. Mrs. Miller, do you know Scotty Mason?"

"Of course." She took the hand he extended. "I was so sorry to hear about your father, Scotty."

"It wasn't unexpected," Scotty said, and bowed his head almost as if he were thinking of kissing her hand. If he was, he stopped well short. "And he's out of pain now."

"True." Mrs. Miller's eyes filled with tears, and she patted the hand that lay on top of hers. "And so is Katie."

A slightly awkward silence ensued. I glanced at Aunt Regina, who gave me a slight grimace, with the corners of her mouth turned down like a sad clown.

We couldn't really walk away without a word, though, so we stayed where we were, and waited. Eventually, Mrs. Miller sniffed and let go of Scotty's hand to pat her eyes with a lace-trimmed handkerchief. "Thank you for stopping in."

"I'm just sorry I can't stay," Scotty said. "If I had known about this, I would have scheduled my father's service for another time."

She patted him again. "You couldn't have known, dear. When your father passed, we had no idea that Katie had been found. It's my fault. I should have waited a week. But we were just so overwhelmed…"

Her eyes filled again.

"Come along, Laura," Aunt Regina said briskly and put her arm around Mrs. Miller's shoulders. "Come and sit down a little before the service starts."

She nudged Mrs. Miller into motion, away from us and toward Doug Miller. "Sorry," I told Scotty, as we stood there and looked after them.

He shook his head, his eyes on the scrolling pictures of Katie, going by. "It's devastating. They kept hoping, all these years…"

Darcy nodded. "That's what she was telling us when you showed up. How she's still living in the house where Katie grew up. How she couldn't leave, just in case Katie came back.

Her husband couldn't handle the pressure after Katie disappeared, so he left—"

"I wondered about that," I cut in. "Whether the police had looked at him for Katie's disappearance back then."

It was Scotty who nodded, not Darcy. "Oh, yes. They were whispering about how maybe he'd hurt her. Katie's mother had already gone to work, and the police thought that maybe Katie's father had done something to her, while it was just the two of them in the house."

"Nobody saw her after she left? On her way to the bus stop?"

Scotty shook his head.

"She wasn't at the bus stop when you got there that morning?" He'd said they took the bus together, right?

"No," Scotty said.

"Did they ever prove that her father didn't have anything to do with it?"

Scotty shrugged. "They never charged him with anything, so at least they couldn't prove that he did do anything."

I looked around the room. "Is he still around?"

"He's dead," Darcy said. "He and Katie's mother broke up a couple of years after Katie disappeared. She said they just couldn't be together anymore. That the only thing they had in common was the grief over Katie, and it wasn't enough. He'd started drinking a lot. They were both depressed. And five years ago he died in a drunk driving accident."

The same kind of accident that had killed Darcy's adopted parents.

"That's sad," I said. Both about Darcy, and that Katie's father had died without knowing what happened to her.

Unless he'd been responsible for what happened to her, of course. Then he knew exactly what had happened.

Although if he'd been dead five years, it wasn't him who had put Katie's bones on the Devil's Backbone in October. So maybe he hadn't been responsible.

"I was hoping Lynn Jeffries would be here," I told Scotty. "Do you know her?"

He looked taken aback for a second before he nodded. "Sure. I know Lynn."

"Have you seen her today, by any chance?"

But he hadn't. "She might be working. It's a workday for some people."

It was. Like my husband. "Do you know where she works?"

"The Wayside Inn," Scotty said. And added, "If you'll excuse me, I should go back to my dad. Nice to meet you both."

He walked away without waiting for an answer, and with a last look at Katie, young and pretty and alive, scrolling by on the big screen.

"His father is laid out in the room across the hall," I explained to Darcy. "Scott Mason. Died of what was probably an accidental or self-inflicted overdose of pain meds a week or two ago. Cancer patient."

"That's sad."

"It's all sad." Both funerals, what happened to Katie, what happened to Katie's father and to Scott Mason. What had happened to Darcy's parents. The fact that my dad—her dad—had died before she even knew he existed. It was all sad, and it all combined to me saying, "Let's get out of here."

"We just got here," Darcy said.

"I know, but we gave our respects to Katie's mother. Katie's dad is gone, so we can't talk to him. I don't see Lynn Jeffries." But I knew where she worked, so I could find her. "And I don't feel like sitting through the service. I didn't know Katie. And I want to go home and hold my daughter."

Darcy looked surprised, but game. "OK. If that's what you want. I don't know anyone here, either."

Except for Aunt Regina, and she was coming toward us,

after having deposited Laura Miller with Doug, who had put her on a chair and was sitting next to her, holding her hand.

"We're leaving," I told Aunt Regina.

She nodded. "I'll come with you. I don't think I can stand much more of this."

Me, either. "Maybe we can go get some early lunch or something." What I really wanted was a stiff drink, but since I was nursing Carrie, that option was off the table. And so was lunch, once I took a look at my watch. It wasn't even ten-thirty yet. "Or brunch."

"The Café on the Square does a nice bellini," Aunt Regina said brightly as we hit the foyer.

The Café on the Square was in Sweetwater, but I guess I'd be willing to drive back there for brunch. I was going to Sweetwater eventually anyway, so why not?

"What about the Wayside Inn?" It would give me a chance to see if Lynn Jeffries was there.

"No bellinis at the Wayside Inn," Aunt Regina said, and I guess that settled it. At least for now.

"You can drop me off on the way," Darcy told me.

"You're not coming?"

She hesitated, but when Aunt Regina and I pinned her with identical stares, she gave in gracefully. "I was thinking you might want me to pick up my own car, so you don't have to drive me back."

Oh. Yes, that made sense. "Sure," I said.

Aunt Regina nodded. "I'll see you girls there."

She must have gotten here early enough to find a parking space in the funeral home lot, because she trotted across the blacktop while Darcy and I skirted the corner and headed back down the street. A few minutes later, we were back in the Volvo, and a few minutes after that, back at Darcy's little ranch house. "I'll see you in fifteen minutes," I told her, just in case she was thinking of going inside instead of following me to

Sweetwater.

She rolled her eyes. "Yeah, yeah."

"She's your aunt too, you know."

"I have no problem with your Aunt Regina," Darcy said.

"*Your* Aunt Regina." I took my foot off the brake and rolled off down the driveway before she could respond.

But she did follow me to Sweetwater, and when I'd parked on the square and made my way toward the door to the café, she was right there, coming toward me from the other direction.

"I guess I'm having a hard time getting used to some things still," she told me by way of greeting, as if we were just picking up where we'd left off fifteen minutes earlier. "I've never spent much time with your aunt."

"Our aunt."

"And I always got the impression she didn't like me."

"I'm sure that's wrong," I said, as I reached for the door to the café. "Aunt Regina likes everybody. She always liked Rafe. She likes Audrey. There's no reason why she wouldn't like you."

"My mother slept with her brother."

"None of which was your fault." I shook my head as I waved her past me into the café. "If anything, she's probably upset that she missed the big denouement in the office this fall. Aunt Regina likes to be in the middle of things. That's why she writes the gossip column for the paper."

"Society column, dear," Aunt Regina's voice said from behind us.

"Right." I rolled my eyes. "Society column."

Fifteen

The Café on the Square does a brisk business on Saturday and Sunday mornings, when the ladies who lunch—and we do have some of those in town—come out for brunch with bellinis. Aunt Regina must have called ahead, because we only had to wait a couple of minutes for a table.

As the hostess led us toward it, I looked around.

The Café is quite a pleasant place. Very feminine, with spindly chairs and tables, elegant ivy wallpaper, and lots of green plants against exposed brick walls. It isn't somewhere I'd ever take Rafe, although on the occasions when he's been here, he's handled himself just fine. He just doesn't enjoy it much.

The place can seat maybe thirty or forty people. All the tables are square with white tablecloths: either small two-tops, or larger four-tops. If you have a bigger party than that, they'll shove two tables together for you.

Nothing like that was going on now. Everything was elegant and subdued, with soft music piping from overhead, soft conversation, and the muted clinking of silverware against china. We were almost to our table when I stopped in my tracks. "Charlotte!"

My one-time best friend looked up with a surprised expression that quickly turned guilty when she recognized me. She swallowed visibly. "Savannah."

"You have some 'splaining to do," I told her, and nodded

politely at Charlotte's mother, on the other side of the table. "Mrs. Albertson."

She nodded back, with a grimace that was a lot more like a… well, grimace, than a smile. "Good to see you."

The statement was so patently false that I was tempted to call her on it. I might have refrained anyway, given where we were, but I had bigger fish to fry. "What the hell do you mean," I asked Charlotte, "by going on a date with my brother without telling me about it?"

"It wasn't a date," Charlotte said.

I fisted my hands on my hips. "What exactly would you call it? You went to dinner with him. At a restaurant. Just the two of you."

Charlotte glanced around. We had attracted some attention. People were watching, although they were doing it pretending they weren't doing it. I could practically see ears twitching as their owners strained to hear. "I don't want to talk about this now."

"Then maybe you should try to answer my calls and texts," I told her.

On the other side of the restaurant—which isn't a big space, but far enough away that they couldn't hear what was going on—Aunt Regina and Darcy were getting comfortable at our assigned table. The hostess was fluttering nervously as she waited for me.

"I'll stop by your house this afternoon," I said. And I included Mrs. Albertson in the statement, since the house was hers, but then I focused my attention back on Charlotte. "And you'd better be there and be willing to talk to me, because I'm not happy."

Charlotte pressed her lips together, but she didn't tell me not to come. Instead she nodded once, her cheeks flushed. I gave her one last scowl before I stalked across the floor toward Aunt Regina and Darcy. The space was small and the tables close together, so the stalking was inhibited by my having to twist and turn so I wouldn't accidentally whack anyone in the head with my purse, but I made a passable impression. And got rid of some frustration at the same time.

"Dear me," Aunt Regina said when I reached the table and flounced down on my chair. "That looked uncomfortable."

Her lips twitched, and her eyes were bright and inquisitive. Perhaps she was scenting a story.

"She went on a date with Dix a few days ago." I twisted out of my coat and left it draped over the back of the chair, since I was sitting on part of it. Mother would have made me hang it up properly, but she wasn't here, so I rebelled in my small way. "Dix won't talk to me about it, and Charlotte's been ducking my phone calls ever since."

"That's between them, surely," Aunt Regina said piously. Which was pretty rich, considering the source.

I gave her a scowl. "Not when one of them is my brother and the other my best friend."

"I thought Detective Grimaldi was your best friend," Darcy said. "She was the maid of honor at your wedding."

"Charlotte lives too far away. And I wasn't sure she'd come." I don't think she's quite reconciled to my marrying Rafe yet. Or at least I didn't think she was reconciled to it eight months ago.

"If you'd made her your maid on honor she would have come," Darcy pointed out.

That was true. Or she would have told me no. Maybe I'd just been trying to avoid that. I could deal with Charlotte not being reconciled to my marriage if we didn't talk about it. If she refused to be maid of honor at my wedding, there'd be no coming back from that.

Although there was also the fact that I'd spent a lot of time with Grimaldi over the past year. And that when it came to my marrying Rafe, she was a much better fit as a maid of honor.

"You think she felt slighted? Charlotte?"

Darcy gave a shrug. Under the coat, she was wearing a pale gray sweater dress that set off her figure and coloring in a very nice way, and under other circumstances I would have told her so.

"She might have," Aunt Regina said. "Wouldn't you?"

Charlotte hadn't asked me to be maid of honor—or matron of honor, since I was married to Bradley at that time—at her wedding. And yes, it had smarted a little. Not a lot, since I'd had other things on my mind—including my not so successful marriage—but a little.

I glanced across the room, to where Charlotte and her mother had their heads together across the table. "Now I feel kind of guilty."

"You didn't do anything wrong," Aunt Regina said. "You're allowed to have anyone you want stand up for you at your wedding. But you might want to consider Charlotte's feelings, and that maybe you aren't the first person she'd confide in right now. Especially since Dix is your brother."

Right. "I told her I'd stop by later."

"Then we'd better get busy ordering," Aunt Regina said, lifting the menu, "so we can get out of here and you can pick up your baby."

Charlotte and her mother left before our food arrived. They didn't speak to us, but Charlotte did glance at me across the room. Since I figured I'd already put the fear of God in her— about me coming over later—I didn't acknowledge it, just pretended I hadn't noticed.

So we had brunch, and Aunt Regina and Darcy had bellinis, and then we parted ways on the square. Aunt Regina was going home to Uncle Sid, who was probably getting done with this morning's round of golf, and Darcy was going back to Columbia, where Patrick Nolan was going to meet her after he finished his traffic duty at the funeral home. Darcy and I waved politely as Aunt Regina rolled off, and then she went in one direction while I went in the other, and got into the Volvo and drove to pick up Carrie from Catherine's house.

The baby turned out to be ready for food when I got there, so I ended up in the family room while Catherine fed the kids in the kitchen.

"How did the funeral go?" she wanted to know after the kids were fed and she could join me.

"We ended up leaving early," I explained, as she sat down across from me, "and going to the Café on the Square with Aunt Regina instead."

Catherine arched her brows, and I added, "Being there was a little weird. And sad. There were pictures of Katie floating across this big screen in the front of the room. Katie at sixteen, you know. Never getting older. Mrs. Miller was crying through the whole thing. And across the foyer there was a memorial for a guy named Scott Mason, who took an overdose of pain killers last week instead of waiting until he died of cancer. And then it turned out that his son, also named Scott, grew up around the corner from Katie. It was all very sad."

"So you went to the Café on the Square and had bellinis instead."

"Not me." I nodded down at the baby. "I enjoyed the crepes, though. And it was a chance for Darcy and Aunt Regina to spend some time together. Darcy is worried that Aunt Regina doesn't like her."

"Aunt Regina likes everybody," Catherine said. "And she loved Dad. How could she not love Dad's daughter?"

Exactly. "Speaking of fathers and daughters… I heard that Katie's dad killed himself a few years ago. Or maybe it was an accident. Do you know anything about that?"

"No more than you do," Catherine said. "He and Katie's mother broke up a few years after Katie disappeared. I imagine something like what happened probably puts a strain on a marriage."

No doubt. Especially if one of the parties was a suspect. "Scotty Mason said Katie's dad was a suspect. Any idea whether he could have done something to her?"

"I never met him," Catherine said. "I keep telling you, Katie and I weren't close. Although I didn't get the impression that she was abused in any way. Physically or sexually."

"I'm sure the police looked into it at the time."

"I'm sure they did," Catherine said, "but your friend Chief Grimaldi would probably be able to tell you that."

Probably. Or Rafe, if he had the file.

We sat in silence for a moment. At the kitchen island, the kids were laughing and playing over cheese sandwiches. I moved Carrie from one side to the other and got her going again.

"What do you think happened to Katie?" I asked my sister.

She looked at me for a second. "Don't know."

"You knew her. At least a little. She left home in the morning. Where did she live?"

Catherine shrugged. "Somewhere in Columbia."

"You've never been there?"

"I don't know how to make it any plainer," Catherine said. "We weren't friends. We weren't close. I had some classes with her, but we didn't talk to each other outside that. I had my friends from Sweetwater. She had hers from Columbia. I have no idea where she lived, other than that it was somewhere in town."

"Fine," I said. If she was telling the truth, it meant she couldn't have gone to where Katie lived to pick her up the morning she disappeared. But I had a feeling Rafe would tell me that this wasn't evidence, and of course he was right. Catherine could be lying. "Katie's mother still lives there, so I'm sure it's in the phonebook. Or I can find it through the county tax records."

"Fine," Catherine answered, her voice clipped.

"Did you know her well enough to know whether she was the type of girl who would have gotten into a car with a stranger?"

"No," Catherine said.

"No, you didn't know her well enough, or no, she wouldn't have?"

She rolled her eyes. "I didn't know her well enough. But I wouldn't have thought so. I mean, we were all brought up not to be stupid, weren't we?"

We had been. And while some parents might not have warned their daughters about stranger dangers, Mrs. Miller had struck me as a decent enough human being. She hadn't seemed like the type to have been too busy with other things to make sure her daughter was as safe as possible.

"So wherever she went after she left her house that morning, she probably went with someone she trusted. Or at least someone she knew."

"I'd think so," Catherine nodded.

That didn't get Catherine off the hook, of course. Katie would have known her, and probably trusted her. Same with Darrell. Same with most of the people she went to school with, I assumed. Maybe some of the neighbors. Presumably her teachers. It was a long list. And I had to assume—and would double check with Rafe when he came home—that they'd mostly been considered and eliminated fifteen years ago.

Catherine hadn't been, though. Darrell might not have been, either, if her parents hadn't known she was involved with him.

"Hopefully Rafe will find some evidence today, that Katie's body was kept on Skinner land all these years," I said, "and that for some reason they moved her into the woods sometime this fall."

"That would be nice," Catherine agreed, "but I'm not holding my breath."

I wasn't, either. "It doesn't make much sense, does it? If they had her hidden where nobody could find her, why not just keep her there?"

"Maybe whoever moved her, did it because she wasn't safe where he or she had kept her."

"Maybe."

I thought it over while Carrie snuffled greedily and while the kids in the kitchen finished up their lunch and ran back upstairs to the media room. "What would that entail, do you think? What kinds of reasons would someone have for needing to move the body after all these years? If it had been safe there all this time, what changed?"

"Someone who was forced to move?" Catherine suggested. "A divorce, maybe? Or someone whose house went to foreclosure? Something they didn't have any control over, you know? They had to get the body out before it was discovered, and the Skinner murders made the Devil's Backbone a good place to dump the bones?"

I nodded. That made a certain amount of sense. "Maybe I should go visit a local real estate brokerage. Or maybe I should just set up some appointments to see some empty houses in town, just in case we get lucky." Here was a benefit of having a real estate license, finally.

"Unless you're Rafe's cadaver-sniffing dog," Catherine said, "I don't see how you'll know that Katie was ever there. If she had been, whoever removed her would have made sure to remove any sign of her."

True. "Maybe I'll just give it some more thought."

"Go ahead and do that," Catherine said, and pushed up off the couch. "I have to go clean up the kitchen."

"And I need to go talk to Charlotte." I put Carrie against my shoulder and patted her back. "If I come up with anything we can do, do you want to know about it?"

"Sure," Catherine said, wiping down the kitchen island. "Anything that'll keep me out of prison."

"I'll see you later," I said, wandering down the hallway with the baby.

"Have a good time," floated down the hallway after me.

I must admit to having some trepidation as I opened the gate and carried the baby seat up the stairs to the big, white Victorian where the Albertsons live. What if Charlotte wasn't here? What if she'd decided she didn't want to talk to me enough that she'd ducked out instead of facing me? After twenty-plus years of friendship, I wasn't sure we would be able to survive that.

And on the flipside, what if she was here and willing to talk, and she told me something I didn't want to hear? What if she told me she was in love with my brother? She must have been, back in high school. They'd dated. For all I knew, they'd slept together, although I'd been careful not to broach that subject. I hadn't been sleeping with Todd, and I'd been happy to believe that Charlotte wasn't sleeping with Dix, either. He was my brother, so it wasn't anything I wanted to discuss.

But what if I had to discuss it now? What if she thought she was still in love with him? What if I had to choose between rooting for my old best friend or my new best friend when it came to who I wanted to marry my brother?

I suppose I could take a step back and not root for either, since it wasn't really my business either way. That was between them—each of them—and Dix. But I wasn't sure I had it in me to be impartial in that way, so I just had to hope that that wasn't what Charlotte was going to tell me. Even if I was horribly afraid it was.

Maybe it would be better if she wasn't at home after all. At least that way I could keep my fingers crossed for Grimaldi and

Dix with no guilty feelings about anyone else.

I pushed the doorbell and waited. After a few seconds I heard footsteps inside, and then the door opened. "Hello, Savannah," Mrs. Albertson said.

"Let me guess," I answered. "She isn't here."

Mrs. Albertson looked surprised. "Of course she's here. You told her you were coming."

I'd told Charlotte I wanted to talk to her before, and it hadn't made a difference, but it would probably be better not to mention that. So when she invited me in, I just stepped across the threshold and smiled graciously.

"You can make yourself comfortable in there," Mrs. Albertson said, waving me into the priest's parlor on the left side of the foyer, "and I'll get Charlotte."

"Thank you." I wandered in, put the baby carrier down on the floor next to one of the chairs, and took the blanket off Carrie. I was in the process of shrugging out of my coat when Charlotte came down the stairs.

She'd changed out of the dress she'd worn at the Café on the Square, and into a pair of leggings and a velvety tunic. I, meanwhile, was still in funeral attire: black wrap dress, black stockings, black boots. Charlotte looked me over. "Who died?"

"Katie Graves," I said. "Sixteen years ago. The memorial was this morning."

Charlotte winced. "Sorry."

"No problem. I didn't know her."

"Why did you go to the memorial?"

She waved me to a seat in the chair I'd already chosen, and curled up on the sofa opposite.

"Rafe's working the case," I said, sitting down. "And I met Katie's parents," or Katie's mother and her husband, "the other day. I guess I was curious."

Charlotte nodded. "Can I hold the baby?"

"Sure." I unbuckled Carrie from the seat and handed her

over. Charlotte cradled her in one elbow and looked down at her.

"She has your eyes."

And otherwise she was the image of her father. "Not much doubt about her parentage."

Charlotte glanced at me. "Rafe has a son from a previous relationship, doesn't he?"

"I'm not sure I'd call it a relationship," I said, as I made myself comfortable in the chair again. "Elspeth talked him into bed once when he was seventeen and drunk and didn't know better. But yes, he has a son. David's fourteen."

"But he doesn't live with you."

I shook my head. "He already has parents. He's been theirs since the day he was born. Rafe didn't find out about him until a year ago. And while he might get a judge to give him custody—maybe—if he tried, it wouldn't be in David's best interest to do that." Or Ginny and Sam Flannery's best interest, either. They loved their son, and had always thought of him as theirs. Just as David thought of himself as theirs. To do anything to change that would be cruel.

"Does she look like him?"

She glanced down at Carrie again. Carrie cooed. Charlotte smiled.

"I imagine she will when she gets a bit bigger." David looked a lot like Rafe had at that age. Or at least a lot like he had a few years later, which was when I first laid eyes on him. Minus the obvious signs of neglect, and the hard edge. David had always been loved and protected. Rafe had had a much harder upbringing, and it had been visible. But apart from that, David looked a lot like his father.

"What's it like?" Charlotte asked.

To have children? "You have a couple of kids of your own. Don't you know?"

She wasn't looking at me, but was focused on tickling

Carrie's chin. "The step-parenting thing. When your husband has children with someone else."

Uh-oh.

"Listen," I said. "I don't feel great about you and Dix going out. You're still married, and he's only been a widower for a little over a year, and I like the idea of him and Grimaldi together. Not that I don't like you. We've been friends a long time, and I want you to be happy. But I'd take it as a personal favor if you'd be happy with someone other than my brother."

And his two daughters. Who—yes—could use a stepmother. But who'd be better off with someone like Grimaldi, who gave them Police Barbies for Christmas and who could teach them that they could be whatever they wanted to be in life, and didn't have to settle for wifedom and motherhood.

Not that there's anything wrong with wifedom and motherhood, if that's what they wanted to do. But they should have the knowledge that they could do something else, too, if they wanted.

"I'm not dating Dix," Charlotte said.

I opened my mouth, and closed it again. And opened it again. "You went on a date with Dix."

"We had dinner," Charlotte said.

Right. A date.

"And talked about my divorce."

Rafe and I had probably talked about my divorce on one of our dates, too.

Not that we'd gone on many. We'd spent plenty of time together, but not on what I'd call dates. But we'd talked about Bradley and myself. It's the kind of thing you cover when you're getting involved with someone new. Bradley and Shelby had probably talked about his and my divorce, too. Before it took place, even.

"I want him to represent me," Charlotte said. "I want to

work with someone I know and trust."

"You should hire Catherine instead." The words were out before I'd thought about them. And because I'd just been contemplating my divorce, I added, "She would have nailed Bradley to the wall by his ba… um… ears if I'd let her."

Charlotte titled her head to look at me. "Why didn't you?"

"Some misguided idea of playing fair," I said. "Or trying to retain my dignity." Pretending I wasn't hurt by the fact that my perfect first husband had found me wanting in the bedroom and had taken up with his paralegal instead. "Do you want to nail your husband to the wall by his ears?"

"I wouldn't mind," Charlotte said.

"Catherine can help you with that. Better than Dix can. He's a man. He has a man's perspective." And like all men, he's protective of his genitalia. He wouldn't want to nail another man to the wall by his, even metaphorically speaking. That kind of talk makes most men wince.

"I thought," Charlotte said, "since we'd been involved once…" She trailed off, and then added, "I mean, we were just kids. But I've always liked Dix. I know he liked me, too. And I thought because of that he might be willing to play hardball with Richard."

I'm not sure Dix has hardball in him. He's a well-brought-up Southern gentleman. Catherine, on the other hand…

"What did Doctor Dick do?"

Charlotte swallowed what was probably a snort of laughter, but might have been a sob instead. "Slept with one of his clients and knocked her up."

Hence Charlotte's question about stepchildren. She hadn't been wondering about Abigail and Hannah at all.

"Bastard," I said.

Charlotte nodded.

"Bradley did that, you know? It wasn't a client," although he'd done that later, but to Shelby and not me. "It was his paralegal, but he screwed around on me."

"I know," Charlotte said.

We sat in silence a minute.

"Why have you been avoiding me?" I wanted to know. "I've been leaving messages and texting you for the past several weeks. You've never gotten back to me."

She flushed. "I didn't want you to know what was going on."

"If you're not going after my brother, why would I care?"

That didn't sound quite right, and I added, "I mean… of course I care. I'm sorry you married a cheating jackass."

That didn't sound quite right, either. "I mean… I'm sorry he cheated. I think you're right for leaving him. But why wouldn't you want me to know? Didn't you think I'd side with you? I married my own cheating jackass. Of course I would understand."

"It wasn't supposed to happen to me," Charlotte said.

I stared at her, eyebrows raised. What the hell—heck—did that mean? Was it supposed to happen to me?

"You married Bradley, and you realized right away that you'd made a mistake."

Perhaps not right away. It had taken a year, and then I'd held on for the best part of another year because I didn't want to give up on the fantasy of my perfect husband and perfect future. It took Bradley leaving me for Shelby before I placed the blame where it belonged.

"But I've been married to Richard for six years. We had a good marriage. Until this happened. And then I realized I was wrong. Because how good could it be, if he was sleeping with his clients?"

Not very good, obviously.

"It wasn't your fault," I said. "When a man cheats, it's never his wife's fault."

Charlotte bit her lip. "I thought it was your fault. That you hadn't been what Bradley needed, and that's why he left you for someone else. And I thought if I was everything Richard needed, he wouldn't have any reason to stray."

I shook my head, even as I tried to process the idea that my best friend had thought my divorce was my fault. "It doesn't work that way."

"You were just so rebellious after the divorce," Charlotte said, sounding amazingly like my mother. "You stayed in Nashville instead of coming home, and you lived by yourself, and then you got involved with Rafe Collier..."

She said it as if I'd gotten involved with Lucifer himself. Or Jed Clampett.

"Rafe's the best thing that ever happened to me," I told her. "And I'd appreciate it if you didn't say his name in that tone. He's worth a thousand Bradleys, and probably an equal number of Doctor Dicks."

"I just meant that he isn't the type I ever thought you'd be involved with."

Me either. And I thanked God every day I'd come to my senses.

"So you didn't want to tell me what happened because you were ashamed."

"Something like that," Charlotte admitted.

"Because while it was OK for me to screw up my marriage, it wasn't OK for you? Glad we got that cleared up."

Charlotte blinked limpid, blue eyes. "It wasn't any kind of reflection on you, Savannah."

The hell—heck—it wasn't. She'd thought she was better than me, because I hadn't been able to hold my marriage together, and she could.

Until she couldn't.

But there was no point in arguing about it. I had divorced Bradley and found Rafe, and Charlotte had no one. So whether she thought I was a screw-up or not, didn't really matter.

"I'm glad you told me. Is there anything I can do to help?"

"Give me Catherine's number," Charlotte said. "Dix wasn't all that keen on helping me, anyway. If Catherine can nail Richard's... um... ears to the wall and get me some real alimony, so I can move out of my parents' house and into something of my own, I'm all for it."

I was all for it, too. I'd let Bradley off the hook too easily four years ago. (Although he was in prison now, so I had nothing to complain about. All his assets were gone, and Shelby, bless her heart, had to bring up their child like any normal person. I wouldn't really wish Bradley on my own worst enemy, but I couldn't help but feel that Shelby had gotten what was coming to her.)

I recited Catherine's phone number from memory. Charlotte wrote it down, and I put my daughter back into the car seat and said goodbye. And went back to my house. The one I didn't have to share with my parents, or my mother, but where my unsuitable husband would be home at some point this afternoon to rock my world.

Sixteen

I was at the kitchen island creaming butter and sugar for the cheesecake we were going to bring to Audrey's house, when Rafe came through the back door looking bedraggled and grumpy, like he'd had a long, not entirely satisfying day. His jeans were muddy to the knees and wet the rest of the way. His boots were probably ruined, and his leather jacket was soaked through to the shirt underneath. As he toed off the boots and peeled down the sodden jeans and stripped off the wet T-shirt that had been clinging to his upper body, he also looked good enough that I forgot all about the butter and sugar and the oven that was preheating behind me.

"Don't mind me." I was doing a little preheating of my own as I looked him up and down and up again.

He cut his eyes to me, and for a second it looked like he might be too tired and pissed off to play along. But then his eyes warmed and his lips curved, and he padded around the island and wrapped both arms around my waist and pressed his front to my back.

He was cold all the way through, cold enough that I could feel it through my clothes. Even his lips were cold when he nosed my hair aside and dropped a kiss on the back of my neck. A shiver ran down my spine, but it wasn't from the cold. His chuckle tickled the soft hairs in front of my ear. "Evening, darlin'."

"Same to you," I said breathlessly. "Is that a cucumber in your pocket, or—?"

"No pockets."

No. So he must just be happy to see me.

Something that became more obvious with every second that went by. "Just stay right there," he told me, hands on my hips, grabbing handfuls of my skirt and lifting the fabric out of his way. "I'll take care of everything."

I'm not sure I would have been able to do anything anyway. I was held in place by his body behind me and the edge of the island in front, and when he hooked his thumbs in the sides of my panties and pulled them down, there wasn't anything I could do or say about it.

Not that I wanted to say anything. Why would I? Who would object?

Although I did manage a breathless, "Here?"

"We're alone, ain't we? The dog don't mind."

She didn't seem to. She had put her head back down on the pillow, and while her eyes were still open, she clearly couldn't care less how we were disporting ourselves.

"I guess it's been a while since we had sex on the kitchen table," I said.

"Who said anything about the table?" Rafe wanted to know.

"Not me," I answered, and let nature take its course.

The cheesecake was late coming out of the oven, but I couldn't really feel too bad about it. The little interlude in the kitchen had been lovely. Rafe is something of an expert at love-making, and entirely aside from that, it was nice to be close to my husband. Nice that he wanted to be close to me. With the whole issue of Catherine and Darrell Skinner and Katie Graves's disappearance hanging over us, last night had been a little tense, and it hadn't made me happy. I don't like it when Rafe and I are on different pages about these things. Most of the time he's very good about seeing my point of view, and we've rarely, if ever, disagreed over a murder investigation. That we did now, and over someone as important as my sister, was tough.

But at the moment we were curled up together on the loveseat in the parlor waiting for the cake to finish baking so we could leave. We were both clean and dry and warm, dressed to impress Audrey and Mrs. Jenkins—or rather, dressed appropriately for a quiet dinner at home with family, since I don't think I've ever managed to actually impress Audrey's Parisian tastes. Rafe's jeans and button-down shirt weren't of a quality to impress anybody—we can't afford *haute couture*—although there was no denying that he filled both out nicely, and looked good enough to eat.

"This is nice," I said.

He made an agreeable sort of noise in his chest. I heard it against my ear.

"Earlier was nice, too."

This time the noise was amused.

"Any particular reason you came through the door wanting to ravage me?"

"Was that what I did?" He didn't wait for me to answer, just continued, "I was cold and hungry and had a bad day, and you looked warm and sweet and like you'd taste good. And you looked at me like you wanted to be ravaged."

"That's definitely going in the book," I said.

"*Bedded by the Bedouin*?" He didn't sound bothered by the idea. "There's a kitchen island in the desert?"

Well, no. There wasn't likely to be a kitchen island in the desert, now that I thought about it. "Maybe I can have him bend her over a camel, or something."

"Sure," Rafe said. "So what've you been up to today?"

Best to start with some of the more innocuous stuff, probably. Not that there was any reason why I shouldn't have gone to Katie's memorial service. But still. "I spoke to Charlotte."

There was a beat. Then— "Really?"

"She was at the Café on the Square when I got there with Darcy and Aunt Regina."

"I didn't know you were gonna have lunch with your aunt and Darcy."

"Brunch," I said. "And we didn't have plans. It was a last minute thing, when we didn't want to stay at the memorial any longer."

"Memorial?"

"Katie's. It took place this morning. Nolan and Vasquez were directing traffic, and Darcy and I went to pay our respects. Aunt Regina was already there."

He straightened up. "You went to Katie Graves's memorial?"

I did the same, and turned to face him. "Any reason I shouldn't?"

"You didn't know her."

"Nor did Darcy. Or Aunt Regina. Or for that matter Grimaldi. She was there, too. Representing the Columbia PD both for Katie and the memorial across the hall."

"Who was laid out across the hall?"

"A guy named Scott Mason," I said. "Paul Jarvis has the case."

He arched a brow at the sound of Jarvis's name. "What happened?"

"To Mason? Not a lot. He was a sixty-year-old man who was dying of cancer and who took his own life with pain killers."

"Why's Jarvis looking into it?"

"Grimaldi gave it to him because you got Katie. She said it was probably a suicide, but it couldn't hurt to look into it."

Rafe nodded, and I added, "I don't know how much of that

was just to give Jarvis something to do, so he'd stop complaining. Although she probably wouldn't waste taxpayer money on an open and shut case. There has to be something about it that's questionable."

"You always take an extra look at unattended deaths," Rafe said. "Even when the dead guy had motive and opportunity to do himself, you gotta look, just in case someone else did it for him."

"What would be the point of killing someone who was dying soon anyway?"

"Sometimes you get people trying to put other people out of their misery," Rafe said. "Mercy killings. Angels of death. Nurses and doctors, a lot of'em. And sometimes you get family members who get tired of waiting for so-and-so to kick the bucket. Whether there's money in it or not."

"That's sad."

He shrugged.

"I think you knew his son," I added. "Or at least he knew you. Or your name."

"Mason's son?"

I nodded. "Scotty. Scott Junior, I guess. We got to talking about Katie, and I told him that Catherine had been in Katie's grade in school and that my husband was a year younger. He asked who you were, and got a sort of funny look on his face when I told him your name."

"Scotty Mason." Rafe looked pensive for a second before he shook his head. "Can't say I remember him. Sorry."

"Don't worry about it." Most people had known who Rafe was in high school. He probably hadn't known all of them. And Scotty hadn't been very memorable. There was nothing I could say about him to jog Rafe's memory. Average height, average weight, medium hair, medium eyes...

"Wait a second." I got up and pulled one of Catherine's yearbooks off the shelf, where I'd stashed them yesterday.

"He's probably in here."

Rafe tilted his head. "What's that?"

"Catherine's high school yearbook." I sat down again, next to him. "I found it in the attic yesterday."

"Find anything else?" Rafe wanted to know, while I flipped pages, looking for Mason.

"What do you mean? Oh… Katie's clothes or backpack or anything like that? Of course not. You can't seriously think that my sister had anything to do with Katie's disappearance. There's nowhere around here to keep a body for sixteen years. And you can believe me, if I knew that there was a dead body on the premises, I would have told someone. It isn't the kind of thing I'd keep secret, even if it did involve my sister."

"What about the ring?" Rafe said.

I glanced at him. "Sorry?"

"You said your sister had a ring like the one we found in the woods. Did you find that?"

I hadn't, as a matter of fact. And that was kind of interesting, now that I thought about it. It would have made sense for the ring to be in the little box with the photographs and postcards and other high school mementos. It wasn't something Catherine would have kept in her regular jewelry box for a decade and a half.

To hide my reaction to the question, I put my finger on Scotty Mason's face. "Here he is."

Rafe pulled the book into his own lap and peered at it. "I dunno."

"I guess he didn't make much of an impression."

Rafe shook his head. "Have you looked through these?"

"Not for Scotty Mason," I said. "I only met him today. I did go through looking for Katie."

"And?"

"She shows up here and there. She was on the school newspaper staff and played volleyball the year before she disappeared."

Rafe nodded. He was flipping pages, and stopped on the Gs to take a look at Katie. Then he kept going toward the front. "What are you looking for?" I wanted to know.

When he stopped flipping and grinned at me, I smiled back. "Oh. Wow, you looked a lot like David. Or he looks a lot like you, I guess."

Rafe in his freshman year, at fourteen or fifteen, was all big eyes and attitude, his face softer than now, but his smirk just as annoying. He'd kept his hair in cornrows back then, something I remembered from three years later, when I'd moved from middle school up to my own freshman year of high school. There was no sign of them here, however, so they must have been a later addition. Later than this, I mean.

"You were cute," I said.

"You didn't think so back then."

As he looked at himself, the corner of his mouth curled up. "I looked like a cocky little shit. If I came across myself now, I'd haul myself in for questioning about anything that went wrong, too."

"Well, the sheriff did that for you back then. And with cause some of the time."

I took the yearbook away from him, and flipped to the back, where the various clubs and activities were. "Here's Katie and the rest of the newspaper staff. This girl—the blonde with the teeth, Lynn—played volleyball with Katie, too. I figure they probably knew each other well."

And I could say that even without mentioning the pictures from the outing in the woods, that put Catherine and Katie together.

"I looked for her at the memorial today," I added, "but I didn't see her. Did the police talk to Lynn or Scotty back when Katie disappeared?"

"They talked to a lot of people," Rafe said. "I don't

remember all of'em, but I can check."

"While you're at it, there was talk about Katie's father being a suspect at the time."

"That's natural," Rafe said.

"Mrs. Miller and her husband split up after Katie disappeared. He started drinking, and then he killed himself—accidentally or on purpose—in a car accident a few years ago."

Rafe nodded. "I remember that."

I must have looked surprised—five years ago, he'd been deep undercover in Memphis or somewhere like that; why would he have kept up with a long-ago disappearance down here?—and he added, "From the file. There was never any evidence against him, but he was home alone with Katie. Katie's mama had already gone to work, so there was only his word for it that she ever made it outta the house at all."

"I imagine the police searched the house?"

"They looked around. There was no sign of foul play. No blood, nothing to indicate she didn't just leave for school the way he said she did. And his day was normal. He came in to work when he was supposed to. He acted just like every other day. So while there was some suspicion, there was nothing to back it up."

"And since Katie's mother is still in the same house," I said, "the body couldn't have been hidden there." Not unless Laura had been a party to what happened to Katie, and that I refused to believe. "I don't suppose Doug Miller…?"

"They met in a grief support group in Nashville," Rafe said. "He moved down here when he married Katie's mother. She didn't want to leave her house just in case Katie came back."

"So the family's off the hook."

Rafe nodded.

"And it wasn't random. Or if it was random, if someone just snatched her because she was available on the street that morning, it was someone in the area, since her bones showed up in the same area sixteen years later. The killer was someone local. And someone who's still around."

"Or was around till a couple months ago."

Like Darrell or one of the other Skinners. Or maybe… "Are you thinking about Scott Senior?" Because Grimaldi had told me that he wouldn't have been able to move Katie's remains onto the Skinners' property in the fall.

"I ain't thinking about anybody in particular," Rafe said, as the oven timer sounded from the kitchen. "But I'd like it better if it was somebody who's still alive and well."

I pushed off from the sofa. "I'd like it better, too, if whoever did it is available for prosecution. It's no fun to discover that someone's guilty of murder when they're already dead."

"No," Rafe said, and followed me to the kitchen.

Audrey, and now Mrs. Jenkins, live in a small Folk Victorian in the same general area as the Albertsons and the sheriff. We arrived right on time, with a still-warm cheesecake and Carrie in tow. Darcy and Patrick Nolan were there before us. Nolan drives a navy blue Charger with white stripes, and it was parked at the curb. He must have brought Darcy, because when we walked in, they were both sitting in the parlor, Nolan on the arm of Darcy's chair.

They make a sort of funny-looking couple. Don't get me wrong, I like Nolan. He's a good guy, and he's obviously enamored with my sister. But she's so striking, and very pretty, and he's sort of ordinary. Tall and lanky, with a prominent Adam's apple and a sort of beaky nose.

He has good shoulders, though, and there's probably a decent physique under the shirt and slacks. He's not built like Rafe, but then most people aren't. They're about the same height, a solid six-three, but Nolan probably weighs twenty or thirty pounds less than Rafe.

He nodded politely enough, anyway, when we walked in.

Gave me a smile and extended a hand to Rafe. "Detective."

Rafe grinned, but took it. "Officer."

They shook. "You're not really a detective," I asked my husband, "are you?"

He glanced down at me. "This month I am. As far as the Columbia PD is concerned, anyway."

Nolan looked curious, but he didn't ask. "Long story," I told him, and he nodded.

"How's the investigation going?"

"About as can be expected," Rafe said. "Every piece of evidence is sixteen years old, half the suspects are dead, and nobody remembers nothing."

That about covered it. He took Carrie off to sit beside his grandmother on the sofa—she touched his face and beamed up at him before bending over Carrie—and I walked the cake through the living room and dining room into the kitchen, where I asked Audrey whether she needed any help with the food. She said no, so I went back into the parlor and took the chair next to Nolan. "Did you grow up here?"

He looked surprised, so I guess maybe I sounded a bit abrupt. "In the area."

"Darcy said you might have known Darrell Skinner growing up?"

"Knew of him," Nolan said. "He was a couple years younger than me. I went to school with Robbie."

The middle Skinner brother.

"Could you see either of them doing what was done to Katie?"

"I don't know what was done to Katie," Nolan said, which was fair. "But if you're asking if I could see either of the Skinners killing her, then the answer is, not really. Art was all grown up when she disappeared, with a job and a wife. He wouldna been driving around picking up teenagers. There's never been any talk saying he liked underaged girls."

I nodded.

"Darrell was an asshole, but he was young, and I don't see him killing nobody. Robbie wasn't above beating women, but he was also older, and I don't see Katie going anywhere with him."

"Even if he told her he was taking her to Darrell?"

Nolan looked blank, and I added, "She might have been sleeping with Darrell. Or at least she slept with him once, that we know about."

"Huh." Nolan thought about it. "Darrell got around some, I did hear that. And I suppose she mighta gone with Robbie in that case. But I don't see Robbie doing that to Darrell. They always were thicker than thieves. If she was Darrell's girl, Robbie wouldn't have horned in on that. At least I don't think so."

Another fair point. "I appreciate it," I told him.

"No problem. Why are you so interested?"

I shrugged. "Just nosy. I usually take an interest in what Rafe's working on."

Nolan nodded. "Anything happen at the memorial today?"

"Not while we were there." I glanced at Darcy. She shook her head. "Did anything happen after we left?"

"Not that I noticed," Nolan said.

OK, then. I left them to talk amongst themselves, and busied myself watching my daughter, my husband, and his grandmother on the opposite side of the coffee table.

Mrs. Jenkins had been living in Sweetwater with Audrey for the past couple of months, and although I'm no expert, she seemed to have settled right in. Only Audrey would be able to tell us whether her Aunt Tondalia knew who Audrey was most of the time—at the moment, it was hard to tell whether she knew that Rafe was Rafe, or whether she thought he was Tyrell, and I was LaDonna, and Carrie was baby Rafe—but she was clean and fed and cared for, and she seemed happy to be here, so things could have been a lot worse.

Dinner was ready a few minutes later, and we settled around the dining room table for *Coq au Vin,* or French chicken stew with braised chicken in wine sauce along with mushrooms and pieces of bacon, if you prefer. It was delicious, whatever you call it, and the company was pleasant, too.

Over cheesecake, the discussion turned back to the memorial, and when I asked, Audrey said that she, too, remembered Scott Mason.

"He was a little older than me, but I went to school with him."

She didn't add that she was sorry he'd died, which would be *de rigueur* for a properly brought-up Southern Belle.

"Didn't you like him?"

"I didn't know him well," Audrey said.

"But?"

She shrugged elegant shoulders inside a black blouse with white polka dots. Audrey's always dressed to the nines, even in her own home while having dinner with family. Her only concession to the occasion was the fact that she'd replaced the four-inch patent leather heels and platform soles with a pair of fuzzy slippers. They still matched the rest of the outfit, and had tiny kitten heels. "But nothing. I didn't know him well. He wasn't friendly. Kept himself to himself, from what I can remember."

"He must have gotten married at some point, if he had a son."

"All sorts of people get married," Audrey said, which was certainly true. "And not everyone who has children is married."

I guess that was true. Audrey'd had a child out of wedlock. I was old-fashioned enough—or my family was—that I'd made it down the aisle before giving birth myself. But there isn't anything unusual about single parents these days. Although thirty plus years ago it was a little different.

"What're you getting at, darlin'?" Rafe wanted to know.

I shrugged. "I'm not sure I'm getting at anything. I was just wondering. His son was there, at the funeral home. Scotty Junior. But there was no wife. So I wondered what happened."

"I think she left," Audrey said, with a tiny wrinkle between her brows. Like Mother, she smoothed it out as soon as she realized it was there. "It was a long time ago, as I recall. The boy was young."

"Do you know why?"

"I imagine she found him difficult to live with," Audrey said. "He wasn't the nicest man in the world, as I recall."

"Abusive?"

"He might have been." She shrugged. "It wouldn't surprise me."

"Why didn't she take the kid with her when she left?"

"How do you know she didn't?" Rafe asked, and he had a point.

"I guess I don't." Scotty could have grown up being shuttled between his parents the way many children are. His mother might be alive and well somewhere, and just have chosen not to attend her ex-husband's funeral.

"Something bothering you about the Mason case?" Rafe asked me later, when we were driving through the darkness toward the mansion at the end of the night. We were both stuffed full of chicken and cheesecake, and Carrie was wide awake in the backseat, watching out the window as the streetlights went by. They reflected in her eyes, and in Rafe's too, when he glanced at me.

"Nothing specific. Or nothing at all, really. It's just the coincidence, I think. That it happened at the same time as Katie's body—or what was left of her—was found."

Rafe nodded, but said the same thing that Grimaldi had said earlier, when I brought up the same thing to her. "Katie—

or what was left of her—was found in November. Mason killed himself a week ago."

"Right around the time when Katie was identified, though."

"Yeah," Rafe said, "but nobody knew that she'd been identified yet."

"You knew. I knew. The sheriff knew. Grimaldi knew. We told Mother and Dix and Catherine."

"You think any of'em woulda told Scott Mason?"

Not really. No one in my family seemed to know Scott or Scotty. If Catherine had spoken to Scotty Mason the night I'd stopped by her house and told her and Mother that Katie had been identified, she hadn't mentioned it, and I think she would have.

Granted, there were other things she hadn't volunteered, so I don't know why I'd assume she'd volunteer that.

Maybe Scott Senior had been friends with the sheriff—they were about the same age—and had gotten the news that way.

"If that was the case," Rafe said, "don't you think Bob woulda been at the funeral today?"

Maybe so. Tamara Grimaldi had represented law enforcement at both funerals, but if Scott Mason had been a personal friend, it's likely that the sheriff would have shown up, too.

"It's probably just in my head," I said. "This idea that two strange things that happened at the same time have to be related. Except they didn't really happen at the same time, and they're not really that strange, either."

Or rather, what happened to Katie was strange, or at least out of the ordinary for our little town, but that didn't mean it had anything to do with a man suffering from cancer who chose to end his life before the cancer could.

"If it'll make you happy," Rafe said, "I can ask Jarvis about it tomorrow. Just to see what it is about it that makes him wanna investigate it."

I'm not sure he wanted to investigate it, to be honest. Or if he thought there was something unusual about it, he was probably just making it up to convince himself, and everyone around him, that he hadn't just been saddled with make-work while Rafe was handling the real case. But—

"You could do that if you wanted. But don't do it for my sake. It's none of my concern. And I'm already happy. You make me happy. I don't need Jarvis for that."

"Good to know," Rafe said, and kept driving.

Seventeen

Rafe took it easy the next morning. It was Sunday, and in a small, Southern town, you can't just go hog wild and start interrogating people on a Sunday morning. Sunday mornings are for church, and for lunch with the family. The Lord rested on the seventh day, and so do we.

So we spent the morning in bed, enjoying each other's company, and Carrie. And when we decided that the others— more pious than we—had had enough time to make it through the church service and out the other side, we got up and got ready for family lunch at the Wayside Inn.

It's sort of a tradition. I'd foregone it during the years I'd been living in Nashville, of course, but I happened to know that Dix brings the girls to church, and Catherine and Jonathan bring their brood, and afterwards, they and Mother get together for food and gossip at the Wayside Inn. At this point, we could probably expect Sheriff Satterfield too, and maybe even Todd and Marley and little Oliver.

"That could be awkward," Rafe said, as he pulled a pair of jeans up over long legs.

"Not as awkward as it used to be." I watched until he'd tucked himself away, and then I went back to my own business of getting dressed, since there was nothing more to see. "They might not be there, anyway. Marley might feel a little uncomfortable around all us Martins."

"Or maybe they just like spending the day in bed," Rafe said.

Maybe so. Either way, they might not be there. And if they were, we'd deal with it. And them. It was easier now that Todd had a girlfriend of his own, and didn't want to damage Rafe anymore, for stealing me away.

Not that he really would have done anything to Rafe, or to me either. He was just excruciatingly polite to me, and gave Rafe "the cut direct," as Barbara Botticelli might say. Pretended not to see him, while making it very clear that he did. But Todd would never engage in any kind of actual damage. Only nutcases do that sort of thing. Or very immature people. And besides, the one time Todd had gotten in Rafe's way over me, Rafe had knocked him on his butt in front of the whole family. I'm sure he hadn't been eager for a repeat performance.

"Did Katie have a boyfriend?" I asked Rafe.

He stopped in the middle of buttoning his shirt to look at me. "You're worse than Tammy. You never stop chewing over whatever's going on."

"And you do? You lived undercover for ten years. I imagine there weren't many seconds out of that decade you didn't think about what you were doing."

He didn't have any response to that, or if he did, he chose not to share it. "No," he said, instead. "No boyfriend. Not that was mentioned in the file. Or that her mama mentioned."

"How about an old boyfriend? Or even a secret admirer? Someone who might have found out about Darrell and decided that if he couldn't have Katie, Darrell couldn't, either?"

The corners of Rafe's mouth lifted, but he shook his head. "Nobody like that. If there was someone, it wasn't common knowledge."

I nodded. "I think we should try to track down Lynn Jeffries. If anyone knows, she might."

He tilted his head to look at me. "We?"

"You. I meant you."

"Sure you did." He grinned. "How d'you know Lynn spent time with Katie outside of school?"

"Saw a picture," I said, hoping he wouldn't ask me to show it to him.

"In the yearbook?"

I shook my head. "Catherine had some of photos in the attic. Not of Katie specifically. Just group photos. And pictures of Greg and Angela and people like that. But Katie and Lynn are in a couple."

Rafe arched a brow. I sighed. "Hold on. I'll go find them."

They were still in my jacket pocket from yesterday, when I'd shown them to Catherine. By the time I'd dug them out, Rafe had finished buttoning his shirt and had scooped up the baby and carried her downstairs. The sight of her tiny dark head nestled in the crook of his elbow, where his bicep was stretching the fabric of his shirt, never failed to give me a warm, gooey feeling in my stomach.

He handed over the baby and I handed over the photos. I got Carrie situated in the car seat while he perused the pictures. "Where's this?"

"Catherine didn't know exactly," I said. "Somewhere in the woods."

He gave me a look. "You noticing how your sister ain't exactly being forthcoming?"

"I noticed," I said. "I don't think she knows where it is, though. One patch of woods looks a lot like another, and it was a long time ago. And I suspect they may have been a little impaired, too."

Rafe nodded. "This is your sister here, right? And here's Lynn. And that's Katie behind her. Likely on Skinner land up in the hills."

I nodded.

"But your sister told us she didn't know Katie, and didn't

know about any connection to Darrell."

"She just didn't want to get involved," I said.

"I'm getting sick of this."

I didn't honestly blame him, but at the same time, I felt I had to defend my sister. "She just didn't want it to get out that she'd had anything to do with Darrell Skinner."

"No, God forbid anybody thinks any of the Martins do anything less than perfect." He gave me a dark look. "I keep waiting for you to come to your senses and get an annulment, you know."

I lost my breath for a second. "That's just mean. First of all, I wouldn't leave you. And second, if I did, I wouldn't try to erase having been married to you. And third, I gave birth to your daughter. How would I hide that?"

"You couldn't," Rafe said, "and some days I wonder if we're gonna get to a point where you're gonna wanna try."

My chest hurt, so I put my fist to it. It didn't help, and when I answered, my voice was unsteady. "Of course I won't. I love you. I married you. And we're not talking about me. *I* never had anything to do with Darrell Skinner!"

The few seconds of yelling startled Carrie, who scrunched up her little face and started crying.

"Shhh. Shhh." I stuck the pacifier in her mouth. She spat it out and kept screaming, her tiny face turning red.

"Give her to me," Rafe said, and snagged the handle of the car seat. "I think maybe she and I'll just stay home and let you go have lunch with your family by yourself."

I stared at him. "That's unfair. If I have to deal with Mother, you should have to, too."

"I'm angry enough I wanna yell at your sister right now," Rafe said, "I don't think I'd better come. Your mama would forget how much she likes me and go back to the way she used to treat me."

And neither of us wanted that. "Are you sure? I don't want

you to have to miss the Wayside Inn." Or Lynn Jeffries.

Although since he didn't know that she worked there, maybe it would be better if I kept that tidbit to myself for now. Because he was right: Mother wouldn't like it if he yelled at Catherine in public. And if he knew that we might find Lynn at the Wayside Inn, he might decide to come after all.

"Darlin'," Rafe told me, and it was a relief that he called me that instead of Savannah, which he only does when things are serious, "you know how much I love places with white tablecloths and several different forks—"

Not at all. He didn't like fancy whatsoever.

"—but I'd rather stay here."

"If you're sure," I said. "I'll only be gone a couple of hours."

He nodded. "Go have fun with your family. Carrie and I'll be fine here by ourselves."

I squinted at him, suspiciously. "Are you looking for an excuse to dig through the mansion for evidence that Katie's body was kept here for sixteen years?"

"'Course not," Rafe said, looking innocent. Or as innocent as he ever manages to look, which isn't very innocent at all. "That'd be crazy."

Yes. It would. But somehow I wasn't sure he realized that.

Or rather, I'm sure he knew that it was crazy to think Katie's body had been hidden somewhere in or around the mansion. We would have known. But I'm not sure he thought it was crazy to suspect my sister of some involvement in the disappearance. "What are you going to do?"

"I figure we'll watch some TV and hang out. Maybe take another look at those yearbooks. Just in case I come up with something you didn't."

"Do you want me to bring some food back for you?"

"We can manage here," Rafe said.

Fine. If he was going to be that way. I wrapped my coat around me and headed out to the garage while he and Carrie and Pearl stayed inside in the warmth of the house.

It had stopped raining, which was one nice thing. But the temperature had dropped a little, so it was now both cold and damp at the same time. I hunched my shoulders and ducked my head as I made my way around the corner of the mansion and toward the old carriage house that serves as our garage.

The mansion is built of brick, and so is the carriage house. So is the sole surviving slave cabin, for that matter. The little smokehouse is a wood structure, though. But the carriage house is a low-slung brick building with four large double doors in it. Because the mansion and all the outbuildings are on the historic register, there's been no electrifying of anything. Everything looks just the way it did when everything was built a hundred and eighty years ago.

I slid the big iron lock aside and leaned back on my heels to open the one set of doors where the Volvo was parked.

It's cold and dark in the garage. There's no insulation, of course, since only cars and garden equipment live here. Rafe's Harley takes up one of the bays. At the moment, his Chevy loaner took up another. The Volvo was parked in a third. In the fourth bay and along the walls are other things. One of the carriages has survived, and is sitting inside the garage. There's some tack and other things hanging on the walls. A metal horse trough sits along one wall. It's been a long time since we had horses on the Martin Plantation, but back in the day, they were everywhere.

I wandered around the interior, trying to see it through Rafe's eyes. Trying to imagine whether there was anywhere he could imagine that Catherine would have stashed a body out of everyone else's sight for fifteen years.

But of course there wasn't. The idea was ludicrous. So I got into the Volvo, drove it out of the garage, kept it running while I went back to shut the double doors behind me, and then I headed down the driveway away from the garage, away from the mansion, and away from my husband and daughter.

The Wayside Inn is what it sounds like: an old roadside inn on the stretch between Columbia and Pulaski. Back in the day, it would give travelers on horseback, who spent weeks on the trip from the Mexico Gulf up to Nashville and beyond, a place to stop for a meal and a stable.

These days, it's been converted to a very fancy restaurant with a German chef. The food is excellent, quite pricy, and the atmosphere is a mixture of old logs, gaslight lanterns, and hard benches, and white tablecloths with ornate silverware and fine china. Mother loves it. I don't mind it, although I'd rather be at Beulah's Meat'n Three with Rafe than at the Wayside Inn without him.

"Where's Rafael?" were the first words out of Mother's mouth when I came in alone.

The rest of the family was already ranged around a couple of tables that had been pushed together in the middle of the room. Todd was not there, I was happy to see, nor was Marley or little Oliver.

The sheriff was present, though, seated next to Mother. "Everything all right?" he asked.

I nodded. "Carrie wasn't feeling well, so Rafe stayed home with her."

I'm not a good, or happy, liar, but I also didn't want to tell them—all of them—the truth about why Rafe wasn't here. There was a chance that the sheriff didn't know about Catherine's involvement with Darrell and with the panty raid, and if he didn't, I didn't want to be the one to tell him.

Mother lowered her brows, and then immediately straightened them out so they wouldn't cause wrinkles. "What's wrong with the baby?"

"Runny nose," I said. It seemed like a reasonable excuse, given the season and weather. "Rafe hasn't had a chance to spend much time with her this week, so he offered to stay home so I could come to lunch."

I looked around for a chair. There was one open next to Dix, so I headed in that direction. That put me at the other end of the table from Mother, and it would be rude to yell, so she went back to talking to Bob instead of continuing to question me.

Dix arched his brows at me as I sat down. "Don't ask," I told him.

"I didn't. Everything OK?"

"More or less."

Catherine was looking at me from across the table, where she was sitting next to Jonathan. I didn't want to go into it with either of them, either, so I just scowled and changed the subject. "I saw Charlotte yesterday. Why didn't you just tell me she wanted you to handle her divorce?"

"Client confidentiality," Dix said.

Since that was an excuse I'd used a time or two in my own dealings with people—maybe even him—there wasn't much I could say to that. "I told her to hire Catherine instead."

Dix looked from me to his other sister and back.

"What?" Catherine said.

"Charlotte's getting a divorce."

Dix opened his mouth, and I continued, "I'm not a lawyer and I don't have to keep it a secret. We're friends, and she shared it with me. She wanted Dix to handle it for her, that's why they went out to dinner, but I told her you'd do a better a job."

"Thanks a lot," Dix said.

"She's right," Catherine told him. "You're too squeamish. When it comes to husbands screwing their wives over, I'm a better choice."

Nobody argued with her. "How do you know her husband screwed her over?" Dix asked instead. "You haven't spoken to her."

"She wants a divorce, doesn't she? If he wasn't screwing her over, she'd still want to be married to him." She glanced at me. "What did he do? Sleep around?"

"Knocked up one of his clients," I said, "from what Charlotte told me."

Catherine smiled. And while she didn't go as far as to rub her hands together, I could tell she was looking forward to this.

The others had already been seated long enough to give the waitress their drink order, and now she appeared with a big tray loaded with glasses. Styrofoam takeout cups with lids and straws for the kids, but real glass for everyone else. I watched as she deposited Mother's sweet tea first, and then the sheriff's cup of coffee. By then I had recognized her, and was twitching as she came closer.

"Problem?" Dix asked.

I shook my head. "No. You've been here long enough to order drinks. Have you ordered food, too?"

"We're about to," Dix said, as Lynn Jeffries stopped beside him. She looked a few years older than she had in the picture, and her masses of curly blond hair were piled up into a messy bun on top of her head. When she smiled at me, she still had twice the number of normal teeth. "Can I get you something to drink?"

"Lynn?"

She nodded, and looked at me a little closer. "Do I know you?"

I shook my head. "Savannah Martin. Collier. You had left high school by the time I started. But you went to school with Catherine."

They looked at one another. And either they hadn't acknowledged one another before now, or just hadn't realized they knew each other. Hard to believe, since Lynn looked quite a lot like she did in high school, and Catherine didn't look all that different, either.

Or maybe that was just my imagination, since I'd seen the change happen gradually. Maybe, to Lynn, Catherine looked like a different person.

At any rate, they gave each other wary nods now. "Good to see you," Catherine said. Lynn murmured something that might have amounted to the same thing, but maybe not.

"I looked for you at Katie's memorial yesterday," I told her.

"I had to work. We were short-handed."

"So short-handed that your boss couldn't let you take off for a funeral?"

She didn't answer. "What would you like to drink?"

"Sweet tea," I said.

She nodded. "I'll be right back to take your orders."

She hurried off before I could say anything else.

"Way to go," Dix told me. "You chased off our waitress."

Hannah's bottom lip stuck out. "I'm hungry."

"She'll be back," I told my niece and pushed my chair back. "Excuse me."

"Oh, great," Dix said from behind me. "Now it'll be even longer before she comes back."

I ignored him, just headed in the direction Lynn had disappeared, and ended up outside the kitchen. When she came out with a glass of sweet tea in her hand, and saw me, she stopped in her tracks.

"Thank you." I took it out of her hand.

"I would have brought it to the table, you know."

I nodded. "I wanted to talk to you."

She folded both arms across her chest. "About what?"

"Katie Graves," I said.

"Why?"

"My husband's working the case for the Columbia PD. I'm curious."

She didn't answer, and I added, "You and Katie were on the newspaper staff and the volleyball team together. And I saw pictures of the two of you—and a bigger group of kids—up in the hills by the Devil's Backbone."

"So?"

"So I thought you might know what was going on back then."

"With Katie?" She shook her head. "If I'd known what happened to Katie I would have told the police."

"I didn't mean that." Because of course she would have. "I just thought, if you were friends, you might be able to fill in some blanks."

Her eyes narrowed. "What kind of blanks?"

"Just some questions I had. I guess you heard that Katie's remains were found on the Skinner family's property after the murders?"

She nodded.

"I know Katie slept with Darrell Skinner before she disappeared."

"How d'you know that?"

"Darrell kept souvenirs," I said. "He wrote names and dates on them."

She made a face, and I added, "I take it that isn't news to you?"

"There's a pair with my name on it somewhere."

In the evidence room at the sheriff's department, but it was probably just as well not to mention that. "Did everyone at Columbia High sleep with Darrell Skinner?" I asked, exasperated.

"No," Lynn answered, "but enough of us did that he had quite a collection."

There was something in her voice, and I tilted my head to look at her. "Were you in love with him?"

"None of your business," Lynn said, and of course she was right.

"Was Katie in love with Darrell?"

She hesitated. "If she was, she didn't tell me."

But if Lynn had been in love with Darrell, and Katie knew, she might not have told Lynn if she felt the same, especially if Darrell reciprocated.

But— "No," Lynn said when I asked.

"Are you sure?"

She nodded. "Darrell didn't love anybody but Darrell."

"I guess it isn't likely that Darrell killed her, then?"

She shook her head. "He wasn't a killer. His brother Robbie could get nasty, but not Darrell. Not that way."

"What way?"

"Like I said," Lynn said. "He was selfish. He'd play girls against each other. Sleep with someone and her best friend the same day. That kind of thing. But he wasn't violent."

"What if Katie rejected him?" She hadn't, of course. At least not the first time. But maybe later. "What if he wanted to keep sleeping with her, but she didn't want to?"

"He wouldn't care," Lynn said. "There was always someone else he could sleep with."

The more questions I asked, the more it sounded like Darrell wouldn't have had a reason to hurt Katie. And the more questions I asked, the more it sounded like some other girl, upset with Darrell, might have committed the murder.

Someone like my sister.

I pushed that thought aside and focused on Lynn. "What did you think happened to her? Back then, I mean?"

"I thought she ran away," Lynn said.

"Did she have a reason to run away?" And we were back to the possibility that Katie's father might have done something to her.

"None I know of." She peered over my shoulder. "Can I go back to doing my job now?"

I nodded. "I'll see you back at the table."

She bustled off, and I headed back to where I'd come from.

When I sat down, Catherine arched her brows at me. Since Dix and Jonathan were engaged in a discussion about sports, I said, "She slept with Darrell."

Catherine made a face. "Welcome to the club."

"She said Darrell wouldn't have killed Katie. That the only person Darrell cared about was Darrell, and that he had fun playing girls off one another. That he didn't make a secret of sleeping around."

Catherine nodded.

"So maybe another girl killed Katie. Someone else who was sleeping with Darrell, and who didn't like the competition."

"Not me," Catherine said.

"I wasn't thinking about you." Although that was the reason Rafe had postulated for why Catherine might have wanted Katie out of the way. But if it applied to Catherine, it could equally well apply to someone else. "I was thinking about Lynn."

Who, in spite of having been close to Katie in high school, hadn't cared enough to show up at the memorial. And who, unless my lie detector was on the fritz, had had feelings for Darrell in high school.

Catherine didn't say anything for a second, just watched Lynn as the waitress came closer and started taking Mother's and the sheriff's lunch orders. (A Southern Caesar salad—it comes with cherry tomatoes—and a gouda meatloaf with smashed potatoes and green beans, if you're interested.)

"I wonder where she lives," I said.

Since she was here at the Wayside Inn, working, it might be a good idea to take a look around her place. Just in case she had a handy airtight container in her garage, that had held Katie's bones all these years.

"Sunnyside," Catherine said. "Or she did when she was younger. Maybe not anymore."

Lynn smiled at Dix and Jonathan. "What can I get you for

lunch?"

They ordered, and she turned her attention to Catherine and me.

"I'll have the roast beef sandwich with potato salad," Catherine said. "Are you still in... Sunnyside, wasn't it?"

Lynn nodded. "What about you?" She turned her body toward me, but without meeting my eyes.

I asked for a turkey sandwich. "Sunnyside is on the west side of town, isn't it?"

"Why?"

"I'm a real estate agent." I dug in my purse for a business card. "I've been working in Nashville for a few years, but we're down here now, and I have to get used to the neighborhoods again."

I found a card and handed it to her. Lynn looked at it, decided I must be legitimate if I had a card, and handed it back.

"Keep it," I told her.

"I'm not interested in selling."

"That's OK." I smiled. "Maybe you'll remember something else about Katie you'll want to tell me."

Lynn looked like she didn't think that was likely, but she dropped the card in her apron pocket.

"Did you buy something of your own," Catherine asked, "or are you still in your parents' house?"

"I'm still in my parents' house, but my parents aren't. They moved to Florida. Excuse me. I have to get these orders in if you want to eat today."

She walked away.

"When she comes back," I told Catherine as I pushed my chair away from the table, "if she asks about me, tell her I went to the bathroom. Hold off as long as you can before you admit that I left. I don't want her coming after me. And it's going to take me some time to get there and get in."

"What about your sandwich?" Catherine asked my back.

"Have it boxed up," I told her over my shoulder as I headed for the exit. "And whatever you do, don't tell her where I went."

Eighteen

Sunnyside turned out to be a nice, quiet neighborhood on the southwest side of town, not too far from Damascus, where Elspeth had lived and Yvonne still did. The streets were winding, the lots middling to large, and there were a lot of trees. Bare now in the throes of winter, but it would probably be a nice neighborhood when spring came and everything was in bloom. And the houses were set far enough apart that breaking and entering might not be too difficult.

Property records are freely available online, if you know where to look for them. As a real estate agent, I have access to databases that makes it even easier. Digging up Lynn Jeffries's address was literally a matter of thirty seconds.

I turned up the driveway and slipped the Volvo in behind the house. And sat in the car for a moment and looked around before I got out.

The house was a low-slung mid-century brick with a built-in garage on one end and a carport in the back, under which I was parked. Three bedrooms, from what I'd seen of the layout of similar houses. Two bathrooms, or maybe just a bath and a half. Not too dissimilar to Darcy's rental, but a bit more rundown. It could use some new gutters, and maybe a good power washing. The brick could have done with some tuckpointing here and there, too.

Lynn had said her parents had moved out, but that didn't

mean she lived alone. She hadn't been wearing a ring, but that didn't mean she wasn't involved with someone. She might have a boyfriend tucked away inside. Or a couple of kids. Maybe a Rottweiler.

There was no sign of a Rottweiler, or any other kind of dog. No pen, no doghouse, no water bowl by the outside spigot. Also no sign of children, or that anyone else shared the house with Lynn. Everything was quiet and looked deserted. After two minutes, when nobody had come to the back door to investigate, I decided I might as well get out of the car and look around.

I started with the back door. It had a big window in the middle, and behind it was a small laundry room with a washer and dryer on one side wall, and a utility sink on the other. A pair of rubber boots sat under the sink along with a bucket with a rag draped across the opening to dry.

I knocked on the door, just to be on the safe side, and while I waited, I peered deeper into the house. At the other side of the laundry room was a door to the kitchen—I saw a vinyl floor, and the edge of an upper and a lower cabinet, and the corner of a counter.

When nobody, animal or human, showed up in response to my summons, I moved on from the door.

Beside the kitchen was a high window that probably belonged to a bathroom, and beyond that a bigger window into a bedroom. After that I reached the corner of the house, and I decided not to tempt fate by peering through the windows on the side or the front, where someone would be more likely to see me. I was curious, but I'm not stupid. Or not stupid enough to tempt fate quite that far. Bad enough that I was here to begin with. I didn't want to be caught peering through the windows in broad daylight. I could only imagine Grimaldi's face if one of her squad cars had to drive out here to arrest me.

So I wandered back toward the Volvo, past the bathroom

window and the back door to the garage.

Unlike the carriage house at the mansion, this garage was attached to the house, or more accurately, they were built as one building at the same time. One of the bays had been motorized, it seemed. There was no lock or handle, and no way to pull the door up from outside. Lynn probably had a remote.

The other bay hadn't been touched. There was a shiny handle in the middle of the door, with a keyhole in the middle of that.

I tried it, having no expectations that it would turn. When it did, I did what anyone would do, and yanked.

The door rolled up with a roar like thunder. Or more likely it just sounded that way to me. When I looked around, with blood thudding in my ears, the sound hadn't caused any of the neighbors to come running out of their houses to see what was going on.

Heart beating fast, I took a step forward, into the garage. It seemed safer, really, to get out of sight than to stay where I was, just in case someone happened to glance out their windows.

The garage was a two-bay, and both bays were empty—or at least empty of cars. Lynn probably parked on the electric side, where there was enough room for a car.

On the other side, a small lawnmower sat off to the side, along with a wheel barrow leaned up against the wall next to several rakes and shovels. One of the shovels was caked with dirt, and that seemed sinister to me, until I remembered that Katie hadn't been buried, just dumped in the woods. The dirt was probably just from gardening.

A bag of fertilizer leaned against the wall underneath a row of hooks with things hanging from them. A coiled hose, small gardening tools with and without claws. An old raincoat, caked with mud, to go along with the rubber boots in the mudroom. I stuck my hands in the pockets, but found nothing except a wadded-up tissue, a couple of pebbles, and an oxidized penny.

A couple of makeshift shelves in the corner held tools of the handyman variety. Hammers—none of them with blood on them—ditto screwdrivers and wrenches. An old, round tin that sported a picture of Danish butter cookies on the lid and Danish landmarks around the sides—I recognized the Little Mermaid on her rock—turned out to hold a variety of screws and nails. I sifted through them with my fingers, but found nothing that didn't belong there.

In the far-back corner of the bottom shelf, half hidden behind a stack of empty flower pots, was something that looked like a dark bundle of cloth, and I squatted to peer at it. And felt my heart start to beat faster.

Not a bundle of cloth. A nylon backpack, black and bulging.

Now, there was no real reason why Lynn shouldn't have an old backpack in her garage. It might be a slightly weird place for it—a closet inside might make more sense—but there was absolutely no reason why she couldn't have held on to her old backpack from high school, and this was it.

Hadn't Rafe said that Katie had been carrying a black nylon backpack when she disappeared, though?

I reached for it, and then hesitated. And pulled out my phone instead. And took a picture of it. And sent it off to Rafe. *Look what I found.*

The response came back promptly. *Where are you?*

Lynn Jeffries's house, I wrote back, and added the address. *In Sunnyside.*

There was nothing more, so after a minute I sent another text. *Should I look inside?*

No! The response came back in record time.

It might be Katie's.

The phone rang. "All the more reason not to open it," my husband told me when I answered. "What the hell are you doing, Savannah?"

"She's waiting tables at the Wayside Inn," I said. "Taking care of the whole Martin clan. She'll be there a while. I figured it was a good time to check out her place."

"You're breaking and entering?"

"Of course not." I sniffed. "You know I don't have the skills for that. The garage door was open."

I could hear the eyeroll. "Get outta there."

I supposed I might as well. It wasn't like the backpack would develop legs and walk away while I sat outside and waited. "Are you on your way?"

"Yes." He bit the word off.

"Good." And then something occurred to me. "What did you do with Carrie?"

He wouldn't have left her home alone. But there was no one else living with us. So who did he give her to?

"She's here," Rafe said.

"In the Chevy? But you don't have a car seat." The only car seat we had was in the Volvo, and that was parked outside.

"You should have thought of that," Rafe told me, "before you went out of your way to get yourself in trouble."

I wasn't in trouble—at least not until he got here—but by now I fervently wished I hadn't called him. My voice shook. "Go back home. Or pull over somewhere and wait for me. I'll come get Carrie. Then you can drive over here on your own."

"Just get the hell out of the garage. We'll be there in a few minutes."

By this point I was hyperventilating, and he must have realized it, because he added, "She's fine, Savannah. I'm being careful."

Of course he was. She was his daughter, too. "I know," I said. "It's just..." Accidents happen.

"Yeah. But I'm taking care of her. I need you to take care of yourself. And that means getting out of the garage before someone sees you."

"No one's going to see me. The neighbors aren't paying attention, and Lynn's twenty minutes away, in Sweetwater."

"Just do it," Rafe said and hung up.

Fine. I made a face at the phone before I dropped it in my pocket, and gave the backpack a last covetous look before I straightened and headed out.

The car came up the driveway just a few minutes later. I heard the driver gun the engine to go up the hill, and got out of my own car preparatory to greeting my husband and daughter.

Rafe pulled the tan Chevy to a stop behind the Volvo, and got out to glare at me across the roof of the car. "Dammit, Savannah. You understand that I can arrest you for this, right? You don't have to be inside the house for it to be a crime. What the hell were you thinking?"

I was thinking that I'd wanted to help. But as I watched him slam the car door and stalk around the Chevy with my daughter—our daughter—slung across his chest in one of her baby slings, the sight blew the thought out of my head. "Is she OK?" I asked instead.

His voice was impatient. "She's fine. She fell asleep when we started driving. She'll be hungry when she wakes up."

Just like always. I indicated the open garage door. "The backpack's on the shelf in the back."

He stalked past me and into the garage, where he bent down, one hand on the baby, to peer at the backpack. It didn't surprise me when he let loose with a ripe curse. "Did you touch anything?"

I shook my head. "It's right where I found it."

I had thought he might give me a pat on the back over that, at least, but he was still scowling. "This is the problem with letting yourself into somebody's garage without permission. We don't have a search warrant for this house. So even if this is Katie's stuff, it's inadmissible."

"Can't we get a search warrant now?" I asked.

"No," Rafe said. "Not without some kind of evidence."

I pointed to it.

He shook his head. "It don't work that way. You can't find the stuff and then get a search warrant to make the search legal. And I can't start searching through people's houses just 'cause I don't like their attitudes. I need some real evidence to go on before anybody'd give me a search warrant. Do you have any evidence that Lynn Jeffries was involved in Katie's disappearance other than her attitude? And this evidence we can't use?"

I shook my head. "I'm sorry. I should have waited for you. It's just that the garage door was open, and I figured, since time was of the essence…"

He arched a brow, and I squirmed. "OK, so the garage door wasn't open. Not exactly. But it was unlocked. So it was sort of open. Just not standing open."

"Lemme guess. Your fingerprints gonna be on the door handle?"

"Um…"

"I don't believe this," Rafe said. He ran a hand over the top of his head, which is his equivalent of running his fingers through his hair. Most of the time there isn't enough hair there to run anyone's fingers through. "Our first real piece of evidence, and you made it inadmissible."

"I didn't mean to!"

He took a breath, and I could feel him work to calm himself down. After a couple of seconds, he reached out and put an arm around my shoulders. "I know, darlin'. It's just a shame, is all."

It was. It really was a shame. "Do you think it's Katie's backpack?"

"Looks like it," Rafe said. "It matches what the police report said she was carrying."

He didn't say anything else, and I waited. And waited. Until I couldn't wait any longer. "What do we do now?"

He sighed. "It's already inadmissible. We might as well take a look at it."

Exactly what I was hoping to hear. "Would you like to do the honors, or should I?"

"I've got the baby," Rafe said. "And you've got a pair of gloves in your pocket. I don't want your fingerprints on the evidence, so put 'em on before you dig in."

Great. I shoved my hands into gloves, and tackled the backpack.

The first thing I pulled out was a pair of jeans. "Levi's. Size 26." She hadn't been a big girl, if they were hers. "Striped shirt. Blue jacket with hood. And a pair of running shoes, size 7."

Rafe nodded. "No underwear or socks?"

"Pair of socks stuffed into the shoes. No bra or panties." And no jewelry or watch or anything like that.

"She might not have been wearing a bra," Rafe said. "Some girls don't."

No. Katie might have been built small. The waist size of the pants indicated that she was a small girl. But even the most dainty of girls don't tend to go commando. And I knew we were both thinking about the same thing. "The date of Katie's pair of panties in the box…"

"Two weeks before she disappeared," Rafe said. "If he killed her, he didn't do it then."

So Darrell Skinner hadn't been the male equivalent of a black widow spider. Good to know.

"Anything else in there?"

I peered into the backpack. Along the sides and bottom were a binder, a couple of folders, a composition book, and some pens and pencils. I pulled out the composition book and held it up. "Katie's name."

Rafe nodded. "Put it back and zip it up."

"Do we take it with us?" I asked, as I fumbled to do as he said. "Or leave it here so you can try to get a search warrant and come back?"

Rafe opened his mouth to answer, but before he could, another voice spoke, from behind us. "Take what with you?"

We both turned on our heels, and Rafe moved automatically to stand in front of me. When he realized he had Carrie strapped to his chest, and was exposing her to danger by trying to protect me, a look of frustration crossed his face.

Not that it looked like there was any danger. At least not at the moment. It was Lynn Jeffries standing in the open garage door, still in her waitress uniform with an unbuttoned down coat hastily thrown over top. She had her hands on her hips, but other than that, and the scowl on her face, she didn't look threatening. "What are you doing here?"

Her eyes found me, and the scowl deepened.

"Columbia PD," Rafe said, going for his badge, which was clipped to his belt. He had a gun, too, in an official holster next to it, but I guess he didn't feel it was necessary to go for that.

"I know who you are." Lynn turned her attention to from me to him. "What are you doing in my garage?"

"Just looking around," Rafe said. "The door was unlocked."

Lynn smirked. "Find anything?"

"As a matter of fact." Rafe took a step to the side, exposing the black backpack. "You wanna explain this?"

Lynn looked at it, and for a second her face went absolutely blank. She blinked a couple of times, but that was all. As we watched, all the color leaked out of her face and left her ghostly pale. "That..." She stopped and ran the tip of her tongue over her bottom lip. "That looks like Katie's backpack."

"And Katie's clothes," Rafe said. "You wanna tell me how they got here?"

Lynn looked at him. And back at the little pile of evidence. And back at Rafe. "I have no idea."

I didn't know about him, but I was inclined to believe her. No way was she able to fake the pallor. The voice, sure. But not the way she'd turned pale at the sight.

And then all my sympathy vanished when she glanced at me and said, "Maybe she put them there."

"I most certainly did not!" I said, offended.

"Prove it!" Lynn shot back.

I opened my mouth, and closed it again. Because of course there was no way I could prove, to Rafe or Lynn or anybody else, that the backpack had been in Lynn's garage when I walked in. Rafe knew—at least I hoped he did—that I hadn't put it there, but I couldn't expect anyone else to believe me.

Grimaldi probably would, come to think of it. So the chances were slim that I'd be arrested. But if Lynn had killed Katie and hung on to the evidence all this time, I hadn't made Rafe's case any easier to prove.

Which was exactly why he hadn't wanted me inside the garage to begin with.

"Why would I try to frame you for murder?" I asked, trying to be reasonable. "I didn't even know Katie."

"Maybe you were trying to help your sister," Lynn answered. "I wasn't the only one who slept with Darrell, you know. She did, too. And she wasn't any happier about sharing him than I was."

There was a pause.

"Any reason I should believe that somebody else put that backpack there?" Rafe wanted to know, and Lynn looked at him.

"I had no reason to want Katie dead. We were friends."

"Friends who slept with the same guy," I put in.

She gave me an unfriendly look, but Rafe asked a question, and she turned to him rather than bother with me. "Did you live here when Katie disappeared? In this house?"

Lynn nodded. "I grew up here. My parents moved to

Florida a couple of years ago, and I took over the house. Before that, I was in a rental in downtown. And in college."

She glanced at the door between the garage and the rest of the house. "If we're gonna talk about this, you might as well come in. I've been on my feet all day, and I wanna sit down."

She headed for it. I glanced at Rafe. He arched a brow, but nodded for me to follow Lynn, so I did.

The door led into a little den, with paneled walls and a fireplace. A drop zone was set up along the wall next to the door, and Lynn dropped her bag on a bench sitting there, and hung her jacket on a hook. "Can I take your coats?"

"I don't imagine we'll stay long," Rafe said. He probably didn't want to deal with trying to get the sling with the sleeping baby off, in case she woke up. I slipped out of my coat, though, although I kept it with me, just in case we had to beat a hasty retreat.

It didn't look like such a thing was imminent. Lynn looked tired and sad, and she dropped heavily into the sofa group curved around the fireplace. "Have a seat."

I perched on the edge of the chair opposite, with my coat on my lap. "You look tired."

"I worked the late shift last night," Lynn said, "and the early shift this morning. I didn't get much sleep in-between. I was supposed to leave early, but then your family came in. And after everybody else had sat down, you showed up."

So she'd been hostile because she wanted to get home and get off her feet, and I'd dragged mine about ordering lunch. "Sorry," I said.

She grimaced. It might have been intended to be a smile, but I don't think so. "I couldn't deal with it anymore, so I left. I'm probably missing out on a nice tip."

She probably was. There were a lot of us Martins (and McCalls), and we all—with the exception of yours truly—had good jobs.

"I don't even care." She leaned her head back against the sofa and closed her eyes. "I just want to sleep."

"Answer a couple questions," Rafe said, "and we'll leave you alone."

He'd sat down in the chair next to mine, with a big hand bracing Carrie. She was still asleep, in spite of everything that had gone on around her.

Lynn sighed, but nodded. "Shoot."

"When was the last time you looked on the shelf where the backpack was?"

"I haven't been in that corner since the end of gardening season last year," Lynn said.

"Anyone else have access to your garage?"

She shook her head.

"You do your own mowing and your own landscaping?"

She nodded, with a look at me. "Don't you?"

I don't, actually. I grew up with landscapers and mowers being brought in, and now Rafe does it. With his shirt off, which is enjoyable as hell—heck—for anyone who happens to be around.

He gave me a ghost of a smile, so he probably knew what I was thinking. "I noticed your electrical panel's in the garage. Have you had any updates recently?"

Lynn shook her head. And I must say I was impressed. It would never have occurred to me to notice that, much less ask.

"Do you always keep the door open?"

She turned to me. "The garage door? Of course not."

"It was open today. Or unlocked, I guess I should say."

"It's not supposed to be." A furrow appeared between her brows.

"When's the last time you remember opening it?" Rafe asked.

"I go in and out of the automated side every day. Or almost every day. The last time the other side was open..." She thought back, "I guess it was probably New Year's Eve. It's the middle of winter, so I haven't done any gardening. But there were a lot of people here that night, and it wasn't very cold. I had both the doors open to get some air going."

"Do you remember locking the door afterwards?"

Lynn thought about it. "I'm pretty sure I did, yeah."

"Where do you keep the key?"

"By the door." She turned to look over her shoulder. "See the little hook there? Next to the jamb?"

I saw the little hook. But there was nothing on it.

"I'm gonna need a list of everyone who was here that night," Rafe said.

Lynn's tired eyes opened wide. "You think someone who was here on New Year's Eve took my key and put Katie's things in my garage?"

"Unless you put them there," Rafe told her, "someone else did. It wasn't Savannah." He glanced at me.

"But—"

She stopped and sunk her teeth into her bottom lip. We waited. "That means someone who was here, someone I know, killed Katie."

Yes. It did. And it can be hard to rat out your friends. So I added some incentive, since I thought she might not have thought of it. "Someone who was here—someone you invited into your home, someone you trust!—didn't just kill Katie, but he or she left Katie's clothes and backpack in your garage to implicate you in her disappearance."

Lynn flushed, and her eyes turned flinty. "I'll get a pen and some paper."

She left the den and went into the other part of the house. Rafe glanced at me and nodded in approval. I smiled back. Maybe I'd gone some little way toward redeeming myself from the mess I made earlier.

It took a couple of minutes, and then Lynn came back into

the den. She was holding a yellow pad that she passed to Rafe. "This is all I can remember. There might have been a few other people, but this is most of them."

I stretched my neck. The list had fifteen or twenty names on it, although several said "plus date." I guess we—or Rafe— would have to ask around about those.

"Anyone we know?" I asked, and he handed me the pad. I glanced at the names while Rafe continued talking to Lynn.

"How many of these folks knew Katie?"

Lynn thought about it. "Maybe half?"

"Mark'em," Rafe said, and I handed the pad over.

"I see Scotty Mason's name on there."

Lynn nodded, a few strands of her hair falling out of her bun and across her face as she made checkmarks alongside some of the names on the list. "We went to school together. I see him once in a while."

"Sad news about his father."

She nodded. "It's been a tough six months for Scotty. Between his dad falling ill and dying, and the Skinner mess last fall, and now Katie… That's why I invited him to the party. I thought it might cheer him up."

"Did he know Katie? And the Skinners?"

"He knew Katie," Lynn said, handing the pad back to me. "We all went to school together. And they lived near one another. Took the bus together in the mornings."

I nodded. Scotty had told me as much.

"And we all knew Darrell. He was a couple of years older than us, but both Katie and I were involved with him, and Scotty knew him, too. We'd all go up to the Skinners' to party on the weekends when we were in high school."

"With Darrell providing the beer and weed," Rafe said mildly.

Lynn shrugged. "I won't deny there was some of that going on. Darrell always had a head for business."

That was one way of putting it, I guess.

We sat in silence for a few seconds before Lynn asked, "Anything else I can do for you?"

I glanced at Rafe. He looked back at me.

"Doesn't look that way," I said.

Rafe nodded. "Thanks for your time. We'll get out of your way now." He pushed to his feet, one hand on the baby, while I ripped the list off the yellow pad. Once he was upright, he extended the other hand to me, to help me up. "If any of these people contact you for any reason," he told Lynn, "give me a call."

"And if any of them knock on the door," I added, "don't let them in."

She stared at me.

"Better safe than sorry," I added.

When we walked out, I heard her compulsively shut and lock the door behind us.

Nineteen

"I didn't get to eat my sandwich," I told Rafe as we headed for our respective cars. "I left it behind at the Wayside Inn. Have you had lunch? Do you want to join me at Beulah's?"

"I'd rather talk to Jarvis," Rafe said. "I don't know that Yvonne'll have much to contribute, darlin'. She was too young to know Katie."

"She might have noticed something. And maybe Jarvis will be friendlier if you make it casual. At a restaurant instead of the office."

"I suppose." He sounded dissatisfied, but he nodded. "I'll follow you over there. And call Jarvis on the way. If he don't wanna go to Beulah's, I'll text you."

"I'll take the baby," I said. "That way, if you have to leave to meet Jarvis, I can take her home." And she'd be properly strapped into her seat.

We spent a couple of minutes transferring the sleeping baby from the sling across Rafe's chest to the seat. I thought for sure she'd wake up, and for a few seconds it looked like she might, but then she settled back down again. I clicked her onto the base in my backseat. "I'll see you at Beulah's."

"Unless I text you," Rafe said, and headed for the Chevy.

By the time I had navigated through Columbia and out the other side, and into the graveled parking lot outside Beulah's, he was still on my tail, though. "Didn't you get hold of Jarvis?"

I asked when I'd gotten out of the Volvo and Rafe was on his way toward me from the Chevy.

He nodded. "He's coming."

"Is he upset?"

"He wasn't happy," Rafe said, grabbing the seat with the baby, "but he's willing to listen. I invited Tammy to join us. Figured while Jarvis might tell me to go eff myself, he wouldn't do it to her."

"Is she coming?"

"She's here." He nodded to a navy blue SUV a couple of places down from where we were walking.

"That's Grimaldi's car?" I'd only ever seen her drive a beat-up, unmarked, burgundy sedan in Nashville. This didn't look like an unmarked police vehicle. It was several years younger and in much better condition than the Chevy.

"Personal car," Rafe said and headed for the door. "C'mon."

I scurried after, with a last look at the SUV.

Grimaldi was sitting in the rear of the restaurant with her back to the wall. Rafe slid in beside her, since he never chose to sit with his back to the door if he could avoid it, and since we'd be packed tightly into the booth once Jarvis got here. Someone would have to sit next to Grimaldi, and I guess he'd rather it be him than Jarvis. That left me to share my side of the table with Jarvis, it seemed. I had the hostess bring me an overturned high chair for Carrie's car seat.

"So what's going on?" Grimaldi asked Rafe when we were seated. "Paul called me after you called him, and told me if I took the Mason investigation away from him, he was going to report me to the city council for playing favorites."

"Christ."

"I told you you're the pet investigator," I said.

He scowled at me. "I'm not the pet investigator. There's no pet investigator."

"You can tell yourself that, but Jarvis obviously believes otherwise."

He turned the scowl on Grimaldi, who told him, "Of course you're the pet investigator. I talked you into coming onboard after I got the job. Everyone knows you're the pet investigator."

"Christ," Rafe said again, but with a completely different inflection this time.

"Don't worry about it." I patted his hand across the table before I turned to Grimaldi. "Is that a problem?"

She shook her head. "I'm allowed to hire or fire anyone I want. And it isn't unusual for a new chief to bring onboard a few people he or she already knows and trusts. Carter did it."

"Are any of them still around?" Or did they leave when Carter went to prison?

"Jarvis was one of'em," Rafe said. "He don't seem like he wants to go nowhere."

No. And the jury was still out on whether he was dirty.

Rafe looked past me to the door. "Here he is now."

I slid out of the seat so Jarvis could sit by the window and I could stay next to the baby. "Detective." I gave him a polite nod.

Jarvis is maybe ten years older than Rafe and Grimaldi. He's stocky, with slicked back, dark hair, and like every other time I'd seen him when he hadn't been sitting at his desk, he was wearing a tan trench coat. Today, since it was Sunday, the coat covered a sweater and casual slacks instead of a suit.

He gave me a look before sliding into the booth. I fitted myself next to him, but left enough space that no part of me was touching any part of him.

Up close, he had a slight bulldog quality. Broad face, pugnacious jaw, button nose. A mouth that turned down at the corners. It might be the way he looked all the time, or it could be the current company.

After he shrugged out of the trench coat, we all sat in

silence for a moment. I guess we were taking stock of the situation and each other. "What's this all about?" Jarvis wanted to know.

Rafe opened his mouth, and thought better of it. He glanced at Grimaldi. She lobbed the ball right back at him, but before either of them could say anything, a gum-snapping waitress with a behive appeared next to the table. "Get you anything to drink?"

"Sweet tea and a turkey sandwich," I said, since by now, the fact that I'd missed lunch was starting to become an acute problem.

Rafe ordered a burger, and Grimaldi and Jarvis settled for coffee, with the excuse that they'd already eaten.

The waitress took herself off, and Grimaldi picked up the reins. "As you know," she told Jarvis, "Collier's been working with Sheriff Satterfield on the Katie Graves investigation."

Jarvis sneered, and while he didn't chant *"Teacher's pet, teacher's pet!"* I think we all heard the echoes.

"I worked the Skinner investigation," Rafe told him, his voice tight. "Katie was found on Skinner land. It made no sense for anyone else to take it."

Jarvis said nothing to that, but he didn't look like he agreed.

"This is my department now," Grimaldi said. "If you have a problem with the way I run it, feel free to leave and find a job somewhere else. I'll give you a recommendation. But I won't have you challenge my authority, and I won't have you refuse to cooperate with other members of the department."

"I'm here," Jarvis said, "ain't I?"

He was; there was no denying that.

"I'm interested in the Mason case," Rafe told him, but before either of them could say anything else, the waitress returned with our drinks. A minute passed while she placed cups and glasses, filled coffee, and dropped cream and sugar on the table.

When she'd walked away again, Jarvis asked, "Why? You wanna take that over, too?"

Grimaldi looked at him, and he had the grace to look ashamed, even if he didn't say he was sorry.

"Scott Mason's name came up in the Graves investigation," Rafe said. It probably wasn't the first time he'd had to deal with a jerk in the line of duty, because his voice was even and his face calm. "I wanna know what's going on with the Mason case."

"I'm making progress," Jarvis said, dumping Splenda into his coffee.

Rafe hadn't ordered coffee, so he had nothing to do with his hands. They were wrapped around the glass of tea the waitress had brought, probably in lieu of wrapping around Jarvis's throat. "What kind of progress?"

Jarvis stuck his spoon into the cup and swirled the coffee around. "Something about it don't smell right."

"Do you have any evidence?"

"Not yet," Jarvis said.

There was a moment of silence. As it lengthened, Jarvis added, "We all know what happened. Mason died of an overdose of pills. His own pills. The empty pill bottle was on the floor. The glass was on the bedside table. His fingerprints were on both. He might have managed to do it on his own. It'd have been difficult, but it's possible. I can't prove he didn't. Nobody can. But I don't think he did."

There was another pause.

"If Mason didn't do himself," Rafe said, "who do you think did?"

Jarvis looked at him, and Rafe sighed. "I'm not interested in your case, OK? I have a case of my own to figure out. Katie Graves ended up on Skinner land sometime between last spring and November. Before that, she was somewhere else. It's likely that whoever put her there decided to take advantage of the Skinner murders to put the blame for Katie on Darrell Skinner. They were involved before she disappeared."

Jarvis opened his mouth, and Rafe shook his head. "If Darrell had killed her, he wouldna put her where she was found. It's too close to the trailers. And if he killed her and kept here somewhere else for sixteen years, there was no reason to move her now."

"And too much of a coincidence that he'd do it just before he ended up dead himself," I shot in.

Rafe nodded. "We already know that the Skinner murders didn't have nothing to do with Katie. Otherwise, I mighta speculated that the Skinners were killed in retaliation for Katie. But that wasn't what happened. It makes more sense that whoever had Katie decided to dump her in the hills after the murders. The Skinners were gone, so they weren't likely to stumble on her, and if somebody else did, it'd look like the Skinners killed her."

Jarvis nodded. A little reluctantly, but he nodded.

"I found Katie's clothes today, along with her backpack."

Grimaldi's eyes widened. She opened her mouth, and closed it again.

"Where?" Jarvis asked.

"A house in Sunnyside. The woman who lives there knew Katie. I don't see how she coulda kept the body there until last year, though. She was sixteen when Katie disappeared. She lived with her parents. And it's a small house."

"Some parents might notice but not say anything," I said. "To protect their children."

Rafe nodded. "And I'm gonna have to track down the Jeffrieses in Florida and talk to them. But Lynn also said she took the bus to school. Whoever took Katie probably had a vehicle."

"Either that, or lived nearby and got Katie into his or her house," Grimaldi added.

"What does this have to do with Scott Mason?"

"Nothing with Scott," Rafe said. "Scotty Junior's looking like a person of interest. He had access to Lynn Jeffries's garage, and he knew Katie."

"Mrs. Miller said he was a neighbor," I added. "He and Katie took the school bus together, so he must have lived nearby."

"Did you do a search of the Mason property?" Rafe asked.

Jarvis shook his head. "Not beyond the bedroom. Everything was right there, out in plain sight. There was no reason to ask for a search warrant. And I wouldn't have gotten one if I had asked."

Nobody said anything for a second.

"So what are you saying?" I asked Rafe. I'm sure the others had already figured all this out—this was their business, after all—but I needed to talk it through. "Scotty Junior gets Katie back to his house, and kills her. We don't know why, but maybe he liked her and she didn't reciprocate. Maybe he just tried to talk to her, and she didn't want to. Maybe he wanted help with his homework, and she wouldn't give it to him."

"Maybe she was sleeping with Darrell and he didn't like it," Rafe said.

"So Scotty kills her. Wouldn't his father notice the dead body in the living room?"

"There are parents who wouldn't go to the police," Grimaldi said distantly, "even over something like that."

I'd take her word for it, even if it was hard to believe. "So Scotty killed Katie, and his father was OK with it—or at least OK enough that he helped Scotty hide the body instead of calling the cops. Years go by. The body rots. Nobody does anything. Then Scott Senior gets ill. And Darrell dies. And Scotty moves the bones to the Skinners' property."

Everyone nodded.

"Mason Senior's illness might have had something to do

with it," Jarvis suggested. "He had hospice nurses coming and going last fall. If Katie's bones were still in the house, Scotty might have wanted them out of the way. Just in case."

That made sense.

"I'm thinking that if Scotty killed Katie, and Scott Senior knew about it," Rafe said, "and he pretty much had to know, I think, if the body was kept in his house—"

I nodded. So did Grimaldi. So did Jarvis.

"Then Scott Senior mighta felt the need to unburden his conscience before dying."

And Scotty might have killed him to keep him quiet. Scotty wasn't dying, and would be looking at a lengthy prison term if he was convicted of Katie's murder. Scott Senior might not care—he didn't have long to live anyway—but Scotty would.

Hell—heck—Scotty could even tell himself he was doing his dad a favor by putting an end to his suffering.

"A bit of evidence would go a long way," Jarvis said.

"What kind of evidence?"

But before anyone could answer, my sandwich and Rafe's burger appeared, courtesy of Yvonne McCoy herself.

"Hello, princess." She smiled at me as she dropped the sandwich. "Hello, handsome." She gave Rafe a flirtatious look, and got a grin in return before she nodded to Grimaldi. "Afternoon, Chief Grimaldi."

Finally she made it around the table to Jarvis and the smile dropped off. "I know you."

Jarvis looked like he'd sunk his teeth into a slice of lemon. "Ms. McCoy."

I looked from one to the other of them. Until now, I hadn't really thought about it, but of course Jarvis was the detective who had stood next to Mrs. Otis Odom and her daughter while Beulah's body was being exhumed. Jarvis had been in charge of that fiasco. At Chief Carter's suggestion, no doubt, since it was Carter Mrs. Odom had sweet-talked into ordering the exhumation. But it had been Jarvis at the Oak Street Cemetery that day, looking for the evidence he'd need to charge Yvonne with murder.

She looked like she wanted to order Jarvis out of his seat and into the parking lot, but she was too good a businesswoman to let her feelings get the best of her. After staring at him for a few seconds—take the 'if looks could kill' cliché as read—she turned back to Rafe. "How're things?"

"Still working the same case," Rafe told her. "What can you tell me about Scotty Mason?"

"Junior?" Yvonne shrugged. Her breasts—much more impressive than mine—moved against the fabric of her blouse. Rafe didn't seem to notice, but Jarvis's eyes snagged for a second before he looked away. "Not much."

"Don't he come in here?"

"Sometimes he does," Yvonne said. "But I didn't think you wanted information on what he likes for breakfast."

Rafe shook his head. "When's the last time you saw him?"

"Funny you should ask," Yvonne said. "He was in here a couple hours ago. Said he needed to fuel up before he tackled clearing out his dad's house."

Nobody said anything, but I could feel the tension criss-crossing the table. So could Yvonne, because she looked from one to the other of us. "What?"

"Nothing you need to worry about," Rafe said, and Yvonne scowled at him.

I waited for her to make the connection, and it didn't take long. Her eyes widened. "Wait a minute. You think Scotty killed Katie?"

"It's a theory," Rafe said. "Nothing more right now."

Yvonne nodded. And didn't say anything more, just stood there and chewed her bottom lip.

"You don't seem that surprised," I said, since she hadn't tried to tell us that Scotty couldn't possibly have done anything like that. When someone I know is accused or suspected of murder, that's usually the first thing out of my mouth.

She glanced at me. "I don't really know him well. He's older than me by a couple of years. I have no idea whether he could have done anything to Katie Graves or not. I didn't know her."

"But?"

"I saw him just after Darrell was killed. I was working the register at the drugstore in Sweetwater. The restaurant was closed while the police," she avoided looking at Jarvis, "were investigating Beulah's death."

I nodded. I remembered that time. The hearing into Beulah's competency had been going on, and when the judge ruled in Yvonne's favor, the Otis Odoms had prevailed upon Carter to have the body exhumed.

"He came in to buy something," Yvonne said. "Not sure I can remember what. Maybe a box of trash bags?" She thought for a second and then dismissed it. "We talked about the Skinners, of course. Everyone who came in did. Just like when Katie disappeared. It was so shocking, and all anyone wanted to talk about."

"Did Scotty bring it up?"

"I was upset about Darrell," Yvonne said. "We weren't together anymore. I was done with him. But I was upset. Scotty asked why. And he didn't seem upset at all. He said something like, they got what they deserved."

Cold. Especially considering that in addition to Darrell, Robbie, Art, and Linda, the dead included sixteen-year-old A.J, eighteen-year-old Cilla, and her boyfriend Matt, who was around the same age.

"Trash bags?" Rafe said.

Yvonne nodded. "I think trash bags. Although it was a long time ago."

"It's a long drive for trash bags. Unless he works in

Sweetwater?"

Yvonne shook her head. "He commutes to Cool Springs. The mall."

North of Columbia by at least thirty minutes. In the opposite direction from the drugstore in Sweetwater.

"He might just have had business in town," Grimaldi said. "Dinner with a friend, a date, shopping to do."

Rafe nodded. "Thanks," he told Yvonne. "Do me a favor and don't tell anybody we talked about this, OK?"

She smiled, although it was a little wobbly. "Sure thing, handsome. Y'all enjoy the food."

She wandered off. Jarvis scowled after her. "She's gonna blab to everyone who comes through the door."

"My wife saved her life once," Rafe said. "I don't think she will."

"And she slept with my husband in high school," I added. "I don't think she will, either."

Grimaldi's mouth twitched, like she was holding back a smile.

"Besides," I added, "she was involved with Darrell Skinner. She knew he was a womanizing jerk, but she loved him. She'll want whoever did this to get caught, so everyone knows it wasn't Darrell."

Jarvis didn't look convinced, but he also didn't say anything else about it. And who could blame him, when there were more important things going on? "He's at his dad's house destroying evidence," he said instead.

There was no need to specify who he was talking about. We all knew. And nobody told him he was wrong. Rafe and Grimaldi just looked glum.

"How do we stop him?" I asked.

Grimaldi shook her head. "We can't. We don't have enough to get an arrest warrant."

"Can't you bring him in for questioning without that?"

"Sure," Rafe said, "but if he hasn't broken in sixteen years, he ain't likely to break now. And once we let him go—and we'll have to, since we don't have enough to arrest him—he'll just go back to what he's doing."

There was another little silence while we all thought about it.

"I could go knock on his door," I said. "I don't think he'd think I was spying on him. Not if I gave him a card and asked about the house."

Jarvis looked confused, so I added, "I'm a real estate agent. I assume he'll be inheriting his father's house. I could ask whether he's thinking about selling it. Or even renting it out. Charlotte wants somewhere to live that isn't her parents' house."

"I don't think Charlotte's gonna wanna live in the middle of Columbia, darlin'," Rafe told me.

"Well, of course not. But it makes for a nice excuse for why I'd be interested. You might recall that I'm not an especially good liar."

His lips curved. "I know about that, yeah."

"If I keep him busy for a while, maybe you'll have time to get a search warrant. And if I see anything weird inside, maybe that would help, too."

Nobody said anything for a moment. I waited for Rafe to tell me that he didn't like this idea, and that he didn't want me to do it, but he didn't say a word. Grimaldi didn't, either.

"You'd have to wear a wire," she said instead.

"Really?" I'd never worn a wire before. It would be a new and exciting experience.

Rafe's lips twitched at my tone, and I looked from him to Grimaldi and back. "You're actually thinking of letting me do this?"

"I don't imagine it would be all that dangerous," Rafe said, "so long as you don't say nothing stupid."

I gave him a look, and he grinned. "I'm not saying I love the idea. But chances are he's not even gonna let you inside the house. If he does, the fact that you're my wife is prob'ly enough to keep him from doing anything to you. And short of another illegal search, which'll blow up in our faces if we find anything we can use as evidence, it's our best shot at getting somebody through the door. He's lived in Columbia his whole life. I'm sure he knows everyone on the police force. It's worth trying."

"As long as you're wired," Grimaldi added firmly. "I'm not sending you into a house with a possible murderer unmonitored."

Fine by me. I didn't really think Scotty Mason was dangerous. He hadn't seemed dangerous yesterday, and he'd been a kid when he killed Katie. Not that that's an excuse, but he'd probably learned some self control since then. It might even have been an accident. And as far as his father was concerned, there was no proof that Scotty had had anything to do with it. Scott Senior might have taken his own life before the cancer took him, and Scotty hadn't been involved at all.

I looked from one to the other of them. "When do we want to do this?"

"The sooner, the better," Rafe said, and Jarvis nodded.

"Just let me feed the baby and spend ten minutes on the computer, so I can tell him how much his house is worth if he wants to know, and I'll be ready."

"I'll get the wire," Grimaldi said, and nudged Rafe out of the booth so she could leave. "Come to the police station when you're ready."

Jarvis got up at the same time and followed her out the door. He gave Rafe a fairly cordial nod before he went.

"Other than those few seconds when Yvonne recognized Jarvis," I told Rafe, "that went better than I expected."

He nodded.

Twenty

Forty-five minutes later, Operation Scotty was underway. Rafe and I had finished our sandwiches, and I had fed and changed Carrie in Beulah's—or Yvonne's—restroom. We had convened at the police station, where Grimaldi had handed me a small, black box. "Your wire."

I looked at it. "That doesn't look much like a wire. I was looking forward to squeezing into a broom closet with Rafe so he could cop a feel while he put it on me. It just goes in my pocket?"

"I can stuff it in your bra if you think it'll be comfortable," Rafe told me, "but yeah. Just drop it in your pocket."

I must have looked confused, because Grimaldi consented to explain. "The kinds of wires you're thinking of—the kind you see on TV, that have to match the skin and be invisible under clothes... we only use those when there's a chance someone will get patted down or strip searched. Mason won't do that to you—"

Rafe muttered something. Neither Grimaldi nor I asked him to repeat it, but I saw her lips twitch. "We'll be half a block away," she told me—and him. "We'll be armed. If anything happens, we can be there in a few seconds."

"I don't think anything will happen," I said.

"As long as you don't do nothing to provoke him."

It sounded like maybe Rafe was rethinking this whole idea

now that it was actually time to put it into practice.

"I won't," I said. "I'll just ask him about his plans for the house, and see if he wants me to walk through it, to give him an idea of how much it's worth. If he says no, you'll just have to try to figure this out another way. But if he does, I'll walk around and open doors and poke into closets and see if I notice anything out of the ordinary."

He didn't look convinced, so I added, "I won't try to get any information about Katie out of him. I won't try to get him to confess. I won't even bring her up."

Rafe nodded.

"You could even be there if you wanted. Say hello, and then tell him you'll stay in the car with the baby, since she's asleep. That would ensure that he wouldn't try to do anything to me, if he knew you were outside."

Rafe looked like he was thinking about it.

"Might also ensure he wouldn't let her in," Jarvis pointed out. He was staying in the background, but still sticking around.

"And you wouldn't be able to hear the conversation if you weren't in the car with the rest of us," Grimaldi added.

Rafe nodded. "Guess we'll go with the original plan."

"All set, then?" I looked at them all. They nodded.

"Take care of the baby," I told Rafe.

"You mean for the next thirty minutes, right?" He didn't wait for me to answer. "She'll be fine. Just make sure you come back in one piece."

I promised I would, although I wasn't really worried about it. What could go wrong? Katie's body was gone. Katie's clothes were gone. Katie's underwear was probably in Darrell's collection. And the police had already seen and confiscated anything to do with Scott Senior's death. There wouldn't be anything left to find in Scotty's house.

I didn't point that out, though, since by now I was kind of

excited about getting to do this. I didn't want any of them to change theirs minds about letting me.

So we transferred Carrie's car seat and the baby herself to Rafe's Chevy, and then I got into the Volvo and drove the few blocks to Scott Mason's house. I kept the voice transmitter on in my pocket, and talked to it. "I'm turning out of the police station. I'm traveling down Broad. I'm turning onto 4th Street. I'm pulling up in front of the house. Now's the time to stop me if the transmitter isn't working. I can see you pulling to the curb behind me. Flash your lights if you can hear me and it's safe to go on."

The Chevy pulled to a stop half a block away, and the lights flashed once. Guess we were good to go. I took a fortifying breath before I pushed the door open and got out of the Volvo. My knees were a little shaky as I headed across the sidewalk and up the path to the front door, but it didn't stop me.

Here in downtown Columbia, the houses were much older and closer together than in Sunnyside. This looked more like downtown Sweetwater, where Audrey and the sheriff and the Albertsons lived, but it was a bit less upscale. Or more than a little. The Mason house was a small clapboard cottage, late Victorian style, with wood rot on the eaves and leaky gutters.

The front door was awesome, though. Heavy carved wood, more than a hundred years old, and with the original twisting doorbell in the center. It worked, too. The sound pealed through the house. I was still admiring the wood carvings on the door when it was yanked open. "Yes?"

Scotty Mason stood in front of me, and he looked very different from yesterday. Now he had a day's worth of beard, his hair was uncombed, standing up in spikes, and he was dressed in sweatpants and a T-shirt.

"Oh," I said, taken aback. "I'm sorry."

His eyes were bloodshot, like he hadn't gotten a lot of sleep last night. Maybe not surprising, if he'd spent the night stashing evidence in Lynn Jeffries's garage.

"No, no." He ran a hand over his face. "It's OK. What's going on?"

"Oh," I said again. "I'm sorry. We met yesterday, at the funeral home. I'm Savannah Martin."

I held out a hand. He gave it a perfunctory squeeze. "I remember."

"I don't think I mentioned it yesterday," I said, taking my hand back and plunging it into my purse, "because I didn't want to be rude at the memorial, but I've just moved back to Maury County."

He nodded.

"This is my card." I handed it to him. "I'm a real estate agent. I've been working for a company in Nashville for the past couple of years," as he could see from the card, "but now that I'm here, I'm going to have to find a brokerage in town to affiliate myself with. Not that it matters. I'm licensed for the whole state of Tennessee."

"What's that gotta do with me?"

"Oh. I'm sorry. I don't know the situation, of course. But I thought maybe you were thinking about selling your father's house. And I thought maybe I'd stop by and give you my card, in case there was something I could do to help."

He didn't answer that. But he also wasn't thanking me and withdrawing, so I kept talking.

"This is a great front door. Original, right? Late Victorian?"

"It's crooked," Scotty said.

It was. But— "Just a little bit. There's been some settling. That's to be expected with a house that's more than a hundred years old." I went up on my toes and peered past him into the foyer. "Nice fireplace, too."

"Would you like to come inside?"

He didn't sound excited by the prospect, but I was. Not only because that was why I was here, but because I genuinely do love to see other people's houses. And this one had a lot of old character going for it, at least from what I'd seen so far. I beamed. "I would love to!"

He took a step back, and I took one across the threshold. My heart was thudding a little extra hard in my chest, but I wasn't really worried. I'd done this before. Gone into houses with people I didn't know. It comes with the territory. The only difference was that this time, we thought the owner of the house might be a murderer. Other than that, it was real estate as usual.

"This is a great foyer." I tilted my head back to look up at the ten foot ceiling and the original light fixture still hanging there.

"It's old," Scotty said.

"Yes, of course it's old. That's what makes it great. I grew up in the Martin Mansion, you know. It's from around 1840." I gave him a bright smile. "I love old houses."

"So what do you think this is worth?" Scotty looked around.

"I'd have to see the rest to give you a solid estimate," I told him, "but I can tell you that prices in this area went up seven or eight percent last year. And there aren't that many old Victorians left. They're popular with the renovation crowd."

Scotty nodded.

"If you wouldn't mind giving me the five-cent tour, I could probably give you a pretty good idea what you could get for it."

The idea of money seemed to appeal to him, because he agreed. "What do you want to see first?"

"Whatever you want to show me," I said, mentally cracking my knuckles.

We started in the front parlor, to the left of the foyer. It had the same tall ceilings as the foyer, and the same uneven plank floors. The house had indeed experienced some settling in the past hundred years, and it was obvious that nobody had done any structural work in that time, because if I'd put a marble in the doorway between the foyer and the parlor, it would have picked up speed across the floor and bounced off the wall next to the fireplace.

The fireplace itself was awesome, though. Dark wood, with an oval mirror above the mantel, and earth-glazed original tiles in shades of brown and green.

"That's gorgeous," I said.

Scotty gave it a disparaging look. "Old."

"Yes. But beautiful."

The tour continued down the hall, past Scotty's bedroom—navy blue and messy—to Scott Senior's, which had a hospital bed still sitting in the middle of the floor.

"This would have to go," I told Scotty. "Some of the furniture can stay, especially the older pieces—unless you were planning to clean the place out—but nobody likes to be reminded of illness and death when they're looking to buy a house."

And although that was as close as I was willing to go to pointing it out, the fact that someone had actually died here wasn't a selling point. Some buyers are sensitive to that sort of thing.

"Is this your dad?"

It was a picture of a family group hanging crookedly on the wall. Mother, father, and young boy. The boy was probably Scotty, at twelve or so. I could pick out some of the same features. He smiled at the camera, but the smile looked anxious.

Scott Senior in the picture looked like what Scott Junior did now, at what I estimated was probably around the same age or a little older, and Mrs. Mason was sort of faded and washed out, with mousy hair and a flower printed dress.

"Were you able to let your mom know about your father?" I asked Scotty. "They separated, right? Do you know where she is now?"

He shook his head. "Haven't seen her since I was fifteen. There's no way to get in touch with her."

He led the way through a door from the hallway into the kitchen. It was also vintage, but not quite as old as the house. Nineteen-sixties, maybe, judging from the cabinets. The tile and countertops had been updated since, probably in the eighties, and the fridge was a pretty recent economy model, white, with the freezer on top. A door led to the formal dining room, and beyond it, I could see the wallpaper in the foyer.

"It goes in a circle."

Scotty nodded.

"What about this? A pantry?" I reached for the door in the wall between the kitchen and dining room. "Pantries are always popular with home buyers."

Scotty lifted a hand, but it was too late. I'd already pulled the door open.

"Oh." I rocked back on my heels, with a distinct lack of enthusiasm in my voice. "You have a basement."

A set of rickety stairs disappeared down into darkness, while a cold breeze wafted up from the unheated depths. It was the kind of place that hinted of earth worms and cobwebs and fungus.

And old bones and other gruesome things.

Scotty reached around me and flipped on the light. "Feel free to check it out."

There was, I thought, a hint of challenge in his voice. Maybe he'd picked up on the fact that I didn't particularly want to descend into the chill under the house. There was no way anyone would be able to turn a space like that into a cozy den.

But I was here to look around, so I forced some interest into my voice. "Sure thing. Basements are great for storage. And they make for easy access to plumbing and the other major mechanicals." I gave him a bright smile before I stepped onto the staircase.

"How's your husband doing with the investigation?" Scotty asked, as he headed down behind me.

I missed a step, and had to grab onto the railing to keep my balance. The wood was rough, and it felt like splinters were digging into in my palm.

I pushed it aside as I thought back. Had I told Scotty that Rafe was working the Katie Graves investigation? I didn't think I had. I'd come into the Mason room at the memorial with Grimaldi, of course, but we hadn't talked about Katie. Or not about the investigation into her death, at any rate.

"You mean Detective Jarvis? He's the one looking into your father's death."

"I was talking about Katie," Scotty said, descending on my heels. His voice was a little funny, but I didn't want to turn my head to look at him. The stairs were steep, and I wasn't sure I'd like what I saw. I won't deny that I felt a little trickle of fear down my spine, though, as if a droplet of cold water had found its way behind my collar and trickling down my back. One good shove, and I'd be tumbling down the rest of the stairs and end up in a heap on the hard-packed dirt floor below.

I did my best to keep my voice steady, like this line of questioning didn't bother me at all. "I didn't realize you knew Rafe was working on that."

"I overheard you telling Katie's mother what your husband was doing on Saturday," Scotty said.

We got to the bottom of the steps and I scurried off the staircase and onto the floor with some relief. And gave Scotty the best natural-looking smile I could muster as I turned toward him. "I guess he's doing all right. He was all over the Devil's Backbone yesterday with a cadaver dog, to see if he could figure out where Darrell might have kept Katie all these years."

"How does he know she was kept somewhere else?" Scotty

asked as he stepped down next to me.

I moved back, trying to make it seem polite instead of a retreat from danger. "Something about the bones never having been frozen." I looked around. Dirt floor, dirt walls, small, deep-set, dirty windows. Not big enough to crawl through. "It's cold down here."

Scotty smirked. "A balmy fifty degrees. Standard underground temperature at ten feet."

This was probably where he'd kept Katie, then. There'd been nowhere upstairs where he might have stowed a body, but there was plenty of room down here.

"Furnace?" I asked, nodding toward the back corner, where something big and dark hulked.

Scotty nodded. "It's old."

Yes, it was. It looked like it had been sitting here since the house was built. "No AC?"

"Just window units upstairs," Scotty said.

A big, old workbench was slotted into the corner next to the furnace. I guess Scott or maybe Scotty had been doing carpentry down here, because there were hammers and nails and things like that scattered across it.

Halfway down the next wall, behind the staircase, stood a big box with a couple of doors with black hinges, and my eyes opened wide. "Oh, my God! Is this what I think it is?"

"Don't touch that—" Scotty began, but I'd already reached for one of the handles, prattling on.

"It's an old ice chest, right? Did it come with the house? Is it original? We have one of these at the mansion, out in the carriage house now, but ours is wood. This one is metal. And it's in really good condition. Do you know how rare this is?"

If it were me, this would be upstairs. And if he wanted to sell the house…

But of course he didn't. I was just pretending. I was really here to see whether I could get a clue as to where he'd kept

Katie Graves's body for the sixteen years between the time he killed her and when he dumped her on the Devil's Backbone.

And here I was, looking at it.

I'd already opened one of the latches. And there was nothing inside. Just an empty space where either the food or the block of ice would go.

I'm not sure what I was thinking. Perhaps that I'd already opened one of the doors, and there was nothing there, so it would be safe to open another.

Scotty opened his mouth, but nothing came out as I flipped the latch on one of the other doors. And stumbled back with a scream when I came face to face with a skull, staring back at me with empty eye sockets.

Twenty-One

The next few seconds were a little disjointed, no pun intended. I fetched up against the dirt wall, and tried to catch my breath. Meanwhile, Scotty took two steps closer and slammed the ice chest door shut. "Now look what you did," he told me. "Didn't I tell you not to open that?"

He had told me that. I tried to keep my teeth from chattering. "That's not a real skull, is it?"

"Of course it isn't a real skull," Scotty said. He smiled, but it didn't come anywhere near his eyes. "It's from Halloween."

"Creepy." My heart rate was starting to settle back down again, and my voice was practically even. To be honest, I was a little surprised that Rafe wasn't already banging on the door upstairs. "Thanks for trying to warn me."

"No problem," Scotty said.

I looked around, more to avoid his eyes than for any other reason. They were bright and inquisitive and fastened on me. Probably trying to determine whether he'd convinced me or not.

For the record, the skull wasn't fake. I'd seen real skulls, and if that was a Halloween decoration, it was the most realistic Halloween decoration I'd ever seen.

And it wasn't Katie's. Hers had been found on the Devil's Backbone along with some of her other bones. This was someone else's skull.

If I opened another door in the ice chest, would I find the remains of yet another body?

While all this was going through my brain, I tried to look and sound natural, like I'd bought his explanation and wasn't worried at all. "I guess there isn't much more to see down here."

"No," Scotty said. "You've already seen it all."

"I guess we should go back upstairs, then." I went to move past him toward the stairs, and had to stop when he didn't get out of the way.

"I don't think so."

"I'm cold," I said, still clinging to the illusion that everything was fine. "If there's nothing more to see here, why don't we go upstairs and talk about the house and how much it's worth?"

He shook his head. "You didn't come here for that."

"Of course I came here for that. I gave you my card. I'm a real estate agent."

"Who's married to a cop," Scotty said.

"Sure. But he doesn't know that I'm here."

Scotty's expression eased. It wasn't by much, but I could see the difference. And that's when I knew that he had no intention of letting me walk out of this basement alive.

Cards on the table, then. I might as well keep him talking, and find out what I wanted to know before Rafe, Grimaldi, and Jarvis burst through the door upstairs.

"Whose skull is that? I thought you just killed Katie and your dad, but it looks like I was wrong."

Scotty looked at me for a second before he smiled. "Nobody. I would have killed Darrell Skinner if I could have got to him, but he was all the way up in the hills, and he was always with his other brothers. So I had to settle for Katie."

That wasn't what I'd asked, but if he was willing to talk about Katie, I guess I'd settle for that. "What happened?"

I kept my ears peeled for sounds from upstairs, for signs that Rafe, Grimaldi, and Jarvis were on their way to rescue me, but so far there was nothing. Hopefully the transmitter hadn't stopped working because we were down here, below ground.

"She lived just over there," Scotty said, gesturing with his thumb in the direction of the furnace. "On the next block. We grew up together."

I nodded, as I surreptitiously shook the voice transmitter inside my pocket. "I noticed you seemed close with her mom."

"All the moms in the neighborhood," Scotty said, with a sudden grin. "Poor Scotty, whose mama ran off."

There was something not quite right about his reaction—why would he think that was funny?—and then it hit me. "Oh, my God. Your mother…"

I glanced at the ice box. "Is that your mother?"

Scotty chuckled. "That's mama."

The skin at the back of my neck prickled. "How did she end up down here?"

"My daddy killed her," Scotty said. "She was gonna leave him and take me with her, and he didn't want us to go."

So he'd killed her. Just like that. "And she's been down here ever since?"

He nodded.

"Why didn't you call the police?"

"What woulda happened if I did?" Scotty demanded. "I'd have nowhere else to go. I'd end up in foster care. And it worked out better, anyway. When I killed Katie and put her here with Mama, there was nothing Dad could do about it. If he told on me, I'd tell on him."

Good grief. "So the two of you lived here for sixteen years with two women rotting in the basement?"

Scotty shrugged.

"Didn't anybody notice?"

As anyone who has ever smelled the stench of a rotting

mouse can attest, it's a pervasive odor. And that's a mouse. Something the size of a human body—even a small one—doesn't decompose without giving off a strong and pervasive—and unmistakable—whiff of death.

"Katie," Scotty said, his countenance darkening.

"Katie realized your dad had killed your mom? That's why you killed her? Because she figured out what happened to your mother?"

He nodded. "Why did you think I killed her?"

"No reason," I said. "I mean, I didn't think you had. There was no reason why you would."

"There was every reason why I would!" Scotty said. "That stupid bitch figured out what happened to my mom. And she wouldn't listen to reason. I tried to tell her that I couldn't turn my dad in, but she wouldn't listen to me."

"So you killed her."

He nodded. "She came over here before school, to try to talk me into it, and I strangled her and put her in the ice chest, and then I went down to the corner and caught the bus. I wasn't even late."

"And when the police came and asked questions, you said you hadn't seen Katie that morning."

He nodded.

"When did you decide to put her—or what was left of her—up on the Devil's Backbone?"

"After the Skinners died," Scotty said. "I kind of hoped she wouldn't be found so fast—or at all—but I figured if she was, it wouldn't matter. Everyone knew what creeps the Skinners were. I figured, if someone found her, they'd just think it was one more thing the Skinners were responsible for."

Sure. No big thing. I mean, if they were growing pot and running a dog-fighting operation, might as well pin a murder on them, too.

"So you took what was left of Katie up there and left her in the woods."

Scotty glanced at the ice box. "There's probably some of Katie left here, too. The bones got kind of mixed up after a while. I took what I knew was Katie's skull and some of Katie's bigger bones, and I left everything else. I didn't want to accidentally take some of my mom."

No, I could quite see why that wouldn't be a good idea. It would have been a lucky break if he had, of course. The case might have been solved a lot quicker. But from Scotty's perspective, very smart.

"And you left her clothes and backpack in Lynn Jeffries's garage," I said.

"I had to get rid of them. I was going to dump them on Darrell, but there were investigators crawling all over everything. So I took them back here. And then yesterday you mentioned Lynn and how you wanted to talk to her. And I thought it made sense to dump them on Lynn instead. She was involved with Darrell in high school, too."

"Darrell got around," I said, as my ears picked up a squeak in the floorboards upstairs. Scotty's gaze turned distracted, and I shifted my weight and rustled my clothes in the hope that he'd forget what he thought he might have heard. "Just out of curiosity, do you know anything about a ring Rafe and I found near where you dumped Katie's body? One of those cheap drugstore rings with a D and a C on it?"

Scotty nodded. "That was your sister's."

"My sister's?"

"Catherine." He grinned. "She threw it at Darrell one night when we were up there. That was when she found out that he'd been sleeping with other girls, too."

"And you picked it up?" No wonder she hadn't wanted to talk about the ring.

He shook his head. "I left it there. I looked for it again when I brought Katie's bones up there, but I guess I didn't remember exactly where we'd been, because I couldn't find it."

"That was why you chose that spot? Because it was where you used to get together when you were kids?"

He nodded.

"What about your dad?"

"He had a tumor in his intestine," Scotty said. "No way to operate. Just live with it until you die. And suffer."

"And he wanted to come clean?"

"He thought it was judgment." Scotty curled his lip. "He found religion and thought the cancer was God's punishment for killing Mom and for keeping quiet about Katie."

"And he wanted to tell someone."

He nodded. "Selfish bastard. It was easy for him. He wasn't gonna go to prison for the rest of his life. I was looking at the next fifty years in maximum security."

"So you killed him."

"He was dying anyway," Scotty said. "I did him a favor."

I wondered whether Scott Senior had thought of it that way. And decided that Scotty might be right. Maybe he had.

I glanced around. No rescuers on the stairs that I could see. And nothing more to talk about, either. "I guess that's it."

Scott nodded. "Now I'm gonna have to kill you."

"I wish you'd reconsider," I said. "You're already in enough trouble, you know?"

"I'm not in any trouble," Scotty said, advancing on me.

I took a step back. "My husband knows I'm here, you know."

"I'll tell him you left," Scotty said.

"He's not stupid. And besides, I'm wearing a wire."

He stopped. "What?"

"Wire." I pulled it out of my pocket and showed it to him. "Voice transmitter. There's a car down the street with two detectives and the chief of police in it. They've been listening to everything you've said."

Or at least I hoped they had. There was no way to tell whether the transmitter was actually transmitting or not. What if I'd spent all this time getting Scotty to confess to everything, and nobody had heard a word?

And then I had to stop worrying about it, because in the second it took me to look down at the transmitter, Scotty flew at me. He knocked me to the ground—I didn't actually see stars, thankfully the dirt floor wasn't hard enough for me to crack my skull open, but I did have the wind knocked out of me—and it was enough for Scotty to land on top of me and fit his hands around my throat.

I flailed, thinking in the back of my head that dammit, this wasn't going to do my coat any good, while the front of my brain was preoccupied with short bursts of thought like "Kick!" and "Hit!" and "I'm going to die!"

Scotty's face was above me, his lips pulled back and his teeth bared, eyes furious as he did his best to squeeze the life out of me. It was hard for him to get a good grip, though, over the scarf I had wound around my neck. If he'd thought about it, it would have made more sense to use that to strangle me, but I guess he wanted to feel my skin under his hands while he killed me.

And then there was a clatter of footsteps on the stairs, and Scotty went flying backwards. And Rafe was there, and he pulled me up and into his arms, and beyond him I could see Jarvis grab Scotty and flip him over on his stomach, and put a knee in the middle of Scotty's back while he struggled to get a pair of handcuffs around Scotty's wrists. Scotty was bucking like a bronco, trying to throw Jarvis off. I don't know what he thought he was going to be able to do if he could get free, because between Rafe and Jarvis—and Grimaldi, wherever she was—he had no chance in hell—heck—of getting out of the basement.

Although that didn't stop him from trying.

"You OK?" Rafe asked into my hair.

I nodded, my teeth only chattering a little. "I knew you were there. I knew you'd get to me in time."

"We heard the whole conversation. Some of it from the top of the stairs."

"I know I wasn't supposed to ask any questions about Katie or the rest of it. But once we were down here, I thought it made sense."

"Once you found that skull, he wasn't gonna let you leave anyway," Rafe said.

That had been my impression, too. Good to have my instincts validated, though. "Where's Carrie?"

"Still in the car," Rafe said.

I took a step back to look up at him. "You left our baby in the car? All this time?"

"Tammy's with her. She's sleeping. And it's only been a few minutes."

It felt like a lot longer than that. I looked around the dank and dirty basement. "Can we go?"

Rafe glanced over his shoulder. Jarvis had gotten Scotty to his feet. He was crying. Scotty, I mean. Tears of frustration, no doubt. "You stupid bitch," he told me. "This is all your fault."

"I would have gotten away with it, too," Rafe muttered, "if it wasn't for you meddling kids."

I couldn't help it, I laughed out loud. "Actually," I told Scotty, "it's Detective Jarvis's fault. He always suspected that something was wrong with your father's death."

"You wanna take him in?" Jarvis asked Rafe.

Rafe shook his head. "He's all yours. I'm gonna take my wife and daughter home."

"You gonna come by later?"

"Yes," I said, when Rafe hesitated. "He'll be by later."

Jarvis nodded and muscled Scotty over to the stairs. We watched for a few moments, to make sure Jarvis had it under control—he did—and then Rafe turned his attention to the ice box. "This it?"

I nodded. "I'll do it. My fingerprints are already on the latch."

He waited while I twisted the latch and opened the door again. The skull grinned out at us, just like before.

"Halloween decoration," Rafe said, "my ass."

Yes, indeed. "I'm sure Grimaldi has already phoned for a crime scene crew. Let's get out of here so I can take my daughter home and get a shower."

"I could join you," Rafe said.

I grinned at him over my shoulder as I started up the stairs. "Some other time. You should go to the police station and help Jarvis interview Scotty. It's your case. You should be there."

"I don't mind," Rafe said.

"I know you don't. But I don't mind, either. And we'll be there when you get home."

I reached the top of the stairs and headed into the dining room with Rafe on my heels. Jarvis was wrestling Scotty through the front door onto the porch.

"It's a shame about the house," I said, looking around. "It has—" I bit my tongue before I came out with that old chestnut, "great bones."

"Maybe he'll wanna sell it to pay for legal fees." Rafe steered me toward the door. Scotty and Jarvis were on their way down the stairs outside.

"Maybe." Although I wouldn't hold my breath. If Scotty had any sense, he'd settle for a public defender and take what was coming to him without quibble. With his mother's skull still sitting in the basement, and some of Katie's bones still down there, too, there wasn't much he could do to wiggle out of this. "The kindest thing anyone could do for this place is to mow it down and build something new on the lot."

"Never thought I'd hear you say that about an old Victorian

house," Rafe said.

"With three murders taking place here, and two bodies hidden in the basement for almost two decades? Nobody in their right mind would buy this place. Might as well put it out of its misery."

We passed through the front door and onto the porch, and already it was a little easier to breathe. Down at the curb, Jarvis was wrestling Scotty into the back of Rafe's Chevy. Carrie and her seat had already been transferred to the back of the Volvo.

"All ready," Grimaldi told me.

I nodded. "We'll get out of your hair."

"I'll drive," Rafe said. To Grimaldi he added, "I'll be back in an hour. Keep him on ice for me."

"He's not going anywhere." Grimaldi glanced at Scotty, now safely tucked into the back of the Chevy, and then at me. "Good work, Ms.... Savannah."

"Thank you, Detective." I grinned.

"Let's get outta here." Rafe slid behind the wheel of the Volvo. A second later the engine turned over.

"See you later," I told Grimaldi, before I slid into the car on my own side and shut the door.

"Ready?" He glanced at me.

"Ready," I said, and buckled my seatbelt as we pulled away from the curb and headed for home.

About the Author

New York Times and *USA Today* bestselling author Jenna Bennett (Jennie Bentley) writes the Do It Yourself home renovation mysteries for Berkley Prime Crime and the Savannah Martin real estate mysteries for her own gratification. She also writes a variety of romance for a change of pace.

For more information, please visit Jenna's website:
www.JennaBennett.com